BAILED OUT

THE ANNA ALBERTINI FILES #2

REBECCA ZANETTI

RAZ INK LLC

This one is for the Voltolini Sisters, whose grandma really was Nonna Albertini: Suzanne, Kathy, Janine, Marie, Ann, Julie, and Lisa. And of course, for Steve—their one brother.

ACKNOWLEDGMENTS

Thank you to everyone who helped to make this book a reality!

Thank you to Tony, Gabe, and Karlina for being an understanding and fun family who let me bounce ideas (often odd ones) off them constantly;

Thank you to Craig Zanetti, Esq. for the help with criminal law and procedure. Any mistakes about the law are mine and mine alone;

Thank you to Asha Hossain of Asha Hossain Designs, LLC for the fantastic cover;

Thank you to Debra Stewart of Dragonfly Media Ink for the wonderful edits;

Thank you to Jillian Stein for being the best social media guru in the history of the world;

Thank you to Stella Bloom for the fabulous narration for the audio book;

Thank you to Liz Berry, Asa Maria Bradley, and Boone Brux for the advice with the concepts for this new series;

Thank you to my incredibly hard working agent, Caitlin Blasdell;

Thank you to Jenn from Social Butterfly, Sara and Gwen from Fresh Fiction, Cissy and crew from WriterSpace, and M.J. Rose from AuthorBuzz for helping get the word out about this new series;

Thank you to Rebecca's Rebels (my FB street team) and their hard working leader, Anissa Beatty;

Thank you to Rebel Katy Nielsen for her creativity with

helping to name my novella in the Lone Wolf anthology (Rescue: Cowboy Style);

Thank you to my constant support system: Gail and Jim English, Kathy and Herbie Zanetti, Debbie and Travis Smith, Stephanie and Don West, and Jessica and Jonah Namson.

NOTE FROM THE AUTHOR

Howdy everyone! Thank you for so much support for his new series of mine. Sometimes, as an author, you have to write something a little different. This series is that for me.

I've loved the emails and FB notes about this series, and I'm happy to keep writing about Anna and her family. Sometimes we need a little bit of humor, right? The next book is called Adverse Possession, and then we have a Holiday book called Santa's Subpoena coming Fall of 2021.

Also, I am a lawyer, and I might live in a small town, but this is in **no way** autobiographical. It turns out that the name Albertini is a distant family name of my relatives, which is pretty cool. However, the story is all made up. The characters are all fictional and so are the towns and counties (like usual). Also, the law is correct. :)

I hope you like Anna's world as much as I do!

Also, to stay up to date with releases, free content, and tons of contests, follow me on Bookbub, Facebook, the FB Rebel Street Team, and definitely subscribe to my newsletter for FREE BOOKS!

Also, I like to pair up with other bestselling authors to cross promote and give away books in our newsletters, so I will be giving away copies of my friends' books coming up. Just go to my website (RebeccaZanetti.com) to sign up for my newsletter.

XO

Rebecca

CHAPTER 1

"*Y*ou're an idiot," I muttered, not too quietly, to my boss.

Nicolo Basanelli shrugged, his shoulders powerful beneath his killer black suit. "Look at the situation as great job security, Anna." He turned and strode up the marble stairway in the courthouse building toward the district courtrooms.

"Ha," I muttered, taking the stairs down to the world of misdemeanors and traffic tickets. I meant the insult. Nick was being a moron. It had been two weeks since he'd fired the entire cache of lawyers in the district attorney's office in our medium sized town, and it was time he rehired them. Cleaning house on his first week as the prosecuting attorney had been his strategy, and right now, it was killing *me*. "I need a vacation," I said to nobody in particular as I pushed open the double wooden doors to the smaller courtroom, furnished in 1980's salmon colored accents.

"I'm with you." Clark Bunne stood from the back bench and straightened his Monte Carlo style gun-metal glasses. "Is Nick any closer to rehiring people?"

I switched my file folders to my other arm and took a quick

1

glance around the courtroom without making eye contact with anybody. "He seems to be holding strong for some reason."

Clark gestured me toward the two tables in front, and I turned on my red kitten heel and strode down the aisle to push open the gate and wait for Clark to come through before closing it. Oh, the gate was attached to railings on either side that only rose to my thighs, but at least they would slow down an attacker for almost a second before he or she could get to us.

I flopped the files on the defense table and drew out a chair.

Clark already had his file folders neatly stacked, and he took the chair he'd keep for the preliminary hearings. "What's up with the red shoes?"

I settled my light-weight blue skirt with a red border of poppies around my legs. The skirt reached just above my knees and was both casual and smart. "The shoes match my outfit."

Clark leaned back, his dark brown gaze taking in my legs and the shoes. "You only wear red when you're in a mood to kick ass."

Huh. I hadn't realized that fact, and since I'd only worked with and against Clark for a month, his attention to detail should be a warning. "I haven't had a chance to look at our cases today, and to be honest, these were the first pair I came across in my closet. I'm running on fumes here."

He shrugged, and I decided to study him. The guy was good looking, but I'd already noticed that. He was maybe an inch over six feet tall, thin, well dressed, and had a smile that no doubt mothers loved. His skin was dark, his eyes an intriguing blend of different browns, and his hair black and short. A month ago he'd shaved it, and either way looked good on him. "What do you wear when you want to kick ass?" I asked.

"These glasses." He reached for the first file folder and flashed me a grin. "Unlike you, I have looked at these cases."

I sighed. "All right." Quickly, I read through the first one. It was a misdemeanor vandalism charge against a junior in high school who'd painted his girlfriend's name on a local water tower. "Mitch

Styles. First offense. How about we scare him for ten minutes and then let him off with a fine?"

Clark nodded. "Sounds good. You be mean, and I'll look worried on his behalf until cajoling you into accepting the plea?"

I set the file aside. "I do like being cajoled."

Clark laughed, and I started, looking up at his handsome face. He had a great laugh.

He caught my gaze. "No."

I blinked. "I didn't ask anything." Then I frowned. I had enough on my plate without dating anybody else right now. "I'm not interested."

"Thank God," he said, and truth to heck, it sounded like he meant it.

"Hey." I tugged on my navy blue jacket. "I'm a catch."

He grinned. "Keep running. You're pretty and interesting and smart, but you're a whole boatload of trouble, and I don't need that right now. Or ever."

How had this conversation gotten so out of hand? I really wasn't interested in Clark. "This is a weird conversation."

"Agreed." He flipped over the next manila file folder.

I did the same. Should I be a little bit insulted? We were around the same age, had both just started as lawyers, and seemed to get along. He was much nicer than the other three men I seemed to be juggling, and at that thought, I shut down the entire idea. I might not really be juggling three men, considering only one was front and center in my brain right now, and I couldn't find him. Aiden Devlin had a reckoning coming for him...if I ever saw him again. He'd disappeared two weeks ago after saving my life and quite possibly ruining me in bed for other men, and my concern had now turned to irritation.

"Well?" Clark asked.

I blinked. "Sorry. Got lost in my head."

The door by the judge's bench opened, and the bailiff strode out. His name was Jay, he was around thirty, and he had a beard most men could only hope to grow. "All rise," he said, his voice quiet with authority.

I stood and took my files over to the prosecuting attorney's table. It was common for the prosecuting and defense attorneys to try and reach some sort of agreement on cases before the preliminary hearings started, so long as the criminal defendant ultimately agreed. We didn't get very far today before Judge Williams strode confidently to her bench and sat, reaching for the gavel. "Looks like a light day."

Thank goodness.

She peered down at us, her brown eyes twinkling. "Ms. Albertini. Has the prosecuting attorney's office hired anybody else yet?"

I huffed out a breath. "I believe it should happen soon, Judge."

"Good." Her skin was a deep brown, her lips red today, and her hair salt and pepper with awesome curl. Her shirt peeked above the judge's black robe and matched her lipstick. What shade of red was it? I made a mental note to ask her later because it was the perfect color. "At this point, it appears as if charging documents are being submitted too slowly," she said, a slight bite in her voice.

My eyebrows rose, and I nodded subtly. Oh, I'd definitely hit Nick with that information and soon. Then I smiled, silently thanking her for the opportunity to kick Nick in the preverbal butt that she'd just given me.

"All right. Let's start with *Elk County vs. June Applebee* for public nuisance," the judge said, perching her glasses on her forehead and reading from a file.

I dug out the correct file and read quickly. After a couple of hours, Clark and I had pled out thirteen cases, set for trial ten more, and had worked in tandem well, even though we'd end up against each other in the trials. But we were efficient, and the judge was quick to find trial dates, so when I picked up the last file and began to read, I was already planning my lunch.

The judge cleared her throat. *"Elk County vs. Danny Pucci."*

I stifled a gasp and swiveled to watch Danny lope to Clark's table.

"Hi there, little sister," Danny gave me a slow wink as he took his seat. I gaped in shock as I stared at my sister Tessa's ex-fiancé.

Danny was long and lean with a crapload of mean. He was the guy who had mothers rushing to shut their daughters behind locked doors before running out to say hello themselves, and his tan brought out the deep green of his eyes. I had the biggest crush on him while he was engaged to Tessa. Until he beat the heck out of her and stole her car. Now I wanted to return the favor.

I liked to believe that my even mix of Italian and Irish genes lent loyalty, spirituality and spunk to my make-up. But in truth they also created fire and a need for revenge. To hurt those who wounded mine. Danny had nearly destroyed my sister. The wild sister.

I checked the hackles rising on the back of my neck and turned toward the judge.

The judge looked our way. "The charge appears to be domestic violence against a live-in girlfriend, but this charging file is terribly light. Ms. Albertini?"

I cleared my throat and leaned down to read the charging documents. Oh, I wasn't going to be nice. "Your records are light, judge." Way too light. It wasn't a surprise, considering the former prosecuting attorney had gotten involved in the drug trade and then was murdered before all of the lawyers were fired. "From the records, this looks like a third offense." Yeah, the asshat should've been charged with a felony. This had fallen through the cracks. I stood taller to take the lumps. "It appears that additional charges are required here, your honor. The state requests a postponement and a week to prepare for a preliminary hearing."

Clark glanced my way, surprise in his eyes. "We could plea this out."

Glass sharp eyes narrowed on mine as Danny stood in faded

jeans and a tan shirt decorated with a dragon spitting fire. "I plead not guilty, your honor. Regardless."

The judge gave me a look that clearly said this was my *last* favor. "It appears we're not ready for a plea. This time. Very well, Ms. Albertini. One week to amend charges." She stood, we all jumped to our feet, and the judge strode gracefully out of the courtroom.

Clark turned toward me. "You okay?"

"Yes." I grabbed the files off my table and ignored his client. My afternoon was swamped, and I had to get through it and fast. I had to find Tessa.

Once I got back to the office, I tried to call but went to her voicemail. Then my first witness arrived to prepare for an upcoming trial, and I had to get down to trying to fix the mess the office had become.

I worked diligently until quitting time and all but ran out the door at five o'clock. Nick hadn't returned from court, and right now, I didn't care.

After an afternoon where my red shoes made me feel like anything but a badass, I swung through Margo's Tai Palace for buckets of calories to take to my sister Tessa's place. I had tried her phone a couple more times through the afternoon, but she must've been working. This was better news given in person... with wine. I'd already picked up several bottles before hitting Margo's.

It was finally summer, and I drove my Fiat with the top down, trying to suck in fresh air and lose the worry. Timber City had about forty-nine thousand citizens, which was the big city to a girl from Silverville. Most of my family still lived in my home-town, fifty miles east through a mountain pass. Tessa lived here, right off the main drag in town in an apartment above Smiley's Diner, where she worked as a waitress.

A lot of people, locals and tourists, strolled along the brick sidewalks in the warm weather now that the workday was finished.

I parked at the curb, grabbed the food and wine, and then walked past the diner entrance to a doorway just around the corner. Using my hip, I nudged it open and walked up the cement steps and through another doorway that led to an alcove with two apartment doors.

Tess's door was the one to the right, and it was ajar.

I stilled. Tessa never left her door open. Panic tried to grab me, but I had to stay smart. Had Danny already found her? No. Maybe she was just putting groceries away or something. As quietly as I could, I set dinner against the wall. Then I walked on my toes across the hard cement to the blue steel door, careful not to let my heels make any noise. My heart pounded, and my lungs tightened painfully.

The massive lump in my throat didn't allow me to swallow. Okay. Tess had to be okay. I reached her door and gingerly pushed it open, listening for any sound.

"Freeze!" A male voice bellowed from behind me.

I yelped and fell against the door, going down to the soft rug inside and coming up fast. Wincing at the pain in my hip, I threw my head back and put my shoulders against the wall.

Then I just stopped thinking as my brain tried to interpret too much information at once.

Tessa stood near the head of a bloody and beaten body, a silver gun in her hand and her eyes wild. At the feet of the unmoving guy stood my pseudo-boyfriend, Aiden Devlin, a man I hadn't seen in two weeks. His beard rivaled that of the bailiff's earlier, but his piercing blue eyes were in a category of their own.

A hard shoulder shoved me, and then Detective Grant Pierce was between me and everybody else, his gun out and pointed at my sister. "Drop the gun."

Tessa, her face whiter than any ghost, gently set the gun down.

I gulped and peered around Pierce to see the body. "Please tell me that isn't Danny Pucci," I whispered, my voice shaking. But I didn't need an answer.

The bloody guy on the floor was definitely Danny Pucci. I looked closer, trying not to vomit. Danny stared back at me, his green eyes unblinking, a hole through the center of his forehead. It took me a second to realize why. It really did.

Danny was dead.

CHAPTER 2

*T*essa's stricken green gaze met mine, and I automatically tried to step toward my older sister.

Detective Pierce pivoted and put me back into the wall with his right hand on my chest, his left hand pointing the gun between Tessa and Aiden. "Both of you turn around and lace your fingers behind your heads," he barked. The sound had me jumping.

I stayed in place. Detective Pierce was almost a foot taller than me with a tough and lanky form, dark blond hair, and an overall cranky disposition. He was probably in his early forties, but it was possible late thirties with just a ton of baggage in his hard cop eyes. His hand against my upper chest was firm, and I wasn't going anywhere.

Tessa immediately turned around and hesitated before lacing her fingers behind her thick reddish-blonde hair. The blonde streaks were new. Her legs in white capris visibly shook, and she looked defenseless in her Baby Yoda t-shirt with the girly cut.

Aiden ignored the detective as two patrol officers strolled into the room, guns out. His gaze raked me head to toe.

I shivered.

Then he slowly, deliberately, turned around and expertly laced his long-tapered fingers against his thick black hair. He'd obviously done so before, and his knuckles were bruised and bloody. He was at least an inch taller than Pierce, and not a thing about him was lanky. He was broad and muscled with a dangerous grace that reminded me of those panthers on television.

The uniformed cops instantly stepped up and each handcuffed Tess and Aiden, turning them toward the door and away from the body.

"Anna?" Tessa whispered, the slightest hint of our mother's Irish brogue in her shaking voice.

"I'm coming," I breathed, barely able to get the words out. What had happened? If Tessa had killed Danny, it had definitely been in self-defense. Why was Aiden there? And why was he wearing bloody boots, ripped jeans, and a Lordes T-shirt? He had belonged to the motorcycle club, but it had been disbanded, with most of the members arrested for running drugs. "Let me go, Pierce."

"No." He holstered his weapon with one hand, keeping the other on me.

I grabbed his wrist. "Tess? Don't say a word until I get there. Ask for an attorney right away. Not one word," I said in a rush of energy, my entire body heating.

The officer ushered my sister out of the apartment.

Aiden stopped cold near the door, forcing the cop pushing him to halt, his blue eyes lightening to glacier cold. "Get your fuckin' hand off her." While Pierce had barked his order, Aiden's was said in a dangerously quiet voice that lowered the temperature in the entire room.

If anything, Pierce pushed me harder against the wall. "Get him out of here."

The uniformed officer struggled, but then Aiden let himself be pushed out the door. There was no doubt in my mind that Aiden allowed it to happen; otherwise there'd be a fight right now.

Pierce took a deep breath, released me, and turned on me. "What are you doing here?" His breath was hot and his eyes even more so.

I blinked but was already against the wall and couldn't step away. "I was bringing my sister dinner." Then my gaze strayed to the dead body, and the smell of coppery blood began to permeate the fog in my head. A sofa pillow sat a distance away with a hole burned through it. It was a pillow my Nonna had stitched with the word 'family' carefully embroidered across it. Now it had a hole in the middle. "I wanted to tell her that Danny was back in town."

Pierce stiffened. "I take it the deceased is named Danny?"

Numbly, I nodded.

"How do you and your sister know the deceased?" Pierce asked as crime techs began to filter into the room, already wearing protective gear and booties.

My brain finally kicked back in. "Sorry. I have to go."

"You're a witness, and you're not going anywhere," Pierce said, anger cutting lines into his rugged face. Oh, he was older than me, and there was no doubt he had a lot going on, but he had asked me out once. Right now, it seemed like a good thing we'd never made that date.

"I'm her lawyer, and I am going now." I tried to put some authority into my voice, although the longer I remained in the room with the dead body, the more I wanted to scream.

Pierce leaned in. "You're a prosecuting attorney, Albertini. You can't be her lawyer. Even if you quit your job, you're a witness, and you can't be her lawyer."

Crap. He was right. My shoulders slumped. "She's my sister," I whispered.

Pierce's eyes softened for the briefest of seconds. "All right. I'll have a uniform escort you to your car, and you drive directly to the station for an interview. I'll be at least an hour here, but I want you in my office when I arrive. You can make arrangements for your sister on the way."

It was the best I was going to get. "Thanks." Without looking at the shiny gun or the battered body, I turned and walked out of the apartment with an officer at my side. She was in her thirties with a cute blonde bob, and she probably would've been pretty had she been smiling. I didn't blame her. There was nothing to smile about.

After she'd seen me to my car, she disappeared back inside the building. A crowd was gathering on the sidewalk, and I pulled away from the curb before anybody could stop me.

Then I quickly dialed a phone number.

"What, Anna? Didn't you get enough of me today?"

"Clark? I need your help." I sped up to make it through a yellow light. "My sister was just arrested, and she needs a lawyer. She might qualify for a public defender, but if not, you can contract with private clients, right?"

"Yeah." His voice went from cajoling to serious. "Where is she?"

Tears threatened my voice, and I shoved them away. This was just too much. "On the way to the police station. I told Tessa not to talk, but she looked scared. Please hurry."

* * *

I TWIRLED the Styrofoam cup around on Pierce's cluttered desk. As a detective in the Elk County Sheriff's Office, he had his own office with a battered desk, two rather nice guest chairs, a plush looking leather chair for him, and a nice window that faced the city park with the beach and Lilac Lake behind him. My office was situated kitty-corner to this building around the park. I'd sat in his comfy guest chair for almost two hours before he arrived, and I'd memorized the pictures of him fishing with what looked like a brother, one with him and a smiling blond woman with the same light green eyes he had, and one of him in his dress uniform. Other than that, case files took up all available space in the small room.

I heard him enter the room before I saw him, and he shut the door, crossing around his desk to sit. His scent of salt and the ocean, even though we were nowhere near an ocean, filtered around. "Did you get food?" As usual, he didn't start with niceties.

"One of the uniforms brought me a granola bar," I said, my head hurting and my mind weary. My phone buzzed for what seemed like the millionth time, and I switched it to silent.

His dark blond eyebrows rose. "I'm sure you called the entire family."

I sighed. "By the time I sat here, they already knew." My immediate family consisted of the combination of two large families from Silverville; the Albertini and O'Shea families. Silverville was settled by Irish and Italian miners, and as most small towns go, there are few secrets. Even from fifty minutes away in the big town of Timber City, word about Tess's arrest would've traveled faster than an August wildfire. "I'm surprised you didn't see anybody when you came in."

"I came in the back door," he admitted, the leather seat groaning as he leaned back. His hair was ruffled, and his eyes battle weary, but he filled out the long-sleeved black shirt like it had been made for him. With the gun and badge at his belt, he all but screamed cop. "Tell me everything."

I looked in the empty coffee cup. The coffee had sucked, but at least it had been something. "I was taking dinner to my sister, you yelled at me, and I fell into her living room. You saw what I saw." My stomach hurt like I'd been punched. "Is Tessa okay?"

"When had you last talked to your sister?" Pierce asked, the slight gray at his temples giving him an air of command.

"Last night," I said, picking at the Styrofoam. His tone was conversational, but there was no doubt he was interviewing me. Definitely fishing for information, and I had to be careful. This was my sister. "I called her when I saw that *The Quiet Man* was on the old movie channel. It's a family favorite."

Pierce rolled his head, and his neck cracked. "You didn't call her after Danny Pucci made his first appearance in court today?"

I caught my breath and hid the reaction as soon as I could. Pierce had done his due diligence before coming to interview me, now hadn't he? "I did call her but didn't catch her. There's no way she killed him." I sat forward, desperation ticking through my veins.

"Really?" Pierce tugged his phone from his back pocket and scrolled along the face. "Danny Pucci was arrested a year ago for domestic battery against one Contessa Carmelina Albertini. She pressed charges, and he got a slap on the wrist since it was a first offense." Pierce looked up, his gaze hard. "I doubt it was the first time he hit her. Hell, Anna. She might have a decent self-defense case here."

Fury nearly choked the fear out of me. Not quite, but close. I slammed my hand on his desk. "Tessa would never shoot anybody. She doesn't have it in her." Probably. Well, maybe. If she was in fear for her life, she'd shoot. I would, too.

"Where did she get the gun?" Pierce asked smoothly.

"That wasn't her gun," I retorted. "That gun was long, silver, and shiny. She has a smaller Lady Smith & Wesson, just like me." Relief caught me with enough smoothness to calm me a little bit. Why would Tess shoot Danny with somebody else's gun? She wouldn't. "I told you she didn't do it."

"How long has Aiden Devlin been dating your sister?" Pierce expertly switched topics.

If he was looking to trip me up, he'd failed. "Aiden and Tess aren't dating. I have no idea where he has been for the last two weeks." It wouldn't do to lie to Pierce right now, and I didn't see a reason not to tell him the truth. "Before you ask, I don't know why Aiden was at Tess's apartment or if he had any prior relationship with Danny Pucci." But I was sure going to find out.

"So you don't know why Devlin's knuckles were as beat to shit as the dead body's?" Pierce asked.

Yeah, I'd noticed that as well. "Nope."

Pierce twirled a pen on his desk. "This isn't looking good for your sister."

Considering I hadn't talked to her yet, I didn't know how bad it looked. "Did you test her hand for GSR?" I asked the question like I knew what I was talking about and hadn't binge-watched Law & Order all day Sunday, where is actually how I'd learned about gunshot residue. A homicide case was way above my pay grade.

"She tested positive," Pierce said, seeming relaxed but definitely not missing anything.

I rolled my eyes. "If she picked up the gun that had been used to kill Danny, then the residue would be on her hand. You know that." I thought that was the truth.

"I also know that only a moron would pick up a gun in that situation," Pierce retorted. "Unless she was frightened by Devlin. But I'd have to ask what he was doing there."

I swallowed. "Did you test Aiden's hand?"

"Yep. Positive as well," Pierce said, watching me like a bird of prey. "According to him, he was target practicing yesterday, but that's all he'd own up to—so far. I'm off to interview him next."

"What about Tessa?"

Pierce shook his head. "She lawyered up right away with Clark Bunne. Wouldn't say a word."

Relief cooled the hot ball of anxiety in my stomach. Okay. Good. "Well, then. I guess I'll go talk to her and figure this out. Let's hope you're as good of a detective as you think you are." With that zinger, I stood.

"Albertini? You'll have to talk to her tomorrow," Pierce drawled.

I stopped cold, still facing him. "Why?"

"Because I just arrested her for suspicion of murder. She's being processed now."

CHAPTER 3

I paused at the door to the station, looking out at the darkened night. Pierce had arrested my sister? Oh, I wasn't sure about him before, but this put us squarely on the opposite side of pretty much everything. Even though I was a prosecuting attorney, darn it.

Either way, I couldn't just leave now. Looking around the reception area, I fumbled in my purse like I'd forgotten something, shook my head, and then returned back up the stairs toward Pierce's office. Just in case anybody was watching, which I didn't really think was happening. Of course, there were cameras, so it wouldn't hurt to be careful right now.

Not that I was doing anything wrong.

Well, not really.

Once I crossed to the second floor where detectives were mainly holed up in their offices, I strode briskly down the hallway to the interrogation rooms. The light for the second one was on above the door, so I whisked around the corner and entered the darkened surveillance room, shutting the door quietly. Then, for some bizarre reason I didn't want to explore, I tiptoed up to the two-way mirror to see Aiden facing me with Pierce across the table from him.

Pierce's shoulders looked tense, and Aiden's expression looked bored.

Oh, this was so not good.

I held my breath, leaning over to engage the speaker system.

"Those are nice bruises on your knuckles," Pierce was saying, his tone congenial.

"Thanks," Aiden said, sprawled lazily in his chair. Apparently the police had confiscated his clothing because he now wore an ECSO, Elk County Sheriff's Office, black shirt that stretched tightly across his spectacular chest. One I had spent hours exploring with my hands and mouth only a couple of weeks ago. He stretched out his right hand, and the knuckles had already turned a painful looking purple.

Pierce tapped a closed case file on the smooth metal table between them. "Once I get the lab results back on Danny Pucci, what are the chances your DNA is found on his body? Say in those bruises around his eyes?"

Aiden lifted one shoulder. "Chances and odds aren't my thing."

I shifted my weight, my heart thundering.

Aiden's gaze flicked from Pierce to directly at me, the blue of his eyes sharp. Oh, there was no way he could see me through the mirror, and no way he could hear me. He did not know I was there.

His lips tugged in a smile.

How did he *do* that?

I made myself exhale and breathe normally so I didn't just pass out right then and there.

Pierce leaned toward Aiden, his blond hair looking more ruffled and shaggier than usual. "I had a nice long talk with Tessa Albertini."

"Did you now?" Aiden drawled, his attention returning to Pierce.

What was it about the bad-boy Irishman that got to me? His hair was black and a bit too long, his eyes sharp and way too blue, and his body one that had been sculpted with a devastating attention with too much muscled detail. In other words, he was just *too*…everything.

And the fact that he'd saved my life when we had been kids would never leave me alone. No matter what happened, he would always have a place in my heart—and that was before we'd slept together, and I'd learned that those romance novels that promised multiple orgasms were actually based on fact and not fantasy.

Who knew? Now I did, and I didn't want the fun to end.

But murder had a way of changing things, now didn't it? I sighed.

Aiden's lips twitched again as if we were on the same wavelength.

How did he *do* that?

Pierce slapped his hand on the file. "Like I was saying, I talked to Tessa Albertini, and she said you shot Pucci. That she walked in right after you shot him."

Aiden lifted one dark eyebrow. "Really?"

"Yeah," Pierce said, satisfaction thick in his tone.

I shook my head. Pierce had told me that Tessa hadn't said a word, so he was trying to trick Aiden. Or get Aiden to say that Tess shot Danny. Turning two people against each other was an old police interrogation tactic, and Pierce could tell any lie he wanted.

Somehow, I figured Aiden already knew this. This wasn't his first arrest—not by a long shot. Although, after our last escapade, when he'd saved my life again, after I'd saved his, he'd promised he was one of the good guys. Since that moment, I'd had plenty of fantasies starring him as an undercover FBI agent, but we'd checked out the FBI, DEA, and DHS, and Aiden Devlin didn't work for any of them.

I stood closer to the glass, taking in his fallen Angel-like appearance. Just who was he?

"Devlin?" Pierce prodded.

Aiden flattened his injured hand on the cool metal table. "If Tessa walked in and saw me shoot the dead guy, how did she get the gun from me?" He leaned toward Pierce this time, his gaze intense. "The Albertini women are a tough bunch, a stubborn bunch, but even the tallest is half my size. You think Tess took the gun from me?"

"Are you confessing?" Pierce shot back.

"Nope," Aiden said easily. "Just following your line of bullshit and trying to see how far you'd spin it."

Pierce sat back. "Fine. Forget bullshit. How about you tell me what happened?"

I caught my breath again. Finally. What in the world had happened in that apartment?

"I don't have anything to say about that," Aiden said.

Damn it.

Pierce pounded the table with his fist. "Damn it, Devlin. I thought you left town. Then you show up back here, wearing a Lordes jacket and standing over a dead body. For the love of Christ, do the right thing and get Tessa Albertini off the hook here. Let's start at the beginning. When did you get back?"

"Who said I left?" Aiden said.

I stilled, and my chest heated. Well, he'd certainly left me.

"I do," Pierce said. "I've been watching for you, and I think you know it. You came back on the radar yesterday along with a whole new crew of Lordes motorcycle members—all moving into the Lorde apartment complex just outside of Timber City."

I reared back. What? I truly had believed Aiden had left the Lordes or that he'd been using them for a job or something. That maybe he was a private detective actually on the right side of the law. What was happening?

Aiden cocked his head. "It's nice to be noticed."

Oh, I could just punch him in the face right now.

Pierce's back looked like one long line of pissed off male. In fact, he reminded me of a Doberman our neighbor at the river had for years. Old Bastard Bud had been the dog's name, and he was always pissed but never bit. Something told me that Pierce was going to bite. "What are you up to?"

Aiden exhaled. "You arrested and are going to put away several members of the Lordes club, so we had to reach out to keep our numbers strong. We patched over a couple of smaller clubs in San Diego, Denver, and Dallas. Good news. More tax revenue for Idaho."

My chest ached. I couldn't believe this.

Pierce shook his head. "Don't tell me. Now you're one of the longest standing members, even though you've only been a Lorde a short time. You gunning for president of a motorcycle club that deals in illegal matters, Aiden?"

"No," Aiden said softly. "I already got the job, Pierce."

I ALL BUT ran out of the station and around the flower-scented park to my car, jumping in and squealing out of the lot. Aiden wasn't going to tell the detective anything, and I just couldn't watch any more. Quickly, I dialed Clark's number.

"Hey, Albertini," Clark said, sounding like he had a mouth full of a late dinner.

I swallowed. "Hi. How did it go with Tessa?"

"Good. She's being held overnight for bond, and the hearing is first thing in the morning," Clark said, taking a drink of something. "She's solid, Anna. She'll be okay."

My sister didn't belong in a cell. But I was a prosecuting attorney and knew many of the police officers, so hopefully they'd look at her as one of their own. One of our own. "What happened in that apartment?" I whispered, my voice shaking.

21

Clark was silent for a minute. "You know I can't break client confidentiality."

"Clark," I snapped, even though I knew he was right. "That's my sister. Talk to me."

"No, sorry. Talk to her tomorrow. That's the best I can do, and you know it." He coughed several times and then took a big drink of something. "Sorry about that. Wrong pipe. Make sure Nick is up to speed on this because you can't represent the State. See you tomorrow." He clicked off.

I wanted to scream. Instead, I fielded calls from our mom, dad, grandparents, aunts, uncles, and cousins before arriving at my sister Donna's house. Although it was tempting to leave my phone in my car, I just couldn't do it. My body felt like it was a hundred years old as I lugged myself to the front door of her Craftsman style cottage in the older part of Timber City.

She had the door open before I could knock. "Come on in." Donna was the oldest at twenty-eight, and whereas Tessa took after the Irish side of our family, Donna looked like the Albertini side with her black hair, soft brown eyes, and definite curves. I'd always thought she looked like a young Isabella Rossellini because Donna had that natural style and grace. I didn't take after either side with my brown hair and grayish-green eyes.

I stumbled inside and threw my phone onto the sofa before making my way to the island in the kitchen, where Donna already had a glass of wine poured for me. "Thanks." I took a deep gulp of the fragrant Chianti and let the warmth hit my stomach and spread out.

Donna perched on a stool and reclaimed her glass of wine. She'd dressed down in faded yoga pants with a matching top, and her dark hair was piled high on her head. Her usual realtor outfit was a snappy suit. "How bad is it?" Worry cut into the sides of her generous mouth.

"I don't know," I admitted, leaning on the marble island. "It definitely didn't look good seeing Tessa with a gun in her hand over a dead body, but I think Detective Pierce wants Aiden to be the killer." I wanted them both free and clear.

Donna shook her head and nudged a bowl of apples toward me. "You hungry?"

"No." I still felt like throwing up.

Donna finished her glass and reached for the bottle to refill. "Do you think Aiden is the killer?"

"I have no idea," I admitted. "I doubt it. If Aiden killed Danny, why would he have done it in Tessa's apartment? And if he'd shot Danny, then how did Tess get the gun? None of it makes sense."

Donna rubbed her left eye. "I don't know anything about the criminal process. What happens now?"

I bit the inside of my cheek. "Tess will have a first appearance tomorrow morning, plead not guilty, and probably have bail set. Since she's been arrested on suspicion of murder, the bail will be a lot, and we'll probably have to hire a bond company." It seemed like the judges in Elk County liked really high bail these days. "I think Judge Williams is the most reasonable, so let's hope she's working tomorrow. Also, there's a chance Nick won't argue for a high bail." I hoped.

Donna swirled her wine around in her glass. "Then what?"

My temples ached. "Then the State will try and put together a case, we'll work on a defense, and we'll see. For now, we need to talk to her to see what really happened." I hated that I couldn't get to her. Or to Aiden. There were too many darn questions.

Donna frowned. "You work for the state."

"I don't care. If I have to quit my job to help Tessa, I will." Although, I was still a witness.

Donna patted my hand, back into big sister mode, even though I was the lawyer in the room. "Let's not do anything hasty until we talk to Tessa and her lawyer, okay? Maybe there's a simple answer to all of this."

The simple answer was that Aiden killed Danny, and Tessa somehow got the gun from him. Then Aiden would go away forever, and that thought was like another punch to the solar plexus. Oh, I knew Aiden was a dangerous guy, but I couldn't imagine him being a cold-blooded killer any more than I could Tess. I looked at the partially empty bottle. "Please tell me you have more bottles than that."

"My wine cellar is stocked," Donna said.

"Can I stay the night?" I didn't want to be alone, and I was sure Donna felt the same way. Besides, when I became really anxious, the nightmares returned, and I just couldn't deal with more right now.

She nodded. "All of the clothes you left here are clean and in your drawer. Your duck pajamas are in there."

I wanted to smile, but my face wouldn't work. I told her all about Aiden and Pierce's interview. When we were finished, she reached down into the cupboard.

"We're gonna need more wine," she said.

CHAPTER 4

$\mathcal{I}$'d headed into work early and waited in my office as long as I could the next morning, hoping to catch Nick before the hearing. He never showed up. Our offices were rather quiet, considering he'd fired almost everybody. Finally, I couldn't wait any longer, so I stood and hustled out of my office to the door, nodding at the receptionist as I hurried outside into the morning.

Donna had lent me a red suit with skirt and jacket to match my red shoes from the day before. The shell was a soft white that I might not return to her.

The heels clip-clopped on the sidewalk around the park to the courthouse, and I climbed the marble steps, stopping short at seeing my cousin standing near a pillar. "Pauley?"

He looked up and then back down, his brown hair smoothed back. At sixteen, he was tall and handsome with startling brown eyes. "Anna. Hi." He tapped his long fingers on his khaki pants in a one, three, two, one rhythm that calmed him. Today he wore a plain white shirt, and when he only wore one color, he was in need of peace and quiet.

I stopped a couple of feet away from him. "What are you doing here?"

"Everyone is here," he said, looking past me to the park.

I exhaled. Okay. That was to be expected. My entire family would need to see that Tessa was all right for themselves. "I need to go inside, P. Do you want to come with me?"

He shook his head. "There are too many people in there. I told my mother I would meet her in the college library across the park."

Timber City Community College took up the third side of the park that wasn't lakefront, and Pauley attended the school at his age since he was brilliant. He was also one of my favorite people in the world, and I knew he wouldn't like to be inside the courtroom with so many people. He was autistic with savant qualities, and I loved him more than I could describe. "Can I come with you?" I joked.

His grin was quick and then gone. "The grandmothers are united."

I gasped. My head spun. "United?"

"United," he affirmed.

In union, in perfect accord, we both crossed ourselves. Holy Mary Mother of God. I couldn't breathe. "Are you sure?"

"Yes. Goodbye." Pauley strolled gracefully down the steps and toward the trails that wound through the city park to the college.

I looked at the closed double doors of the courthouse and fought the very real urge to run back to my office. This was worse than I'd feared. "Okay," I whispered to myself. "This is okay. I can handle this." Sucking up courage, I barreled up the remaining steps and through the door, all but running down to the lower floor, where only the first appearances took place in misdemeanor court. After the first appearances, felony cases then took place in the district courtrooms upstairs.

My head swam, but I pushed open the double doors in the courtroom in which I normally worked. Today, one entire side was packed full of family members on the benches, as if they were attending a wedding and were on the bride's side. Today it was the defendant's side. The other side of the wide aisle just held a couple of people I didn't know, including two Lorde's members with long hair and the Lorde cut on their powerful shoulders.

Donna stood from the back row and grabbed my arm. "The grandmothers are *united*."

"I heard," I whispered, my voice trembling. Taking another deep breath, I angled my head to see our grandmothers standing in front of the first bench, shoulder to...head. Yep. Right next to each other, an invisible shield all but cascading out from them. "Holy Mother."

Donna pulled me out of the aisle. "I know." Her voice remained hushed, although many of our relatives were talking loudly to each other in front of us.

I didn't know what to do. Instead, my eyes remained glued on the two. Nonna Albertini and Nana O'Shea couldn't be more different if they had made a lifetime attempt at it. Nonna was tall with black hair, incredible brown eyes, lovely olive-toned skin, and a no-nonsense approach to life. There was not a doubt in my mind that she had a wooden spoon in her massive leather purse, and it'd be a miracle if she didn't clap Nick on the ear with it during the hearing.

Nana was only five feet tall, had reddish-blonde hair, pale skin that turned red from a breeze, and soft green eyes. She believed in magic, fairies, and everything in between, and there was a fair chance she'd end up putting a spell on Nick if he didn't do well today.

The grandmas were the same age and had been enemies from high school for a reason I'd never truly heard since neither one of them would talk about it. When my folks had gotten together, most of Silverville had picked a side and then gone to war...until Donna had been born and they'd shared blood. From that time, the grandmas had tolerated each other because they loved the same people, but usually that was as far as it went.

When they united, they were a force beyond this world. Kind of like two magnets that somehow figured out how to mesh together when it's a physical impossibility.

Donna leaned in. "Do you think they'll grab Tess and run?"

"I wouldn't rule anything out." For sure, I wasn't getting in their way. I fought the very real urge to cross myself again. "How mad are they?"

"Neither has said a word," Donna whispered.

Oh, Lord. I needed a sedative. Next to Nana stood my mom and dad. The grandpas stood in the second row, behind their wives and out of the line of fire. Yeah, they weren't dumb. Then too many family members to name took residence in the remaining rows.

The doors opened and Nick walked inside, two case files in his broad hand. He stopped short. "Oh, Jesus," he whispered.

I nodded.

He looked down at me, his tawny eyes sharp. "United?"

I grimaced. "Apparently."

Then to Nick's credit, he threw his shoulders back and kept moving to his table. I had to give him that. He'd graduated from Silverville in the same class as Donna, gone on to college on a football scholarship, and then had become a lawyer while in the service. Now he was home and making a name for himself, no doubt so he could run for office someday. If my grandmothers didn't curse or kill him.

Donna leaned toward me. "He has combat experience, right?"

"I think so," I said, ignoring the low pull in my abdomen from his courage.

The doors opened and Clark rushed inside, quickly making it up the aisle to his table just as the bailiff entered and told everybody to rise for the judge. We were all standing already.

Judge Williams walked inside, and relief cranked through my

anxiety. Okay. That was one good thing. She took in the court-room and then sat, reaching for her glasses. "Everyone sit. Please. Full house today, Mr. Basanelli?"

Nick nodded. "Apparently so, Judge."

Everyone sat, the sound loud enough to remind me of fans at a football game.

The judge read the first file. "*Elk County vs. Aiden Devlin.*"

Deja Vu. Seriously. I watched as the side door opened, and the bailiff drew Aiden inside toward Clark. After his night in jail, Aiden looked surprisingly refreshed. He still wore the borrowed dark t-shirt and sweats, and the handcuffs looked just right on his wrists.

He reached Clark and stood beside him.

Donna cut me a curious look. I shrugged. It was Clark's job to defend people, but I thought Aiden would hire his own attorney. For now, at this first appearance, I guess it didn't matter.

The judge looked at Aiden. "You're charged with suspicion of first-degree murder. Do you understand the charges against you?"

"Yes, your honor," Aiden said, his very slight brogue proving he'd lived in Ireland until moving to Silverville to live with his grandparents when he'd been a wild teen. They had both passed on, and Aiden had left town at eighteen, already on the wrong side of the law.

"How do you plead?" The judge asked.

The entire courtroom seemed to still.

"Not-guilty, your honor," Aiden said calmly.

Nonna yelped and moved back as Nana rushed past her, toward Aiden.

The bailiff launched into motion, but Aiden held up both hands, stopping him. It was Jay, and he looked back and forth, clearly at a loss what to do with my minute grandmother.

Aiden turned toward her. "Mrs. O'Shea?"

She stood behind the short railing in the empty front bench and leaned up toward his face. Her cushy body vibrated in her flowery dress. "Did you kill that man?" she asked, Ireland heavy in her voice and her body ramrod straight.

"No, ma'am," Aiden said, his voice gentle.

She stared at him, right in the eyes, and he let her. Finally, she reached over the railing and patted his arm. "I always thought you were a good boy, Aiden Devlin. Glad to know I was right." Then she turned and made her way back to her spot on the other side of the aisle.

For the briefest of seconds, Aiden's mask dropped. Vulnerability glowed in his sapphire colored eyes, and he looked like the sixteen-year-old boy who'd saved me from a monster.

Donna breathed out next to me. "Oh," she whispered. "I see it now."

My heart took the hit. "You didn't see him before?" I mean, come on. The guy was hot sex on a stick with a side of badass and untamable male.

She slipped her arm through mine. "I didn't really see *him*."

Yeah, I got that.

Then his gaze lifted and met mine across the many rows of vacant benches on his side. Warmth slid through me from my ears to my toes, heating several important places on the way.

Donna gulped.

The judge banged her gavel. "Mr. Basanelli?"

Nick cleared his throat, looking tall and dangerous in another black suit—this one with an aqua colored power tie. "The defendant is a flight risk, your honor. In addition, the defendant is a known member of a criminal motorcycle club that just had several members arrested and charged."

Clark reared up. "The defendant wasn't charged because he didn't do anything wrong. In fact, Mr. Devlin saved Mr. Basanelli's colleague, Ms. Albertini, by risking his own life. He runs a business in Spokane, and he has no intention of leaving town. I request the defendant is released on his own recognizance."

They argued back and forth, and finally the judge set bail at three hundred thousand dollars.

Donna tugged me closer with our entwined arms. "What does that mean?"

"It means he's out ten percent of that if he gets a bondsman," I said.

"Thirty thousand dollars?" Donna hissed. "Where are we gonna get that kind of money for Tessa?" She didn't wait for an answer. "If we all pool extra money, we can find it. I don't want to risk all of mom and dad's retirement. I can figure this out."

Aiden looked over his shoulder at the two Lordes' guys and gave a short nod. "Thank you, your honor." Then the bailiff escorted him away and brought in Tessa.

I jumped to my feet just as the rest of my family did the same. She was dressed in cute jeans and an ECSO long-sleeved T-shirt, her hair was in a ponytail, and she looked like she'd gotten some rest. Unlike Aiden, she wasn't cuffed. Thank goodness. Tessa looked at the family and then sighed, her chest moving.

She took her place next to Clark and looked at the judge, who ran her through the charges like she'd done Aiden and then asked how Tess pled. Tessa pled not-guilty.

The judge looked at Nick. "What does the state argue?"

Nick didn't hesitate. "The defendant has been charged on suspicion of first-degree murder. She was found standing over the body of her ex-boyfriend, in her apartment, with a recently discharged weapon in her hands. We don't have ballistics back yet, but the victim was killed with a nine-millimeter, and the gun fits. The defendant has access to a lot of family members with substantial resources, and the state considers her a flight risk. We ask that she is held over without bond."

Muttering echoed up along my side of the courtroom. Nonna reached in her purse, and the bailiff immediately put himself in her path before she could reach Nick with the wooden spoon in her hand.

I couldn't believe it. Fire lanced down my throat, making my tongue hurt. Oops. I'd bitten it.

Donna tightened her grip on me. "They won't make her stay in jail, will they?"

Clark chuckled, and the sound was reassuring. "That's the most ridiculous thing I've heard all day, your honor. Ms. Albertini does have plenty of family, as you can see. That is a strong tie to this community, and she has no plans to go anywhere. Ms. Albertini has a clean record, and this is her first offense. In addition, her sister is a prosecuting attorney and has dedicated herself to pursuing the law. Not only that, but Tessa didn't shoot anybody. We request she's released on her own recognizance."

The judge read through the file. "Very well, Mr. Bunne. Bail is set at one hundred thousand dollars."

I breathed out. "Okay. We can come up with ten thousand amongst all of us." Now we just had to find the bondsman and get my sister out of jail.

CHAPTER 5

I left my family at the police station to await Tessa's release, making them promise to call me the second she was free. I had to get to her. For now, I was going to kill my boss.

Even the clipping of my heels sounded angry as I hustled around the park, up the stairs, and into the prosecuting attorney's offices. Nick stood at the reception desk, flipping through a stack of messages while the young receptionist smiled up at him like he'd created ice-cream or something. He looked over his shoulder, and his jaw tightened. "My office." Then he turned and strode down the long hallway, beyond the conference rooms, and to his corner office that looked over the building next to us, the beach, and the lake.

I followed, my throat hot. When we entered his office, he strode around his desk, and I slammed the door with all the fury finally let loose.

"What in the holy fuck were you thinking?" I bellowed at the top of my lungs, truly not caring who heard.

His eyebrows went up, his chin went down, and his eyes

narrowed. "I was doing my fucking job." He had a pretty good bellow.

Unfortunately for him, half of my family was Italian, and an Italian man losing his temper and raising his voice did nothing but piss me off more. "That wasn't your job. That was a travesty and a heavy handed smackdown," I yelled, stomping past the guest chairs to face him across his desk.

His teeth ground together, and his eyes glittered. He planted both hands on his desk and flattened them in what I feared was an attempt to keep from grabbing me. He had big hands. "Sit the hell down. Now."

Oh, I didn't think so. "No."

His nostrils flared, and he jerked his fancy black suit jacket off to drape over his chair. Then he yanked his tie loose and slowly, carefully, unbuttoned and rolled up the sleeves of his pressed white shirt. The taut muscle beneath his shirt moved nicely. When he'd apparently tamed his temper, he exhaled. "Where do you work?"

I blinked. He was threatening my job? Oh, I wasn't sure I wanted this job. "Right this second? In this office."

"Right." His forearms were tanned and strong, and frankly, the whole rolling up the shirt was kind of sexy in a threatening way.

I tried really hard to push the unwelcome intrigue out of my head. I was not interested in Basanelli, no matter how rugged, sexy, and dangerous he was. "Your point?"

"Your sister is a defendant, and I knew Clark Bunne would do his job and remind the judge that Tessa doesn't have a record and has strong ties to the community." Nick pulled out his chair and dropped into it, for the first time looking tired. "I also knew that Judge Williams likes you and would go easy on the bail, but not too easy. We had to avoid any sense of favoritism here, and if you'd pull your stubborn head out of your spectacular ass, you'd know that."

Oh. All right. I deflated and stepped back to sit in one of the leather guest chairs. "You think my ass is spectacular?"

"You know I do," he said, warmth finally filtering through his tawny eyes. Then he pinched the bridge of his nose. "You are, however, more trouble than I think any woman could be worth."

Also a fair statement. "I, ah, shouldn't have yelled at you. I mean, you are my boss."

He sighed. "When has that ever stopped you?" He sat back and studied me with those intelligent eyes. "How close was I to getting a wooden spoon to the head?"

"The spoon was in Nonna's hand, but Jay intercepted her," I admitted.

Nick grinned. "I guess I owe Jay a bottle of Scotch. Good to know." Then he sobered. "Here's the deal. I have Celeste creating an ethics wall between you and this case because I can't afford for you to take a leave of absence right now."

I shook my head. Celeste was Nick's paralegal, and she pretty much ran the office. If she wanted me away from a case, there wasn't anything I'd be able to do. Right now, I needed to know everything the state had on Tessa. "She's my sister, Nick."

"Don't care," he retorted. "You're screened from everything having to do with this case. In addition, I strongly advise you to tell your sister that you can't discuss the case with her. You are not her attorney. Keep that in mind."

I swallowed. Since I was positive my sister hadn't shot Danny, anything she told me wouldn't harm her case. "You're really going forward with the prosecution?" It shouldn't hurt, but somehow, my chest still ached.

"Yeah. At the very least, we have to figure out who killed Pucci, and there's a chance it was Tessa." Nick reached for a gold pen to tap on the desk. "This is the last time we'll discuss this case until it's over, Anna. Don't ask me, don't look in files, and don't ask the paralegals for information. You're screened."

I could quit my job, but that wouldn't solve anything. "Fine."

"And stay away from Aiden Devlin. He's a defendant once

again, and this office has had enough bad press lately. I don't need one of my prosecutors associating with him. Got it?" Nick had a good glare when he wanted.

I nodded. There really wasn't an answer, and it wasn't like Nick knew I'd burned up the sheets with Aiden before he'd left town. That was private, and apparently that was over. Plus, I had no intention of staying away from Aiden right now. Oh, we were done on a personal note, but I was going to find him and get the truth about Danny Pucci from him.

Then I'd say goodbye.

Quite possibly with a kick to the groin.

* * *

It was after five when Nick finally finished piling cases on my desk in an obvious attempt to both bury me with work and keep the office running smoothly until he got off his butt and hired more attorneys, so I drove directly to Donna's house where she and Tessa were already into a bottle of wine and an extra-large Vinnie's fully loaded pizza. I threw my briefcase and purse on the sofa and grabbed a slice before Donna could hand me a plate. "Did you send the family home?"

Tessa nodded, her hair still in the ponytail and her eyes mellow from the wine. "Yeah. We had a family meeting with a lot of yelling and swearing, and then they went home. I'm supposed to keep everyone informed."

I swallowed without chewing and coughed, quickly recovering and going slower. The food was delicious. I pulled up a chair at the island, patted Tess on the shoulder, and took a deep breath. "All right. If you killed Danny, don't say another word to anybody."

She rolled her eyes. "I didn't kill Danny."

That's what I had figured, but it didn't hurt to ask. "Okay." I tried to put my lawyer hat on when all I wanted to do was snuggle down with my sisters and get lost in a movie. But this was serious, and I was the one with the law degree, so I had to grow a pair. "Tell me what happened."

Tessa finished her slice of pizza, took a deep drink of the Cabernet, and exhaled. "There isn't much to tell. I got home, and my door was unlocked."

"Open and unlocked or shut and unlocked?" I asked.

She pursed her lips. "Shut and unlocked. I slipped my key in, discovered the door was unlocked, so I twisted the knob." She shrugged, still looking young in her goofy T-shirt. "I do forget to lock it sometimes, so I wasn't worried. In fact, I was thinking about a million things and stepped inside, almost shutting the door before I saw...Danny on the floor." She gulped as if trying not to puke. Her face paled.

I tried to keep my voice level. "Okay. What happened next?"

"I kind of froze," Tessa admitted. "I dropped my purse on the ground and just stared at him like I wasn't sure what I was seeing, you know?"

"Yeah." Boy did I ever know. "Then what?"

She rubbed her eyes. "I heard a noise to the left, by his feet, and I just reacted. The gun was on the floor next to Danny, and I grabbed it and jumped toward his head and away from the noise. It was all instinct."

"Where was the gun when you grabbed it? By his head, his feet, what?" I kept my voice level even though fear for my sister made my throat hurt.

She frowned. "It was kind of by his shoulder. Not touching him but right next to him."

Donna poured more wine for the three of us. "Didn't I read somewhere that leaving a gun at the scene was smart, so long as you wiped it down? That it was better to drop it, if it's untrace-able, than take it after shooting someone?"

That sounds good, but hell if I know. It also sounds like some-thing off a television show." I checked out Tessa's coloring to

REBECCA ZANETTI

make sure she wasn't too pale, and light pink still lingered in her Irish-looking cheeks. "What happened next, Tessa?"

"I, um, caught sight of Aiden, who I hadn't even realized was in the room. So I grabbed the gun, pointed it at him, and I didn't recognize him right away with the beard." She shivered and rubbed her hands along her arms. "Then you came inside, and the police were there yelling at me to drop the gun. So I dropped the gun."

What questions should I ask her? "Did Aiden say anything?"

She shook her head. "Neither of us had time to say a word."

I bit my lip. "Aiden's knuckles were bruised. Do you have any indication that Aiden hit Danny or shot him?"

"No," Tessa said quietly. "Except that they were both in my apartment and kind of bloody." Her very green eyes darkened. "How much trouble am I in?"

I patted her hand. "I don't know, but since you didn't kill Danny, we'll figure this out." I ran through the scene in my head. "How long had you been away from your apartment, and think really hard on whether or not you locked your door before leaving."

"I was gone for a couple of hours—just shopping. And I think I locked the door, but I might not have." Tessa reached for her wine.

"Good. Give me a list of where all you went during the afternoon, and we'll find any security cameras that caught your image." If we could establish that she wasn't anywhere around when Danny was killed, she'd be okay. Of course, we had to be able to determine when he'd been shot. "When was the last time you talked to Danny?"

Tessa went from pale to tomato red.

Ah, crap. "Tessa?" I asked.

She looked away. "I talked to him just yesterday."

I shut my eyes and then slowly reopened them. "For how long?"

She ducked her head. "I don't know. Maybe for an hour?"

38

Donna's lips tightened, but when she spoke, her tone was gentle. "Tessa."

Tess sighed. "I know. I've been talking to him on the phone a few times the last month. He said he's gone through anger management and changed, but we were just talking as friends and nothing more. I promise. I'd never try for something more with him."

Donna looked at me. "Is it bad that they've been in contact recently?"

"It isn't good," I admitted. "Did you invite him over, Tessa?"

"No. I didn't even know he was in town," Tessa burst out. "He has been living in Washington state up in the mountains, and there was no discussion about him visiting. I promise."

Okay. We could deal with this. "Do you know of anybody who would want Danny dead?"

"Besides anybody he ever dated?" Donna asked dryly.

"No," Tessa said. "He never mentioned being scared or worried about anybody. In fact, I think he's made some good friends where he lives now and seems much more grounded. Like he's finally found himself."

I couldn't quite make sense of this. "Then how was he arrested here for domestic violence of a girlfriend? His hearing was yesterday."

Tess stilled. "I don't know anything about that. He's dating somebody in town?"

I had to get my hands on that file. "It seems like it. We need to find out who and what happened. Is there anybody else in town that Danny would be talking to these days?"

Tessa shrugged. "I don't know. He had some friends in the bar where he used to work, so maybe there? Also, I guess, Aiden Devlin? What was he doing at my apartment, and what was their connection to each other?"

Excellent questions. I rubbed my left temple, which was beginning to ache. "I have no idea, but I'm going to find out. I promise."

CHAPTER 6

*A*fter a night of not sleeping well, I drove away from my sweet cottage with the lovely view of Tamarack Lake. Tamarack was much smaller than Lilac Lake and yet no less busy on this Saturday at the beginning of July. I rented the guest house of a much larger estate from old friends of my parents who were actually rarely in Idaho. The rent was cheap so long as I kept an eye on the main house, dock, and grounds, which I happily did.

At the moment, I'd much rather be going to the lake with my sisters for a Saturday of playing on a boat, but duty called. My heart rate was up and my anxiety flaring, and the most uncomfortable sense of anticipation tingled through my hands on the steering wheel. I'd called Aiden that morning and left a message when he hadn't picked up. After waiting most of the day without receiving a response, I'd texted him that I was on my way to his apartment complex on the border of Idaho and Washington state. If I didn't find him there, I'd head to the Lorde's garage north of Spokane.

I was finding him whether he liked it or not.

My phone rang when I was just a mile away from my house. "Hello."

"Don't even think of coming to the Lordes apartment complex," Aiden said.

Every nerve in my body short circuited from his low voice with the slight brogue. My heart twinged. Man, I'd missed him these past two weeks. I'd thought we were starting something, and now I wasn't even sure who he was. I tightened my hold on the steering wheel. "We need to talk."

"There's nothing to talk about," he countered.

Ouch. I winced at the direct hit to my heart. Okay. He really didn't care and was done with us. Done with me. I sucked in air and then let it out. "That's where you're wrong, asshole." Crap. Calling him a name gave away that I was upset. Shoot. I sucked at this. "I want to know what happened." I really wanted to dive headfirst into a gallon of ice cream and cry for a while, but I wasn't going to let him know that.

"Upon advice of counsel, I can't talk about what happened," he said evenly.

I rolled my neck to keep from screaming at him. From asking what the heck had happened that we'd gone from wild sex and half-promises to...this. To nothing. I hated being confused, but a girl has her pride. "Okay. Here's the deal, Aiden. My sister is in trouble, and you're involved, and I'm not going to stop until I find you." I let my voice lower this time. "I will find you. I'll hunt down every place you work, every place you might be laying your head at night, and I'll beat the bushes around everyone who even thinks they know you."

"Beat the bushes?" he drawled, humor coming across the line.

My temper spiked even higher. "It's an expression, dumbass. But I meant every word. If I have to, I'll place ads in the newspapers, call the radio shows, and plaster your face all over town with wanted posters. Want to try me? *Do* it."

"Jesus Christ, Angel," he snapped.

Yes! I silently gave myself a high five. I got to him—pissed him off. Now who looked like they weren't controlling their temper?

41

And hearing him use the nickname for me that he'd given me over a decade ago barely hurt at all. Nope. "I hardly see what the Almighty has to do with this, Aiden," I drawled, trying very hard to keep the triumph from my voice.

He sighed, and the sound was long suffering. "We have to meet off the grid. I'll call you when I have time."

"Nope," I retorted. "I'm on my way. Either meet me now, or I'll keep searching until I find you. Trust me when I say that I'm determined." It wasn't just that I wanted to see him, either. This was now a battle of wills, and considering he'd pretty much kicked me in the heart, I wasn't going to lose. No matter what.

He said something in Gaelic that sounded rough. "Fine. I'll come over tonight."

Oh, hell no. "You're no longer welcome at my home, and I'm done messing around about this. I'll arrive at your apartment complex in about twenty minutes. Be there." I hoped I felt half as tough with him in the room as I did right now when miles separated us.

"I'm nowhere near there right now and couldn't get to Idaho if I wanted," he growled. Yeah. Growled. How the heck did he do that?

"You're lying," I muttered.

"I'm not," he countered. "I promise I'll come by tonight and we can talk all you want, although there's not much to say."

Oh, he was just being a complete dick. Sometimes it was becoming more difficult to remember that he'd saved my life when I was ten years old. Last month, I'd decided to save his, and I thought I had to some degree. "Why are you doing this?" I asked, turning onto the freeway.

Silence. Heavy and thoughtful and just like Aiden. "Doing what?" he asked finally.

"Don't be obtuse," I said. "You can be as big of a jackass as you want, but don't pretend to be a moron. Why, Aiden?"

"Some things just have to be the way they are," he said, almost sounding regretful. Almost. "I got caught up in you and forgot the rest of the world. Don't get me wrong—I enjoyed myself. But reality always comes back, Angel. You know that."

Know that? I didn't even know what the heck he was talking about right now. "Aiden?"

Movement sounded over the line. "I have to go. I'll be at your place after dark." Then he disengaged the call.

After dark? What was he—a vampire now? I bit my lip and tossed my phone to the passenger seat. The top was down on my car, the sun was out and on my face, and I felt like crap. My phone rang again, and I pressed speaker. "Hello."

"Hey there. Had a feeling I should call," my cousin, Lacey, said. She was Pauley's big sister and always had a sixth sense when it came to me.

I sucked in air. "You were right." Lacey was my best friend and had been since we'd been in diapers. We shared our whole lives, including the worst day for us both. The day I'd been kidnapped, and Aiden had saved me. "How's the bullet wound healing?"

"I'm fine." Lacey worked as a cop in Detroit and had been shot the month before. "Tell me about Tess."

I gave her the entire story, which she'd no doubt already heard from her mom. "What I can't figure out is what Aiden is doing," I admitted.

"Talk it through with me," Lacey said, horns honking around her.

I turned off the freeway toward the apartment complex. "Okay. He was a member of the Lordes Motorcycle Club, and they were part of a drug running operation. He turned against them and saved me, which resulted in many of the members being charged and most taking plea bargains." Which kept them nicely in prison.

"Okay," Lacey said. "So far, so good. Then he disappears for two weeks and shows back up in Tessa's living room over a dead body."

43

"Yeah," I said. "Not only that, but apparently he's been traveling around and gathering new members for the Lordes. Why would he do that? He was out, they were over, and he could've made a fresh start." It hurt that he hadn't taken his second chance. Or third. Or however many chances there had been for him.

She sighed. "I checked every contact I could find with the FBI, and he's not one of them, Anna. He's not undercover or some hidden hero. Get that out of your head right now."

"I know," I said, lying my ass off. "So what's he doing?"

"Well, there's only one reason he'd want the Lordes back together. Something is happening." Lacey was quiet for a few heartbeats, and I heard more horns honking in the background. "They'd be stupid to still be in the drug trade, but criminals are often stupid. There's a reason he has recruited more members, and I doubt he needs a brotherhood. Have you talked to Detective Pierce about it?"

"No," I admitted. "For one thing, Pierce doesn't trust my loyalty to Aiden, which I understand. But Pierce did say something about keeping an eye out for Aiden, and he seemed to know about the Lordes regrouping." Yeah, I needed to track down Pierce and get him to talk somehow. "First, I'm going to talk to Aiden."

Lacey was quiet for a few minutes, no doubt struggling between her knowledge as a cop and her knowledge of me as her cousin. "Just be careful, okay?"

"Definitely." I pulled into the main area in front of the Lordes apartment complex, which was vacant. Silent and still, although a new Lordes banner hung from a balcony on the second floor of the two-story building to the south. "I'll call you later. Bye."

"Bye." Lacey sighed as she hung up.

The apartment complex consisted of two buildings angled toward each other with the parking area in the middle and a forested area across the street. Fields stretched out behind the buildings, and nobody else lived near. The place probably had been built in the seventies, and bullet holes still marred one side of the structure from the gun fight we'd been in last month. I shivered.

Gathering my rapidly dwindling courage, I stepped out of my Fiat to the warm asphalt and looked around. Heat shimmered between the buildings, and not an ounce of breeze calmed the sun beating down. Taking a deep breath, I strode in my flip-flops to the northernmost building and climbed the steps to the second floor, walking past several apartments to Aiden's.

His blue door was faded, and the doorknob seriously scratched through the metal. Okay. This was trespassing, and I was an officer of the court since I worked in the prosecuting attorney's office.

But we had been lovers, and maybe I was just visiting him. Yeah. That'd go over like a fart in church. I twisted the knob. Locked. Darn it. I knelt down and studied the wimpy lock. Well, what the heck. Drawing a credit card from my purse, I sliced it down through the side of the door to the lock and then twisted the old knob hard.

It opened easily. Yeah, sometimes the lessons from my Uncle Gino came in very handy as long as my mom never found out about them. That would teach Aiden to have such a cheap lock. I mean, it's like he wanted somebody to break in. It's possible I was actually doing him a favor.

With that thought giving me courage, I pushed open the door and stepped inside, instantly holding my breath.

Quiet reined. The place felt...empty. Worn sofa, rickety wooden coffee table, and old television on an even older wooden stand. Dust covered every surface, but the carpet looked fairly clean. It was a gold shag that had mellowed to more of a rust color, and it was a little crunchy under my flip flops.

The picture of a teenaged Aiden and his Grams still sat on the end table by the sofa, and the cheap plastic blinds were up on the one window, showing a view of the dried fields extending to the west.

I gulped in the quiet, shut the door, and turned toward the one bedroom to the right. His bed was made with a thick blue comforter, and the sight caught me off guard. Did bad guys make their beds? A damaged plastic white clothes basket perched in the corner with dirty clothing piled in it.

Still holding my breath for some unknown reason, I opened the closet to see clothes neatly hung with shoes beneath them. His leather jacket and leather cuts were side by side. I ducked down to rifle through his shoes, but there wasn't anything out of the ordinary there. Man, he had big feet.

Turning, I shut the closet door and searched under his bed. Just dust.

Finally, I opened the one drawer of the particle board bedtable by his bed to find condoms, Chapstick, and a matte black gun that looked like a Glock, but I was no expert.

Talk about prepared for anything.

I fought a hysterical giggle. If he had sex and then had to shoot somebody, at least he'd have moistened and protected lips from the Chapstick.

The roaring of motorcycle pipes echoed through the peaceful day outside, and I slammed the drawer shut and froze. Just completely froze. My entire body electrified, and I took a deep breath to prevent the heart attack that was probably coming for me. What had I been thinking to break in?

Heavy footsteps sounded and then paused by Aiden's outside door. It slowly opened.

I winced and moved out of the bedroom, more than ready to give Aiden a piece of my mind.

It wasn't Aiden standing there.

CHAPTER 7

"Well, hello." The guy in the doorway filled it completely. His brown hair hung to his shoulders, his eyes were a shade lighter than his hair, his skin was tan, and his jawline was strong. Several scars lined the right side of his temple, and he looked like he'd spent a lifetime in the boxing ring leading with his face. He wore jeans with oil stains across the left knee, motorcycle boots, and a dark T-shirt that had seen its share of time. "I believe you're trespassing." He had a very slight Spanish accent.

I set my stance. "This isn't your apartment, so I doubt you'd know who was trespassing. From where I'm standing, it's you." My heartbeat thundered in my ears and my knees wobbled, but I kept my expression calm. In my cut off jean shorts, pink tank-top with the pretty flowers across the bottom and flip flops, there was no way I was going to scare this guy. I might be able to bluff my way out of this before Aiden arrived, and at the moment, that seemed like a good thing to do. "If you don't mind, my boyfriend is waiting for me at the police station. He's a detective nicknamed Killer."

The guy at the door grinned. "That's a good nickname. Mine is Saber."

I frowned. "Saber like the company from The Office? The one that bought Dunder Mifflin?"

The grin widened. "No. Saber like I enjoy slicing people all the way through."

I barely kept from gulping. Saber and I were not going to be friends. "Get out of my way." It was time to stop being nice.

He didn't move. "I'm pretty sure Aiden doesn't have a bitch. Want to tell me why you're here?"

"I'm nobody's bitch," I said calmly, wishing I'd brought my gun from the car. I could get to the one in Aiden's bedroom, but it'd be close as to whether or not Saber could get to me first.

"Okay." He reached for his back pocket, and at that second, I moved. I leaped into the bedroom, yanked open the drawer, and turned around with the gun pointed to the doorway that Saber suddenly filled. What was it with this guy and filling doorways?

He looked at the gun and then pressed a phone to his ear. So he'd been going for a phone and not a gun. Good to know. "Devlin? Yeah. There's a cute brunette holding a gun—your gun—on me in your bedroom."

The fact that Saber thought I was cute shouldn't relieve me, but it did just enough to steady my aim. "Get out of my way. So far, today has been peaceful, and I'd hate to have to shoot you, Saber." My voice quivered just a little.

He listened, and then his gaze raked me. "Frilly tank top, flip flops, and really short shorts."

"Hey. These aren't that short," I protested, wildly wondering if I could survive a jump from the second-story window from Aiden's bedroom. Probably not. "Get out of my way." Slowly, I lowered my aim to his left leg. "I will shoot you."

"If you shoot me in the leg, you still have to get by me to reach the outside door and freedom," Saber said reasonably. He listened to the phone for a minute. "Can I have her?" Then Saber's face fell.

"Fine. I won't touch her so long as you're making a claim." Hand to truth, he looked sad. "What do you want me to do with her until you get here?"

"I have a gun," I bellowed, shaking it wildly. "Get out of my way, Saber!" Was he touched in the head?

He listened and then nodded. "I have a message for you, lady."

I figured. "What is it?" Hopefully Aiden once again would tell me to get the heck out of there. Right now, I was on board with this plan.

Saber frowned. "I don't want to say that. The chick has a gun on me." Then he listened some more. "Fine." He cleared his throat, his gaze drifting to the gun. "First, and the most important thing, is that Aiden said not to shoot me."

I put my other hand to the gun to steady my aim. "Aiden isn't exactly on my list of people I'm listening to right now."

Saber swallowed. "All right. He says that he's just a few minutes away and would very much like for you to stay here and wait for him since you're here already." A loud ruckus erupted on the phone, and Saber winced before pulling it away from his ear.

"What did he really say?" I asked, the adrenaline flooding my body making me feel lightheaded.

Saber shook his head. "Point the gun somewhere else."

"No," I said. "Now tell me what he really said, or I'm aiming for your foot." I lowered the barrel of the gun.

Motorcycle pipes ripped through the day.

"Thank God," Saber said, sliding the phone into his back pocket. He hesitated. "Devlin's pretty mad. You seem like a nice girl, even though you won't put down the gun. I hope you understand him."

"I don't," I admitted. "What about you? You're obviously a new member. Why become a Lorde and move to Idaho?" If Aiden had just arrived, there was no way I could get out of there, so why not dig for information?

Saber rubbed the scruff on his chin. "He made me an offer I couldn't refuse."

Wonderful. "I don't know what that means. Where are you from?"

"California," Saber said.

I tilted my head, lowering the gun even more. "You were in a club that got patched over? By a group that barely had any members?"

Saber shook his head. "Nope. I've never been in a club. I love to ride, though."

So Aiden was recruiting new members who weren't even in clubs? How did that make any sense? "What kind of an offer did Aiden make you?"

Saber smiled again, but his gaze didn't move from the gun. "Not a lot motivates me, pretty lady. But a guy hits an age when comfort matters, you know?"

"So, money?" I asked. "What are you guys into these days?"

Movement sounded, and Aiden suddenly stood behind Saber. He'd shaved off the beard but already had a five o'clock shadow. "Leave," he said.

Saber gave me a sympathetic wince, turned, and quickly exited the apartment. When he closed the outside door, silence descended.

Aiden's chin lifted. "You have one second to put that gun down."

I was a woman who should live in a bubble. Surrounded by family, still living close to where I grew up, working hard in a secure job. But one moment years ago had blasted that bubble apart, and I knew it was all a mirage. Danger could be anywhere, whether you lived in a bubble or not. Right now, it was standing right in front of me. "I think I'll keep the gun," I said, the shiver ticking down my back feeling like ice.

Aiden's eyes were a combination of so many blue hues that a true description wasn't possible. Right now, they were harder than the sharpest edge of a new blade. His black hair was thick and curled beneath his ears, having grown out a little bit the last couple of weeks. With his black motorcycle boots, faded jeans, and dark tee stretched across his rock hard chest, he looked like the proverbial immovable object—with an edge that might just slice through a girl. He was a good foot taller than me, about a hundred pounds of pure muscle bigger than me, and if I had to guess, a boatload of more danger than I could ever hope to be. Worse yet, he was sexy. Oh, he shouldn't be. But I knew, firsthand, what he could do with that firm mouth and those broad hands.

"Now, Angel," he said softly, that Irish brogue hinting at his heritage.

I'd already learned that when Aiden got quiet, when he went tense, he was more dangerous than another man in full and loud temper. So I tightened my hold on his gun. Even though he was scaring the crap out of me, part of this was about my sister. "We're going to have a little talk. Did you kill Danny Pucci?"

Aiden's jaw tensed. His gaze didn't so much as flicker from mine. Then he stepped forward. Slowly, deliberately, he prowled right toward me with the grace I'd admired in him from his youth.

I took a step back. Damn it.

He kept coming, and I had a split second to decide whether to pull the trigger or not. Then his hand was on the gun, and the weapon was out of my hands. His scent of leather, motor oil, and male washed over me in a remembrance of much better times.

The gun was instantly tucked at the back of his waist and his free hand wrapped around the front of my neck, lifting me up.

I gave a very unsexy squawk as I rose to my toes and my eyes widened on his.

His nose almost touched mine. "When I tell you to stay away from somewhere, you fuckin' do it. Tell me you get me." His voice was so rough it went hoarse.

Flutters whipped through my abdomen in a combination of fear and something I really didn't want to admit to. It definitely wasn't fear. There was something about him that scared people, and I got that, but I didn't want to be one of them. From day one with him, I'd wanted to be different than everybody else. Yeah, I was screwed up. No question. "I'm not afraid of you," I whispered, the slight shake in my voice telling a different story.

"Then you're not nearly as smart as I'd hoped." His fingers tightened but still didn't hurt me. "What do I have to do, Angel?"

"For one thing, stop calling me Angel," I admitted, wanting to plant my mouth against his to remind him of our time together. "For another, tell me what happened so I can clear my sister." And him. I didn't think he'd killed Danny, and I was going to find out the truth whether he liked it or not.

"You ever been spanked?" he asked.

I caught my breath. Oh, definitely not my thing. "Don't even think it. I have no problem pressing charges for a battery, Devlin," I retorted, my butt already tingling. "Now stop trying to scare me away because it obviously isn't working. Try something else."

His nostrils flared, making him look like a warrior from years gone by. "You are the most stubborn person I've met in my entire damn life," he muttered.

"I know." Something eased inside me. A flare of panic that had surprised me with its intensity. "Did you kill Danny?"

He shook me just enough to show how close to losing his temper he really was. Then he released me. "No." He took a step back and shoved both hands in his pockets as if he was afraid he'd grab me again. "You can't be involved in your sister's case, and we both know it. So back off and let everyone else do their jobs for once."

"Why were you in Tessa's apartment?" I persisted, back down on my flip-flops and searching for even ground. "Tell me what happened."

"No." He stepped to the side. "I'm not discussing it upon advice from counsel. Now, if you don't mind, I have to get ready for a date."

I burst out laughing. Full on, from the belly, surprising even me.

His dark eyebrows rose.

I caught my breath and put a hand to my stomach. "Oh, Aiden." I coughed a couple of times. "I don't give two shits if you're dating somebody. If you think hurting my feelings is going to get me to crawl into a hole and hide from this, then you don't know me at all." Plus, I didn't believe him. If I did, I *would* be seriously wounded. But he just seemed to be trying too hard to get me to back off. Why? I could never turn away from a puzzle. Ever.

He looked at me like I was nuts. Yeah, I'd seen that look before.

I smiled, finally relaxing. "Scaring me didn't work. Hurting my feelings didn't work. The only thing that is going to work is for you to tell me the truth."

"The truth?" He scrubbed a hand through his thick hair. "All right. Here it is. You were the one good thing I've done in my entire life, that day a million years ago, and I thought I could revisit that. Be a hero once more."

"You were," I whispered. He'd turned against his whole club and driven a car hauler full of drugs into a dangerous situation to save my life just a couple of weeks ago. "You are. This isn't making any sense to me." It felt good to be in his space again, even though I was more confused than ever.

He shook his head, his eyes darkening to a deep sapphire. "That's just it. I'm not. I'll hold that one day forever, and I'll keep a part of you with me, but our lives are too different. We're too different. You have to move on from us, and you have to let the justice system take care of the case. Tessa didn't kill Pucci, so she'll be okay. So will you." His words were soft, as was his voice.

I'd been dumped before. Never like this. "I guess there isn't much more to say." Not that I wasn't going to help my sister, no matter what. Then I walked by him, my bewildered heart slightly breaking—but I still wasn't completely buying it. Until I opened his outside door and nearly walked right into Jolene O'Sullivan.

"Oh." She stumbled back and caught herself before focusing on me, recognition dawning quickly. Then a catlike smile spread across her still lovely face. Her eyes were blue, her hair a natural blonde, and her figure cheerleader tight. "Things never change, do they?" She looked over my shoulder at Aiden. "Seems like old times, doesn't it, sweetheart?"

CHAPTER 8

$\mathcal{I}$ somehow made it to my car and out of the parking lot before bursting into tears or throwing up or both. My hands shook on the steering wheel as I drove down the quiet road to get a far enough distance away before calling Donna. Or Lacey. Yeah, Donna. My sister hated Jolene as much as I did—or at least she had years ago.

Just as I reached for my phone, it buzzed. "Hello," I said, keeping my eye on the road.

"Anna? It's Thelma. Are you still coming by today?"

My chin dropped to my chest, but I still watched the road. I'd forgotten. "Yeah. In fact, I'll be there in about fifteen minutes or so." My voice shook, and I cleared it.

"Great. I have to run to the store for a better suitcase and then go visit my new flame before I leave him for weeks because he's going to watch my cat while we're gone, but Georgiana is here to give you directions. Drive carefully, honey bun." She fumbled for a minute or so and disengaged the call.

I sighed and fought back tears. Okay. Aiden really had picked up his life without me. Jerk. Fine. I would go do the favor for the elderly ladies and then get drunk with Donna. It was a tequila night, for sure. My mind fuzzed as I drove toward the retirement community where Thelma and Georgiana lived. I'd met them during a case, and they'd kind of adopted me as a granddaughter, which was awesome because they baked a lot and I loved cookies. Since they'd helped solve a drug case, they'd earned a financial award from the federal government, so they were heading off for a three-week Alaska adventure that included a cruise.

The bright and oddly painted homes in the Sunnyside Retirement community failed to amuse me for once. I pulled into the driveway of a white duplex with beige trim on one side and bright pink on the other. I stepped out of my car and headed for the pink side, my body feeling like it had been through my Uncle Sean's woodchipper.

Georgiana opened the door on my first knock, took one look at me, and yanked me against her very ample bosom. "What happened?"

That fast, I went from tough to full on tears. She drew me inside to the sofa and patted my hand as I told her the entire story. "I know that girl power matters, and we should stick together, but Jolene was always such a...witch," I hiccupped. "I was ten years old when Aiden rescued me from that kidnapping, and he was sixteen, but he let me hang out with him for two years as one of the gang." I'd felt cool and safe as his friend.

"Go on," Georgiana said, rubbing my leg. She was very tall and rather round and looked festive in a flowered dress with bright blue sandals.

"Jolene was a year younger than him, and she slept with Donna's prom date the night of the junior prom," I said, trying not to wail it.

"What a bitch," Georgiana agreed, her brown eyes narrowed. "What happened after that?"

I sucked in air and wiped my face off. "Then she started dating Aiden, and while he was nice, she was just mean to me. Acted like it was a pain to have a ten-year-old around." Which, frankly, it probably was. But Aiden was always kind, and so were his friends. "Seeing her at his place today…"

Georgiana sighed. "We should put off our trip and take this wench out."

Humor bubbled up through my heartbreak, and I leaned over to hug her. "That's kind of you, but you deserve a vacation, and I have another murder to solve." Before she could offer to help, I held up a hand. "I'll call you if I need backup. For now, tell me which plants to water and how much. I'll be careful."

Georgiana brushed back her dark hair that normally was streaked liberally with gray. Today the highlights were a bright pink.

I gulped, really taking her in. "Did you let Thelma do your hair?" There was no doubt the pint-sized Thelma was a little creative. Or a lot creative, actually.

"Yes." Georgiana blushed and patted her head. "It's wild vacation hair." She sighed. "Let's bury ourselves in a pound of brownies as I go over the directions. I find that chocolate always helps a broken heart."

Chocolate could help anything.

She went to grab a huge dish of brownies with homemade chocolate syrup, and I dug in as if I could ease all pain with sugar. Frankly, it helped. We went through the litany of different plants and flowers I'd need to water while they were gone, and I tried to explain that I'd do my best not to kill them, but I wasn't good with plants. Double checking that the outside flowers had gotten enough water from the automatic sprinklers was my best chance at success.

Finally, she wound down. "Let's have more brownies."

I didn't have the energy to fight the idea, and besides, it wasn't like anybody would see me naked any time soon. So we dove into the brownies again, and it was getting dark by the time we finished. Her hug was comforting as she let me go, walking me to my car.

"Have a great time," I said, feeling better after letting it all out. And eating copious amounts of chocolate.

She smiled. "We will. Forget that Aiden Devlin. You should be with a nice Italian boy, anyway." Of course, Georgiana was a Lambertini, so she might be a little biased.

"Maybe." I waved to her as I drove away, wondering where I could find the same indoor replacement plants if I accidentally killed some of theirs. The ladies were so kind, and I didn't want them coming home to dead plants.

I sighed, heading home, feeling much better. Kind of like I was floating. As I reached Tamarack Lake, her words kept drumming inside my head. A nice Italian boy would be a good thing, at least for half of my family. It wasn't a terrible idea, and once Tessa had told me that the best way to get over a man was to find another one. That thought totally made sense right now. So I skipped the turnoff toward my cottage and kept driving around the lake, stopping at the luxurious Blueridge Condos overlooking Bear Bay. A warning ticked in the back of my head, but it didn't make sense, so I ignored it.

Then I strode up the stairs and knocked on the first door.

The door opened almost instantly, and Nick Basanelli stood there in a tank top with jogging shorts. A military tattoo spread across his left bicep. His chest was broad, his muscles corded, and his legs very nice for a man.

So I leaned up right into him and pressed my lips to his. The world spun. Gasping, I stumbled back, turned, and puked right into his potted hydrangeas by the door.

* * *

To his credit, Nick tangled his hand in my hair and held it back from the flowing chocolate. No hesitation, no surprise—just full on helping me out like he'd been expecting me to show up, try to kiss him, and throw up. When I was finished, he lifted me, turning and kicking the door shut behind us.

His hold was solid as he moved into the living room and then the kitchen to place me on his cool marble island. "How much chocolate did you eat?"

"A lot," I gasped, trying to lean away from him because no doubt I smelled horrible.

"I've never seen that much chocolate come back up from anybody, and we had a dog that got into my mom's Valentine's stash one time." He stepped back as if sensing I needed some space.

The room spun around me, and I dug my hands into my bare thighs. Embarrassment competed with a light-headedness. "I am so sorry about this."

His upper lip quirked. "About killing that nice pot of flowers my neighbor gave me or about trying to kiss me first?"

Oh God. "Both. Definitely both." Aiden's face swam across my mind, and I pushed thoughts of him ruthlessly away. Whatever we'd had was now over. "I may not have thought all of this through."

"Maybe not." Nick leaned in again and then paused. His brows drew down, and he stepped closer to me. "What's going on with your eyes?"

"My eyes?" I blinked, and my stomach rolled over. What was happening?

"Yeah." He leaned in. "They're bloodshot, glassy, and dilated. Did you hit your head?"

Just then, my phone buzzed, and I jumped.

In one smooth and rather cool motion, Nick reached behind me and drew my cellphone from the back pocket of my cutoff shorts. He clicked the speaker button to answer, sliding the phone onto the marble. "Anna's phone."

"Oh my. Oh my goodness." Thelma's voice came over high and panicked. "Oh my. Who is this? Is Anna okay? Oh no."

Nick's eyes had turned a deeper brown and sharpened instantly. "Who is this?"

"It's Thelma," I explained, trying not to sway on the marble. The world fuzzed around me, and all of the hurt from earlier dissipated. I sniffed the air. "Hey. Smells like pizza. Do you have pizza? I could use a slice." Wait. What were we talking about? The counter swayed beneath me.

Nick instantly caged me on the counter, one hand on either side of my hips. "What's going on?" He had his grumpy boss voice back, and I missed his sweet and humorous one already.

Thelma sighed. "Georgiana gave you the wrong brownies," she whispered.

"Ah shit," Nick muttered, leaning back. "How much did you eat?"

I bit the inside of my cheek. "Of pizza? None. Where is it?"

His face morphed just a bit, and it wasn't pretty. "Thelma? Talk now, please."

Thelma rushed on using a bunch of letters and abbreviations that didn't make a lick of sense, and all I could think about was pizza. Finally, Nick ended the call and promised everything would be okay.

I blinked up at him, my mind so calm I wouldn't be surprised if I were emitting Theta waves. It felt like the calm before the hurricane. "Bye, Thelma." She may have been gone for a few minutes at that point.

Nick leaned in, looking at my eyes. "Have you been high before? Eaten edibles?"

"Nope." I liked his place now that the moving boxes were gone. It suited him. Long lines, awesome view of the lake, sleek furniture. "Why? Are you putting edibles in the pizza?"

"No." He rubbed his chin. "Let's get some water in you."

My stomach lurched again. I clapped a hand over my mouth. "Um."

He lifted me fast and jogged to the guest bath, setting me down on a deep grey mat and flipping the toilet lid up. "Hold on a—"

But I was already heaving liquid brownie mix into the bowl. I levered up on my knees and ralphed, my entire body moving with the exertion.

Gentle hands gathered my hair away from my face, keeping it out of the way. I don't know how long I threw up. It seemed like forever. Finally, my body was just heaving on its own. "I'm dying."

"You're not dying," Nick said, rapidly braiding my hair.

Wow. Had Nick Basanelli just actually done that? Braided my hair? I started to lean my head down, and he stopped me. "Hold on. Take a few deep breaths. I'm going to get you some water and a washcloth. Do not put your face on the toilet seat."

Oh, I could die. Seriously. I waited, and then sounds ticked around me, toward me, through me. The room swam and came in and out. Nick returned and wiped off my face before giving me some water. I drank, and the skin prickled on my arms.

He took the glass away. "I'm thinking your system doesn't like recreational edibles."

The words didn't make a lot of sense. The hurricane landed inside me. Fear grabbed me and held tight. "They're coming for her, Nick. You have to save her." I grabbed his arm. "Please." This day had gone so darn wrong, and it was getting worse.

He handed me the water again. "What are you talking about?"

I lowered my voice, panic rushing through me faster than the chocolate had. "Tessa. The dead body. Please. He's coming to get me, and I need your help. Please help me." Oh man, they were coming from every direction.

Nick grasped my hand and drew me to my feet. "All right. You're having a reaction I don't like, and we're going to see a doctor. You're paranoid for a moment, but you'll be okay."

I pulled away—or at least I tried to pull away. There was nowhere to go. "No. I'm not paranoid. Please. I can't see a doctor. I'm a prosecuting attorney, and apparently I ingested drugs that are legal in Washington but not Idaho. You know that." Finally, my brain was kicking back in. Even so, my skin still crawled. "Please, Nick. Call Tessa. Jareth Davey is going to get to me through her. I know he is."

Nick stiffened at Davey's name. "Honey, Jareth Davey is in California. He can't get to Tessa, and he can't get to you." Jareth Davey was the monster who'd tried to abduct me as a child, and he starred in every nightmare I'd ever had.

"You don't know that," I whispered.

Nick led me out of the guest bathroom and up the carved wooden stairs to a master bedroom with an amazing view of Tamarack Lake. "I can't call Tessa. She's a defendant in a possible murder case, Anna. I'm the prosecutor."

I turned and grabbed his arms. "Please. Her number is on my phone. I need to know she's okay."

He hesitated and then sighed. "Fine." He led me into a master bathroom fit for royalty and pushed me around a series of stones into the shower. He flicked on the water.

Warm and then really warm water washed over me, and I coughed, ducking my head. The chills started to subside.

"I'll get you towels and something to change into," Nick said.

"Call Tess," I said, closing my eyes, unable to get rid of the feeling that my sister was in trouble because Jareth Davey was coming for me. Nick disappeared, and I stripped out of my sopping wet clothing, trying to force my brain to take back over. The terror wouldn't leave me. I was in danger. Everything in my cells knew this. I also knew that I was having a reaction to those stupid brownies.

Where was my gun? I needed to get it out of my car. Then everything would be all right.

CHAPTER 9

*M*y hair was wet. Smooth sheets, the good kind, surrounded me. Wait a minute. I blinked, scrambling for reality. "Gun. I need my gun," I whispered.

"Shh. I have your gun," Tessa whispered, wiping my hair back from my face.

"Tess?" I tried to sit up, but she put her hand to my shoulder.

"Yeah. It's me. You're having a bad reaction, but you're going to be okay. Just take deep breaths." Her familiar scent of lilacs surrounded me.

I breathed deep. "Is it really you? You're safe?" I tried to open my eyes, but the room spun around, and I had to shut them.

She chuckled and patted my shoulder. "It's me, and we're both safe."

My stomach clenched. "Where are we?"

"We're still at Nick's. I think he's on social media telling people he has two out of the three Albertini girls in his bed right now."

Even though the paranoia and nausea still edged toward me, I smiled. "He'll be a legend."

"He already thinks he is," she whispered.

I chuckled, keeping my eyelids closed. Was that interest in her voice? Maybe? The two of them were opposites, which could be a really good thing. I was suddenly very glad I hadn't landed that kiss earlier, although it was too bad about the flowers. "Tessa? Don't leave me, okay?"

"I wouldn't think of it." Her cool palm felt my forehead. "Just rest, okay? I'll stay here with you. Sleep now."

I loved that her voice sounded the most like our mom's, although mom's brogue was stronger. "Don't tell mom about the edibles," I groaned.

"Oh, don't worry," Tessa said. "This one would be too hard to explain."

Wasn't that the truth? Finally, my body began to relax, now that I knew Tessa was safe and that Jareth Davey couldn't get to me. I sighed and snuggled down in sheets that smelled a little smoky and woodsy...just like Nick. "He called you."

"Yeah," she said softly. "He didn't want to call, and he's kept his distance, but it was nice of him all the same."

It had been a while since I'd taken on a challenge that didn't have to do with the law or dead bodies. Tessa had been alone for too long, and I wasn't sure why. Guys asked her out all the time, and she rarely accepted the invitation. It was probably because Pucci had been such an ass.

With that thought, I slid into a sleep that included bright colors, sparkling horses, and swiftly moving clouds shaped like dragons. I awoke a couple of times throughout the night, double checking that my sister was still there, sleeping quietly beside me.

Then I'd fall back asleep, my stomach better but my head hurting a little bit.

It wasn't a surprise when the nightmare found me.

I was ten years old again, and ropes tied my hands to the dashboard of a muddy four-wheeler while my kidnapper drove through narrow trails away from the river, where I'd been skipping rocks with my cousin. When the guy had grabbed me, Lacey had rushed toward him, but he'd pushed her down. The sound of her head hitting the rock still echoed in my mind.

I pulled on the ropes and looked toward him, my ears ringing and my stomach hurting. "You have to let me go. Please."

He had a big nose, narrow brown eyes, and dirty brown hair. "No. I need a bride."

I coughed and held on as he turned too quickly, and I was rocked against the door. "I'm only ten. It's too young to be a bride." Fear tasted like metal at the back of my tongue. Had Lacey been knocked out? Or had she been able to get back to the family campground and let my dad know I was taken?

God, I hoped she was all right.

The guy kept driving for at least an hour, and I hadn't managed to loosen the ropes at all. "Who are you?" I asked, trying to listen for help. Was anybody coming? Tears pooled in my eyes but I couldn't stop them.

"Jareth Davey," he said, turning again onto a trail that was barely there. "I won't hurt you. But I need a bride."

I didn't believe him. If he didn't want to hurt me, he wouldn't have pushed Lacey down or tied my hands together. What if my dad didn't find me? I sucked in air.

The sound of a helicopter pierced the nice Spring day. Was it for me? Were they coming? Then the sound of four-wheelers and dirt bikes echoed around the mountains. It was Memorial Day weekend, and there were a lot of campers, but maybe those were looking for me.

What if I never got free? My legs shook. This had to be a bad dream.

"Shit," Jareth said, driving the machine to the right and aiming toward a weathered cabin that seemed to almost go into the rocks. I hadn't even seen it before. He parked beneath some trees, undid my rope, and then carried me toward the cabin.

I screamed and punched him, fighting and trying to fall to the ground. He kept going and opened the door, hurrying inside where it was quiet. Would anybody even see the cabin? I punched him in the throat.

The cabin only had one room with a kitchen that had a hotplate and several mismatched pans on a counter. A bare mattress was on the floor with one pillow and a dirty looking blanket. I punched him again in the throat, and he put me down.

"We're married now," he said. He was crazy. I'd heard about how some people could go nuts and make up their own rules, and I think that's what happened to this guy.

I ran toward the counter and grabbed a heavy pan to ward him off. It was heavy and hurt my shoulders, but I held on so tight my fingers hurt.

He laughed and walked toward me.

Panic caught me around the throat, and I swung, hitting him in the side with a loud thud. He fell back, and his face turned an ugly red. Then he jumped for me.

The door burst open, and a dark-haired boy ran inside, smashing into the man so hard they rammed into the opposite wall. The boy started punching Jareth Davey in the face, neck, and stomach, grunting wildly each time. Jareth hit back, and blood flew from both of them.

I dropped the heavy pan and screamed for help. The boy was from the high school, and I'd seen him around town.

He grabbed the pan and swung it, hitting Jareth right in the face. The bad guy fell back, and his eyes closed.

I gulped and tried to breathe. My legs wanted to run but I couldn't get them to move. Everything froze.

"You okay?" the boy asked, breathing heavily. His blue eyes focused on me, and a bruise was already forming above one of them.

"No," I whispered, my voice shaking.

"You will be." He took my hand and pulled me toward the door.

I clutched onto him, holding as tight as I could.

"My dirt bike is outside. I'll take you home," he said.

I sniffed and hurried toward the door and away from the bad man. We had to get out of there before he woke up. I swallowed and tried not to cry.

The boy looked down and smiled. "I'm Aiden. You're safe now. I promise."

I jerked awake and sat up, noting the sunlight pouring through the sliding glass door that led to a small balcony. Tamarack Lake sparkled merrily this morning, the slight waves shining like diamonds. I sat up and pushed my hair away from my face, taking inventory.

My head ached a little, but my body felt okay and I no longer needed to puke. The paranoia was gone. What a crazy trip I'd taken. Yeah. I always reacted oddly to medication, so it wasn't a surprise that I'd had the extreme trip of the night before. What had I been thinking to show up at Nick's place?

Dishes clattered, and soft voices wafted up the stairway.

I used the bathroom, finding a new toothbrush already waiting for me. After taking care of my teeth and trying to finger comb my curls away from my face, I gave up and walked toward the stairway, noting the too-long sweats and roomy JAG T-shirt that covered me.

Pausing, I rolled up the bottom of the sweats so I wouldn't break my neck on the stairs down to the kitchen. Then I descended, sniffing as the smell of breakfast hit me.

I was starving and had to hold the waistband to keep the sweats up.

Passing the living room, I gingerly walked into the kitchen where Tessa sat at the counter with Nick scrambling eggs at the stove. Both were smiling.

Oh yeah. I had a thought about them the night before.

Tess turned. "There you are. How was the trip?"

I grinned and took the stool next to her. "I was just thinking the same thing."

She felt my forehead. "No fever. It figures you'd have a horrible reaction. Remember when you tried penicillin in kindergarten?"

I nodded. The allergic reaction had been very unpleasant. I leaned toward her. "Thank you for coming last night."

"Of course." She smiled and touched temples with me. Today her blonde hair was up in a ponytail, and she also wore a NAVY T-shirt with what looked like jeans she'd probably worn the night before. In fact, Tessa looked just right in Nick's shirt. I returned her smile.

Nick dished up eggs and handed us plates already ladened with bacon and buttered toast. "How are you feeling?"

Basanelli looked good in the morning with wet hair curling around his ears, mellowed brown eyes, and barefoot. Yeah. I studied him with new eyes. There was so much potential with him. Plans started to form in my mind. "Much better. I think I owe you both an apology and a thank you."

He poured orange juice into three pretty blue glasses that no doubt had come from his mama. "I'm just glad you came here and didn't drive to Las Vegas or something."

I chuckled and accepted the juice before turning to Tessa. "He braided my hair last night when I was done throwing up. How impressive is that?"

Her green eyes danced, and she looked toward Nick. "You know how to braid hair?"

A slight red wandered across his very Italian cheekbones. "I have many female cousins, and believe me, I spent my share of time babysitting when I was in high school. I can also paint fingernails like an expert." The grin he shared with my older sister warmed me throughout.

Oh, this might have been a good thing after all.

I dug into the eggs. "I take it you two have some sort of agreement not to discuss the case and the fact that you want to put her in jail, Nick?"

He lost the grin. "We aren't discussing the case. Period."

Tessa ducked her head and ate more eggs, not noticing that his gaze had strayed to her again.

I hid my smile and finished my breakfast. Nicolo Basanelli was a bloodhound on a case, and I had no doubt he would've discovered the truth no matter what. But having him being especially inspired by my very pretty sister was a good bonus at the moment.

Nick studied me. "How are you feeling? I still think we should consult a doctor."

"I'm fine." Truthfully, I felt okay now. "No aftereffects, and I'll be careful next time."

He shook his head. "Did you eat the entire pan of brownies?"

Tessa tried to stifle her laugh but then gave up. "We had to throw those poor flowers away."

Heat filtered into my face, but it was nice to hear Tessa laugh, considering the week she'd just had. "I'll get you new ones." I took my empty plate to the sink. "I have to get going. Don't let me keep you guys from relaxing."

Tessa jumped up and brought her plate over. "I need to go, too. I'm still a defendant, you know."

Well, that was true. And now I was starting to care about Basanelli's future—just in case my sister was in it. "All right." I fumbled a little and managed to thank Nick again before heading out with my wet clothes safely tied in a plastic bag.

Tess's car, a newish Volkswagen Bug that she'd leased, sat next to mine. "Don't even think it," she said, nudging me toward my car.

I gave her my most innocent look. "What?"

"Nothing." She didn't bite. "I let mom know we wouldn't make the family barbecue today in Silverville because we both have to work. Wasn't sure if you'd feel up to going."

"I don't," I admitted. I loved my family, but being around a lot of people right now didn't sound like fun.

She nodded. "I really do have to go to work, and then I'm staying in Donna's guest room if you want to come by for dinner. The police haven't released my apartment yet."

I paused by my door. "Thanks for coming, Tess."

A slight wind off the lake blew a couple of tendrils from her ponytail to dance around her smooth skin. "Always." She smiled and jumped in her Bug.

Oh, I finally had a project. Slipping into my seat, I started my car and headed away from the condos and around the lake to my cottage. Who should I get as an accomplice? I had to be careful who I chose. My thoughts were still clamoring around when I parked and walked by the pretty smattering of Petunias I'd planted that led to my front door, catching sight of a large figure lounging on my porch. "Aiden."

His gaze raked me, head to toe. "Nice clothes. Basanelli's?"

CHAPTER 10

W hy did my entire body react to him? My toes tingled, my fingers clenched, and my abdomen flipped over. Yeah, I'd had a crush on him for years while he'd been away, but then we'd gotten together, and I knew how he kissed. How he had the ability to concentrate so fully on me that I felt both safe and challenged in the same second. So inspired. I drew in air. "What are you doing here?"

He stretched to his feet like a lazy panther. Today he wore ripped jeans, motorcycle boots, and a washed-out green tee that showed his impressive biceps. Motorcycle riding clothing. Interesting.

"I wanted to talk to you," he said.

"You have my phone number." If he had ridden his bike, where was it? Down the road and behind a tree? Why?

"This is *in person* information." He glanced at the rolled up sweats again, and his jaw tightened until a vein showed along his neck.

I reminded myself to breathe in through my nose and not mouth so my body wouldn't freak out and think it was under duress. Yeah, I'd learned that in a yoga class, but right now, the adrenaline flooding my system wanted me to mouth breathe. "What is it? I'm kind of busy today. Please get to it." I sounded properly frosty.

A smile tugged at his mouth. "Sleeping with your boss is a bad idea."

"Sleeping with you was a worse one," I countered quickly.

"I don't disagree," he said mildly, the narrowing of his blue eyes showing more emotion than did his level tone. A light scruff covered his jaw, and my palms twitched to rub along it as I had done so before. "Let's go inside."

Considering the borrowed sweats were too big and about to fall, I held the waistband in place and strode for the door in my flip flops that thankfully had been spared the chocolate horror. I dug my key out of my purse to unlock the door. "Fine. I can give you about five minutes." He had saved my life, after all.

His sigh stirred my hair as he followed me inside and shut the door. "Do you want to change first?"

Well now, sometimes I can be a jackass. It's a fact, and I guess I should accept it. "Nope. I'm good." Hitching the sweats up, I ambled for the breakfast nook and sat across the table that my Nonna Albertini gave me, still wearing Nick's clothes. "Please. Sit."

Aiden watched me and then took a seat, overwhelming the oak chair that was a hand-me-down from my Nana O'Shea. I used to like how he did that, but right now it ticked me off. He cleared his throat before speaking. "When I was in California—"

"Recruiting new members for your drug-running motorcycle club," I interrupted.

His chin lowered a fraction and made him look a little more dangerous than he had on my porch, which frankly was already plenty dangerous. "All of the drug runners were arrested, and we don't do that anymore."

"Right. So you recruited all of these new members to do…

what?" I slightly turned my head as if I wanted to hear him better. "Well?"

"God, you're a brat," he muttered.

Brat? I was aiming for full on bitch. "Sorry. I forgot how mean and nasty you like your women."

He smacked his hand against his forehead. "Jesus, *Aingeal*. I'm not seeing Jolene O'Sullivan. She was a snake in high school, and we have not kept in touch, so I can't vouch for whether or not she's still a calculating shrew. Maybe she is, or maybe she isn't. Either way, I don't know."

I wish that didn't make me feel a heck of a lot better. I so wish my heart didn't just flutter, warm, and thump like it had been asleep for the last day. "Then what was she doing at your apartment?" Yeah, I had no right to ask. But I did, anyway.

He lifted a shoulder. "Hell if I know. She said she was back in town, heard I was back, and wanted to meet up. Since I had not planned on being at my apartment—" His voice lowered into a growl as he reminded me of exactly why he'd been there— "I had other plans to return to and couldn't stay and find out what she really wanted."

"Oh," I said rather lamely.

He looked pointedly at the JAG shirt covering my chest. "Not that you took some time off to grieve whatever we had."

I sighed. "I didn't sleep with Nick."

"Oh?" One of Aiden's eyebrows rose.

"Yeah. Not that it's any of your business because it isn't, but I ate too many brownies that turned out to be laced with a bunch of letters I didn't recognize, but I'm sure was different cannabis stuff. Then I went to Nick's, threw up in his flowers, and had a paranoia attack. He put me in a warm shower and called my sister, and we both slept over."

Aiden just looked at me. "I really wish I wasn't able to follow that. Where did you get the brownies?"

"Thelma and Georgiana," I admitted. "Georgiana gave me the wrong pan."

His mouth twitched, and he leaned over to grasp my hand. "I don't want to hurt you, Anna."

"Then don't." I loved how much bigger his hand was than mine. "Tell me the truth. Are you an undercover FBI agent?"

"No." He snorted. "God, no. Why would you ask that?"

"Because I don't want you to be the bad guy," I whispered. "You're too good to be the bad guy." I straightened. "In fact, you told me that you weren't the bad guy. Remember?"

"Yeah," he said softly. "When I'm with you, I don't feel like the bad guy."

That was both sweet and kind of sad. "Are you an informant to the FBI? The CIA, DHS, Secret Service, or the DEA?" I asked hopefully.

He grinned. "I am not an informant for anybody, sweetheart. Not my style, and I think you know that."

True. Aiden didn't seem like he took orders from anybody. "The Lordes were disbanded. Why in the world would you rebuild them?" I asked, trying to push away the hurt that caused me.

His gaze roamed my face. "We weren't disbanded. Only weakened. The brotherhood means something to me. We have strength in numbers, and we run several legitimate businesses, including the garage in Washington. I couldn't let all of that go."

I didn't get it. Not at all. "Why not?"

"I don't have what you have," he said softly. "No parents, no siblings, no aunts and uncles and cousins, and so on. It's just me. Just me and the brothers I've found."

"I would've shared mine," I countered. At some point, anyway. "I get it, I really do. But the Lordes have also been shady in the past—especially with the running of drugs. Are you saying you're going all the way legit?"

"I'd like to," he said.

That sure wasn't a yes. Why was this so difficult? "Is the fact that you're not legit why you dumped me?"

He didn't answer.

All righty then. I guess that was an answer. "Why were you in my sister's apartment standing over a dead body?"

Aiden removed his hand. "We can't talk about that, and you know it."

"Did you kill him?" I just didn't see Aiden as a cold-blooded killer. Oh, I had no doubt he'd kill in self-defense but not like that.

Aiden leaned back. "You think I shot him, dropped the gun, and then let your sister pick it up and point it at me?"

Well, since he put it like that. "No. So why not tell me what happened?"

"Advice of counsel," he said, the stubborn tilt of his jaw all Irish.

"Baloney," I said. "You wouldn't listen to a lawyer to save your life. You wouldn't listen to anybody. So why won't you tell me the truth?" I just couldn't get into his head about this.

He glanced at the quiet lake past my deck. "Because I want you to stay out of this. You're a lawyer and a pretty new one. Not a cop, not a criminal, and not somebody who should be pursuing whoever put one bullet through Danny Pucci's head."

The man wasn't wrong. I crossed my arms. "Now listen—"

"No. You listen." He crossed his arms, and his muscles bulged in a much nicer way than mine. Well, if mine bunched at all. "The last time you tried to investigate a case, you nearly died. We both did. Let the cops do their jobs, and you do yours. Okay?"

"Right now, the cops have arrested my sister," I reminded him.

"And you're not her lawyer," he reminded me right back.

Also true. I sighed. "Why are you here, Aiden? If you're not willing to tell me what happened with Pucci, what do you want to say?" I was done with the warnings from him.

He rubbed the bridge of his nose like he was getting a raging migraine. "When I was in California, I looked up Jareth Davey at the residence Nick Basanelli found for him."

A pit of ice dropped into my stomach. "You found Davey?" I whispered.

"No." Aiden studied my face, watching my reaction. "Davey hadn't been there for a least a week, and the landlord had no idea where he'd gone."

I licked my lips. Twice a year I received cards from Jareth Davey at an old post office box in Silverville. One on the anniversary of the kidnapping, which had been just a couple of weeks ago, and once at Christmastime. Then a few weeks ago, I'd received a card at my cottage for the anniversary. Here. Davey had found me and then disappeared again. "Why did you look him up?"

Aiden just stared at me.

I blinked, the chill in my stomach spreading out. "What was your plan?"

"I don't know, but my goal was to make sure he left you alone forever," Aiden admitted. "I don't like that he'd been here."

"Yeah, but that was after the newspaper picture of Nick and me was on the front page, and Davey was ticked I was dating somebody, or he thought I was." I took some solace in the fact that I wasn't dating anybody right now, so Jareth Davey had no reason to seek me out. Not that I wasn't ready. I'd prepared for his return my entire life, from the second I could aim a handgun. "Truth be told, I'd like to get it over with," I said.

"No. I'll take care of him before you do," Aiden countered. "That day changed us both."

Apparently not. "If that day had truly changed you, you wouldn't be a criminal," I said quietly. "Or you wouldn't be involved with criminal activity to the point that you can't date who you want."

His cheek creased in a way I wish wasn't sexy and adorable. "Who says I can't date who I want?"

"I do." I lifted my chin. "I wasn't the only one snuggling on the sofa and watching movies, and I wasn't the only one in that bed. You like me."

His grin widened. "I do like you. A lot."

That ice started to melt. "This protecting me for my own good is a bunch of bullshit, Aiden Devlin," I said. "I'm a big girl who can make her own decisions, and I think you know that. In fact, I think you're backing off because you're not sure of yourself. Did this get too real for you?" I was kind of shooting in the dark, but my instincts with him were usually pretty close to target.

"Maybe," he allowed. "Either way, it wouldn't work. My life, your life, and the future. I'm definitely not a picket fence type of guy, and you're all family, no matter how tough you act."

"It's not an act," I said, feeling settled for the first time in days. "I am tough, and at the moment, I'm a heck of a lot stronger than you. At least I'm not afraid to take a chance."

His bark of laughter was a surprise that somehow warmed me. "I take chances all the time." Then he sobered. "Though not with you. I know you don't get it, but that day in June years ago was the one good thing I can hold on to. That I did something right, and maybe my soul will be okay for it. I can't let you get hurt now."

"You're not responsible for me," I reminded him.

He exhaled. "That's not how I see it."

The fact that he felt responsible for me didn't give me warm fuzzies. Nope. Not at all. My phone buzzed, and I slowly drew it out from my back pocket to see Tessa's smiling face. "Hey, Tess. Everything okay?" I answered, still watching Aiden.

"Yeah. After my shift, Clark wants to meet and go over my case, and I thought you'd want to be there. In fact, can we meet at your place? Donna is having some get-together with her realtor pals to plan the week ahead. Remember when we didn't work on Sundays?" Tessa sighed.

"Sure. Bring a late lunch, would you?" I asked, already knowing she'd bring something from the diner.

She laughed. "Yep. Bye." She clicked off.

Aiden cocked his head to the side. "You're not going to stay out of this, are you?"

Now I smiled at him. "Not a chance in hell."

CHAPTER 11

I couldn't get the thought out of my head that once again, we had no clue where Jareth Davey had gone as I helped Tessa clean up the mess from our late lunch.

Clark sat at the table and spread out a couple of manilla files along with a legal pad as we started to get down to business. He looked up at me, serious and studious with his badass glasses on. "I'm not sure you should be a part of this." Then he paused, held up a hand, and shook his head. "Let me rephrase that. You definitely should not be a part of this, and we all know it."

I tossed the washcloth into the sink and followed Tessa to the table to sit. "Our only worry is that if Tessa says something incriminating, then I don't have attorney-client privilege with her. Since she hasn't done anything wrong, she won't say anything incriminating."

"It's not that simple," Clark said, his eyes a deep brown against his smooth skin. Today he wore a blue golf shirt with pressed dark jeans and somehow still looked dressed up.

Tessa drew out a chair. "I'm fine taking the risk and want Anna here. I'm the client, right?"

"Right," Clark said grimly, reaching for his yellow pad. "Just keep in mind this is against legal advice from me. For now, I've made a formal request for the evidence against you and should be getting that through official channels later this coming week. However, I also talked to a buddy over in the department and got an early and unofficial copy of the file."

I leaned back. Impressive. Clark hadn't been in town very long, but apparently he'd already made some good connections. "You're a smart guy," I mused.

"I know," he said absently, rifling through papers.

Also confident. "Where did you go to school?" I asked. We'd worked kind of with and against each other for over a month, but we'd never taken time to grab coffee or anything. Of course, most of that time I had been learning the ropes, getting kidnapped, and then dealing with a stalker.

"University of Washington for undergrad and law school," Clark said, pulling out a piece of paper. "You?"

"U of I and U of I," I said. "How did you end up in Timber City?"

Clark looked up. "They had a job opening, and I have student loans." His gaze moved to the lake that was now busy with boats and jet skis. "And I like it here. Good summer and great winter sports." Then he looked at Tessa. "You talked to Danny Pucci more than once. When did he start calling?"

Tessa blushed a light pink, which looked crimson beneath her pale Irish skin. "A couple of months ago. He said he was sorry and had learned to deal with anger. I talked to him a few times, and then he asked me out again, and I said no." She shrugged. "I was happy he'd been working on himself, but some things you don't forget even if you forgive."

I nudged her glass of water toward her. "Good for you."

"Yeah. Great," Clark said, perusing the paper. "The phone records show ten calls over the last couple of months, which isn't too bad."

I started. "You already have phone records? The police have those?"

Clark nodded, his gaze knowing. "Yeah. I noticed that as well."

Tessa looked from me to Clark. "What does that mean?"

"It means that the police were already monitoring Danny Pucci," I said quietly. "Do we have any idea why?"

Clark shook his head. "Nope. My source didn't know, and I was hoping you'd try to get it out of Pierce. He seems to have a soft spot for you, and he's the main detective on the murder."

A soft spot? That was a soft spot for Pierce? "I'd hate to see his enemies," I mumbled.

"True that," Clark said, sliding the paper away. "Walk me through what happened again."

Tessa did so, and it was the same exact timeline she'd given me. "I have no idea why Aiden was in my apartment," she finished.

Clark chewed the inside of his lip. "Has Aiden been there before?" He didn't look my way.

"No," Tessa said, her voice clearly distressed. "Not at all."

Clark nodded. "All right. Danny was arrested for battery against Kelsey Walker, who he'd moved in with about a week ago. According to the police report, they've been dating on and off for a while."

I frowned. "Kelsey Walker? From Walker's Funeral Home?" The Walker family had owned the place for several generations; I was pretty sure.

Clark twirled his pen. "Yeah. She's the youngest daughter, and she works there. I hope to interview her this week if I can get ahold of her." He scribbled a few notes on his legal pad. "Tessa? Did you know Danny was dating Kelsey or that he'd moved back home?"

Tessa shook her head. "I didn't know he was dating anybody, and I've actually never met Kelsey. I've heard of the Walker family, though. They're from here and not Silverville, and I remember playing against a couple of the Walker kids in volleyball and soft-ball, but not Kelsey."

"I think she's the youngest," I said, trying to run through my memory. "Maybe even a year or two younger than me." My phone dinged, and I grasped it to read the face. Then I read the text again. "Oh crap."

"What?" Tessa asked.

I looked up, my nerves tingling. "It's a text from mom. She forgot to tell me that Uncle Sean is on his way over to give me the piano she bought from Mrs. Stangleton's estate sale the other day. It's an upright, and I guess mom had been trying to find one for me that fits here?" That was sweet. I'd had no idea she'd been looking. But the timing was so bad.

"Oh," Tessa breathed, looking from me to Clark and then back. "How much time do we—"

The doorbell rang.

"Hurry." I rapidly pushed the papers all together as Tess tried to help.

"What is happening?" Clark asked, straightening up.

I gulped. "Uncle Sean is here, and he's a little rough. Don't take it personally, but he won't be nice."

Clark stiffened now. "Because I'm black?"

Tessa's mouth dropped open, and it took me a second to catch his thinking. "God, no," I said. "It's because you're a lawyer." I scooped the files together and looked frantically around for a place to stash them. The doorbell rang again.

Clark frowned. "You're a lawyer, too."

Tessa jumped up. "Uncle Sean thinks that's a phase, and she's his niece, so he can't just kick her out of the family." She calmly took the stack of papers, walked over to the sofa in the living room, and shoved them underneath a cushion.

The door burst open, and Uncle Sean strode inside. "Annabella Fiona? You okay? Yell out if you need help."

I hurried toward my massive uncle. "I'm fine, Uncle Sean.

Everything is good." We'd each been named an Irish and Italian name, and Sean liked to use them both with us. I reached him and wrapped my arms around his solid middle. Sean was my mom's older brother, and while he cherished her, I still wasn't sure he'd forgiven her for marrying an Italian instead of a good and solid Irishman. But he loved us, and I adored him. He was an amazing uncle and a terrific dad to both Lacey and Pauley. I leaned back and took in his grizzly face. "I didn't know you were coming."

"I like to surprise my girl." He patted my back with a hand the size of a ham. Sean had been a boxer in his younger days, and he had the face to prove it. Nose that angled to the side, a scar by his lip, thick gray hair that covered another scar by his temple. But my mom's green eyes smiled back at me, and I felt at peace.

"Come on in," I said.

He looked over my shoulder, released me, and made a beeline for Tessa. "Contessa Carmelina. Are you okay? Do I need to kill anybody? Did the police find who put that dead guy in your apartment?"

Tessa hugged him. "I'm fine and no to everything else you just said." Her voice was muffled against his barrel of a chest.

He released her and turned to Clark. "Hello. Who are you?"

Clark stood and extended a hand to Sean. "Clark Bunne."

They shook hands, and Sean smiled. "Are you dating one of my girls here?"

Clark coughed, turned red, and coughed some more. Finally, he shook his head. "No. They're lovely girls…but no." His expression pretty much said it all.

Sean sighed and released Clark. "Yeah, I know. They're a handful. I mean with the kidnappings and dead bodies and everything."

Clark took a couple of steps back. While he was a few inches taller than Sean, my uncle had a good fifty pounds of hard earned muscle on him. On everyone, pretty much. Sean had been a boxer and then a stope miner who ran a jack leg. In Idaho, you learned real quick not to mess with a stope miner or a logger. That's just common sense.

Sean widened his stance. "Then why are you here?"

Clark, to his credit, didn't hesitate. "I'm Tessa's lawyer. We're trying to get her out of this mess."

The atmosphere changed. Sean shook his head. "You're young, healthy, and you seem smart. Why in the hell would you become a lawyer?"

I winced and Tessa nudged him in the ribs, but Sean didn't even twitch.

Clark tilted his head. "My dad was a lawyer trying to make the world a better place, and he was shot and killed in front of a courthouse. I like the law, enjoy strategy, and want to help people."

Well, that was just sweet. I hadn't known any of that.

Sean harrumphed, and his gaze dropped to the logo on Clark's golf shirt. Then he rocked back on the dusty cowboy boots beneath his jeans. "Northern River Golf course outside of Seattle? Have you played that?" He stepped toward Clark.

Clark nodded, and a slight grin tipped his full lips. "Yeah. One of my law professors was a member, and he took a few of us."

Sean straightened. "I've heard it's amazing. That the third hole has a water hazard that you'll never forget."

"It's beautiful, man," Clark said, his eyes sparkling. "I only got to play it twice, but it was incredible."

Sean scratched his chin. "Are you any good?"

"I'm a seven handicap right now, but I'm starting to practice more," Clark said, looking toward me.

I couldn't help him out. Years ago I'd stopped trying to figure out what Uncle Sean was thinking.

Sean smiled wide. "My partner for the member-guest at Silverville broke his arm falling out of a tree yesterday. The tournament is next weekend, qualification round on Friday, and all the entry fees are paid. What do you say? Want to team up?"

Clark's brows rose. "Um, that sounds like fun?"

Sean leaned forward and slapped him on the back, nearly knocking him over. "Everyone has faults, Bunne. Yours is being a lawyer, and the good thing is that you don't have to be one forever, right? We can talk about that some other time. For now, let's golf. We'll have fun."

Clark paled a little, but he did seem interested. "Next weekend? Sure. I haven't played Silverville before, but it sounds like fun."

Tessa cut me a look. Talk about two opposite players. Clark was organized and sweet, whereas Sean...wasn't. Oh, I loved him, but he didn't exactly have a gentle touch.

"Good. Very good." Sean smiled. "I'm glad you're here. Come help me move in this piano, would you? I wasn't sure how I'd get it in by myself, so it's great you're available." He turned toward the doorway, his boots clomping on my wooden floor. "Now moving furniture. That's honorable work. I bet we can find you a good moving company to work for if you give up this law stuff."

Clark paused and then followed him.

"We can help," I said, hustling after the two men. Moving a piano wasn't easy, even if it was an upright, as my mom said this one was. It had been a while since I'd played, and the idea that she knew that warmed me throughout. It wasn't a bad way to deal with anxiety. "We're coming."

"We've got this," Sean called out.

I sighed and stopped by the door.

Tessa chuckled. "You know he won't let you help move a piano. It's Uncle Sean." She looked around the room and pointed to the long wall by the front door that led to the master bedroom. The utility room with washer and dryer was on the other side. "That's the only place it'll fit." She rubbed her wrist. "Um, should we give Clark a heads up about golfing with Sean and his friends?"

"Maybe? I don't know what his alcohol tolerance is," I admitted. "I think I've seen him having drinks with a couple of attorneys after work, but I've never seen him do shots. We should at least make sure he has a good base before heading over. We can meet him for breakfast before he drives to Silverville and the golf course."

She smiled, but worry still pinched her eyes at the corners.

"We're going to figure Danny's murder out, Tess. Don't worry." I wouldn't stop until we got her clear of the charges against her. At least now I had a couple of avenues to pursue. "Nick is excellent at his job. He'll find out the truth. Also, he couldn't stop looking at you over breakfast."

She rolled her eyes. "I told you not to go there."

"Why not?" I turned to face her and ignored the swearing coming from my grunting uncle as he hefted a piano down my walkway with a rapidly sweating Clark.

"For one thing, I thought there was something between the two of you," she said.

I shook my head. "Nope." Yeah, there had been some flirting and a drunken kiss a while back, but that was before I'd jumped off a cliff with Aiden. And now that I knew there was a chance Tess might be interested in Nick...he sure looked brotherly to me. Well, in an incredibly sexy way. "I think you might like him."

"No way. Nick is a lawyer, for Pete's sake. A football hero, a Navy hero, and now a prosecuting attorney hero." She craned her neck to watch our uncle. "I'm not. We wouldn't make a good couple."

That was the dumbest thing I'd ever heard. "Okay," I said instead.

We'd just see about that.

CHAPTER 12

*M*y Monday morning hearings went smoothly, and I dodged into my office to drop off my files, nearly running right into Alice Mitchell. She stepped back.

I gasped and leaped for her. "You're back. Tell me you're back for good."

She hugged me and laughed, looking beyond perfect in her pink suit with the tan shoes. Alice was around thirty-five, was happily married with three kids, and had been my mentor for my first month at the prosecuting attorney's office until Nick had gone and canned anybody who'd worked there while the former dirty prosecuting attorney had been in charge. "I'm back. Nick hired me this morning."

Thank goodness. I released her and looked up the several inches to her smiling face. Her pink lipstick matched her suit in a way I could only hope to emulate someday. "I'm so glad."

"Me too." She tugged her Coach briefcase farther up her arm. "I have to run to court but we should catch up later? Maybe lunch tomorrow?"

"Absolutely." I fought the urge to hug her again as she hustled out of the offices. Finally, Nick had come to his senses. My stomach growled, and I glanced at my phone. I had time for a quick bite, so I turned and followed Alice outside before anybody could stop me. Once standing on the clean and very warm sidewalk, I strode along the manicured park toward the lake, stopping at McQuirk's Deli, which took up the entire first floor of the building between my offices and the beach. Businesses took residence on the second floor.

I grabbed a pre-made salad and waited for a chilled latte before heading outside toward the beach, where I managed to snag a small picnic table beneath a tree. Kids laughed while playing in the water, and a boisterous game of volleyball entertained me as I tried to breathe in the nice weather and relax. Now that Nick was finally hiring other attorneys, hopefully my workload would lighten.

"Hi." Jolene O'Sullivan slipped onto the bench across from me with her sandwich and soda.

I coughed on my latte.

She grimaced. "Yeah, sorry about that." She spread the napkin out and placed the wrapped McQuirk's sandwich across it. Today she wore white capri pants, a pretty blue silk shirt, and silver jewelry. Her blonde hair was back in a ponytail, her makeup minimal, and her eyes sparkling. "Not only for that. Sorry I was bitchy the other day. Old habits die hard, you know?"

I didn't know. Instead, I took another sip of my latte and wondered what mercurial gods had put Jolene smack down in the middle of my peaceful moment.

She took a bite of her club sandwich and closed her eyes, humming in pleasure. After she chewed, she smiled. "Man, I missed their sandwiches while I was in Boston."

I sipped my latte. What should I do? Did I still owe her a punch in the face for sleeping with Donna's boyfriend? It was ages ago, he'd been a moron, and no doubt Donna had moved on. But she was my sister, and maybe Jolene was right that old habits did die hard. I wanted to punch her for making my sister cry. Yeah, I'd always thought she was aptly named, and the lyrics for *Jolene* ran through my head.

Jolene smiled. "Okay, fine. Here's the deal. I wasn't nice to you, and I know I hurt your sister, but give me a break. That was a long time ago. My folks were fighting all the time and got divorced, and you all were this one big happy family, and I was a jerk and struck out. I'm sorry."

Well. I'd been much younger than her and hadn't known about any of her home life. "I was probably a pain in the butt tagging along with you teenagers all the time," I admitted.

She chuckled. "You were, but honestly, I was a little jealous of how nice Aiden was with you. He only looked at you like a little sister, but he was genuinely amused by everything you did. He really did like you."

Yeah, I'd thought so. We'd had a friendship that had made me happy.

Her smile made twin dimples show on her pretty face. "I heard that friendship changed lately. Quite a bit."

I lifted an eyebrow.

She took a drink of her soda. "There are no secrets in Silverville, even for somebody who moved away eons ago."

Wasn't that the truth?

"So, are you two dating now?" Her words were a little too casual.

"Why?" I asked.

She shrugged. "Part curiosity and part noticing that he's hotter than ever. I love a bad boy." Her face fell. "Although, that's usually my downfall, you know?"

Did I ever. "I accept your apology, but I really don't want to talk about my love life," I said.

She nodded. "I get it."

"Are you moving back here?" Sure, I was curious.

"I'm thinking about it." She ate more of her sandwich. "I'm

here cleaning out my Grandma's condo since she passed on, and now that I'm here, it feels like home. Much nicer than the city."

My heart jerked for her. "I'm sorry about your Grandma." I hadn't heard. The idea of losing one of mine made everything inside me hurt.

"Thanks," she said softly. "Me, too." Then she finished her lunch. "Okay, I can't help it. The gossip mill is crazy. Did you really find Aiden and your sister standing over the dead body of Danny Pucci? I dated him, you know. Before I started dating Aiden in high school."

I swallowed quickly. "You did? Did the two of you stay in contact?"

She took a sip of her drink. "Yeah. You know. We were Facebook friends and messaged once in a while. In fact, he'd said he was coming home, and we made arrangements to meet up in person."

I leaned toward her, my body going on alert. "Did he say why he was coming back?"

She lowered her voice. "Yeah. You first."

Darn it. Fine. "I can't confirm anything, but rumors are usually true. You know that Tessa didn't kill Danny, though."

"I don't see Aiden murdering anybody like that, either," she said quietly.

I nodded. "Totally agree."

She finished her lunch. "That's quite a conundrum, right? Finding the guy you're dating and your sister over the dead body?" She wrapped up the garbage. "Only you, Albertini."

I snorted. "Yeah. No kidding." I finished my salad. "Tell me about Pucci."

She took lipstick out of her handbag and swiped a deep maroon across her lips. "Danny had been in trouble in Nevada and came home for a fresh start. He didn't say what had happened, but he did say he had a line on a good job here. Something about the Lordes. I think he might've been joining the club."

Had she been hoping to see Pucci or Aiden when she'd shown up at the Lorde's apartment building? My expression must've looked inquisitive because she blushed.

"Yeah, I was looking for either one of them. It'd be nice to see a friendly face." She took a deep breath.

I could understand. For the first time, I smiled. The past was the past, and part of being a teenager was making mistakes. "I can be a friendly face, too. Welcome home, Jolene."

* * *

I BALANCED the two lattes carefully as I smiled at the cop handling the reception area at the police station and strode up the stairs to Pierce's office. A ruckus came from the farthest interrogation room, so I dodged into his office to stay out of the way in case the scuffle made it down the hallway.

He looked up from a smattering of papers across his thick wooden desk. His eyes were bloodshot, his sandy-blond hair mussed, and his hands broad on the papers. An instant smile tilted his lips as he caught sight of the drinks.

Taking that as an invitation, I strode inside and kicked the door shut behind me with my black pump. "Howdy."

"Hi." His gaze didn't move from the drink.

I handed over the latte and took one of the vacant leather chairs across from him, more than ready to drink my second one of the day.

He tipped his head back and drank rapidly. Then he set it down, rolled his shoulders in his pressed white dress shirt, and kicked back in his chair. "Why are you bringing me coffee?"

I had never been a game player. At least not with people. X-Box was another story. "I need to know where you are with my sister's case." I took a drink of my hot latte, which was slightly better than the cold one had been for lunch.

"You know I can't really talk to you about it," he said, watching me.

I studied him right back and paused in my interrogation. "You look tired, Grant," I said. There were new lines fanning out from his eyes, which were a bit bloodshot.

"When I moved to Timber City, I figured it'd be a slower pace than Los Angeles," he said, drinking more of the latte. "So far, I've been wrong."

I think it was the first time I'd actually seen Grant Pierce with his guard down. He was an interesting guy, and if my plate wasn't full with Aiden Devlin and heartache right now, I might try to flirt a little bit. Instead, I went the safe and friendly route. "Have you taken a vacation since you've been here?"

He shook his head. "No. Not sure where I'd go right now."

That sounded a little sad. I glanced at the pictures on his desk. "You have what looks like a brother and a sister. Where are they?"

He tapped a pen with his free hand. "Brother in Wyoming and sister in New York City. Both busy and I'm hoping to get them here to relax instead of going there."

I took a moment to breathe, which is something apparently he needed to do as well. "Why don't you invite them here this month, since it's the best time of year to visit? You could take a week or two off and show them around." People flocked to northern Idaho in July.

He lifted a shoulder. "Maybe I'll do that after I figure out who shot Pucci in the head."

Well, that was an opening, and we both knew it. I exhaled. "What do you have on Pucci's murder? You can talk about it because I work for the prosecuting attorney's office." Before he could object, I held up a hand. "This wouldn't get you in trouble. Just me."

"Maybe I don't want to see you in trouble," Grant muttered.

"Is there something I shouldn't know?" I asked, taking a chance.

Pierce glanced down at his papers. "Not really, to be honest." He reached into a drawer and brought out a bright and fluorescent pink file folder that was somehow glittery. My name was written neatly on the tab, and he handed it over.

Wow. That was a lot of sparkle. I took the folder and flipped open the top. "What is this?"

"Everything on the case," Pierce said, drinking more of his coffee.

I gulped and looked up at him. "I don't understand."

He shrugged. "I knew you'd come looking, and I also knew you had access to most of this from your office, although that'd get you in trouble. So I saved us both a ton of time and dancing around and just compiled it."

My chest warmed, and hope burst through my chest. "You don't think Tessa killed Danny." Oh, I knew she hadn't done it, but relief lightened weights I hadn't realized hung heavy on my shoulders.

"I'm not ready to say that," Pierce said, his eyes beyond green in the small office. "My instincts are usually on track, and I don't think she did it, but I've been wrong before. I haven't cleared her or Devlin. It doesn't make sense that he'd drop the gun for her to take, but maybe he'd been ready to leave when she came in the door. So you need to continue to keep your distance from him until we arrest somebody."

At that second, I knew that not every bit of evidence was in my pretty pink file folder. I couldn't blame Pierce for that, though. He'd been more than generous. "This is nice of you."

"Yeah, it is. Remember that in the future," he muttered. "Besides, at some point, we have to turn over everything to your sister's attorney, and you'd have access anyway." He cleared his throat. "The only prints on the gun were Tessa's, but the lab pulled a different set off the bullets. It doesn't come back to anybody in the system, including Devlin."

Okay. That was good. Very good. Not great, because anybody

could've touched the bullet, but it was something.

I rifled through the papers and found Kelsey Walker's information and address on the bottom sheet. Excellent. "Thanks for the address on Kelsey. I want to talk to her."

"We've cleared her for the murder. She was at the concert down in the park with about a hundred witnesses," Pierce said. "Feel free to talk to her, but go gentle because Pucci really did a number on her. I don't think she would've held firm with the battery charges against him."

I always went gentle. "This is the pinkest file folder I've ever seen."

He chuckled. "I found it in the supply closet, and it reminded me of you."

I rolled my eyes. "Anything interesting in here besides Kelsey's alibi information?"

"Yeah. Pucci has quite the sheet with all sorts of crimes for your reading enjoyment. In addition, his phone records show that he was in contact with Tessa as well as Aiden Devlin. A lot of contact." Pierce finished his latte and tossed the paper cup into the garbage, which was across the room.

"Three points for you," I murmured. Wait a minute. Pierce looked like a weathered good ole boy surfer from California sometimes, but there wasn't a doubt in my mind that he'd reached the level of detective because of sharp intellect and well-honed strategic abilities. What was missing from the file? "If you're trying to get to Aiden or the Lordes, I'm not the way to go," I said, looking up to meet his gaze directly.

"I have no doubt if it comes down between your sister and Devlin that you'll save Tessa." His chin lowered, and he looked every inch the cop. "Please listen to me for once. The last place in this world you want to be is between me and Devlin, Anna. Even if he didn't take out Pucci, he's involved in the entire situation, and none of it is pretty. This time, he's going down. Stay out of the line of fire."

CHAPTER 13

$\mathcal{K}$elsey Walker lived in one of the stylish brick apartment buildings in the older part of Timber City. Trees were mature, sidewalks were cracked, and the lawns were cute and small. I stood on her weathered gray porch and knocked on the charming round-topped door.

Shuffling sounded inside, and then the door opened.

Whoa. I stepped back. "Hi, Kelsey. I'm Anna Albertini from the prosecuting attorney's office, and I'd love to ask you some questions, if that's okay with you."

She studied me for a moment. Kelsey looked to be in her early twenties with green eyes and dirty blonde hair back in a ponytail. She looked a little bit like Tessa, except for a monstrous black eye that extended down her cheek in odd purple and yellow striations.

"Come in," she said.

I followed her inside and shut the door behind me. "Thanks." Now that I was there and she'd let me in, I wasn't sure exactly how to proceed.

She gestured toward the sitting area that held a soft yellow sofa and chair set in front of an older fireplace with a painted white mantle. "Have a seat."

I took the chair and she took the sofa, putting one leg beneath her. Today she wore blue shorts and a white tank top that showed bruises down both arms and around her wrists. Another set of bruises stood out on her pale neck, showing where Pucci had apparently tried to strangle her. "Are you sure you're up to this?" I asked, my heart aching for her.

She rolled her eyes. "I'm fine. Just a little sore with nothing broken. At the very least, I'm still alive." Spirit glowed in her eyes.

Even so, I couldn't take advantage of her. "You don't have to talk to me if you don't want. I'm here more in a personal capacity, although I am a prosecuting attorney."

She set a light blue sofa pillow on her lap. "I didn't kill Danny."

"I know. The police have cleared you." The buzzing of a lawn-mower filled the quiet afternoon outside. "Who do you think killed Danny?"

She shrugged and then winced as obviously something ached. "Heck if I know. He wasn't the nicest guy." She looked up, and the bruise on her cheekbone made me want to punch Danny in the face. Too bad he was dead. "You're Tessa's sister, right?"

I nodded.

"You're the youngest Albertini?"

"Yeah," I said. "Well, the youngest in my family. Donna's the oldest, then Tess, then me."

"I'm the youngest, too," Kelsey whispered. "It's like I'm always screwing up."

I got that. "The fact that Danny was a jerk isn't your fault. Do you blame yourself? If you do, I know a heck of a shrink. It's our cousin Wanda." Well, cousin a bunch of times removed. But she helped me all the time. "Danny's problems were his and not yours." I leaned toward her. "My sister Tessa is the strongest and smartest person I've ever met, and she dated him."

"I think she's still dating him," Kelsey said, her green eyes shallow with what looked like pain. "That's what we were fighting about when things got...out of hand."

My heartbeat increased. "I know they talked a few times, but Tess said they weren't dating. That she'd never date him again."

"That's probably true," Kelsey sighed, looking down at the pillow. "But they were talking, and when Danny wanted something, he usually got it."

I couldn't argue with that. "How long did you date Danny?" Should I say that I was sorry about her loss? As it looked to me, she was lucky the bastard was dead. Saying that was probably a bad idea at the moment.

"Next week is our two-month anniversary," she said quietly. "He wasn't all bad, you know. It's just, sometimes when he drank, he got so angry. But there were good times, too. I loved riding on his bike with him." A slight color finally filtered into her too pale face. "You know what I mean."

I blinked. "I do?"

"Sure. Aren't you dating Aiden Devlin?" She leaned forward. "Is it true he's the president of the Lordes now?"

The breath heated up my throat. "I'm not sure on either front."

She made a sympathetic sound. "Then you're probably not dating him. When those guys cut a girl loose, they do it completely. I'm sorry."

I tilted my head and tried really hard to ignore the truth of that dagger to the heart. "Danny wasn't a member of the Lordes, was he?"

"No." She smiled. "They were just doing some business together."

Finally we were getting somewhere. "What kind of business was Danny in?"

She shook her head. "I don't know. It wasn't like he shared that kind of information, you know? But we rode with Aiden and the Lordes a few times, and I know they had something in the works."

"Drug related?" If the Lordes were running drugs again, I was going to shoot Aiden.

"I don't think so," Kelsey murmured. "I overheard one of the guys approach Aiden about drugs while we were camping out one night, and Aiden was very clear that the Lordes were out of the drug trade."

"What guys?"

"Danny had a lot of business partners." For the first time, Kelsey looked away. Her blush intensified.

I watched her carefully. "Like who?"

She didn't look back at me.

Was she scared or just being careful? "You can trust me," I said.

"I can't trust anybody," she said quietly, folding her hands on the pillow. "Danny kept me out of his business."

I so didn't want to ask the next question, but I couldn't help myself. "Did anybody ride on the back of Aiden's bike? Was he, um, camping out with anybody?"

"No."

Relief filtered through me with a speed that should be embarrassing.

She shook her head. "In the few times I've seen Aiden, I've never seen him with a woman. At the camp out, a couple of women made moves on him, and he didn't take anybody up on the invite that night. Not that I saw, anyway. I heard through the Silverville grapevine that he was dating you, so I figured that was why. I guess not."

"Tell me more about this camp out," I said. Just what were Aiden and Danny into, anyway? "Where was it and what was going on?"

"Hello?" The front door opened and a slightly, very slightly, older version of Kelsey walked in with her hands ladened down with bags. "I brought groceries and stuff to make for dinner since I gave you the day off." The woman paused at seeing me, and her green eyes narrowed. "What's going on?"

Oh, I recognized the big sister over-protective look in a second. I had two of those. "I'm Anna."

"That's right. The youngest Albertini?" She walked toward the compact kitchen and dumped several grocery bags on the counter. "I'm Krissy. I played volleyball against your sister Donna when I was a senior and she was a freshman, I think." Krissy's eyebrows lifted. "How is she, anyway?"

"Good. She's selling real estate in town and is doing well," I said. "How about you? She'll ask when I see her."

Krissy started unpacking the goodies. "I'm great. Took over the business for dad two years ago." She shrugged. "Being a mortician grosses some people out, but I like it. There's peace and comfort with helping people through grief, and I like working with Kelsey, who manages scheduling and the office." Her voice didn't change. "Why are you here, Anna?"

I cleared my voice. "I'm not here officially."

"Yeah. I figured." Her eyes sparkled. "Sisters, right?" She shook her head. "Kelsey has an alibi for when Danny was killed, and the police have cleared her."

I couldn't help it. "What about you, Krissy?" I kept my voice calm, too.

Her grin was instant. "Well, given the chance, I would have absolutely put a bullet in Danny Pucci's head, but unfortunately, I was at the park concert with Kelsey that night and have about a hundred alibis to prove it." She started putting groceries away as if she knew exactly where everything went. "Although I wouldn't mind shaking the hand of whoever did end that loser's life."

I nodded. I'd felt the same way after he'd hurt my sister. "Where's the rest of the family?"

Krissy chuckled. "You're barking up the wrong tree for suspects, though I get it. I don't remember Tessa well, but she certainly never seemed like a murderer." She shook out a bag of grapes into a bowl and set it on the table. "Kami is in New York at graduate school, Kylie is in London on an externship, and Katrina

99

is still in Malibu learning how to surf." She shook her head. "I've always loved the free spirit of my twin, but I don't get how she doesn't settle down with some security."

"Anybody else in the family who might've wanted to hurt Danny?" I asked.

"Everyone," she said easily, looking at her sister's bruised face. "But our folks are traveling through Europe with a group of friends and have been for a month, and any distant cousins we have don't live here. If I were you, I'd look more into that motorcycle gang Danny kept hanging around with."

"Club," I said absently. "They're motorcycle clubs."

"Whatever," Krissy said. "But for now, how about you leave my sister alone about it? She wasn't involved, and she has some healing to do." It was said as a question but sounded like an order. A big sister order.

Kelsey shifted on the sofa. "She's just trying to help *her* sister, Kris."

"I get that," Krissy said. "However, Danny Pucci was into some dicey shit, and the last thing you need is for his enemies to come after you."

Kelsey paled. "That's true. Although I don't know anything about what he was in to." Her gaze shuttered. "Except for Tessa. He definitely seemed to still be into her, even though it sounds like she wasn't on the same wavelength, according to you, Anna."

"I hope not," I said, meaning it. "I'm sorry you had to go through all of this."

"It's my own fault," Kelsey said.

"It is not," Krissy and I said in unison.

Then Krissy sighed. "Since you're talking to Anna, you should tell her everything, Kels."

My stomach clenched. "Everything?"

Kelsey ducked her head and stared intently at her pillow. "Fine. Your sister is lying to you, and I told the police the full story. But it doesn't mean she killed him, you know?"

I couldn't breathe. "What do you mean that Tessa is lying? She never lies to me."

"She's probably embarrassed," Kelsey said, still not looking at me. "The whole thing is embarrassing, and if she feels half as stupid as I do about Danny, then I'm sure she wouldn't want you to know they were on a date last week and got into a big fight at Dunphey's Bar. He came back with a split lip and said Tessa hit him, and he also had fingernail scratches down his neck."

So that's what Detective Pierce left out of the pink file folder. "Are you sure it was Tessa?" I asked. My sister didn't lie—especially to me.

"Yeah. Danny told me that." Kelsey plucked at a string on the pillow. "I'm sorry."

"It's okay," I said, angry with a hint of hurt. "I don't know the right way to ask this, but is it possible Danny lied to you? I mean, he knew you weren't happy he was talking to Tessa, and it seemed like he enjoyed causing pain."

She swallowed. "Yeah, it's possible. But there's something about Danny, you know? I mean, there *was* something about Danny. No matter how mean he got, he could turn on the charm in a second and convince you that he'd change. That you could help him be a better person. He really wanted Tessa back, I think."

Until Tess told me otherwise, I believed her story. So the question was, who'd hit Danny? "Was he interested in anybody else? With the fingernail scratches, maybe there was another woman?"

"It's possible." Kelsey pressed a hand to her temple. "Krissy? Would you toss me the Advil?"

Krissy gave me a look. The look. The "it's time you left" look.

I patted Kelsey's hand. "Thank you for talking to me. Really quickly, before I leave, could you tell me about this group of guys Danny worked and camped out with?"

"No." Krissy finally made a move from the kitchen. "My sister already told you she doesn't know anything about Danny's friends, and enough is enough. Somebody *murdered* him, Anna. If

101

it was somebody he was in business with, Kelsey has already told you all she knows." She opened the door.

I smiled at Kelsey and stood, heading for the door. "Okay." There wasn't anything else I could say.

Krissy waited until I was on the porch before speaking again. "Tell Donna hi for me. And again, if you really want to pursue this, talk to the Lordes motorcycle gang."

"Club," I said, turning and heading down the steps. "Thanks, Krissy." Oh, I was heading to find Tessa right now.

CHAPTER 14

$\mathcal{M}$y sister wasn't at work or at Donna's apartment, and she didn't answer her phone. A healthy headache was already thrumming at the back of my neck as I drove out to Thelma and Georgiana's to water their plants before heading to my peaceful cottage on the lake. Once home, I filled a crockpot with frozen Irish stew and sat at my kitchen table to read through the sparkly pink file folder while waiting for my sister to call.

Danny Pucci had been arrested several times for assault and battery, twice with a weapon in hand. Once a knife and the other time a gun. He'd also been arrested for burglary, attempted kidnapping, possession of illegal firearms, robbery, harassment, and stalking. Most of the charges failed to stick because witnesses seemed to either change their minds or disappear. Just wonderful. It was no doubt that he'd had many enemies, most of whom probably wanted him dead. The biggest question was why he'd been found in Tessa's apartment.

Something told me that could be the key to this whole thing.

I finished my stew, cleaned up my kitchen, and sat back down to sketch out a game plan when my phone finally rang. "Hello."

"Hey. Sorry I missed you earlier. I was with cousin Wanda the shrink and then forgot to bring my phone in from the car," Tessa said, sounding harried.

My shoulders slowly unfurled from their position up by my ears. "I was an hour away from calling in Donna."

Tessa snorted. "Point taken. I'll be more careful with my phone."

We both knew she wouldn't be more careful. In fact, Tessa was terrible with her phone and usually left it somewhere in town. Most of the restaurants knew what it looked like and to call her to pick it up after she'd been there. "Kelsey Walker said you had a date with Danny and ended up giving him a split lip and scratched neck the night before he beat the crap out of her."

Tessa was quiet.

I dropped my chin to my chest. "It's true?"

"Of course it's not true," she exploded. "How could you think that? I did talk to him on the phone a few times, as you know, but I'd never go on a date with that asshole again. He punched me in the face and stole my car, remember?"

I winced. Tessa's temper was closer to the surface than mine, but it was no less impressive. "Sorry. It's just what Danny told Kelsey, probably to hurt her feelings. He still wanted you, apparently."

"He was never going to get me," Tessa retorted. "Although, I would've taken the chance to punch him, you know?"

"Yeah." I spun a piece of paper around with my finger. "She told the police that, just so you know. I feel like Detective Pierce thinks you're innocent, but he'll follow up on any lead he can find."

"Well, that's a dumb lead," she said. "I didn't go on a date with Danny, and I assume Pierce will find out who really split Danny's lip. I wonder, though. Who else was he dating?"

I shook my head. "Who knows. He was cute and charming until the asshole side came out."

"That's the truth," Tessa said. "You can apologize now."

"For what?" I retorted. "I didn't accuse you. I just told you what Kelsey said." I could feel her rolling her eyes.

"Whatever. You sound like a lawyer," she said.

"I am a lawyer." I grinned into the now darkened night outside my sliding glass door.

She laughed. "Fine. Have you tried the piano yet?"

I glanced to where the upright sat against the wall near the door. It was weathered with a well-played look that did invite me to play. "I've been waiting for you to call while reading through a case file about Danny. Now that I know you're alive and well, maybe I'll take a break."

"Anna, I don't want you to get fired over this," she said. "I know you want to help, but I didn't kill Danny, so I'm sure Pierce will figure that out. Maybe you should do what Nick said and stay out of it?"

"Yeah. Maybe I should," I said noncommittally.

She sighed loudly. "It's not just me, is it? You're trying to save Aiden again."

Was I? "I don't know. At the very least, I'd love to know what he's doing." I'd never been able to turn away from a puzzle, and right now Aiden Devlin was a mystery that needed solving. A hot, sexy, frustrating mystery. "Once you're cleared of this, I'll have to really sit down and figure out if I want to help him or not."

"You already helped him with the drug charges," she said quietly. "If you owed him from what happened when we were young, which I'm not sure you did, then you've repaid him by far. You might have to let him go."

"I know," I said softly.

"Why don't you go out with Nick Basanelli?" she asked. "He hits all the marks."

I shuffled the papers back into some semblance of order. "Two lawyers dating? That's a disaster."

"It's better than a prosecuting attorney and a crook," she returned.

"Nope. I think you and Nick make a much better couple," I said. "You're a great balance to each other. I think you'd bring a lot of light into his life, and he'd bring some much needed order and adventure to yours." Yeah. I could totally see them together.

"Not in a million years," she said. "We don't have anything in common, and you know it." The sound of a door closing echoed over the line. "Donna's home with ice cream. Want to come over?"

Ice cream sounded wonderful. "Thanks, but I have to work early tomorrow." I eyed the piano. "Bye." She said bye and hung up.

I moved to the piano and lifted the cover, wandering my fingers lazily across the keys. The thing was nicely in tune. Humming, I started to play a couple of early Bon Jovi songs before moving on to songs from a few movies. Playing relaxed me, and I let myself drift for a while.

A hard pounding on my front door had me jumping.

I stood and hurried to the door to peek through the peephole. Aiden? He was looking down. I opened the door and he stumbled in, looked around, and dropped to my floor. Blood dotted his neck and down one leg.

"Aiden?" I looked quickly outside, didn't see a threat, and slammed the door to lock it.

He groaned. "Were you just playing the theme song from Jaws?"

* * *

ADRENALINE FLOODED ME. "Do I need to get my gun?"

"No." Aiden rolled over and plucked a stick out of his thick hair. Groaning, he sat up and put his back to the wall next to the piano. His jeans were ripped, and blood covered a hole near his knee. "Leave the gun safely in the bedroom." Wincing, he reached behind his back and drew out a Glock to set beside him. "You can use this one if you want."

"I prefer mine," I said, noting the sticks and branches stuck in his hair and on his dirty T-shirt. "What happened to you?"

He planted a scratched and bloody hand on the floor and pushed himself to stand, where he wove for a second on his feet. "I was riding my bike and got hit by a car."

I winced and leaned in to look at his too blue eyes. His pupils looked okay. I leaned to the side to study a scrape along his neck and a bruise already forming adjacent to his right eye. "I'll call the police." Then I turned toward the kitchen table where I'd left my phone.

He stopped me with a hand on my bicep. "No police."

I shut my eyes and exhaled. No police. Why didn't that surprise me? I turned to face him. "Aiden."

He released me and pulled some brambles off his shirt near his way too packed hard abs. "I didn't see the car and have nothing to help the police find the driver. Besides, I don't think the police really want to help me right now."

"If there's somebody out there running people over, we need to call it in," I said.

He looked up, his gaze meeting mine and nearly knocking me back. Man, his eyes were blue. Like a deep and dark pool of night with a hint of sapphire. "Oh, the driver was aiming for me, *Aingeal*. He or she isn't out there looking for other motorcyclists to knock into trees." His jaw hardened along with those eyes. "I'll take care of it."

I shivered. Why was a threat said with a slight Irish brogue all the more dangerous? "Did the car follow you or were they waiting close to my place?"

"I think they followed me," he said, kicking off his dirty boots near the door.

I crossed my arms to keep from reaching for him to check his injuries. It was so difficult being a grownup sometimes. "Why were you riding my way?" Might as well face him head on.

He sighed. "I wanted to see you. It's a mistake and I know it, but I don't like this...discord between us."

Discord? Freaking discord? My arms dropped to my side. "Are you, or are you not, involved in more illegal activity?"

"I'm not," he said, for a moment looking like the kid who'd rushed into a cabin and beat up a monster to save me. Blood dripped over the neck of his shirt. "Do you mind if I jump in the shower? I'm bleeding all over."

"Do you need stitches?" Against my better judgment, I leaned forward to look at his neck.

He shook his head, and a couple of brambles fell onto my floor. "Just a bandage or two. Do I still have some clothes somewhere?"

I rubbed my chest. "Yeah. In the bottom drawer of the dresser." I wasn't quite to the point of burning the clothing he'd left during our few weeks together. "Have you eaten?"

"No." He turned for the bedroom and disappeared.

Sighing, I trudged into the kitchen and quickly heated up some of the stew. What was I going to do with him? Why wouldn't he level with me? Against all rationality, I believed him when he said he wasn't doing anything illegal. Yet he'd answered in present tense. Was he planning to do something illegal?

If not, why was he trying to stay away from me when he obviously wanted to be with me?

Maybe a baseball bat to the head would help. Or a wooden spoon. My Nonna was famous for smacking people on the head with her wooden stirring spoon, and for once, I saw the advantage of the practice. Somehow, I doubted Aiden would fall in line if I walloped him with a spoon. Even so, the thought cheered me.

The shower stopped in the other room and I bustled around, gathering my papers and setting the pink file folder on the counter and out of the way. Then I ladled soup for him and waited.

And waited some more.

After about fifteen minutes or so, I went into the bedroom to check on him. Aiden lay on my bed on his stomach, his arm flung out, bandages from my medicine cabinet across his neck. His torso was bare and led to his phenomenal butt in boxer-briefs. His shoulders were wide, his waist tapered, and his entire bruised body one belonging to a badass. His black hair was wet and combed back, already curling over his ears.

I sighed, my heart doing a flippy odd thing it only did for him.

Even his bare feet were somehow sexy and masculine. His face was half snuggled into the pillow and half facing the sliding glass door, his eyes were shut, and he breathed evenly.

How did you get a guy out of your heart when he looked like that? When he'd saved your life more than once?

I left the room and shut down the cottage for the night, making sure all of the doors and windows were locked. The A/C was on, so I left the windows closed, considering somebody had rammed a car into the guy in my bed.

Said guy didn't move while I got ready for bed. The air conditioning kicked on as I slid beneath the covers, nudging him in the shoulder. "Aiden. Get under the covers."

He mumbled something, rolled over, and slid beneath the sheet. In a move I was hoping he'd make, he tugged me into his body and spooned around me. His sent of leather, oil, and male surrounded me along with the oddest sense of Ireland. Of rolling hills and wild ocean crests.

"Tomorrow we are talking," I murmured, meaning it as my eyelids closed.

He placed a soft kiss behind my ear, and the damn sensation shot right to my heart.

Seriously.

CHAPTER 15

*A*iden was playful very early in the morning. This I knew well after our time together. So when I awoke with his hand sliding down my arm and his erection very firm against my butt, it wasn't a surprise. In fact, usually it was an excellent way to wake up.

"Don't even think it," I said, my voice breathy and not convincing, even to my own ears.

"Too late. I'm thinking it." His lips were close to my temple.

Desire shivered through me, landing in all the right places. Okay. I had to strike fast and right now. "I love you, and I want to have your babies, Aiden. I'm thinking five or seven because I like odd numbers. Unless you want four." Even as I messed with him, I could see little black-haired babies with incredible blue eyes running around and causing chaos. Yeah, I was a complete dork.

"Three kids, tops." His warm palm slid beneath my tank top and flattened against my abs. "Four if the first three are girls, God help me."

Yeah. One thing I often forgot about Aiden is that he called every bluff. I both liked and hated this about him. "I'm thinking a big wedding, white dress, huge cake, flower girls." My voice trailed off because I could actually see it all. I'd always been a dreamer, and Aiden Devlin had starred in his share as I'd grown up. Not that I was ready for all of that, but still.

He cupped one breast and nearly had me orgasming right there. "Nope. On my bike, headed to Vegas, quick wedding and honeymoon somewhere on a beach." His very talented fingers tweaked one nipple, and he bit the top of my ear. "And you promise to obey me during the vows."

Electricity arced through my entire body. I tilted my head on the pillow to allow his mouth better access, which he quickly took advantage of to place kisses down the side of my neck. "You know that will never happen."

"Your loss." His hand moved along with his mouth, and he slid beneath my plain white panties. "Now's the time you kick me out or keep me for the morning." His voice was rough with a hint of hoarse. Deep and rumbly.

I shut my eyes as his fingers unerringly found the right spot. Electricity careened through me and my entire body started to burn for him. "If I keep you, I'm just using you for your body."

"I can live with that." He pulled me onto my back and then kissed me, his mouth as talented as his fingers. In fact, his entire body was talented, and he knew how to use it. More importantly, he knew exactly what to do with mine.

After too many years to count dreaming about him, the reality of touching him was so much better. He was hard everywhere, and I liked that I could slide my hands down his flanks and make him suck in a breath. Somehow, Aiden made me feel both powerful and feminine.

Then he traveled south, kissing between my breasts and paying each enough attention that I was almost begging for more, before heading even farther down.

"I could do this all day," he murmured right before his mouth found my clit.

My agreement might've been a little loud.

The first orgasm took me hard, the second long, and the third with a power that made me whimper. Then, and only then, did he find a condom and let loose inside me, on his knees with his arm around my waist and lifting me to him.

He was powerful, masculine, and at the moment...all mine.

I cried out his name this time, completely spent.

So when we moved to the shower for one last round, my brain was mush but my body ready for him once again. Finally, I stumbled out of the shower and tried to find clean towels.

Oh, I was going to be so late for work, but really, who cared? It was difficult to stress out after multiple orgasms. I dressed in gray slacks with a white frilly shirt, acutely aware of slightly sore spots on my body in inappropriate places. Razor burn from his angled jaw covered my thighs, which explained the pants and not a skirt. That would drive me nuts all day in a skirt.

Aiden dressed in one of his black T-shirts and a pair of jeans from his drawer, finger combing his hair back with one broad hand that was still bruised. "I'll make coffee while you finish up." He paused and then leaned over to kiss me, his lips firm and lingering before he wandered toward the kitchen.

He might as well just take my heart with him. This was too hard, but I didn't know how to stop. I didn't want to stop, to be more accurate. "Tell me you're not doing anything illegal," I whispered as he reached my doorway.

"I'm not doing anything that's against the law." He didn't turn around to face me, and he didn't move. "Trust me, Angel. That's all I can tell you." Then he was out of sight.

If he was lying, he was good at it. Or maybe I just wanted to believe him. Yeah. I definitely wanted to believe him. That either made me a moron or somebody who should learn to trust her own instincts. I wish I could say which one was true, and it seemed only time would tell. Time and proof.

I finished with my hair and met him in the kitchen where he

waited with a mug of coffee for me. Aiden looked just right in the morning light in my kitchen. "Thanks."

He glanced outside at the sparkling and still quiet lake. "Do you want to grab dinner tonight?"

My heart jolted. "Are you asking me on a date?" I tried for casual and teasing, but my stomach was flipping summersaults.

"Yeah." He tucked one thumb in his jeans pocket in a cute tough-guy move that I'd only seen in movies. "Whoever is after me knows I was on the way here, so it seems dumb to try and keep you at arm's length." He rolled his neck. "I don't want to stay away from you. All right?" Now he sounded defensive and totally adorable.

"All right," I said softly. "However, considering you're still a suspect in a homicide and I'm a prosecuting attorney, how about we have date night here? You can cook dinner."

He cocked his head to the side, and his eyes warmed. "I'll *grill* dinner. Deal?"

"Deal." I couldn't wait to tell Tessa about this, but I kept it cool. Or at least, I tried to keep cool. "If we're dating, we can't have so much of a wall between us. It doesn't work for me, and it shouldn't work for you. Why were you in Tessa's apartment standing over a dead body?"

Aiden shook his head. "This is such a mistake." He downed the rest of his coffee. "I was with Danny because we were going to grab a drink and catch up. We were the same age in school and hung out a little bit years ago. He had to drop something off at his girlfriend's place, and I didn't even know it was Tessa's apartment. He went inside, I waited in my truck, and then I got tired of waiting and headed up to see the door open and him dead on the ground with the gun next to him. The shot had obviously been muffled by using that pillow that was by his head."

My mouth dropped open. "So you went inside?"

"Yeah. I heard movement and got inside just in time to see somebody jump out the window toward the fire escape. I moved toward them, Tessa came in and grabbed the gun, and then all hell broke loose."

I gulped. "Who was it?"

"I didn't see anything but movement and maybe dark clothing." Frustration coated his words now. "I also have no clue what Danny was dropping off. He might've just wanted an excuse to see her, and from what you've said, she wasn't really his girlfriend."

"Why didn't you tell the police any of this?" I asked.

He lifted a shoulder. "Why would I? I can't corroborate any of it, and it's not like Pierce wants to help me out. Plus, I don't like the next obvious question."

I asked it anyway. "What kind of business were you doing with Danny?"

"None. We're old friends from back in the day." His gaze didn't flicker.

"I know you were working with him to the point that you went on rides and camped out together," I said, finishing my coffee. "Lie to me again, and we're done." Sometimes I could sound like such a badass. Which I ruined by yelping when Aiden hooked a finger in my shirt and yanked me toward him, his mouth taking mine.

Hard and fast and deep.

He kissed me for so long that I couldn't think and then didn't care about thinking. Only feeling. Man, he could kiss.

Finally, he released me to let me breathe, and I stared up into his eyes. A darker rim of blue surrounded his Iris. "I won't lie to you again," he rumbled.

What? Lie? Oh yeah. "Good." I straightened my top and tried to get my body under control. We'd gone four times that morning, and I was ready for a fifth. Sometimes I wondered if Aiden was even human. "So tell me what you and Danny were really doing together that night."

"We were going for a drink." Aiden wiped my pink lipstick off his mouth with his thumb in a too sexy move that should be filmed. "It's the truth. As for anything else about Danny, I'm under advice of counsel not to discuss my association with him. Protect both of us and stop asking, Angel. We don't have attorney-client privilege."

That was true. "I'm going to keep digging on this."

"How about you stop digging and I promise that if Tessa gets caught up in this, I'll confess to the murder and keep her off the hook?" Aiden turned to rinse out his mug in the sink.

I handed mine over to him. "That ruins my plan of a big wedding and five to seven kids of yours. So, no."

He grinned and turned to face me, leaning against the sink. "It's fun to joke about, but my life doesn't lend itself to that ideal, and you know it."

I lifted one eyebrow in a move I'd learned from my mother. "I figure you're a work in progress, if you want the truth. Or maybe you're just a phase. I don't know yet."

A dimple flashed in his right cheek. "You think I'm a phase you're going through?"

I looked him up and down, truly enjoying our banter. "You're a hot bad-boy. That's a well-known phase for a lot of good Catholic girls."

His chuckle warmed all of the private places he'd explored on me that morning. "You know, my Grams would've loved you."

Well. Direct hit right to the heart. Yep. "I think my Nana O'Shea already loves you," I said instead of jumping his bones and begging him to marry me. I was not even remotely ready for happily ever after, even if he was in a different situation. My body wasn't agreeing with me right now, though. "In fact, don't most women adore you?"

"Huh. Not touching that one." He took my hand and started toward the door. "Considering my bike is in a bunch of trees right now, do you mind dropping me off in town on the way to work?"

"Sure. What's your plan then?"

"To call the guys and have somebody come help me with the

bike." He waited on my front porch for me to lock my door and then took my hand again.

I paused. "Is Tessa in danger?"

He studied me for a moment. "I don't think so. She didn't see who killed Danny, and apparently she wasn't in his life, so she should be fine."

That was a relief. We wandered to the driveway where I'd left my Fiat.

A blue car idled across the road, set against a backdrop of pine trees. A long camera poked out, already snapping photographs.

Aiden shoved me behind him, and tension vibrated down his back. "What the hell?"

The driver snapped several more pictures and then sped off.

Aiden looked over his shoulder at me. "Any clue who that was?"

I slowly shook my head. "You or me?"

He shrugged, anger glimmering in his eyes. "Dunno. That wasn't an undercover cop car, and it didn't belong to anybody I know. The driver wore a hat and was too far away to identify."

"Was it the car that ran you off the road last night?" I asked.

"Nope. That was a truck, actually." He sighed. "I could be wrong, but private detective seems the way to go. But was he looking at you or me?"

I shivered. "I don't know."

"It wasn't Jareth Davey," Aiden said, pulling me abreast of him and tucking me safely against his warm and solid body.

"You don't know that," I said over the new lump in my throat. Davey had found me last month and left a note at my place. Right now, apparently he was no longer in California. Maybe it was time we finally had that showdown.

Aiden stared down the now empty roadway. There wasn't anything else to say.

CHAPTER 16

J alternated all day at work between stressing about the weird photographer in the car and wanting to dance a little jig that Aiden and I were back together. Or at least trying to be together. After a hectic morning of court hearings and then an hour of investigating a case through our computer system, I finally had time to call Tessa.

"Yo," she answered, sounding sleepy.

"Yo. Did I wake you up?"

"No. Well, not really. I'm laying out on Donna's back deck and might've fallen asleep, even though her douchey neighbor keeps peeking over the fence. What is up with that dude?"

I remembered Donna saying something about the old fart being a jerk. "Do you think I have a hero complex with Aiden?" I asked, leaning back in my chair.

Movement sounded as she obviously turned over on the lounger. "Yeah. Is that bad?"

I reached in my desk drawer for some lip balm. "I'm not sure. It might blind me to problems."

"Do you feel blind to problems?" she asked.

I swiped the tube across my mouth and then tossed it back in

117

my drawer. "I'm not sure. I fantasized about him for so long growing up, and now he's here in person."

"Hmmm. Well, pretend you didn't know him before now. What would you think?"

"I'd think he's sex on a stick with a side of overprotective badassness," I said instantly.

Her chuckle eased something inside me. "You're over-thinking this. Honestly. Are you picking out china?"

Well, we had been joking about that earlier, but not really. "No."

"Then just enjoy the ride and see where it takes you," she said softly. "He seems like a good guy, so long as he didn't murder Danny. I don't think he did, you don't think he did, and you might as well either get him out of your system or see what you two could have."

I relaxed and kicked my feet up on my messy desk. "You give the best advice." My sister really was good with people and insights. She got that from our mom. "You'd make a great shrink."

"Ha," Tessa said. "That'd require years of school, and unlike you, I didn't love school. At all."

True on both counts. "Have they released your apartment yet?"

"No," she said. "But I'm not ready to go back yet, anyway. I'm having fun at Donna's with her wonderfully peaceful pool. You should come by for dinner tonight before my shift."

Heat filtered into my face for no good reason. "Aiden is grilling dinner at my place."

"Oh," she teased, making the word sound like it had several syllables. "Aiden is *grilling*."

"Shut up," I said, my face heating more.

"You shut up," she naturally returned. "Do we need to have the sex talk again?"

Considering the last time my sisters had given me the sex talk, they'd convinced me that somehow too much sex would make my nose disappear and I'd have a hole in my face. I didn't think so. I was eleven at the time. "You guys were kinda mean, you know."

"Look who's talking. You might be the youngest, but you always came up with the best pranks," she said.

I chewed my minty lips. "Keep that in mind, Contessa."

She laughed. "Have fun tonight, and call me tomorrow. Bye." She clicked off.

I felt better about everything after talking to her, so I turned back to work and managed to draft several pleadings and begin a response brief to a motion to suppress. My office phone rang toward late afternoon, and I absently picked it up. "Anna Albertini."

"Um, hi, Anna?"

I paused as I recognized her voice. "Kelsey?"

"Um, yeah." She cleared her throat but her words still slurred. "So, I, um wasn't sure who to call. It's, um, it's my fault."

I leaned forward, my heart thundering. "Kelsey? Are you okay?"

Something fell in the background. "Um, it's my fault. I shouldn't have told them. You don't understand." Her voice trailed off.

I fumbled for my cell phone in my purse. "Kelsey? How much have you had to drink?"

She hiccupped. "I had Vodka. It's Danny's favorite. I was just mad at him about your sister, and I, um, shouldn't have talked about everything. I was so stupid. I can't live with this." She hiccupped again.

"How much vodka?" I paused with pressing 9-1-1.

"Just a little." She sighed loudly, and her voice trailed off. Something clattered. "Shit. My pills."

Oh no. "Don't take pills. Stop, Kelsey." What was she doing? I punched in the numbers. "Are you at your house?"

"Yeah." A loud clattering came across the line. Then dead air. Nothing.

The 9-1-1 operator came on and I gave Kelsey's address while grabbing my purse and running out the door and into the late afternoon to my car around the building. I sped through town to the older part and arrived behind two patrol cars and an ambulance with their lights flashing red and blue.

Neighbors had already come out on their porches to see what was going on.

I parked behind a cop car and ran down the sidewalk and up the steps to Kelsey's open door. "Kelsey?" I yelled

"Hey." A strong hand clamped onto my arm and jerked me to a halt. "Hold it."

I stumbled and looked up into dark eyes set in a square face. "Bud." The uniformed cop was built like a linebacker and looked tough with his buzz cut and big muscles. "Um, hi." Last time we'd worked together, I'd gotten him choked out and then shot.

"What are you doing here?" he asked, pivoting to put his body between me and the kitchen.

"I'm the one who called it in," I said, craning my neck to see past him. "Is Kelsey okay?"

Just then, Kelsey walked out of the kitchen with a bag of ice on her cheek. "I cannot believe you called the paramedics. I just tripped and fell." With her bruised face and pale skin, she looked like she should sleep for a year.

I winced. "Sorry. You said something about pills."

She rolled her eyes. "I spilled my vitamins on the floor and then tripped and dropped the phone." Her voice still slurred, and she wove unsteadily on her feet.

A paramedic helped her to the sofa. "Keep drinking water."

She looked over at Bud and smiled. "Hello."

"Hi." He eyed her and then me, and swear to goodness, it looked like he was weighing whether or not to leave me with her.

"I'm not that dangerous," I protested.

He rolled his eyes.

I straightened as tall as I could, which wasn't nearly as tall as

Bud. "Why didn't you call and ask out Donna, anyway?" The guy had expressed interest in my sister a couple of weeks ago but hadn't called her.

"I've been out of town recuperating from our last case together, and I also had some family stuff to handle," he said, giving a tough guy nod to the other cop. "We're good here. I'll walk you out, Albertini."

I shook my head and drew free. "I'll stay here with Kelsey for a little while." What in the world had she meant about causing Danny's death? Now that I knew she wasn't trying to harm herself and wasn't in any danger, my mind turned to the murder. "Thanks, Bud. Bye."

He shook his head but exited the home along with the other emergency personnel.

I winced once the house became quiet. "Kelsey, I'm really sorry." But I'd probably do the same thing again in the same situation. "I thought you were in danger."

She flopped on the sofa and kicked her bare feet onto the table. Then she set her head back. "If you could make the room stop spinning, I'd forgive you."

"I can't control gravity, but I can get you some water if you want." Without waiting, I went into her cheerful kitchen and poured some water from a pitcher already on the table to take to her. I handed the glass over and sat in the matching chair. "What did you mean that you caused Danny's death?"

Motorcycle pipes sounded down the road outside.

She sat up immediately and dropped her feet to the floor. "Shit. You need to go."

I paused. "What? Why?"

The motorcycles stopped outside the house, and running steps echoed up the stairs. The door burst open, and Krissy skidded inside, wearing skinny jeans and a tank top that showed off her cut biceps. "Are you okay?"

I blinked.

121

Kelsey nodded. "Yes. I'm fine. It was just a misunderstanding."

Krissy's gaze swung to me. "What are you doing here?"

I started to answer her when two big and broad men strode into the room and shut the door behind themselves. It took me a second to recognize Saber. "Hey," I said.

Saber looked me up and down, today wearing jeans and a T-shirt with the Lordes logo over his left pec. "Hey."

My gaze switched to the guy next to him. He was handsome with dark blond hair, brown eyes, and scruffy beard. He stood to about six feet tall and had a wide chest. Half of a tattoo wound down his left arm with the other half hidden by the short sleeve of his shirt. It was a crest of some sort with a dagger extending from what might've been the edge of a heart. "Who are you?" he asked.

"I'm Anna. Who are you?" I didn't stand yet.

His gaze flicked to Kelsey. "Why the hell were the cops here?"

She somehow paled even more, and my heart rate kicked into gear. I stood, partially putting myself between him and the sofa. "I called them. As she said, it was a misunderstanding. How did you know the cops were here?"

His head turned slowly so he could face me directly, his gaze hard. "It's time for you to leave, Anna." He took a menacing step toward me.

Krissy grabbed his arm. "It was a misunderstanding, Rich. Let it go."

He shrugged her off hard enough that she stumbled back.

"Hey." Saber didn't move, but he seemed close anyway. "She's Devlin's. Just so you know."

Rich looked me up and down. "Her ass hasn't been on the back of his bike that I've seen."

Saber just looked bored. "Just sayin'. She's Devlin's property. Crossing him right now would be a bad idea, but it's your mistake to make."

All right. That didn't sound encouraging, and right now, I wasn't going to argue about being Aiden's property, which I so was not. But the idea might get me out of there. "I think I'll go find him now," I said. "Kelsey? Why don't you come with me? We can grab an early dinner." A buzzing set up in my head.

"She's fine," Krissy said, moving forward to sit on the sofa by her sister to take her hand. "Just fine. It's all good, right?" She wasn't as pale as her sister, but her eyes darted from me to Rich and back. "Sorry about the misunderstanding, Anna."

It was a good cue to leave. Yet I hesitated. "Kelsey?"

Kelsey leaned into her sister. "I'm fine. Don't worry. It was just a rough day, and I'm sorry I called you. Please forget it."

I didn't feel right leaving her, but at least she was with her sister.

Saber opened the door. "Bye, Anna."

Well. Okay, then. I turned and advanced toward the doorway with my head held up and my steps measured when I really wanted to run. "If you need me for anything, give me a call, Kelsey." I walked out onto the porch, and the door shut quietly behind me.

I hurried to my car and slipped inside, pausing to look back at Kelsey's house. Saber stood on the porch, watching me with no expression on his face. I started my car and drove away, quickly dialing Pierce's number with one hand.

"Detective Pierce," he answered.

"Hey. Have you found any connection between Danny Pucci's death and Kelsey Walker?" I asked, turning the car toward the main drag of town.

Papers shuffled. "No. I mean, he beat the crap out of her, so we've been looking into anybody who'd want to take him out, but so far, everyone of interest has had solid alibis. Why?"

I told him about the afternoon, including that she thought it was her fault that Danny was dead.

Pierce was silent for a few minutes. "Could mean nothing. Survivor's guilt and all of that, but I'll ask her to come in for an interview anyway. Maybe I can say the police spent valuable resources making sure she was okay and that we want to talk to her."

"I'd like to be there for the interview." I almost turned for my office and at the last second realized it was after quitting time. Kind of. I usually did some work at home at night, but tonight I was getting grilled something. Probably steak? "What do you say?"

"I say you need to clear that with your boss," Pierce said. "Real quick, answer one more question. Was this Rich guy a Lordes member?"

"I don't think so," I said. "I can find out, though."

Pierce coughed. "That's okay. I can do my own work, Anna. Try and stay safe, would you?"

"I'll do my best," I said, clicking off. I'd done my duty by calling the information in to Pierce, so now I could enjoy a nice dinner with Aiden. Our conversation would be pleasant and lead around to good ole Saber and his buddy Rich. Of course, there wasn't a doubt in my mind that Saber had already contacted Aiden.

I sighed.

CHAPTER 17

There's nothing like watching a hot guy make dinner. Aiden had his own recipe for marinating steaks, and watching him flip them over in my Pyrex dish as the grill heated up outside made my abdomen go all squishy again. "You know, I don't think it'd be that difficult to domesticate you," I mused.

He glanced up and flashed a grin that had my ovaries flipping over. "Not a chance."

I tried not to melt. He stood at my kitchen counter with a half-finished bottle of Jackleg Stout beer from a brewery over in Silverville. Not only had he brought all of the groceries, he'd brought beer and a good bottle of Leonetti Cabernet. It was one of my favorites, but I was a girl on a budget and rarely got to indulge. The wine had been breathing on the counter, and he poured me a glass, handing it over.

I sniffed deep and moaned.

He chuckled, grabbed his beer and the steaks, and opened the sliding glass door. "It's a nice night. Come keep me company."

I'd be lying if I didn't say the whole domesticated moment didn't start spiraling little daydreams through my head. "I'm not ready for anything serious," I muttered to myself as I followed him outside to the deck.

He flipped open the lid of the grill. "This is an excellent grill. Nicely done."

I shrugged. "I can't take credit. Uncle Sean brought it over the second I moved in, and he pops in once in a while to grill something and make sure I've kept it nicely clean." I'd used it as well, but I preferred cooking and baking to the grilling, for some reason. The deck had a round table with four chairs that I'd found the perfect daisy-decorated cushions for, and I drew out one to sit.

It was only around eight at night, so the lake was still bright and sparkly, although the sun was going down.

Aiden put the steaks on the grill and stepped back, drinking his beer. When he seemed satisfied all was well, he turned toward me. "So. How was your day?" His indigo colored eyes didn't give anything away.

"The usual," I lied, sipping the wine.

"Right." His T-shirt had the same Lordes logo above his left pec that Saber had worn.

I eyed him. "Did you guys get new shirts or what?"

"Yeah. Saber says hi, by the way."

I sipped slower, enjoying the deep wine. "Who's Rich and what's his connection to the Lordes?"

Aiden studied me for a minute. "Rich isn't a Lordes member."

"I'm aware of that fact," I said. "However, he's riding with one of yours, and I believe you've been camping with him. Or at an encampment." It wasn't like those guys were spending weekends fishing Steelhead out of the river. "What's going on?"

Aiden checked the steaks and then looked back at me. "The Lordes are doing some business with Rich's people, and it's all legal, so stop worrying about it."

I cocked my head to the side. "Who are Rich's people?"

Aiden shrugged. "I think members of his family and some

good friends. They have two master brewers and an investor, and they want to create a series of micro-breweries in the Pacific Northwest." He held up his bottle. "Give these guys some competition."

I almost choked on my drink. "The Lordes are investing in microbreweries?" Yeah, I sounded properly incredulous.

"Yeah. I told you we're going legit, and we have a pretty good distribution system already in place." He shrugged. "Now that we're not distributing illegal drugs, why not go for the legal ones like beer?"

There was a thread of logic there, but Rich hadn't seemed like a business guy to me. He'd seemed like an asshole. "Where does Saber fit in?" I hadn't been able to get a handle on the guy.

"He's about to be a full member of the Lordes," Aiden said. "He doesn't know jack about microbreweries, but we have strength in numbers, and I'm not about to let the club disappear. Saber will make a good second, and I like that he knows how to cover my back."

Second. "So you are becoming the president of a motorcycle club." That would complicate my job, to be sure. Even if they were legit.

"Already did," Aiden admitted. "Somebody had to take over, and I want the brothers to head in the right direction, so it came down to me." He turned back to the steaks.

"You're not telling me everything," I said quietly.

"Nope," he agreed, not looking back. "I'm working on it, though."

I took a moment to remind myself that Aiden hadn't been a Lordes member when they'd been running illegal drugs. His club in Portland had been patched over by the Lordes, and he'd moved back home. He had a rap sheet, and it was ugly, but he'd once hinted that all wasn't what it seemed. "When are you going to fully level with me?"

"I have," he said, looking over his shoulder. "I'm not doing anything illegal, but there are some things from the Lordes past, from my past, that you're better off not knowing. It's the truth." He sighed and went for the kill shot. "You either trust me or you don't, *Aingeal*."

I took another drink and let the potent flavors warm my stomach. "Rich seems like a jerk."

"Rich is a jackass with good connections," Aiden agreed.

"What's his connection to Krissy Walker?" I eyed the steaks to make sure he wasn't burning them.

He flipped them over. "They've dated for a while, I think. Before you ask, Danny Pucci was working with Rich, and I figure that's how he met and started dating Kelsey, which did not end well. Pucci had a temper that he never got under control."

I bit my lip. "Do you think Rich had anything to do with Danny's death?"

Aiden shook his head. "I can't figure out what that'd be. Danny had a lot of enemies, and I'd bet one of them caught up to him. I wish I'd been watching the street and entrance to Tessa's building the day he was shot, but I was answering texts on my phone and was parked down the street."

I narrowed my gaze. "What could Danny have possibly been doing with Rich and his micro-brewery plan? You said they worked together."

"Danny was Rich's third cousin on his mom's side," Aiden said easily. "Family pressure for a job, I assume. They didn't even like each other, but that's the other reason I know Rich didn't have anything to do with Pucci's death. You don't kill family. Well, usually."

My phone buzzed, and I drew it out of the back pocket of my jean's shorts. "Hello."

"It's Nick. Get to the office. We have a serious problem." Without waiting for an answer, Basanelli hung up. I looked at the steaks and sighed.

Aiden crossed his arms. "Who was that?"

"My boss," I said, standing.

Aiden's eyes darkened even more. "Oh, we're gonna have to talk about that guy, aren't we?"

* * *

I saw no reason to change my weekend clothing when I'd been ordered to work on a Sunday night but felt a little off as I walked into the quiet offices still wearing cut off shorts and a tank top. "Nick?" The hallways were dark as I moved to the big office on the end and opened his door.

He sat in his chair, a tank top revealing his muscled arms and a pissed off expression revealing more than I wanted. "I can't believe you."

Well, that could mean anything. I shut the door and strode into the office to sit on the other side of his desk, noting the nice view of the darkened Lilac Lake outside his wide window. Nothing came to mind that I'd done lately to elicit that reaction, and surely calling for help when I had thought Kelsey was going to self-harm wouldn't make him mad. "Could you be more specific?"

"More specific? Sure." He turned to the monitor of his computer and started to read. "This is online now, and the print edition hits the *Timber City Gazette* first thing tomorrow."

I swallowed. "I'm in a newspaper article?"

Nick barked out a laugh and turned the monitor so I could see a picture of me taken that morning holding Aiden's hand beneath the headline: "Possible Corruption in the Prosecuting Attorney's Office."

My belly cramped. "Oh, crap." The photographer that morning worked for the paper?

"Yep," Nick said, his voice low as he turned his monitor back to himself. "Shall I paraphrase it for you?"

I winced and tried not to puke. Everyone would see Aiden leaving my place in the morning with us holding hands. And by everyone, I meant my family. They'd know I'd slept with Aiden. I was a big girl, and a grown-up and had privacy and all, but no girl wanted her Grandpa to know she'd tangled up the sheets with a hottie Irishman who might be on the wrong side of the law. "Go ahead."

Nick kicked back and looked at me and not the monitor, obviously having read the gist enough. "Let's see. Anna Albertini, who found both Aiden and her sister standing over a dead body, who works for the prosecuting attorney's office, is having an illicit affair with the prime subject in the murder—a guy who belongs to a motorcycle club that was just disbanded for distributing drugs. Can you say conflict...of...interest?"

A headache started in my shoulders and shot up my neck to my head. "Um."

"Yeah. Um." Nick's dark hair was standing on end as if he'd yanked on it, and his usually mellow brown eyes held a sharp edge.

"Shouldn't they have tried to contact me for a comment?" I asked lamely, trying to drum up anger instead of embarrassment and dread.

"Why yes," Nick said, sarcasm heavy in his tone as he leaned back to read from the article. "Anna Albertini confirmed that the rumors surrounding this situation are true and that her sister did not murder Danny Pucci."

What in the world? I leaned forward.

Nick continued, "Ms. Albertini also confirmed that she found her lover and her own sister standing over the dead body of Mr. Pucci. Mr. Pucci was arrested in the past for assaulting Ms. Albertini's sister as evidenced from court files."

I couldn't breathe. "I didn't confirm anything. Who wrote that?"

He faced me again. "The byline says Jolene O'Sullivan."

"Oh, that bitch," I muttered. When we'd had lunch by the

beach. What had I said to her? "I didn't confirm anything, and I had no clue she was a reporter."

"This is her first story," Nick confirmed. "Apparently she got the job last week and moved here. She didn't tell you that you were on the record?"

"No," I burst out. "Not only that, she's twisting my words. I never said those things." Yet I hadn't denied finding Tessa and Aiden standing over Danny Pucci's body, and there was no way to deny that I'd been leaving my cottage in the morning while holding Aiden's hand. That was there in black and white. "What can we do?"

Nick shook his head. "There's no law that a journalist has to identify herself when getting quotes, but most organizations have a code of ethics that require it."

My fingernails cut into my palms when I curled my hands into fists. "She didn't write anything that's technically false, so I don't have a case for libel."

"Okay." Nick pressed his palm to the bridge between his eyes and closed them for a minute. "Here's the plan." He sat back and looked at me, obviously thinking it through fast. "You have no comment on this. Period. We'll issue a press release tomorrow, and by we, I mean me and the office. You will say nothing. Do you understand?"

I nodded. Saying nothing seemed like a good way to go for me right now. I couldn't believe Jolene had set me up like that.

Nick's expression didn't alter. "You're also taking a leave of absence."

I jerked. "No, I'm not. That's not fair."

A muscle ticked in his jaw. "Anybody else would be fired. I like you and you helped me out big time with that last case, and you're a good lawyer when you stick to the job. But this does scream of a conflict of interest, so until Devlin is either convicted or cleared, you're on leave. I don't have a choice here, and you know it."

"But Nick—"

"You're sleeping with a murder suspect, Anna." His chin rose along with his voice. "Both Devlin and your sister were arrested and are out on bond, and I thought we could screen you from the case, but this is too much. Having a relationship with Aiden Devlin is a mistake, and it shows poor judgment. I can't have that here."

Yeah. That'd probably screw up his chances to run for governor someday. Anger flushed through me, mostly because he was right and I was wrong. I'd screwed up on the professional front.

On the personal front, I wasn't sure yet.

Hopefully this would be worth it.

CHAPTER 18

I ate cold steak for a late breakfast the next morning while sitting out on my deck. When I'd returned home after my disastrous meeting with Nick, Aiden had been gone, and the kitchen had been cleaned up perfectly. He'd left me a steak in the fridge along with rolls on the counter. I'd texted him to check out the online article with a warning that it would be in print in the morning, and he hadn't texted back.

That worked for me at the moment.

I looked up just as Donna and Tess walked along the trail up from the lake, both in shorts over swimsuits.

"We have drinks, food, and suntan lotion in the boat," Donna said, a wide-brimmed hat covering her dark hair and protecting her skin. "Get your suit and let's go."

I finished chewing. "I take it you saw the newspaper?"

"Yep," Tessa said, glancing at my half-eaten steak. "We figured you'd be taking the day off."

"Nope," I said. "I've been forced into a leave of absence. I can't go back to work until Aiden is convicted or cleared."

Tessa rocked back on sparkly flip flops. "Cool. Do you still get paid?"

I frowned. "I'm not sure. Guess I should figure that out." There was no way I was getting my sisters out of there, so I stood. "I'll go get changed. Whose boat did you borrow?" We had plenty of relatives and friends with boats, but so far, none of us had invested in one.

"We just rented the pontoon boat from the marina," Tessa admitted. "Seemed like a fun thing to do, and they gave us a discount since it wasn't being used today. The sound system rocks."

I didn't much care how I looked and the headache hadn't abandoned me, so I put on a plain black bikini with coverup, threw my hair into a ponytail, and snatched a pair of flip flops out of my closet that I was pretty sure belonged to Donna. After tucking sunscreen and a hat in a beach bag, I grabbed a notebook and my phone before meeting my sisters on the deck. "I just realized that my phone hasn't been ringing like crazy."

Tessa nodded, her eyes sparkling. "We told the grandmas to spread the word that we've got this, and everyone needs to leave you alone for now."

Gratitude for my two older sisters nearly had me tackling them both in a hug. "I love you guys."

Donna slung an arm over my shoulder. "This will all be okay."

"Yeah," Tessa said, turning to lead the way down to the dock and waiting pontoon boat. "I'm thinking we build a potato gun and knock Jolene's head off her body with it. What do you think?"

I chuckled. It had been years since we'd built a potato gun. "I'm thinking that's assault and battery. Besides, the last one we built didn't have that kind of power." We'd built more than our share and shot potatoes into the river or lake growing up. All you really needed was potatoes, PVC pipe, hairspray, and a lighter. "However, I wouldn't mind figuring something out with her."

"Oh, we will," Donna promised grimly, untying the boat. "But today, we're going to go float in the middle of the lake, tan ourselves, drink some alcohol, and relax. It's a day off for us all."

My mind was spinning too fast to relax completely, but a day on the lake was appealing. We boated out to the middle and just floated. The pontoon boat had two loungers in the back along with a sun deck. Donna and I took the loungers, and Tessa flopped across the sun deck face down with her Irish skin already freckling. Her blondish-red hair glowed in the full sun.

I let my mind drift a little bit for about half an hour before speaking. "Nick Basanelli couldn't stop looking at Tessa the other morning. I feel like they have a connection."

"Shut up," Tessa said drowsily.

Donna reached for a bottle of water from the ice chest settled between us. "They do make a nice couple. What's wrong with him, T?"

"Nothing." Tessa didn't so much as open her eyes. "We're just too different."

"Opposites attract," I countered, reaching into the cooler for an iced coffee. "Tess thinks he's all a hero and stuff, and she isn't and doesn't like school."

Donna rolled her eyes. "That's dumb." She winked at me.

Yep. We were going to come up with a plan. It felt good to have something positive in the future, although Tessa was stubborn to the nth degree, so it wasn't going to be easy. Getting Nick on board would probably be easier, but he also seemed to have a whole hottie bachelor thing going on.

Tess stretched and turned her head to face us. "What did Aiden think about the newspaper article?"

I drank down the potent coffee. "We haven't talked about it yet." Yeah, that was a little weird. "He was gone last night, and I left him a message but haven't heard back. Maybe he's dealing with the Lordes and him dating a prosecutor?" Not that those guys seemed to care what each other did, really. "We'll catch up later." I hoped.

Donna reached for more sunscreen and tossed it at Tessa. "You're turning red already." The tube bounced on the sun deck.

Tessa shifted to sit and then slathered on the cream. "I wish I would've gotten the Italian skin." She burned like all of the Irish family members.

Donna never burned and instead turned a lovely tan shade. I, on the other hand, didn't burn like Tess or tan like Donna. I was a mixture in that my body got mostly tan and my face burned, so I had to be careful in the sun. With my brunette hair and odd gray with a hint of green eyes, I didn't look like anybody in the family. "I'm not sure what heritage my real father, the mailman, had," I said. It was an old family joke.

Tessa chuckled. "That's funny, but you look just like our great, great grandmother. I found a bunch of old pictures at mom and dad's, and I keep forgetting to bring it to you. She had brown hair and gray eyes, too."

Huh. I hadn't known that. My face started to tingle so I held out my hand and caught the sunscreen when Tessa threw it. I was relaxed and feeling much better about everything, so my mind started to work again. "When you were dating Danny, did you know a guy named Rich? One who has a tattoo on his arm and rides motorcycles? Maybe is into some sort of beer business?"

Tessa finished rubbing sunscreen into her legs. "You mean his cousin Rich? Tall guy, good looking, quiet?"

"Yeah. What's his deal?" I slathered my face with the cream.

She kicked her legs in front of her and stretched her neck. "He always seemed like a jerk to me. He runs training for militia groups planning for the end of days."

I coughed. "Like those survive-a-zombie-apocalypse weekends?" I'd seen a couple online.

"No. More serious stuff that involves real weapons. Most of the attendees are fat dentists who roll around on the ground during the weekends and pretend they can take Rambo."

I perked up. "Seriously?"

"Yeah. His business is located east of Spokane past the airport in Washington, and they train in the Idaho mountains. Danny worked for him to make a little extra money before getting in trouble and leaving. By getting in trouble, I mean hitting me and taking my car. Asshat." She crossed herself. "May he rest in hell."

I snorted. "I wonder if they were training the Lordes? Or the new members of the Lordes?" It was a connection between Aiden and Danny, but I didn't see Aiden needing help rolling around a mountain or learning to shoot a gun. But he did have a bunch of new members, so who knew? "What's the name of the business?"

"I can't remember," Tessa said. "Something about militia strategy and training or something like that. I really didn't pay a lot of attention."

Okay. "What about Rich's last name?"

Tessa thought about it. "Pucci, even though they're distant cousins."

It was a start. I rubbed excess sunscreen down my pinkening arms. "Was he dating Krissy Walker when you were seeing Danny?"

Tess pushed a curl away from her face. "You know, they were dating back then. Yeah. Danny and I saw them at Vassallo's bar one night when we were still getting along, and it seemed kind of like a first date situation? It was a little awkward, and they didn't invite us to sit with them. Are they still dating?"

My mind spun with the possibilities. "Definitely." All right. Guns, militia, training...now we were getting somewhere. I needed to figure out a way to speak with Kelsey without her sister around.

"Stay out of my case," Tessa said, turning onto her back. "Why don't you take some time off and relax?"

"I don't know how," I admitted. "But I'll try."

And I did. We spent most of the day on the boat with good food and drinks until Tessa had to go to work. My sisters dropped me off at my dock, and I wove leisurely up the trail to the guest cottage, happily warm and slightly sunburned. My brain had relaxed almost all day, so ideas started coming at me faster than I expected. I needed to somehow diagram the situation like Nick had taught me to do with an earlier case.

I had an old bulletin board in the garage, and I hurried out to tug it free of a bunch of boxes I hadn't bothered to unpack from law school. It was old and scratched and nowhere near as cool as the magnetic whiteboard Nick used for trial. I lugged it inside and looked for a free wall. After scoping out my entire cottage, I could only find one big enough.

My laundry room led from the garage to the path through the living room to the kitchen. One side held the washer and dryer along with a small counter, while the other wall was bare. I'd always thought the owner had meant to put in a full counter, possible sink, and some cupboards there because there was definitely room, but this had never happened. So right now, I just dumped my shoes there when I was tired. It was the perfect wall.

It took me some time, but after finding a hammer and nails, I secured the board across the entire wall. Yeah, it was a big board. Then I took the case file and put up pictures. One of Danny Pucci in the middle with Tessa on one side and Aiden the other, a blank box with Saber's name next to him. I connected Danny and Aiden both to Rich and to the Lordes and the militia training group.

I took a step back and studied the board before plastering pictures of Krissy and Kelsey on the board along with connections. I had to print out pictures from Facebook for them, but it worked.

My phone buzzed as I was studying my handiwork, and I answered it absently. "Hello."

"Hi, Angel. Sorry I didn't call earlier. It's been a day," Aiden said.

The sound of his voice warmed me to my slightly sunburnt toes. "No kidding. I'm on leave apparently." I leaned back against the washing machine.

He was quiet for a moment. "I'm sorry about that?"

Well, at least he'd phrased it as a question. I grinned. "It does give me more time to help you and Tessa out of this murder charge."

His sigh was long suffering. "I have a few things I need to do but can be over about ten tonight if you want some company."

"Sure." I nearly bit through my tongue to keep from asking what he had to do and what he knew about the militia training group, but I'd learned before that Aiden would get himself shot before he brought danger to my door. I needed to find out all I could before I asked him about Rich. "I'm going to cook spaghetti and will save you some if you're hungry later."

"Thanks, baby." He hung up.

Baby? He'd called me that before, and it sounded sexy in his deep voice. But should I like it? Was it sweet or chauvinistic? From the curling of my toes and the warming of my private areas, I guessed my body thought it was sweet. All right. Sweet worked for me.

I kept staring at my murder board and then pinned one more picture in the far right corner. I'd searched for it on the Internet and took the profile picture from Jolene O'Sullivan's Facebook page. Oh, I didn't think she was involved with any of this, but I still wanted to keep her in mind.

Just in case I found a potato gun.

CHAPTER 19

a knock on my door at midnight had me stumbling out of bed to open it for Aiden.

"Sorry I'm late," he said, heat from the night washing in with him.

I blinked, my body awakening at the sight of the shadow covering his bad-boy jaw. "Are you hungry?" I mumbled.

"Yes." He stepped into me, easily lifting me and kicking the door shut. His head swooped down, and he kissed me, striding toward the bedroom.

Fire lashed through me, strong and unexpected as I kissed him back, my thighs clamping to his hips. I wore a light tank-top with matching shorts, and somehow the top flew over my head while he was still kissing me. Then he dropped me on my bed, and his shirt careened through the air.

He leaned over me, his mouth finding mine. Firm and deep, he kissed me. God, I loved how he kissed.

My shorts and panties were quickly gone, and he kissed his way down the center of my body. I had the quick thought that he was really good at this and then I quit thinking completely as his mouth found right where I ached for him.

After two orgasms where I'm pretty sure I felt the entire galaxy tip, he levered over me after putting on a condom. "Remind me to get another box of these," he murmured, sliding inside me and having to go slow to let my body take him. Yeah, Aiden was gifted.

"Urg," I agreed, sliding my hands through his thick hair and around to his neck. I loved a tough guy neck for some reason.

Then he was inside me, pulsing and deep.

I closed my eyes at the exquisite feeling. He kissed me again, this time taking his time. When Aiden went all in, he did it with a vengeance. Even so, there was an edge to him that shot my heart into a full-on run. "Aiden?"

"Yeah." He started moving, fast and hard, taking me in a way he hadn't done before.

I held on as pleasure swamped me until I could barely breathe, and when the world detonated and sheeted white, I whispered his name. He dropped his forehead to mine and shuddered with his own climax. I went limp and let my arms drop. Wow. Just wow.

He kissed me again and then withdrew, striding into the bathroom to take care of the condom. When he returned, he slipped us both beneath the sheet and curled around me, his big hand caressing down my arm. "You okay?"

"Urgle," I said, not caring that I had lost the ability to speak real words.

His chuckle eased something inside me.

"Are you okay?" I whispered, clasping his hand, my butt to his groin.

"Yeah." He kissed the back of my head.

My eyelids grew heavy. "You seemed tense when you got here."

"I'm not now," he said, a smile in his voice.

That simple statement shouldn't have swamped me with the girly pleasure that it did, but I basked in it anyway. "Did the guys give you a rough time about the newspaper article?"

He stiffened and then relaxed behind me. "The guys?"

141

"You know. Saber and the Lordes."

"No," he said, sliding his arm around my waist and pulling me even closer. The heat from his muscled chest brushed against my slightly sunburned back. "They had a few comments, but then I punched one of the prospects in the face, and the comments stopped."

I opened my eyes to see the darkened lake outside. "You did what?"

"Different groups communicate in different ways," he said, stretching lazily. "I communicated my displeasure with his comment, and he stopped commenting."

I shook my head and relaxed right into his heat. "I'm fairly certain you shouldn't admit to committing an assault and battery to a prosecuting attorney."

"The prosecuting attorney happens to be an angel, and since she's naked, there must be some sort of exception to the rule of self-incrimination." His hand flattened across my abdomen in what felt both protective and possessive. "Not that it matters because I was in Washington state and out of your jurisdiction." The lazy humor in his voice warmed me while the casual state-ment of violence should bother me on some level. Right now, it was difficult to feel anything but satisfied.

"About the article," I said sleepily.

"One of the things I like about you is that you're not all chatty after sex." He nipped the top of my ear.

I settled. "Don't be an ass. If I want to talk, we're talking." I yawned. Then I paused. "What else do you like about me?" Yeah, I was a dork.

"A lot," he murmured. "I like that you're a softie for old ladies who poison you, that you fight for family even though it's gonna get you fired, that you try to be tough when you're a marshmallow for kids, puppies, and lost old bastards in court."

Okay. Now I was getting all squishy and warm. "Oh."

"I like that your eyes are gray or green, depending on your mood. In the moonlight off the lake, when I'm inside you, they're almost silver."

My heart flipped over and almost hurt. Aiden Devlin being sweet might be too much for me. "Okay."

"Your brain intrigues and scares the shit out of me at the same time. You're too smart for that heart you have, and somehow you make it all work and so far have survived." He kissed my ear again. "And your ass is the perfect curve for my hands. Now can I go to sleep?"

I was unable to think of anything to say. There were slight tears in my eyes and a lump in my throat, and I tried really hard to convince myself that allergy season had continued into the summer.

As if he knew exactly how vulnerable I was suddenly feeling, he tightened his hold. "Go to sleep, *Aingeal*. I'm not going to let anything bad happen to you."

I cuddled into him, but it was a long time before I slept. Sure, I'd had a crush on him for over a decade, and yeah, I knew it was a huge risk to be with him right now with my job and his life. I'd rushed right into something with him, wanting to feel everything I knew he could help me feel. I wanted to know him—the real him—and I hadn't given the consequences a second thought. This was the first time I came face to face with one harsh reality.

Aiden Devlin could absolutely break my heart.

* * *

I WAS STILL off kilter when morning arrived and was almost grateful Aiden received an early text message that had his jaw tensing before he kissed me and quickly headed off to take care of whatever business he was in—something I really should figure out. As I showered and dressed for the day, I really wanted to put on kick ass red heels. However, considering I was wearing white capri's and a flowered blouse, it'd look too weird.

An extra pump of mint syrup in my coffee lifted my mood as I drank the entire mug while sitting on my washing machine and studying my murder board.

No new answers came to me.

So I hopped off and returned to the kitchen, slipping on my favorite blue Betsey Johnson sandals and heading out to handle a very nice Thursday. The weather was in the low eighties with a slight breeze, and I drove to Thelma and Georgiana's to take care of their plants before driving across town to Kelsey Walker's house. She didn't answer the door, and by the darkness of the house, I figured she'd gone to work.

I was actually jealous. Work would be great.

So, planning quickly, I stopped for hot lattes and a bear claw before parking at my office and striding past it toward the police station fronting the park. A wink to the guy at reception had me up the stairs and in Pierce's office without any problems. "Howdy, Detective," I said, stepping inside.

He looked up from his computer, sighed, and leaned back in his chair. "Is that a bear claw?"

"Yup." I handed over his latte and the pastry before taking a seat across from him. "I'm not above bribery."

Today Pierce was dressed down in a polo shirt and beige slacks with his badge at his belt. His hair was smoothed back, his face clean shaven, and his green eyes clear and alert. "Bribing a police officer is a crime, Albertini." I'd noticed he'd started to use my last name more, probably to distance us. He'd asked me out in June and apparently regretted it, although we'd never made that date. "Although a bear claw is the way to do it."

I caught sight of the front page of yesterday's paper at the edge of his desk. "Are you going to lecture me?"

"Would it do any good?" He hummed happily as he dug into the donut.

"No," I admitted.

He shook his head. "You wouldn't be the first woman to dump her career over the wrong guy. I figure I'll be helping you out when I finally put Devlin away for good." He reached into his desk drawer for a file folder, this one a bright and sparkling purple. "I printed out Devlin's rap sheet for you, just in case you'd like a reminder." His eyes were hard, but his voice resigned.

"Huh." I took the folder. "Where are you finding these bizarre folders?"

"In the supply closet," he said, finishing the bear claw and reaching for his coffee again. "They pretty much scream your name to me, so there you go."

I didn't need to see the rap sheet again. Sometimes it kept me up at night.

"Let me remind you," Pierce said. "Armed robbery, grand theft auto, drug distribution, assault, and battery—all with not nearly enough prison time. In addition, he was a person of interest in several homicides connected to the motorcycle gang he rode with in Portland before they were patched over by the Lordes."

I flattened my hand over the file folder. "Yeah, and I'm not buying it all. There's no way he wouldn't have done more time for those crimes." Yet, the prison system wasn't the best right now, and felons were let out all the time.

"You know I can have him picked up any time for a weapons violation, right? Felons can't have guns," Pierce said.

"I don't think he has one," I said. "At least on him, and he's not going to admit to having one."

Pierce sighed. "Tell me you really haven't convinced yourself that those charges are fake. I've checked with every contact I have with the FBI and DEA, and Devlin isn't working for them. He's not even an informant."

Yeah, so had Nick. They were both trying to help me out, but my instincts had to count for something. "If they are true, then he's turning his life around." I sounded lame, but I couldn't help it.

"He's trying to remake the Lordes into pursuing legitimate businesses."

"Bullshit," Pierce said bluntly. He shook his head. "Just stay out of the way when we take him down. I'd hate to pinch you as an accessory for anything."

"You're not being a very nice friend." I jerked my head toward the very nice latte I'd purchased for him.

He rolled his eyes. "We are not friends."

Well, that hurt a little bit. "What are we, then?"

He shook his head. "Until you get fired, we're colleagues. I'd try to help out any woman throwing her entire life away like this."

When Pierce wanted to be a condescending ass, he excelled at it. Even so, I held back on calling him on it. "Have you received the autopsy report on Danny Pucci yet?"

"Yep." Pierce finished his latte and tossed the empty paper latte cup toward the garbage can in the corner, easily nailing it. "Pucci died from a bullet to the head, which is not surprising. He had lacerations from a beating from a day or so before, more bruises from a beating a week or so before, and a nice amount of meth in his system."

"Meth? Great," I muttered.

"Yep. Your boyfriend was hanging out with a guy high on meth, and didn't you say the Lordes were out of the drug game?" Pierce rifled through the myriad of case files and pieces of paper across his desk and pulled one from the bottom, nudging it my way. "Take a look at Pucci, just so you know who you're dealing with."

I opened the file folder to see pictures of Pucci that clearly showed the bruises and cuts. "Ouch."

"Weren't Devlin's knuckles torn from what had to be beating on somebody?" Pierce asked casually.

There wasn't a good answer to that question, so I didn't bother. I peered closer at the picture of the tattoo on Pucci's upper arm. "That looks like the same one I saw poking out of his cousin Rich's shirt." It was a heart with a sword through the middle and some initials above it. "What's BGC?"

"Dunno yet," Pierce said, reaching for a piece of paper. "I haven't been able to get Kelsey Walker or her sister to talk to me about either Pucci or this Rich fellow. But you've now given me a place to start. Thanks for that."

CHAPTER 20

*a*fter giving Pierce a tip I hadn't known I had, I drove back to Kelsey's house, and she wasn't home. Taking a chance, I maneuvered through the main area of town and then farther north to Walker's Funeral Home. The place was a large white building attached to what looked like a nondenominational church, set about two miles from the Elk County cemetery. Bright and beautiful flowers extended around the grounds, and big pots overflowing with Petunias were set up on the wooden porch with its two white and charming columns.

Majestic groves of tamarack and different species of pine extended on both sides, and a couple of pretty blue spruce trees stood tall on the front lawn. It was peaceful and welcoming. During the heated day, Robins bobbed all over the grassy area, and I could see the edge of a birdbath.

I parked in the lot to the side and walked along the cobbled way to the front door, opening it and stepping inside the main foyer. Heat blasted me.

Kelsey looked up from behind an antique desk in the small reception area, her hair frizzing around her head and her suit jacket hanging over the back of her chair. "Anna." She paled and wiped sweat off her brow. Serene pictures of fields and animals graced the wall behind her, and gentle music played in the background.

I grimaced. "Whoa, it's hot in here. The A/C is out?"

She blew hair out of her face. "Yeah. We have somebody coming to fix it, but the place was shut down all night, and it's hotter than heck. Hopefully they can fix it fast because the generators only work on the embalming and crematorium levels, and the last place I want to hang out is down there. It's so creepy. What are you doing here?"

I walked toward her and drew out one of two thick white leather chairs on the other side of her desk. "I was hoping you'd talk to me." The heat wafted over my skin, prickling and making my shoulder blades itch. It was way too hot in there, but it made sense that the place was built solidly with the dead bodies and all. No wonder the heat was trapped. "It's cooler outside. Do you want me to open the door?"

"No. I have all the windows open because they're screened. We can't risk bugs in here by opening the door. Can you imagine a fly buzzing around during a funeral?" She blanched, her blue eyes wide. "We had a skunk make it inside one time, and people decide to sue you when a skunk ruins their funeral. Trust me."

"Good point." I should've brought a latte or something, but I didn't know what Kelsey liked. She had a half full bottle of what looked like flavored water next to her. "I'm hungry, and it's hot in here. Do you want to grab lunch? I'll buy."

"I can't. Have work to do." She tapped several peaceful cream-colored file folders into a neat square with her pretty pink nails. She wore a light white sleeveless blouse and what looked like blue capri's that matched the jacket she'd ditched. Her makeup was soft and her blondish-red hair in curls that frizzed wildly, and in the heated day, she looked a lot like Tessa. Apparently Danny had had a type.

I gentled my voice. "I totally understand and apologize for

149

bugging you at work. Just a couple more questions. Are there plans for Danny's funeral?"

Her eyes started to glisten. "Yeah. We're having something small on Sunday. His cousin wants it to be family and close friends, and I'm going to say some nice words about him. He was a good guy beneath all the problems, and I hope he's at peace now."

So the funeral would not open to the public. "I really am very sorry for your loss."

"Me too," she said, a tear caught on her lashes. "His cousin is paying for a nice headstone and for him to be buried in the cemetery down the road. It's so much more peaceful than the old one across town." She wiped her eye clear. "At least this way I can visit him sometimes."

"That'll be nice. This has to be driving you crazy, and I'm so sorry about that. Do you have any idea yet on who killed him?"

She sighed. "Besides your sister or boyfriend? Nope. My guess is that he was bugging Tessa, and she killed him." Kelsey blanched. "Sorry. But that's my guess."

"Tessa wouldn't kill anybody," I said, not sure if Aiden would or not. Yeah, he probably would, but it would have to be in self-defense. "I know she didn't." When Kelsey glanced at her watch, I pushed on before she could ask me to leave. "What's the deal with his cousin, Rich? He seemed a little over the top at your house."

She glared. "He's hurting that his cousin was murdered. So am I." It wasn't a subtle hint.

"I know, and I'm sorry. Surely you'd do the same for your sister, and try to follow up with any leads," I said, feeling for her. This really did suck.

"Yeah, I would." She looked up and faced me directly. "I don't know who killed Danny, Anna. If I did, I'd tell the cops because I cared about him. I know he had problems, but I still loved him." Her hands shook, and she put them in her lap. "I hope the police find out who did it."

"Me too," I said softly. "Before I go, what does BGC mean? It was on Danny's tattoo on his arm."

She tilted her head. "How do you know about his tattoo?"

I couldn't think of a gentle way to give her the truth. "I saw the autopsy report." My stomach ached. "I'm sorry." Then I cleared my throat. "I think it was the same tattoo that Rich has on his arm, but I didn't see the top of his, so I can't be sure. Was it the same tattoo, and what does it mean?"

She glanced down at her nails. "Um, I'm not sure if it's exactly the same tattoo, and I don't know what the initials mean. I think I remember some story about them getting drunk in Vegas and getting tattoos." She snorted. "The initials are probably something stupid like the first names of their first loves or something like that. I asked Danny once, and he just said it was dumb and wouldn't tell me the truth. So I stopped caring about it."

That did sound dumb, and I couldn't determine if she was being honest. "Is there any chance this business Rich and Danny were involved in could've led to his death?"

"I don't see how," she said, looking toward her computer. "It's just a tactical training business. You know, self-defense, wilderness survival, basic weaponry. They train corporate travelers, preppers, people in high pressure and dangerous jobs. They hired some good ex-soldiers to handle the weapons because they can't due to their records. They were smart about the business, and it makes money. Why would anybody want Danny dead?"

"I don't know," I admitted. "I don't know much about him. Could there be a different ex-girlfriend in his background who might've been mad at him?"

"Not that I'd know of," she said.

A door to the side opened and Krissy walked in, wearing scrubs with her hair up in a ponytail. "Any news on the A/C guy?" she asked before she saw me.

"Not yet," Kelsey said, stiffening.

Krissy's gaze landed on me and narrowed. She held a couple of bottles of cleaning solution in her hands. "What are you doing here?"

"Just talking to Kelsey to see if we can figure all of this out," I said. "Is there a way you'd answer some questions?"

"No," Krissy said, glancing at her watch. "I'm busy, and so is Kelsey." She focused on her sister again. "Did you get the programs for the Daily and Johnson funerals printed yet?"

"Yes." Kelsey tapped the top file folder. "I also finished the obituaries for our website and updated the notification for the county of the times you want to run the crematorium." She grabbed a notepad. "Lana can't be here until ten the day of Mrs. Daily's funeral to do her makeup."

Krissy grimaced. "That won't give her much time, but that's not my problem."

I cleared my throat. "You two work well together. It'd be fun to work with my sisters, but we've all chosen different careers."

Krissy slowly turned to look at me as if irritated I was still there. "Your middle sister is probably going to prison for murder, and you know it. Now, please leave. Let the police do their jobs and stop trying to cover for your sister or your lover. Nice picture in the paper, by the way."

It was hot enough that the heat filtering into my face would just mix with the rest. "Thanks so much. The news reporter is an old friend. Tell me about *your* lover. Rich seemed intense."

She sighed and rocked back on her tennis shoes as if needing to stretch. "He is, and I like him that way. Now leave before I have you arrested for trespassing, and don't think for a second that I won't call the newspaper to report the arrest. They can follow up on your earlier article, and your old friend can expand her fanbase. I couldn't believe the number of clicks on that online article. I will call her, Anna."

Ouch. Good threat. I scrambled to think of anything to ask that wouldn't tick Krissy off, but nothing came to mind. So I turned back to Kelsey, who was a much softer sell. I got the feeling that she wanted to do the right thing but didn't know what it was right now. "All right. If you have anything you want to talk about, please call me."

Krissy looked at her sister. "I need some help in the back room." Then she turned on her tennis shoe and disappeared through the doorway. Apparently the eldest Walker sister didn't like me much.

I stood. "I'm sorry if I got you into trouble."

Kelsey grinned and stood. "She's always like that, and when Rich is cranky, she's cranky. Don't worry." Then she walked to follow her sister, tossing carelessly back at me. "Good luck with the case, Anna."

I watched her go but couldn't reply as she walked away. The tattoo visible beneath the strap of her sleeveless blouse, directly over her right shoulder blade, was of a heart with a sword through the middle.

The letters BGC and PROPERTY were clearly inked right above it.

CHAPTER 21

y mind spun as I drove away from the funeral home. Kelsey had lied to me about the tattoo. Why? What in the world could BGC stand for? I quickly dialed Pierce and got his voicemail. "Hey, it's Anna. Kelsey Walker has the same tattoo as Pucci and probably Rich. Thought you'd like to know." Then I hung up and tried to plan my next move. The only thing I could think to do was head out to Rich Pucci's business and see if he'd talk to me.

As I swung back toward town, my phone buzzed. "Hello."

"Hey Anna, it's Aunt Rachel. I heard you're on a leave of absence, and I need a favor." Her voice was chipper. My aunt had married Uncle Sean when they were both still teenagers and was often the calm in the storm of the Irish side of our family. Probably because she was mostly Swedish.

"Sure. What's up?" I asked, speeding by a tourist going way too slow.

"Pauley is in a session with Cousin Wanda, and I'm stuck on the other side of the pass. A truck carrying salmon turned over." A honk sounded.

I flipped a quick U-Turn to head back to the main area in town. "I can pick him up and take him to lunch."

"Wonderful," she breathed. "I'll call Wanda to give him the heads up so he isn't surprised. I really appreciate it. He's a little off because one of his college classes was canceled after the professor came down with Shingles, so it'd be better if you took him to your place and not a busy restaurant. I'll meet you there."

"You've got it." I turned down Main Street. "Grab me a couple of salmon steaks if it doesn't get too hot, would you?" Whenever a food truck turned over near Silverville, the locals all rushed out for the food before it could go bad, and the truck drivers were on board with it because wasted food was bad for everyone. Last year a whole truck of prized lobsters turned over, and we ate like kings for a week.

I slid into a spot at the curb of a building holding different businesses in the middle of Main Street. Cousin Wanda Versaccio's psychology practice was on the third floor. She was my fourth cousin twice removed, or something like that, but a shrink in the family was a shrink in the family. I saw her whenever I got too stressed out or worried about life, and especially about Jareth Davey.

After parking, I jogged up the stairs to the third floor. At the end of the hallway, a frosted glass window in her worn oak door allowed light to come from her office. I quietly opened the door to a freshly painted waiting area adjacent to a new wall that had been put in just a week before to separate the reception area and Wanda's office, which right now had the door closed.

I took a seat on a new chair with pillows covered with pink flamingos and reached for the nearest magazine to leaf through.

The door opened when I was halfway through a quiz on whether or not the hot guy in my life was a keeper or not. Maybe it was better not knowing. "Hi."

Pauley walked out, today wearing pressed jeans and a blue golf shirt. "Hi." He appeared relaxed, so obviously he'd been given a heads up that I was coming. "Salmon all over the road." He shivered.

That was a good point. "No kidding." I stood.

Wanda moved behind Pauley and perched her glasses on her nose. Her black hair was up in a messy bun, and she'd chewed half of her lipstick off. She was in her mid-thirties but looked younger. "Tell your Grandma Albertini to stop trying to set me up with single women. I just got divorced, and the last thing I want is to start dating anybody, especially a pilot. I don't like flying."

I took a step back. While I liked Wanda, I wasn't getting between Nonna and romance. "Sorry. We don't have a pilot in the family. You're on your own, Wanda."

Pauley strode toward the exit, already several inches taller than me even though he was only sixteen. His brown hair was perfectly cut. Where he got the darker hair, considering his mom and sister were blondes and his dad a redhead, we'd never known. Kind of like me.

"I will see you next Thursday at ten a.m., Cousin Wanda. Ten a.m. Yes. Ten a.m." He walked out into the hallway.

I hurried after him, keeping somewhat of a distance to give him space. I often needed it after pouring my guts out to the shrink, so he probably did, too.

We reached the sidewalk, and he paced toward my car.

I stepped up to his side. "Do you mind going with me?" It seemed that sometimes people forgot to ask Pauley what he liked, so I always made the effort. Maybe being the youngest kid came in handy that way for me.

"No." He opened the door and slid onto the seat. "I am hungry." He looked straight ahead, his dark brown eyes staring out the window.

I walked around to the driver's side and sat, starting the car. "What sounds good, P?" I drove away from the curb.

"Lil Bear," he said, drumming his fingers on his pants in a familiar three times, two times, three times set of taps. "I would like a cheeseburger with ketchup, pickles, and tomatoes. No onions or mustard or mayonnaise."

"Okay." I knew how Pauley liked his burgers but let him set things right in his head, anyway. We made it through the drive-through and back to my cottage without any more discussion, and then we ate contentedly on the outside deck watching the action on the lake.

Finally, Pauley finished his fries, which he did not like with ketchup. "I saw the picture of you in the paper."

I sucked down my vanilla shake. "Yeah? I didn't know the photographer was there."

"You are dating Aiden again." Pauley neatly folded the paper that had covered his burger into perfect squares.

"Yes. I like him." I crumpled up my paper and tossed it into the takeout bag. "I hope he's not a criminal."

Pauley reached for his strawberry shake, which he'd saved until he'd finished his lunch. "The article said that he's a convicted felon, so that makes him a criminal."

I swallowed more of my shake. "Huh."

"*Huh* is not an appropriate answer." He drank his shake. "You do not seem like you would date a criminal."

"Thanks?" I stirred my straw to break up some of the frozen brew. "I feel like he isn't a criminal. At least not anymore. People can change, right?"

Pauley watched a couple of jet skis on the lake. "I do not believe people truly change. I could be wrong."

I grinned. "You rarely are wrong."

"That is true." He set his wrapper and now empty French fry container into the bag. "How are you doing proving that neither Tessa nor Aiden killed Danny Pucci?"

Apparently Pauley had read the entire article. "Not well," I admitted.

"Would you like my help?" he asked. "I am much smarter than you."

I chuckled. "Although that's true, it's not polite to say it."

"You do not mind." He stood and carried the garbage into my kitchen to properly dispose of it.

I ran through what was on the murder board. Nothing gory or any bad pictures. I followed Pauley inside. "I have a case board set up. Maybe you can see connections I haven't." I led him into the laundry room and hopped up on the washing machine to wait.

Pauley stood against the dryer and studied the connections across the board. "This is weird in the laundry room."

"I didn't have any other wall that would work except my bedroom, and I didn't want this in there." The last thing I needed to see in the morning was Danny Pucci's face on a murder board. Plus, Aiden spent time in my bedroom and had never set foot in my laundry room, which also mattered for some reason I couldn't quantify. He didn't need to know all of my business. "Do you see anything?"

Pauley didn't so much as twitch. "You are missing one person."

I straightened as anticipation lanced through me. "I am?"

"Yes." He reached for his wallet and took out a picture. I already had Tessa on there but couldn't see past his back to the picture. Moving forward, he placed it on the board and drew connections between it, Aiden, Tessa, and Danny Pucci. Then he stepped back.

I exhaled. It was a picture of me that he'd taken at a family picnic a couple of years ago. My heart started thundering for no good reason, so I took several deep breaths like I'd been taught. In through the nose and out through the mouth. "I know my connections to Tessa and Aiden, obviously. Why Danny?"

"He was in court with you, and he hurt your sister. Also, you were the first person through the door before the police, and you are a witness that Aiden and Tessa were in the room."

Pauley really had read the entire article.

I didn't like seeing my picture on the board, but Pauley had a point. "I don't have a connection to the Lordes or Rich Pucci, or the Walker sisters."

"You are connected to the Lordes through Aiden and to Rich through Danny," Pauley countered. "The Walker sisters are connected to Danny and Rich. You are all connected in one way or another."

Maybe, but an argument could be made for most people in that case. I grabbed the notepad I'd left on the counter and quickly sketched out a terrible reproduction of the BGC tattoo before jumping off the washing machine and pinning it next to the picture of Danny. "This tattoo is on Kelsey Walker, Danny Pucci, and Rich Pucci," I said. "Any idea what BGC stands for?"

Pauley scrutinized the drawing. "No. Does the mortician Krissy Walker have the same tattoo?"

"How did you know she's a mortician?" I asked.

"I overheard my mother and your mother discussing the article," he admitted. "Your mother is hoping you're not making a huge mistake with Aiden Devlin, and my mother is furious with the reporter who wrote the article." He slid his hands into his pocket. "Your father thinks you're still a virgin, according to what your mother said to mine."

I coughed.

Pauley rocked back on his heels. "Fathers are purposefully blind, I have decided. Even so, I believe everyone would like for you to keep your private life out of the newspaper."

"I'd like that, too," I grumbled.

Pauley nodded as if his job was done. "You did not answer me. Does Krissy Walker have that tattoo?"

"I don't know." I stepped closer to the board. "She is dating Rich Pucci, so it's possible."

"Do not try to figure out how to get her naked," Pauley warned, his upper lip twitching a minuscule amount. "You are in enough trouble right now, and assault or battery or perhaps harassment would give Nicolo no other option but to fire you. You need your job to buy shoes that make you happy."

I wanted to nudge him but contented myself with smiling. "Shoes make a lot of people happy."

"Helloooo," came from the other room as my front door opened.

Pauley and I jumped and scrambled out of the laundry room as if we'd been caught sneaking cookies from Nana O'Shea.

"Aunt Rachel." I hurried toward her for a hug. She was the exact opposite of Uncle Sean with her petite frame and sparkling brown eyes.

"Hello." She hugged me with one arm and then handed over a grocery bag that smelled like fresh salmon. "I got you some good pieces that were protected from the gravel." She angled her head to the side. "What were you two doing?"

"Nothing," I said, while Pauley looked down at his perfectly tied tennis shoes.

Rachel's chin lowered. "You had better not be getting Pauley involved in a case. Last time you both got kidnapped."

"I totally agree." I took the bag toward the kitchen. Having Pauley study a board in my laundry room wasn't exactly getting him involved. "Do you want to stay for dinner?"

"Can't," Aunt Rachel said. "We have plans tonight in the valley. How was your session, Pauley?"

Pauley looked up at her and then looked away. Many autistic people didn't like keeping eye contact. "It was good. People get Shingles, Cousin Wanda is happy being single, and Anna is probably not a virgin." He moved to walk toward the door. "Thank you, Anna. Goodbye."

CHAPTER 22

$\mathcal{I}$ stared at the board that now had a picture of me on it while dialing Aiden's number.

"Hey, Angel," he answered.

Heat flew throughout my body. I liked that. A lot. "A truck turned over in the valley earlier today."

"What'd we get?"

I grinned. "Salmon. My aunt brought me several steaks. Are you up for dinner tonight?"

"And then some," he said, his voice low and rough.

A shiver wound its way through my entire body. Oh, this was so bad. "All right." I cleared my throat because I'd gone all hoarse for some reason. "What time?"

The sound muffled, and a gunshot echoed. Then he was back. "I'm going to be late—probably ten-ish. Do you mind eating that late?"

I stiffened. "Was that a gunshot?"

He kept silent.

"Aiden?"

"I promised not to lie to you, remember?" His voice came

through muffled again, and I swear I heard another gunshot. "We're not doing anything illegal."

"Where are you?" I asked.

"I have to go. I'll see you tonight." He clicked off.

Why was Aiden shooting guns somewhere? Not that shooting was unheard of in Idaho. But still. Why the secrets? Was he up working with Rich Pucci again? I had to figure that guy out as well as the tattoo. Maybe Aiden knew what the tattoo stood for. Interesting.

Well, I had some free time, so it was time for answers. I grabbed my purse and keys before heading out to the garage and starting my Fiat. The drive away from Tamarack Lake toward Timber City was peaceful and sunny in the afternoon light, and I found myself relaxing a little even though I was on the hunt. I headed toward town and then turned to the west, driving down the quiet residential street and by Kelsey Walker's apartment building. Since it was still before five, I didn't expect to see her, and the place was dark.

There was a small park at the end of the street, and I maneuvered my car into a parking spot away from the road and partially hidden behind a sweeping birch tree. Then I sat and waited. A few green leaves from the tree fell onto my hood.

I called and chatted with my mom and both grandmas, enjoying their outrage at Jolene O'Sullivan. If they had concerns about me, they didn't show it. The support was overwhelming. Then I called both of my sisters, who were working and couldn't talk for long. I called Lacey in the big city and reported that I'd spent lunchtime with her brother and that she should come home to work. Of course, I had to leave her a message.

My stomach growled around six. Darn it. Why hadn't I brought food on the stakeout? Pursing my lips, I dialed another number.

"Hi, Anna. What's up?" Clark Bunne asked.

"Well, I'm on a stakeout, and it's for your client, so I wondered if you wanted to join me and talk about the case," I said, watching a few kids skateboard down the street. "Maybe you could bring dinner?"

His sigh was a little much. "You know we're on opposite sides of this, or at the very least, you're a witness?"

"Yeah, but I'm on leave, and I have a theory," I said. "You're a charming guy, and I think you might be able to get somewhere with Kelsey Walker when I haven't. What do you say?"

"Fine, but I'm only bringing you dinner so you can give me a better heads up about your Uncle Sean and what I can expect tomorrow during the qualifying round. Tell me where you are."

I gave him directions and disengaged the call as Kelsey drove toward me and parked at the curb in front of her apartment. She hopped out with her jacket over her arm, grabbing her purse and a bottle of water before shutting the door. A couple of minutes later, her older sister parked behind her. Krissy drove a silver BMW. Interesting. I hadn't realized that fairly new morticians made that much money. Of course, her family did own the funeral home and mortuary.

Krissy carried bags of takeout food that looked like tacos, and my stomach growled some more. She walked into the apartment without knocking.

My sisters did the same thing.

About twenty minutes later, Clark parked his old Chevy behind me and hustled up to my door, handing over a bag before taking his seat.

"I love Fred's Thai," I said, digging in right away.

Clark handed over two sodas, and I put one in my cup holder. "This is weird. Does the prosecuting attorney's office do stakeouts?"

"Yeah. We do whatever we need to do in order to get justice within the law." I munched happily on noodles out of the carton. It was our office motto and had been for as long as anybody remembered. "You guys don't watch clients or witnesses?"

"Not usually." Clark reached into the bag and drew out some type of chicken dish. "What are we watching for?"

"I'm not sure." Man, Fred had added extra spice this time. My stomach protested, but I kept eating anyway. It was delicious. "If nothing happens, I think you should go visit and ask some questions." I ran him through everything I knew as well as the description of the mysterious tattoo. "What do you think?"

"I'm not sure. Did you do a google search of the letters?" he asked.

"Sure. Lots of businesses and a movie or two, but nothing that would make sense as a tattoo on any of these people."

He took a drink of his diet soda. Interesting. The guy didn't have an ounce of extra fat on him and he drank diet. "I can try to talk to them, but they don't sound all that welcoming."

Motorcycle pipes ripped through the peaceful evening.

"Here we go," I said, sitting up straighter.

Rich and Saber came into view and parked their bikes behind Krissy's BMW. I pointed them out and explained who each man was to Clark.

He frowned. "So Rich is with this training business, and Saber is with the Lordes, and you keep seeing them together?"

"Yeah," I said. "I'm starting to wonder if Saber and Kelsey have something going on because Krissy is definitely with Rich Pucci." What a name. Seriously.

"Does Aiden know?"

"I'm not sure," I admitted, my stomach hurting a little bit. "I'll ask him tonight about Saber as well as the tattoo. Maybe he knows something." Although, it wouldn't be the first time Aiden didn't share information with me. We needed to get over that if we were going to keep seeing each other.

Unlike the rest of the world, Clark didn't open his mouth and give me his opinion about Aiden.

I waited, ate more noodles, and then waited some more. "All

right. Why aren't you lecturing me about dating Aiden? I know you must've seen the newspaper article, and our business runs on gossip, so you obviously knew I'd been put on leave because you didn't ask me about it when I said I was free for a stakeout because of the leave."

Clark swallowed more soda. "I knew about the forced leave within ten minutes of Nick kicking you out of the office. Gossip is crazy in the judicial corner."

I finished the noodles. "No lecture?"

"I have a younger sister, Anna. No lecture."

I turned to study him. "Interesting."

"Yep. She does what she wants, especially when it comes to dating. I learned a long time ago to stay out of the way unless she asks me to step in." He shrugged. "Besides, what do I know about dating? I choose the wrong woman every time. Believe me. I'm trying to break that habit, but it's difficult."

My ears perked up. "Really? Tell me more."

"No." He finished off the chicken dish. Then he kicked back in his seat. "How long do we just watch?"

That was a good question. "I'm kind of interested if Saber stays when the other two leave. If he's dating Kelsey, it might be a way in to get information, considering he works for Aiden." That was if Aiden cooperated with me, of course.

Clark shut his eyes. "Fine. Wake me when something happens." Then, in less than a minute, he fell asleep. His breathing was even, and his body relaxed.

It was impressive. It usually took me forever to go to sleep.

I settled back and let my mind drift to the case, to Aiden, and to a couple of other cases I had coming up. One might go to trial, and it'd be my first real trial.

Motorcycle pipes down the street jerked me awake, and it took a second to remember I was in my car. It was dark and quiet, save for the pipes.

Clarke sat up and rubbed his eyes. "What time is it?"

I glanced down at my phone. "It's around eleven. We fell asleep."

He cocked his head to see better as everyone drove away from the curb. "Looks interesting."

I started my car. Krissy drove her BMW, Rich his bike, and Saber drove his bike with Kelsey on the back. "Looks like they are dating." There was something about a woman on a man's bike in motorcycle clubs, but I'd never paid much attention. I waited until they'd all turned around and drove off before slowly following.

Clark grinned. "This is kind of fun."

"Yeah. They're probably just going for a drink or to get dessert or something," I said. But if so, why was Krissy in her car and not on the back of Rich's bike?

The moon provided enough light for me to follow them at a distance, and when they turned down the long and private road to the funeral home, I turned off my headlights.

Clark shook his head. "This is so not a good idea."

"I know," I whispered, leaning over the steering wheel. "Though the big question is, why are they going to a funeral home after dark?"

"Something kinky?" Clark muttered. "Or illegal. Or maybe they just left something at work."

"Something all four of them have to go and pick up?" I didn't think so. I pulled off the road onto a grassy area and then drove as close to the trees as I could. "We need to go on foot from here. They'll notice the car."

Clark blew out air and stepped out of my car. "This is such a bad idea. We're trespassing."

I quietly exited the car and shut the door. "Don't you want to know what's going on?"

He looked at me over the convertible, and his eyes glowed in the moonlight. "Yeah. Doesn't make it right, though." He hesitated. "Isn't this place also a crematorium?"

I gulped. "Yeah." They couldn't be burning bodies at night,

could they? Dread and a terrible anticipation twirled through me as I walked out to the long driveway and headed toward the sprawling building. Crickets chirped around us and in the far distance, a coyote howled.

Clark kept pace next to me. "What's our plan here?"

"Not sure yet," I said, edging close to the building, which was quiet. Lights went on toward the back. "This way." I hurried around the side, but the windows were fairly well protected with a shield of crimson pigmy all around the perimeter. The prickly and painful bush provided an excellent barrier to anybody trying to get close to the windows. "Shoot."

Clark eyed the brambles. "Huh. I've never seen plants used as home security. That's brilliant."

"That's Idaho," I agreed. "You should see the bushes my dad planted around our entire house once we were old enough to sneak out at night. There was no way."

Clark kept away from the bushes. "What now?"

The sound of a truck rumbled up the long drive. I froze for a second. "Um, hide." I ran for the trees on the side of the building, and Clark hurried after me. We reached the grove and ducked down, watching as the truck drove around the other side to the parking lot.

"Crap. Come on." I led the way through the trees around the perimeter and the back of the funeral home building to the other side, where the back of the truck was already half in the loading dock. We crouched down again and tried to see what was happening.

Clark leaned over my shoulder. "Are those coffins?"

I ducked my head to see better. Two hefty-looking men were unloading coffins, and both Saber and Rich jumped in the truck to help. "I think so?" Why would Walker's be accepting coffins at night? "They have a display room to buy them, but don't you think this timing is odd?"

"Maybe not, but having Rich and Saber here is weird." Clark

brushed some leaves off his arm. "Though they might be helping their girlfriends."

It didn't feel right. In fact, seeing coffins unloaded by a couple of burly guys late at night felt downright creepy.

We watched for about thirty minutes, and then the truck loaded up and drove away. A little while later, the lights went off, and everyone returned to their vehicles. Rich carried a large box to place in Krissy's trunk before jumping on his bike. Krissy followed him and shut the loading dock door.

"That's why they brought the car," Clark whispered.

I really wanted to see what was in that box. They all drove off, and silence descended again.

"What now?" Clark asked.

I took a deep breath and studied the person-sized door next to the loading dock one. "Now we go check out those coffins." Swallowing rapidly, I trekked toward the building.

CHAPTER 23

To his credit, Clark didn't argue. It kind of surprised me, but then again, when you saw coffins being unloaded at night, even a straitlaced guy like Clark had to be curious. I crouched at the door and twisted the knob. Locked. I sighed. Then I twisted it. It was an old lock, no doubt in place for years. "Here goes nothing. Again." I reached for my license in my back pocket and slid it into the vertical crack between the door and the frame.

"Does that really work?" Clark whispered. His eyes glowed a light brown against his darker skin in the moonlight.

I pushed the card in further. "Yeah. I've done it before."

"Great," he muttered. "This is crazy."

"Only if we get caught," I said, realizing that this was crazy. Crap. We couldn't do this. We were attorneys and officers of the court. "You're right. Let's get out of here." I started to remove the license when a bang came from inside.

Clark jumped. "Oh no. Were there people in those coffins?"

Another bump and then the sound of something falling over came through the building. Panic seized me, and I bent the card toward the doorknob, slipping it under the slant-latch and forcing it back into the door. I twisted the knob, and the door opened. "Hello," I yelled, running inside the loading area, which was empty.

Clark hurried after me. "If somebody is here, yell," he bellowed.

Thank goodness he was with me for this.

I ran up the steps to another door, which opened easily to the display room illuminated by the moon through several windows. At the far end, several open coffins were already on display. The newly arrived ten or so coffins were stacked over to the right of the room. I hurried toward them. "They're shrink wrapped." I knocked loudly on the nearest one.

Nothing.

Clark went for the next one, which looked like a light hazel in the soft moonlight. He knocked gently. "Hello. Is there anybody inside? We're here to help you."

I held my breath, trying to listen for any sound.

He leaned over and pressed his ear to the top. "Hello?"

A bump echoed from an open door that I thought led to the reception and gathering area, and then a sleek black cat wound its way toward us.

Clark stood straight and then moved closer to me. "There's a black cat in a fucking funeral home."

It was the first time I'd heard him swear, and I had to bite back a laugh. The cat looked at us with bright green eyes. I shivered. So we'd heard a cat? That wasn't justification for breaking and entering. We had to get out of there. "Um, we should probably—"

"I forgot to feed Romeo," Krissy was saying clearly from the loading area. "Hey. I thought we locked this door."

Clark grabbed my arm, his entire body going stiff.

I looked wildly around and jumped for a door right beyond the stacked coffins. "Here. Closet." I opened it, dragged him inside, and shut the door as quietly as I could. The room was dark and smelled musty. Definitely a closet.

"We did lock it," Rich was saying outside. A light flipped on and filtered between the bottom of the door to my feet. "I know we did."

"Obviously not," Krissy said. "Romeo?" she called out.

The cat meowed loudly as if ratting us out.

Clark sucked in air.

I glanced over at him, but it was too dark in the closet. My nose tickled from all the dust.

"Need...sneeze," he whispered, the sound muffled.

Oh, God. "No," I hissed as quietly as I could, turning toward him and grabbing what turned out to be his arm.

His body bunched and he lifted his arm, sneezing into it.

"What the hell was that?" Rich said.

Darn it. I froze in place, but my heart started beating so fast I could barely breathe. We were so trespassing right now. There was no way out. Well, we had thought we'd heard a noise that might be a body in a coffin? That would never hold up in court.

"I'm ready. Let's get out of here and deal with the mess tomorrow," Krissy said, her voice becoming louder as if she was moving back into the room from the reception area.

I prayed silently in my head and promised God I'd never break and enter again if He helped us out of this. Krissy wanted to leave, so hopefully Rich would go along.

"I thought I heard something," Rich said clearly.

Nope. Nothing. I tried to mentally send reassurances to Rich, just in case that worked. I doubted it, but this would be so bad if we got caught. All they had to do was leave, and I'd never do anything like this again. Ever. In fact, I'd start going to church twice a week. For a while, anyway.

Clark sucked in air, vibrated in place, and then sneezed so hard he fell sideways. Something clattered and I turned to grab for it, my hands raking across a wooden shelf. I stopped the clattering and held a ceramic...urn? "It's an urn," I whispered. "We must be in a storage room for them."

171

He sneezed again, going into a wild fit of continuous sneezes. He fell back and hit the shelf. Something dropped, and dust flew all around us. Thick dust. He coughed. "Shit. Is that?"

"Huh?" I tried to hold still.

The door opened, and the light flicked on.

I caught sight of Clark just as he saw me, and dust covered him. No. Ashes with a couple of very small bone fragments on his shoulder. He looked down, sneezed again, and then let out a girly scream I'd only heard on roller coasters. He pivoted back and hit the shelves on the other side of the small room. Boxes holding remains and old urns rained down, crashing into each other and breaking apart.

I yelped and tried to leap out of the way, but cremated ashes coated me, head to toe. A heavier fragment landed on my nose, and I battled it away so hard that I poked my eye.

Clark fought crazily, back and forth, trying to get out from the cloud of burned dead people.

Oh, God. I coughed. This couldn't be healthy.

He jumped around like something was stinging him, his eyes wide and crazed. "Dead people," he bellowed, twisting and turning. He slid through the thick gray material on the ground and crashed into the still attached shelves on the other side of the closet, which came tumbling down. "Oh, God. Dead people ashes," he yelled, jumping around like a burnt puppy.

More thick material with small bone fragments blew around the entire room, and I ducked as Clark swung out in a panic.

"Stop," I yelled at him through the murk. "You're only making it worse." My skin crawled as if a million ants swarmed me, and I tried to smack away the mess.

He paused, sucking in air with the insane look only seen in rabid wildcats.

Nausea rolled through my stomach and I turned toward the door, ashes falling from my hair.

Krissy held up her phone and snapped several pictures.

A siren quieted the crickets outside. They'd called the cops? My shoulders slumped and more material fell to the floor, where my shoes were already covered.

Clark pushed past me. "Is this dangerous? I need a shower. Where's the shower?"

Rich shoved him back into the room with one hand on his chest.

Clark skidded through the thick pile on the floor and nearly ran into me. "We're covered in ashes. Breathing ashes," he bellowed, his back vibrating crazily. A little drool slid out of the side of his mouth and mingled with the dust, creating a ball of ash near his bottom lip. Particles danced through the air, landing on us.

Krissy lowered her phone. "You're covered in pulverized bone fragments. The term 'ashes' is inaccurate."

"Bone fragments?" Clark whispered, frantically trying to wipe down his arms and shirt. "Oh God, Oh God. Fragments? We're breathing in dead people? Where's the shower?" He lunged at Rich, who moved out of the way, disgust on his face and both hands up to ward Clark away.

"Ahhhh," Clark yelled, his arms waving wildly as he ran toward the reception room, leaving a cloud of what still looked like thick ashes behind him.

"Clark," I yelled, running after him. He was leaving a trail as he barreled through the reception room, peeked into the ceremonial room, and then ran through another doorway and down some steps to the basement. The crematorium was probably down there, and I so didn't want to go into that room. "Stop. Seriously." I coughed and sneezed, trying not to think of the combination of dead people ashes covering my entire body.

Clark tripped and tumbled, coming up and not losing a step but leaving a perfect palm print of ashes on the wall.

He skidded down a hallway and turned into a green tiled room with a smooth cement floor circling a drain. He lunged for a sink set into a white Formica counter and flipped on the faucet, leaning over to frantically splash water onto his face.

I paused and looked at the two sheet-covered tables and then the machinery on the counter as well as the many closed cupboards. We were in an embalming room. At least the tables were vacant.

I sneezed and tried not to think about whose remains were just in my nose. "Clark?" I croaked out.

He turned, and now a muddy paste covered his face and his shirt. "Ashes," he whispered, turning to toss more water all over him, thickening the concoction even more. It was a shade lighter than his dark skin, and it seemed to be hardening pretty quickly.

I gulped and grit ground between my teeth. "That's not helping."

He groaned and reached for the hand soap, lifting it above his head and pumping the soap all over his very short hair. Bubbles popped through the air. It glopped onto the muddy mixture and slowly slid down the sides of his head, covering his ears. His shoulders slumped.

Krissy leaned to my side, lifted her phone, and took another picture.

"Freeze!" The voice was loud and aggressive and came from the doorway behind me.

Clark froze. So did I.

I partially turned just as Krissy snapped several more pictures of me. Then she and Rich stepped out of the way, and a uniformed Bud Orlov came into view.

Bud looked us up and down before holstering his weapon. "You have got to be kidding me."

Clark whimpered behind me.

I blinked pulverized bone fragments and ash out of my eye. "Hi, Bud."

CHAPTER 24

*C*lark and I were put into the same cell at the police station after having taken showers in the gym in the basement. We both wore ECSO shirts and sweats, and Clark had used a razor to shave his entire head. His skin looked a little raw from the scrubbing he must've given it, and if he didn't stop knocking his head against the wall, he was going to get a concussion.

I cleared my throat from my perch on the bench across from his bench. "This probably isn't so bad."

He opened one eye. "Are you kidding me?" Red patches wound down his neck into the T-shirt.

"Did you use a Brillo pad to clean your skin or what?" I'd need to get him some decent lotion. It was the least I could do.

He growled. At least it sounded like a growl. Or maybe it was more of a low grunt. Yeah. That was it.

"I'm sorry about this," I said.

"It's my fault. I take full responsibility." His eyes were bloodshot, and I hoped he hadn't put soap in them to wash out the ashes. "I knew better, and yet we still trespassed. Worse yet, I really was worried that there was somebody in that coffin. Do you think insanity is contagious?"

"Not really." I chose to ignore the statement that implied I was insane and had passed it on to him.

He frowned. "Why do you think they haven't booked us yet?"

I'd been wondering the same thing. "Maybe it's some sort of professional courtesy, but there's no way Krissy Walker won't press charges." I didn't want to think what she was doing with the pictures right now. My mother would be mortified if she ever saw them.

The door down the long hallway opened, and soon Detective Grant Pierce came into view. His hair was mussed, his clothing casual, and his eyes pissed. "It's two in the morning."

It had taken a while to shower. "Why are you here?" I asked. There wasn't a big mystery right now.

He ran a hand through his sandy-blond hair, ruffling it. "For some reason, I get called in when you find yourself in another situation like this one." He angled his neck to see better. "Did you wash off all of the dead people?"

Clark grunted again, but this time he sounded pained.

"Yes," I said. "I don't suppose it'd help if I told you we thought somebody might be in danger before we entered the premises?

Pierce glanced at Clark, who nodded vigorously. "It normally would not help."

I frowned. "Isn't there some law against storing cremated remains at the funeral home?"

"Actually, the law says the opposite. In Elk County, crematoriums have to hold unclaimed remains for up to ten years, and they have to make an effort to find family members. After ten years, they can petition the county to have a burial," Pierce said.

I looked at Clark. "Did you know that?"

"Of course not," Clark muttered. "Who would know that? Honestly. However, I do know what the sentence is for criminal trespass as well as malicious mischief to property. I'm not sure what kind of charge messing with and commingling the remains of the deceased carries, however."

I winced. "Pierce? What are we being charged with?" I didn't want to know, but as soon as I did, I could start thinking of a defense. It was my first charge and no doubt Clark's first offense as well, so hopefully we could plea bargain something down. However, we were both lawyers, and often the law needed to make examples out of us. It couldn't look like we were being granted favors from the state. My stomach lurched. "Grant? How bad is it?"

"It should be terrible," he said, no sympathy on his suntanned face. "However, for some inexplicable reason, Krissy Walker has chosen not to press charges."

My heart leapt while my chin dropped. How was that possible? She'd obviously been irritated with us, and she'd called the police right away. "That's odd. Why would she do that?"

Pierce lifted one muscled shoulder. "I don't know. It's a gift horse, and you should take it."

"Yeah, but..." I stood and grasped the cell bars. "It's weird, right? The only reason she'd want to drop charges is to let this thing die and not bring attention to the funeral home. Something is going on with her and that Rich Pucci. This is interesting."

Pierce took a step back and eyed me warily.

"What?" I asked.

He didn't say anything.

Or, for goodness sakes. "I got all of the ashes and bone fragments washed off, Pierce." Although my skin was still crawling a little bit. Then I looked over my shoulder at Clark, who still slumped against the wall. "Why do you think Krissy is being nice?"

Pierce coughed. "I wouldn't say she's being nice." He pulled his phone from his back pocket and held it up to show me the screen while still remaining feet away. "Her first call was to one Jolene

O'Sullivan at the paper, and the online article has already gone live. You really did take a long shower."

The picture of Clark and me in the closet covered in ashes covered the entire screen. "Oh, crap," I murmured.

Pierce nodded. "The print version will come out tomorrow morning, and you know Friday morning is often the biggest news of the week here in our little county." He looked down and scrolled through. "There are several pictures in the online version, anyway. What were you doing at that sink, Bunne?"

Clark groaned.

I tried to drum up righteous anger. Or irritation. Or anything. Nope. Just mortification. "Krissy isn't trying to stay too far under the radar if she sent the story to the press." So why did she let us off the hook?

Pierce unlocked the door and swung it open. "While I'm of a mind to let you two spend the rest of the night in here, there are no charges and I don't have the energy right now. Get out."

I hurried out with Clark on my heels.

Pierce stepped away. "Bud is waiting to escort you back to your vehicle, and he's in a really bad mood." Pierce seemed to brighten a little. "Have fun with that."

I grimaced but followed him down the hallway, noting that he stayed a safe distance from us. It wasn't like we were infected with ghosts now. "Thanks, Pierce." At his grunt, a much more irritated one than Clark had issued earlier, I fetched my belongings at the front desk and hurried into the warm night. Or morning. Whatever.

Bud made us sit in the back of the patrol car and didn't chat on the way out to my partially hidden car by the funeral home. Clark rested his head back on the seat and didn't talk, either.

My phone rang, and I cringed before answering. "Hello."

"Hey, sweetheart. I was up early talking to a friend on the East Coast and saw the article. That Jolene O'Sullivan is such a rotten person. Terrible. I'm so sorry," Nana O'Shea said cheerily.

My body relaxed, and a tear might've poked the back of my eye. "Thanks, Nana. It was a misunderstanding."

"Oh, I'm sure of that, sweetling." Her Irish brogue was soft in the early hour. "You'll need to drive over in the morning for a smudging. Don't argue with me."

Clark perked up. "Smudging?" Apparently my partner in crime had a good sense of hearing because my grandma wasn't that loud on the phone.

I put her on speaker. "Clark is here, Nana. He wants to know about smudging."

"Oh, good. I was going to get your number from Anna, Clark. You must come to Silverville in the morning for a sage smudging and then some energy work. After what you've been through, we're going to want to make sure nothing...clung after being spilled. The sage will cleanse you. It even has anti-bacterial properties, if you need a science based reason to visit me. What do you say?"

"Yes. Definitely. We'll come and get smudged," Clark burst out, the words tumbling over each other. "I have the day off and am supposed to golf with Sean in the afternoon but can be smudged all morning."

I looked at him, unable to keep the surprise off my face.

He didn't even look at me, his attention solely on my phone.

"Good. See you then." Nana knew when to hang up when she was ahead.

Bud pulled next to my car and stepped out to open the door and release us. "Try to stay out of trouble."

I edged away. "Are you going to call Donna or what?"

He didn't answer.

I frowned. "She's not like me. Don't let my life interfere with your love life."

Bud blushed deep enough I could see it in the moonlight. He turned, sat in his vehicle, and then drove quickly away without saying a word.

Clark shook his head and settled into the seat of my Fiat. "What time are you picking me up tomorrow morning?"

I sighed. "How about eight? That way we could get a little sleep."

"Oh, I'm never sleeping again," Clark muttered.

* * *

I PULLED into my driveway after dropping Clark off at his car, and I was unsurprised to see a motorcycle resting in front of the garage door. There had been a few texts from Aiden asking where I was, and then one saying that the article was out, so he figured I was safe. I limped along the flowers to the front porch. Why I was limping, I had no clue. But after the night I'd had, limping made sense. I unlocked the door and moved inside to see Aiden sprawled on the sofa.

He blinked awake and looked up. "Nice picture in the paper."

It was almost three in the morning, and I needed sleep. "How did you get in?"

He sat up. "You're not the only one who can force a lock." With his hair ruffled and his blue eyes sleepy, he looked like a mellow predator who was thinking about springing. He stretched his impressive arms and chest.

My mouth watered, even after the night I'd had.

He looked me over, and my body tingled. "You okay?"

"Yeah." Then I studied him, and thoughts crashed into me. "Wait a second. Are you the reason Krissy didn't press charges? I mean, did Saber talk to her or something?"

"Or something." Aiden stood and stretched again. His T-shirt rose to reveal his cut abs. "I called Rich directly, and he did me a solid. I am *not* happy that I now owe a favor to Rich Pucci, Angel."

Aiden being not happy gave me more tingles, for some reason. Man, I was screwed up. "I'm sorry about that." I hadn't asked for the favor, but pointing that out would make me seem ungrateful, and I was very grateful I hadn't been charged for trespass and malicious mischief, for starters. I moved toward him. "How can I make it up to you?"

He stiffened and moved away, slight alarm flaring a lighter hue of blue in his incredible eyes. "I have some ideas, believe me. We'll talk about them tomorrow."

Oh, he had to be kidding me. I put my arms on my hips. "Are you joking right now?"

He swallowed, and that tough guy neck moved. "What?"

Seriously? I stepped forward, and he stepped sideways and away from me along the sofa. "I'm not infected with anything," I protested.

"I didn't say you were." The shadow along his cut jaw showed a couple of days growth. "I have to get going but wanted to make sure you were all right."

I shook my head. "Unbelievable. Fine. I'm getting smudged by Nana O'Shea tomorrow morning. Does that make you feel better?"

"I don't know what you're talking about," he lied, heading toward the door and away from my cremated dead people cooties. "Although if I did, that would make me feel a lot better." His brogue emerged when he was tired, and right now it was rough and sexy. He'd only lived in Ireland until he was a teenager, but sometimes the brogue returned. He paused by my front door and turned to face me. "It was stupid breaking into that funeral home. Tell me you get that." His tone strongly suggested that I get that.

Sure, I'd been trying to help Tessa as well as Aiden, but that wasn't a good reason to break the law. "I wasn't going to go inside, but we heard something and thought somebody could be in danger." How was I supposed to know a cat was moving around?

"Then you should've called the fuckin' police," he said, his voice quiet.

I had already learned that when Aiden was angry, truly pissed, he became quiet and still. Right now his voice was way too soft and his body unmoving. "How much trouble have I created now that you owe Pucci a favor?" I asked.

"You don't want to know, and that's how you pay me back. Stay the hell away from Rich Pucci, his girlfriend, and her sister. Do you understand me?" His jaw ticked, and he looked every bit as dangerous as I knew him to be.

Yet he didn't scare me. Well, not really. "I'm fairly certain I don't have a choice." Then to make a point, I walked toward him.

"Good. Bye." He slipped outside and shut the door behind himself.

I smiled. Maybe having dead people cooties wasn't such a bad thing.

CHAPTER 25

I still felt a little off all morning, and neither Clark nor I talked much as I drove over the pass. After dropping a still twitching Clark off at Nana O'Shea's house, which was set against a mountain and had fields extending out, I meandered across the small town to a house closer to the main river. My Grandpa would already be out for the day, and I figured a talk with my Nonna Albertini might help put things into perspective. Thick logs made up their home, a couple of pickup trucks lined the area by the super organized shop, and an extra-large USA flag flew high and proud from its own pole in the center of the yard.

Grandpa Enzio had been a CB in World War II, and boy, did he have some stories to tell. I made a mental note to find and spend some time with him this weekend.

My Nonna Albertini opened the door before I could knock. "Hi." She leaned in for a hug, smelling like flour.

"Hi." I hugged her back. "What are you cooking?"

"I'm making raviolis for the barbecue on Sunday." She gestured me inside and headed back to her kitchen.

I followed happily, shutting the door and sinking into the

REBECCA ZANETTI

familiar smells of family. I reached her kitchen, and she tossed an apron toward me.

"I saw the paper." She began kneading the dough again. "That was quite the picture."

I finished tying the apron and walked over to mix ingredients, which she'd already set out on the light yellow countertops that were the same as they'd been when I had been a toddler. It was like she'd known I'd be stopping by. Or maybe she'd figured that one of her many grandchildren would be visiting and would dig in to help cook. I'm not sure how, but she had the ability to make us all think we were her favorite. I, of course, actually was her favorite. "I made a mistake," I admitted.

She snorted and kept working the dough to make into pasta. Liberal gray streaked her black hair, and she'd piled it on top of her head to cook. Glasses that she'd had for at least a decade perched on her nose and her Mediterranean skin was smooth except for the generous laugh lines extending from her deep brown eyes. I'd always thought she looked a little bit like Sophia Loren and wished once again that I favored her somehow. We might have the same shape to our eyes. I hoped.

"Go on," she encouraged, looking over her shoulder.

I also wish I had her height. She was almost five-foot-nine, which would be so cool. "We heard a noise in the funeral home and should've called the police but went inside instead. I was worried about Tessa and Aiden."

She kept working the dough and let her silence prompt me to continue.

I sighed. "Fine. I was also curious and really wanted to see what was in those coffins."

"You know all about cats and curiosity," she said, leaning to the side and surveying her work.

Yeah. One thing I loved about Nonna was that she didn't beat around the bush. Oh, she'd cover my back with any enemy and she could be terrifying, but when it was just the two of us, I didn't get away with a thing. "Yeah, and I ended up covered with dead people."

She barked out a laugh. "Don't tell me. You have to go see Fiona next."

"Yeah. Clark is with Nana right now."

It was nice of Nonna not to roll her eyes too hard. She'd never been all that agreeable to Nana's energy work. So I changed the subject and told Nonna all about tough guy Grant Pierce and deadly Aiden Devlin and how they'd both been afraid to be near me the night before. By the time I was finished, she had to wipe her eyes from the laughter. I grinned. "Maybe I could bottle ashes and sell them as men repellant. There's a market for that, right?"

"Absolutely." She pushed her glasses up her nose. "Are ashes like that dangerous to inhale?"

"No. Clark checked it all out, and it's fine. There's nothing dangerous in the remains, even if we swallowed some." The idea made me want to puke, but at least it wasn't serious. "Kind of switching topics here, but I have to tell you, Nick Basanelli couldn't stop looking at Tessa the other day." There was no need to mention that I'd tried to kiss him, thrown up in his flowers, and then had slept over.

She began to beat the dough with a little more force than was necessary. "Nicolo tried to put Tessa in jail until trial. He is on the list." She made a spitting sound over her shoulder and away from the food.

"No. He was trying to help her," I protested, mixing together the cheeses. "Honestly, Nonna. He had to appear tough to protect both Tessa and me, so he could stay on the case and help her. I'm sure he'll clear her soon." If I didn't get to it first.

She paused. "Really?"

"Yes. He's trying to help, and he's a very good lawyer who served in the military, you know."

"I did know that," she said, turning back to her task. "He's also quite nice to look at. Of course, most Italian men are, you know."

"Yes." There was no other answer, and Aiden was Irish and not Italian. But if I helped fix Tessa up with Nick, that would count for something. "Also, Tessa's acting like she isn't good enough for Nick." Direct bomb hit right there.

"What?" Nonna straightened up and turned. "What did you say?"

I nodded as if I couldn't believe it. "Yeah. She said something about he's a hero and is a lawyer, and she isn't any of those things. It was crazy."

Nonna's shoulders went back. Like way back. "Oh, I do not think so."

It might seem like I was throwing my older sister under the bus, and I kind of was, but she was an amazing, brilliant, beautiful woman and if she didn't see that, she deserved to have Nonna on her butt.

Mission accomplished.

* * *

I met Uncle Sean in Nana's living room just as Clark emerged from Nana's basement, where she kept her energy rooms. "Hi." I hugged him, and he lifted me off my feet in his return.

He dropped me. "Who do I need to hurt because of that article?"

I sighed. "I'm at fault and don't be mad at Clark. He really did try to be the voice of reason."

We both looked at Clark. He had stopped twitching and appeared almost back to normal with his creased black shorts and blue golf shirt. His eyes were clear and his shoulders relaxed, and he smelled a tiny bit like sage.

My Nana bustled behind him and raced toward Sean to hug

him. "Now, you take care of Clark out there on the course, Sean. I mean it."

"Yes, mom." Uncle Sean was more careful with his hug to her. Then he clapped Clark on the shoulders. "Let's go. I want a chance to practice putting." He glanced over his shoulder at me. "Clark's staying at our house, and you're more than welcome."

I grinned. "Thanks, but I'm staying with my folks tonight. I've embarrassed the family again and need to give mom a chance to handle me."

Sean winced. "Out of my three sisters, she's the most dangerous. Always remember that." Then he all but dragged Clark out the door.

Nana grinned. "Being the most dangerous is a good thing." Her reddish-blonde hair curled around her shoulders, and her pale skin was a little pink today. She was short at my height and had the loveliest green eyes. They were as clear as any pure emerald. "I like Clark."

"Me, too."

"He has a very bright aura. Have you noticed?" She gestured me toward the wooden staircase leading down.

"No, "I sighed. I'd tried to see auras my whole life but had never managed to see them. It was supposed to be easy. "I've been trying really hard but still haven't seen any."

She followed me, her footsteps light on the stairs. "Stop trying so hard."

I reached the bottom and turned right into a magical room with pyramids, waterfalls, crystals, cushions for meditating, and a comfortable table with a soft blanket. "I don't know how to stop trying so hard. It's what I do."

Calming music poured through the invisible speakers.

"I know." She lit some sage and wafted the wand over me. "This is your time. Take a deep breath, relax, and try to go inward." Then she saved me again before setting down the fragrant bundle. Her small hands kneaded my shoulders. "Oh, my. You are tense."

"I was covered in dead people," I admitted. "It's a little creepy."

She patted my back down, smacking my shoulder blades. Then she stepped back. "All right. On the table. Let's work with your chakras and make sure they're open, and nothing unnecessary is clinging to you from the ashes."

I plopped up on the table and relaxed, shutting my eyes. My mind wandered to Aiden, to the case, to my family as Nana did whatever she did to move the energy through my body. I wasn't sure if I believed in Reiki or energy work, but I always felt better after working with her.

Or maybe it was just being with her in her space. Either way, I let myself sink into the relaxation.

When she was finished, I felt more centered and slightly off balance. Of course, I never lay still that long. I followed her up to her bright and shiny kitchen with its stainless steel appliances for a cup of magical tea. Well, it was huckleberry tea, but it tasted magical.

She sat at her round table and gestured me to sit. "Want to talk about it?"

"Sure." I gave her the whole story from the night before, told her about the case so far, and then gave up the truth about Tessa and Nick.

She sipped her tea. "Tessa is doubting her worth? That's not good. I'll need to get her in here."

I nodded. "Totally agree. I think she and Nick would make a great couple."

Her mouth twitched slightly. "Well, he's not Irish, but even I can see he's a good man. Speaking of good Irish men, how is Aiden Devlin?"

I drank more of my tea. "I think he's trying, but he's definitely still keeping secrets. What do you see in his aura?"

"It's good," she said. "Bright and pure with some darkness

throughout, which I'd expect. Everyone has shadows, and he has more than his share, but I don't see anything bad. It can't be good for him to keep secrets."

Oh, I'd give anything to get Aiden into Nana's energy room, but even I couldn't expect that much of a miracle. "I think maybe my job makes him a little nervous," I admitted.

She chuckled and the sound was tinkly and happy. "Your job, or just you? Come on. These escapades aren't because of your job." Then she reached to the side of the table for one of her Tarot decks. "Why don't we do a reading and see what's going on?"

"Sure." I kicked back and learned that I was on a journey and needed to go deeper and trust myself. I loved it when Nana read my cards.

She was so positive and encouraging.

After hugging her, I headed to my parent's house to spend the weekend, which culminated in the weekly Sunday barbecue at their house. I hung out with Pauley as usual, and while I was disappointed that Nonna hadn't hooked Nick for dinner, I knew he'd be there sometime in the future. Probably when the case against Tessa had concluded.

Finally, Clark and I found ourselves driving back over the pass to Timber City.

He was slightly sunburned and very mellow in the passenger seat.

I smiled. "It was nice of you to let Uncle Sean keep the trophy you guys won."

He shrugged. "Sean did most of the heavy lifting, and we only won third place. Even so, he has a trophy case with an empty spot."

I chuckled. "Shocking. What vocation did he finally talk you into doing?"

Clark smiled. "He's still working on it. We're in a tournament the week after next, so I'm sure he'll have some good ideas."

My phone buzzed, and I glanced at the text. "Nick Basanelli would like to see me in the office first thing tomorrow morning."

Clark lost the smile. "Yeah. I figure you and I are both going to have a rough day."

I sighed. So much for our weekend away from reality. It was coming for us and fast.

CHAPTER 26

I clip-clopped into the office wearing my red heels and a navy blue suit, my argument running through my head. It was fairly quiet for a Monday morning, but it was early yet. I hadn't slept well, and Aiden hadn't called, so I'd been both lonely and stressed out. But now I was wearing kick-ass shoes, and I was ready to rumble.

The receptionist grinned at me, and I grinned back. She was young and seemed to enjoy a good joke, as did I.

"Go on back and good luck," she whispered.

I high-fived her and strode down the long hallway to Nick's office. After knocking softly on the door, I poked my head in.

His jacket was already on the clothes tree, his shirt cuffs were already rolled up, and his hair was already looking like he'd been yanking on it. He motioned me inside while still talking on the phone. "I understand and will get back to you as soon as possible. For now, get off my ass." He set the phone in the cradle none too gently.

Oh, I wanted to run. Right now was not the time to talk to Nick. I took a step backward.

"Sit down, Anna." He gestured to the leather chairs on the

other side of his desk, which was littered with case files, pens, papers, and what looked like an empty container of antacids. "Please."

I sat and crossed my legs. "I'm sorry about what happened." Nick was a decent guy, and maybe I could throw myself on the sword. In fact, I really was sorry. "It all got out of hand."

"I understand. I have two younger brothers." He sat back in his chair.

Relief ticked through me, and I let my hands relax. "That's right."

He studied me, both intelligence and wit in his eyes. "However, you need to submit your resignation. I'm sorry."

My throat dried up, and my mouth dropped open. "What?"

His gaze didn't falter. "Either you resign, or I fire you. It's up to you. Your record will look better with a resignation, and mine will look better if I can your ass. I'm trying to help you right now."

"Nick—"

"Do you really think I can keep you on after the newspaper article where you were caught trespassing and tearing up a closet holding cremated remains?" His voice rose.

I winced. "No. I get it." Even though I didn't get nailed, I did get caught.

"You're lucky I intervened with the Bar and said to just give you a warning. They wanted to do an investigation, and I cut it off at the pass. This time." He scrubbed a hand roughly through his hair, his brown eyes blazing. "I won't help again, so knock it off."

"Okay." It was fair, and I didn't want to blow anything that might happen with Tessa.

"Good." He pushed a piece of paper across his desk. "Here's your letter. Sign it."

The resignation letter was quick and to the point without admitting anything or going into any details. I signed it quickly, instantly feeling adrift. "I probably will be unable to get in with one of the bigger firms right now," I mused.

His grin was quick. "True. Give it a little time, and everyone will move their attention elsewhere, so long as you stay out of the news."

That might be difficult with Jolene watching my every move, but so long as I stayed out of trouble, what could she do? I stood. "Nick? I really am sorry about this. I know I caused you a lot of problems, and I know you're covering for me as much as you can."

He also stood. "Listen. I'd do the same for either of my brothers, so I can't judge you. But I'm your boss, and I have to let you go."

"I know." I smiled. "I'll go pack up my office."

"It's already done." He reached for a closed box. "I was pretty pissed last night when I got the *first* call after the story went live online, and I needed something to do. I didn't break anything."

I took the box, my stomach clenching. "Thanks for this." It would've sucked to have had to pack up my office with everyone there during the day. "If you broke anything, don't worry about it."

"I said that I didn't break anything." He studied me, looking much more approachable now that I'd resigned. "You're smart, and you're an excellent lawyer with very good instincts. Don't let one setback keep you from becoming the trial attorney we both know you're meant to be."

Okay. That was sweet. He should be yelling at me right now. "Thanks." I carried my box to the door.

"Anna? I'm going to miss working with you," he said, retaking his seat.

I looked over my shoulder. "Ditto. But who knows? Maybe we'll still get a chance to hang out." With that thought percolating in the air, I strolled back down the hallway to say my goodbyes. He had to know that Tessa was awesome, right?

I finished saying goodbye to everyone and walked out of the building toward the sidewalk, turning around the building toward the parking lot.

Clark sat on a curb with a box next to him that looked just like mine.

I faltered and then approached him. "Oh, no. You too?"

He looked up. "Yep. Signed a letter. You?"

"It was already written for me." I set my box down and sat on the curb next to him. "This sucks. It's my fault and I'm sorry."

"I walked inside that funeral home on my own, and that was my fault." He lifted his face to the sun, once again wearing his tough glasses. Apparently they hadn't worked any more than had my red heels. "I'm not sure what to do now. Nobody is going to hire us here in town, and I love it here." He looked at me. "What now?"

"Now? I've never been fired before, but I think we're supposed to get drunk," I said thoughtfully.

He winced. "My liver might never recover from the weekend spent with your uncle and his golfing buddies. Are you sure we need to get drunk?"

"I'm positive." I stood and held out a hand to jerk him up. Then I looked around, not seeing his car. "Where do you live?"

"At an apartment on Oakwood. I usually walk to work." He reached for his box.

I hefted mine beneath my arm. "Perfect. Let's take these boxes to your place and then walk to Dunphey's Bar at the end of Oakwood. Or would you rather go to Vassallo's?" The two bars were across the street from each other.

"I don't care," he said, slugging his possessions toward my car.

"Let's go to Dunphey's," I said. "It's cheaper and we're unemployed."

Clark sighed in a way that was becoming very familiar.

* * *

I CAN HONESTLY SAY it was the first time I'd spent an entire day and three meals in a bar. By nightfall, we were good and drunk and full of greasy bar food. My purse almost strangled me, but I got it strapped crossbody before heading outside into the darkness. We tripped our way back down the long street to Clark's apartment, and motorcycle pipes ripped through the evening.

"Huh." I stumbled and looked over my shoulder. "Is that Aiden?"

Clark grabbed my arm to keep me from falling and then hiccuped before tripping over a raised edge on the sidewalk. He fell onto a flowerpot in front of a jewelry store, pulling me with him. "You called him," he slurred.

I reared up. "I did not."

Aiden pulled to a stop at the curb, his eyebrows raising. "How much did you two drink?"

"A bit." I wove to my feet and helped Clark stand. Kind of. "What are you doing here?"

"You called me," Aiden said, parking his bike. "You said that you and bunny were fired, and you needed a ride home. Then you promised me all sorts of fun if I came and got you."

"I—"

"You did," Clark said before I could finish protesting. "Honestly. I had to shove my fingers in my ears." He clamped a hand around a decorative light post. "And I have asked you repeatedly to stop calling me Bunny."

Aiden held out a hand. "Aiden."

"Clark Bunne. *Bunne*," he emphasized. "Like bun but fancier." He hiccuped and shook Aiden's hand.

I snorted. "Bunny. It fits you. They're fierce hunters, you know."

"I don't hunt," Clark returned, releasing Aiden and leaning against the light post. "We might've had too many Makers Mules. They were good, though."

"They were." I smiled so wide my cheeks would've hurt had I been able to feel my face. "We got fired."

Aiden crossed his arms. "Where do you live, Bunne?"

Clark pointed down the street. "Just a few blocks. I'll head home and you've got Anna. Good luck, Buddy."

Hey. What did that mean? "I need my box with all my office stuff," I said. "Let's take my car, and you leave your bike, Aiden."

"Not a chance in hell." Aiden reached out a hand. "Get on, Angel."

Well. I liked it sometimes when he got bossy, didn't I? Shaking my head, I moved for the bike, grabbed his muscled arms, and somehow slid into place.

Aiden handed back a helmet that had been hanging on the handlebar. "Helmet."

"You're not wearing one," I protested, taking it.

"Helmet," he repeated.

What a butt. I shoved the darn thing on and then rested against his back, tucking my arms around his waist. Man, he felt good and warm. We drove slowly for several blocks, and I opened my eyes to see that we were escorting Clark to his apartment. He had some dirt on his knees. Had he fallen again? I missed it.

Finally, Clark tripped up the stairs of his place and then was inside.

I flattened my hands over Aiden's abs. "That was nice," I said. "Walking Clark home. I think he had too much to drink." I hiccuped again and felt rather than heard Aiden's sigh.

He clamped a hand over both of mine on his stomach and pulled away from the curb, taking the easier backroads out of Timber City toward Tamarack Lake. I closed my eyes and breathed in the fragrant summer air, feeling free and safe at the same time.

Even drunk, I'd called Aiden. There was a lot about him I didn't know, but I trusted him. I might've drifted off a little because the next time I opened my eyes, Aiden was lifting me off his bike, and the helmet was already off my head. "Hey. That was fast."

He carried me toward the front door. "Keys?" Without waiting for a response, he dug into my purse and pulled them out, unlocking my door. Balancing me, he stepped inside and locked the door before setting me on my feet.

I wobbled but remained upright. "When are you going to level with me?"

He ducked his head to better study my eyes. "Go get ready for bed, and I'll find you some aspirin and water. You're gonna have a headache in the morning."

Ha. I was half Italian and half Irish. I might have a mild twinge in my temples, but a hangover wasn't in the cards yet. "Are you staying the night?"

"Is it okay if I stay the night?" he asked.

I nodded.

"All right." He nudged me toward the bedroom. "Get ready for bed."

I kicked off my heels and padded barefoot into my bedroom, and prepared for bed before sliding beneath the covers. Aiden appeared with a glass of water and a pill, and I took them, waiting until he got into bed with a satisfied sigh. "How come we never stay at your place?" I cuddled into his side.

"My place is a dump and you deserve better," he said, settling around me.

That was sweet, but I wasn't sure it worked for me. "We should stay there sometime."

"Fine, but you won't like it. The Lordes party late every night. I don't even like it." He kissed the top of my head. "Go to sleep."

I yawned as the room spun a little around me. "What's your business with Rich Pucci?"

"Sleep, Angel. Nothing else but sleep right now," he said softly, running a palm down my arm. "I'm exhausted and you're drunk. Sleep now."

My eyelids closed even as I struggled to stay awake. We needed to talk. Why did it feel so right to be next to him like this? "Aiden?"

"What?" Now he sounded grumpy.

"Will you be here in the morning?"

He kissed my head again. "Yeah."

Fair enough. I fell into a wild sleep where I rode unicorns through the golf course. After several great dreams, I tipped into the nightmare of Jareth Davey and becoming his wife. I sat up, gasping, holding the sheet to my chest. Dawn had broken outside, leaving the lake sparkling like diamonds.

"Jesus Christ." Aiden sat and pulled me close, tucking me against him. I shuddered and gulped in air, trying to keep my heart from blowing up. "I have to take care of that guy, Angel. You can't live like this." He stroked my hair away from my face, and he was so gentle I wanted to cry.

Instead, I took another deep breath. "It's okay." Jareth Davey was biding his time, but someday he'd be back. I was ready.

Aiden's phone buzzed on the table, and he answered it. "What?" He stiffened. "No." He waited. "Fine." He hung up.

"You have to go," I said, sorry to be losing him.

"Actually, *we* have to go," he muttered. "Remember that favor to Pucci? He just called it in. Get ready, Angel. You're going to court again."

CHAPTER 27

*O*kay. My head did hurt. A lot. Maybe mixing the bourbon with the tequila and red wine throughout the day had been a bad idea. I stumbled in my white kitten heels into the courthouse, walking up the beautiful marble stairs to the district courtroom where I didn't belong. I was still a misdemeanor attorney. "What is going on?"

"I don't know," Aiden said, dressed in jeans and another Lordes T-shirt. "Pucci said to meet him here and act like a lawyer. Since you are a lawyer, I figured you could handle it."

All right. So Aiden was a mite cranky. I wasn't sure if it was because he'd picked me up seriously drunk with another guy last night, or if I had said anything to tick him off, or maybe because Pucci was giving me orders. Either way, his jaw was tense, his shoulders back, and his muscles rigid. A tough-guy vein bulged in his left hand.

We reached the district court level, where Pucci and Krissy Walker sat on a bench outside of courtroom three.

"What's going on?" Aiden asked.

Pucci smiled. "I fired my attorney because I figured Anna would come cheaper. So get me out of this. You work for the prosecuting attorney's office." His hair was slicked back, and he looked all right in beige dockers and a white golf shirt.

"I was fired yesterday." I pushed my unruly curls away from my face and tried really hard not to burp up tequila. "You can't be in trial today."

"He is," Krissy said, standing next to Pucci. She wore a white pantsuit that didn't have a smudge on it.

This was crazy. I strode over to the list of cases with assigned courtrooms tacked to the bulletin board to read. "*Elk County vs. Richard L. Pucci*," I read out loud. "Set for trial today." My stomach rolled over, and I swear some bourbon popped on my brow. I turned back to him. "We can't go to trial today. Where's your attorney?"

Pucci shrugged. "I don't know. I told him if he showed up I'd break all his fingers, so I guess he didn't show up. He was a hack, anyway. Didn't even have a good plan for trial."

Crap. I leaned back to read the sheet. "Okay. You're fourth set." That could be good.

Krissy tucked her blue Chanel purse against her side. The gold hardware was stunning. "What does fourth set mean?"

I gulped down panic. "So many cases settle right before trial that the court sets several for the same day and time. There are three before us, so if any of those goes, we get rescheduled."

Aiden nodded. "So Pucci's case will get rescheduled."

"Maybe," I said. "There's a good chance the others have settled. We can't do this. I won't do this."

Pucci leaned in toward Aiden. "Control your bitch, Devlin. You owe me." He grabbed Krissy by the elbow and shoved her toward the courtroom. They quietly entered.

"No way am I helping that asshole," I hissed.

Aiden grasped my arm. "Yes, you are. We owe him one, and I don't have time to piss him off right now. I need him doing what I want."

"Why?" I asked, jumping on the advantage. "Tell me why you need that jackass."

Aiden's eyes burned a deep blue. "All right, Angel. Here it is. I owe him a favor, and he's asked that you represent him. If you refuse, I've reneged on a deal, and he'll be angry. I'm not afraid of Pucci, but he'll come after me, and I'll have no choice but to put him down. Is that what you want?"

My mouth dropped open. What was this? Sons of Anarchy? "Are you crazy?"

"No, but I am in a bind. So are you going to do this or what? Can't you go in and explain that you were just hired and need weeks to prepare?" His hand remained firm but gentle on my arm.

I didn't like any of these alternatives. "What business are you doing with him?"

"He's training my guys in tactics," Aiden said.

"Why?"

Aiden made that growling grunt sound that he made a lot around me. "Let's just say that I might've pissed off a couple of clubs when I recruited in California. My guys need training and fast."

What? "Are you kidding me? You're setting up for a motor-cycle club war?" My voice rose.

He winced. "Quiet it down. There won't be a war. The best defense is one that shows you can mount a hell of an offense if necessary. The stronger we look, the safer we are."

I cocked my head to the side and studied him. Clear eyes, unmoving body, no signs of deception. "I'm pretty sure you're full of crap," I said.

His eyebrows rose, and a glimmer slid through his eyes so fast I barely caught it. Respect? Intrigue? "It's time."

I glanced at the stately clock on the wall and huffed, walking into the courtroom and sitting by Pucci. Aiden sat next to me, and I straightened my light blue skirt that I'd paired with a white shell and pretty floral jacket.

Judge Grizzio was already seated, so there must've been a hearing or two before this. The judge was in his late forties with shocking white hair, intelligent blue eyes, and a fit physique from playing basketball. A bailiff stood to his right, the court reporter was in front of him, and his clerk sat to the side taking notes. He shuffled case files on his desk before speaking. "All right. We're about fifteen minutes behind today already."

His clerk handed him a piece of paper.

The judge read for a moment. "Okay. We have settlements in the first two cases set for trial today. The third set is *Peterson vs. Milton*, Elk County Case CV-21402. Are we ready to go?"

Two attorneys and their clients moved up to the tables past the short balcony barrier. "Yes, your Honor."

Oh, thank goodness. I let my body relax.

The judge looked at the attorneys. "We're set for one day. You still think you can be done today?"

"Yes, your Honor," both attorneys said in unison.

Shit.

The judge looked around. "All right. Then we'll have the *State vs. Richard Pucci* start at nine a.m. tomorrow."

I stood up. "Judge? If I could be heard?"

Everyone looked at me, and I tried not to blush too hard.

The judge motioned for the attorneys and parties up front to sit so he could see better. "All right. Who are you?"

I tried to steady my nerves. So the judge didn't read the paper. Good to know. "I'm Anna Albertini, and I was just retained as the defendant's attorney. As in five minutes ago. I request a continuance for a couple of weeks to get up to speed."

Alice stood from the back of the courtroom. "Alice Mitchell from the prosecuting attorney's office, Judge. The defendant in this case has fired three attorneys, gotten seven continuances, and somehow managed to get witnesses to forget their original statements. Enough is enough. The State is ready to go tomorrow."

The judge flipped through what looked like a fairly substantial case file. "Agreed." He looked up at me, and his eyebrows were as white as his hair. "We're on for tomorrow, Ms. Albertini. Let your client know that if he fires you, he's on his own because we're still going forward with trial." He banged down the gavel.

Wonderful. "Thank you, Judge." I moved down the aisle to the door, at the moment not caring if anybody followed me. Of course, Aiden, Rich, and Krissy were right behind me. As was Alice.

"I'll be right back," I said to the gang before heading over to my friend. "Hey, Alice."

She typed something into her phone and looked up. "Hi, Anna. You have a case already. Good job."

Okay. That was a little snide. "Thanks so much. I don't suppose you'd agree to a continuance for this case? Just for a week?" I'd never even been to trial.

She shook her head, her eyes determined. "No. This is a bad guy who's done bad things, and he's played the system enough. Two of my witnesses are gone. Just up and gone from this area. That's suspicious, and it's scary, and even though I've been out of the office for a month, I started this case, and I'm going to finish it."

I had no chance against an experienced trial attorney. "What are the charges, anyway?"

Her mouth dropped open and then quickly snapped shut. "He didn't tell you?" She shook her head. "It's a felony weapons charge, although we pled in the alternative for a misdemeanor. In fact, if he pleads guilty right now, I'll go for the misdemeanor. One year in jail."

"Just a sec." I had no clue if it was a good deal or not, and I was so used to being on the other side of this. I hurried back to Rich. "The state—"

"I'm not taking a plea," he said, cutting me off. "Period."

Krissy stepped closer. "Rich, maybe you should listen—"

"Shut up," he said, still looking at me. "When I want your input, I'll ask for it."

Krissy subsided and I disliked this guy even more.

Rich smiled. "You're going to get me out of this. For now, go tell her no."

Temper flicked down my back, and I gave Aiden a hard look but turned on my heel to go refuse the state's offer. Then I stomped down to the records area on the lower level and requested the entire case file, which took half an hour and thirty dollars to gain more copies. There was no doubt Pucci wasn't paying me back.

When I walked outside, Aiden and Pucci were talking quietly over by a wild rosebush while Krissy sat on a bench in the sun. I strode toward her and sat with the very heavy case file in my hands. "Why do you put up with that?"

Dark glasses covered her eyes. "I love him. Surely you get it. Aiden isn't much better."

I looked at the two men. They were both good looking with an aura of danger. "He doesn't put his hands on me or tell me to shut up."

She smiled. "You just started dating, so don't be so superior. You also don't cross Aiden, if you haven't noticed. Try it and see what happens." She kicked back. "Rich is a good guy who's had some hard times. He has some anger issues, but we're working through them."

Man, she sounded like her sister had about Danny. Did the Walker girls have a type or what? "None of this is okay. You get that, right?"

"Talk to me when you toss Aiden Devlin to the curb," she returned, wiping imaginary dust off her pristine white pants. "And you can thank me for not pressing charges any time."

"Thanks." I stood as the men strode toward us. "This is your case file, and I'm going to need most of the day to get caught up." I directed my attention and anger at Rich Pucci for now. "Unless you want to go apologize to your former attorney, who most certainly will know more about this case than I could learn in a week, and beg him or her to represent you in court?"

Pucci flashed his teeth. "Nah. I think you can handle it. You get me off, and this will square the balance sheet." He glanced at Aiden. "And set us up for more. Got it?"

Aiden looked bored. But I knew him better. "More of what?" I asked.

"None of your business," Pucci said. "Just do your job. The last guy who looked at my file said it wasn't a very strong case against me, so I expect to win this thing. All right?"

"Then hire the last guy," I retorted.

Pucci lost the grin. "Why would I do that? I'd much rather watch your tight ass in front of my table during a trial."

Aiden lost the bored look. He moved fast, grabbing Rich's lapels and lifting him up on his toes. The air electrified. He leaned in. "Mine." This was definitely a growl with no semblance of a grunt. Every hint that he was a deadly man mingled into that absolute truth right then and there.

I couldn't breathe.

Pucci blinked. "Got it. Geez."

Aiden released him with a small shove.

Pucci straightened his shirt and took a slight step back. "I was just joking, Devlin. Jesus. Take it easy, would you?"

"I've put up with a lot from you, Pucci," Aiden said slowly, his eyes a burnished blue. "But that's a line you never want to cross again. Trust me."

I shivered.

Krissy stood and edged closer to Pucci, her glasses on her head and her eyes wide on Aiden. Apparently she'd never seen that side of him.

Aiden turned toward me, and I barely kept myself from stepping away. "What's the plan?" he asked.

I tried to talk, but nothing came out. So I cleared my throat and tried again. "I need the afternoon, and then we should all meet up to plan strategy and talk about witnesses if we have any." I didn't even know what laws were at play here. I also didn't like getting forced into doing this, so I needed some space and time to think about my options.

Aiden's jaw clenched. "Fine. We'll meet after dinner at the Lordes apartment complex. Seven tonight." Without waiting for agreement from Pucci, he took my hand and started walking away from the courthouse.

I couldn't help but look back over my shoulder, and damn if Krissy Walker wasn't smirking at me. "See?" she mouthed.

CHAPTER 28

$\mathcal{W}$e walked around the corner toward my car, and I jerked my hand free. "I'm out. Right here and right now." I turned to face him, caught again by the unreal mixture of blues in his eyes. "Seriously, Aiden. Thanks for talking Krissy into dropping the charges, but if she needs to go press them, she can. I screwed up, and I'll face the consequences. But you and me? Start talking right now and tell me everything, or I'm gone." I meant every word, and it freaking hurt. I loved having him in my life.

His nostrils flared and he stiffened. Then he took a deep breath. "Fine. Here it is. I—"

"Devlin." Pucci came around the corner with Krissy trying to keep up in her mile high heels. "I've changed my mind. Let's go prepare for this stupid trial at the compound."

Two dusty trucks drove into the parking lot, both with a couple of guys in the front seat. Shotguns, or maybe machine guns, were mounted behind them.

Aiden slowly turned his head to look at Pucci, and whatever was on his face had Pucci swallowing nervously. "You brought back up?"

Pucci rolled his eyes, but his movements were still a little jerky. "Of course not. It just seems to me that your woman there might need a little extra encouragement, and having you both in our camp would be beneficial. All of my witnesses are there, anyway." He smiled, although his gaze still darted to the two trucks as if to make sure they were still there. "Besides. She's my lawyer now, and I'm covered by privilege, right?"

I had a split second to make a decision. Aiden had been about to tell me the truth, and in my gut, I trusted him. Against all logic, and with the full realization that I might be strongly influenced by the fact that he'd saved my life as a kid, I still chose to trust him. "Yes. If I represent you, then you're covered by attorney-client privilege." Of course, if I had a hint that he was going to harm himself or somebody else, I was duty bound to notify the police. There was no reason to tell him that, however.

"Good." He looked toward my car. "I'll have one of my guys drive your car out for you, and you two can ride with us in my truck. It's the black Dodge over there. Devlin? We can finish up our business arrangements while your girl is planning brilliant trial strategy."

Business arrangements? It appeared I was finally going to get answers.

Yet Aiden didn't move into action. He set his jaw and seemed to be thinking. Then he looked down at me, and his eyes softened. "No. She's not coming to the compound." Resignation and determination crossed his expression. "I'll blow it all for you, Angel. I ain't risking you."

Before I had time to even start to unpack that very sweet statement, something pointy prodded me in the side. I glanced to see Krissy there and something shiny in her hand. "Oh, come on," I muttered.

She looked over at Pucci. "You want cooperation, right?"

Pucci paused. "Uh. I appreciate the help, honey, but I don't think guns in ribs was necessary here."

"Oh." She sounded like a disappointed toddler. "I was just trying to help."

I grit my teeth together. "Then get the gun out of my side, would you?" A quick glance down proved that the safety was on. What a ditz.

She faltered but didn't move very fast.

Two motorcycles roared into the parking lot, and I recognized Saber on one of them. The other guy was new, had several scars across his face, and a tattoo of what looked like a gun on his neck. They both wore T-shirts with the Lordes logo on them.

Aiden exhaled quietly.

Pucci looked them over. "Your men can come, Devlin. Let's get this done."

"She doesn't come," Aiden said, reaching quickly and snagging the gun from Krissy.

"Hey," Krissy protested in almost a whine.

Aiden handed me the gun. "I'm not supposed to have weapons, and neither is Pucci," he said quietly. "At least not in front of a police station."

Pucci moved forward and patted Krissy's shoulder. "It's okay. Thanks for trying to help."

She preened. I swear to God, she preened.

Pucci tucked an arm over her shoulder and tugged her close. "Listen. We got off to a bad start today, and I apologize. I'd like to finish up our business, and we need to be at the compound to get the ball finally rolling. I have trial tomorrow, and my witnesses are all at the campground, so it makes sense for my new lawyer to come with us. I guarantee her safety."

Saber cut his engine. "That sounds good to me."

Aiden gave him a look.

The other guy looked at me, then at Pucci, and then at Aiden. "We can cover her. This is business, Devlin, and we need the money. It's up to you, but her safety was just guaranteed in front of witnesses."

Aiden's expression didn't change, and now I was so curious about this mysterious compound that I could barely stand it. Plus, since Pucci needed me for trial the next day, it did seem like I was pretty safe. "It's up to you, Anna," Aiden said. "Whatever you decide goes."

I wanted to ask what *he* wanted, but obviously whatever this business was he thought he needed to get done. "It'll be easier to prepare for trial if I can speak to the witnesses beforehand." That was the understatement of the century.

"There we go," Pucci said. "All right. I hope you're a good lawyer." He turned toward the black truck.

I looked up at Aiden. "Does he know I've never been to trial?"

After all the tension, it felt good to hear Aiden laugh.

* * *

THE COMPOUND WAS MORE than an hour away up in a thickly forested area in the next northern county. For some reason, leaving Elk County made me feel nervous. Aiden and I sat in the back seat of Pucci's truck with Krissy in front with him, and nobody spoke. So I read through the file on the ride. Pucci had been charged with violating Idaho Code §18-3316, which prohibited felons from possessing a firearm. I flipped through papers. "What were the felony convictions?"

Pucci turned the vehicle down yet another dirt road through more trees. "Robbery in California, felony assault in Wyoming, and felony domestic violence in Texas." He smiled at Krissy. "It was a bogus charge, and she was sleeping with the judge, I'm pretty sure."

Krissy nodded. "I'm sure."

My stomach lurched. "All right." I read through the complaint. "You were in Dunphey's bar, there was an altercation, and you took it outside for a fight." Three witnesses saw Pucci take a gun from an ankle holster and wave it in the guy's face. By the time the police had arrived, Pucci and his guys had taken off, but people knew who they were. "Were the witnesses all from the bar? Had they been drinking?"

"Yep, and one of them has left the state." Pucci grinned. "Guess it got too cold in Idaho."

I so did not like this guy. Suddenly, I missed my job as a prosecutor. I would've loved to have put him in prison. "Witness intimidation is an even more serious charge, Rich. Just a caution from your very temporary lawyer." I'd go to court the next day, but that was it. Plus, I wasn't feeling a lot of pressure right now. Losing this one wouldn't hurt at all. Although, I'd do my job.

A galvanized steel single swing barrier gate arm came into view. It wasn't unusual to see such gates in forested areas, and most were maintained by Fish and Game, at least in Idaho. This one was alarming because of the man standing to the right of it holding an automatic rifle. One of the big and black ones that probably had initials for a name.

Pucci waved, and the guy lifted the arm for the gate. We drove through and kept going to another manned gate, which opened and then we drove toward a compound.

I looked at the main lodge and the surrounding quaint cabins. "Is this where you do your wilderness training?"

"Yep," Pucci said.

It was kind of charming—except for the armed guards at the gates. There was no reason for them to be there if all Pucci was running was a business training folks how to survive. I kept my thoughts to myself for now.

Pucci parked in the dirt next to the rough hand-forged wooden lodge. "No tourists right now. Everyone here is one of my people in the organization." He looked over the seat at me. "You're gonna want a collar on her unless she wants to play."

My entire body jerked. A collar? I reared up and Aiden clamped a hand on my thigh hard enough that I jumped. Any words I had been about to say stuck in my throat.

Pucci laughed. "This is gonna be fun to watch. We party hard, lawyer lady. The chicks here are here on their own will to play and have a really good time, and you are more than welcome to join in. In fact, Devlin, I wouldn't mind trading for a night."

My ears heated and my stomach rolled.

"I don't share. Thought I made that clear," Aiden said, sounding bored again. "That's absolute, Pucci. Let your men know it, because if anybody so much as breathes on her, I'll gut them right there and hang the entrails from the nearest tree. It's important to feed the squirrels, you know. Winter will be here in a few months."

I could actually feel the color drain from my face, leaving my skin cold. This was so out of my experience. Out of my world. I wanted to look at Aiden for reassurance or guidance, but I also wanted to appear cool, when I so was not anywhere near okay with any of this. My legs tingled as a panic attack threatened. I snuck a sideways glance to watch him.

"I'll spread the word," Pucci said, opening his door. "But you're gonna want to lock her down when the party starts at night, just in case."

"I have plans for her," Aiden said carelessly. Or at least it sounded careless. But the way his body was on full alert, and the way his gaze roamed the full area around us was anything but that. He pulled me toward him and stepped outside, keeping me at his side. "Cabin?"

Pucci pointed to the third one from the main lodge. "You can have that one, but your men will have to stay in the main bunkhouse unless they hook up with someone who has a cabin."

"Good. I'll get her settled." Aiden took my hand and moved toward the cute little cabin.

"Same. Let's meet in ten in the main lodge," Pucci called out.

Aiden kept walking and I did the same; my kitten heels solid on the firm dirt trail. Trees rose all around, and a campfire was already going a little beyond the lodge. A lazy river wound behind the cabins, visible as we approached.

Two identical looking men strolled, or rather patrolled, right by us. They both stopped and looked me up and down. Aiden stiffened and set his stance.

"She's pretty, Devlin," the first said. "I get first dibs tonight."

His twin smiled and showed a gap in his front teeth. Okay. They weren't identical. My mom had told me that everyone was beautiful in their own and unique way.

She hadn't met these guys.

They had to be in their early forties and had both cut their hair short, dyed it red, and had used enough mousse to spike it up through the rapture. Their eyes were a beady brown, their noses too big for their slender faces, and their clothing dirty. Like they hadn't showered in a month.

Aiden sounded bored again. "I don't share. Pucci is spreading the word, but feel free to try me. I haven't gutted anybody in a while, Rhino."

The guy with the gap in his teeth was nicknamed Rhino? Seriously. The men didn't back away like any intelligent human would have.

"You'd look good with a BGC PROPERTY stamp," Rhino said to me. "That makes you protected by the entire brotherhood. You'd be ours."

His brother nodded. "Then you'd get all of this." He gestured to them both.

I burst out laughing. Oh, it was totally inappropriate and probably stupid, but it was a natural defense mechanism.

Their expressions darkened.

Aiden took my hand, and we walked past them and closer to the cabin. "You okay?" he asked quietly.

"Not sure," I said honestly. "Let's get inside and talk."

"No. The place is wired for sure. I'll try to find cameras and bugs later, but for now, watch what you say and definitely don't

213

take off your clothes for any reason." He strode up the stairs to the door as if he was in complete control, while Saber and the other Lordes guy flanked us.

It was like something out of a movie that I'd missed the first fifteen minutes of.

He opened the door and stepped inside first, scouting. "Looks good." Then he drew me in.

It was adorable, actually. Queen bed covered with a red quilt in the corner, sweet kitchenette, sitting area with a fireplace, and a bathroom by the kitchen. I headed for the round table between the kitchen and living area. "Looks like my new office."

He nodded. "Just stick to your case and nothing else, Angel." In other words, no investigating. "I'll have a guy on the door all day, and if you need anything, ask him. It'll be either Saber or Drag, and if it's anybody else, start yelling for me."

I winced. My head spun. Yep. Here came the panic attack.

CHAPTER 29

J worked for a couple of hours familiarizing myself with the case and the witness statements. From the police report, all of the witnesses on the prosecution's side had been fairly intoxicated, and I could work with that.

A knock came on the door, and I looked up as Krissy and Kelsey walked inside with what looked like sandwiches.

Kelsey smiled shyly. "I brought, um, supplies from town. Do you want salad, turkey, or pastrami?"

"Turkey," I said, stretching my neck. "Thanks." I looked at the sisters. "I'm glad you're here. Since you're both on the defense's witness list, I'd like to talk about your testimony tomorrow."

Kelsey shifted and handed me the sandwich. "I'm nervous because I've never been in court. Does the other side yell at you like they do on television?" She drew out a seat and plopped the salad in front of herself.

Krissy rolled her eyes and grabbed three diet sodas from the fridge before joining her sister at the table. "Nobody is going to yell at you." She popped open her soda and unwrapped the pastrami sandwich. "How's the trial prep going? I've never gone to court, either."

I took a bite of the sandwich and chewed thoughtfully before swallowing. The food wasn't as good as McQuirk's, but it would do. "So far, so good. It's my first trial, and Pucci is nuts to want me as his attorney."

Krissy shrugged. "Rich knows what he wants and usually gets it."

I studied her. "I really don't understand. You're a mortician, and you own a business. Why would you let him boss you around like that?"

She chuckled. "Look who's talking. You're representing a guy you can't stand because your boyfriend told you to."

"Asked me to," I corrected, fully understanding there was very little difference. "Although your point is well taken." I leaned in. "Do you think Rich could've killed Danny?" I'd been mulling it over all day once I saw how dangerous and organized Rich's business was.

Kelsey gasped. "No. They're family."

Krissy shook her head. "Rich and Danny were cousins, and Rich is furious somebody killed him. He has feelers out all over and plans to take out whoever did it." She looked up. "You're sure Tessa didn't shoot him?"

"I'm sure," I said, fear slamming into my gut. "She'd never shoot anybody, and I know Aiden didn't do it, either." I looked at Kelsey, taking advantage of the fact that the sisters were finally talking to me. "You knew him better than anybody, right? Who would've wanted him dead?"

She ate more of her salad. "I really don't know. I loved him, and we were together a lot, but he liked women. Many women." She looked down, and her face turned pink. "I thought I could change him, you know? But he wanted to get back with Tessa, and if you're right that she wasn't the woman who scratched him in the bar, then he was seeing somebody else, too." She looked toward the door. "Plus, he definitely plays at the parties that Rich has here."

"Have you played?" I asked.

She shook her head. "No. I loved him and nobody else."

That just completely sucked. "You deserve better, Kelsey."

Krissy nodded. "This might sound hypocritical, but I totally agree. Danny wasn't worth your time."

Kelsey glanced at her sister. "Maybe Rich isn't worth yours."

"Maybe not," Krissy sighed.

I was getting somewhere. The Walker girls were smart and nice, and somehow they'd gone down the wrong path, which I could easily relate to doing. Hopefully I wasn't doing the same thing right now. Doubts swirled around my head, and I pushed them away. "How about when all of this is over that I grab Tessa and Donna, and we all head over to the coast for a weekend? Just girls away from the bad boys we keep choosing?"

Kelsey perked up. "I'd love it."

Krissy kept chewing and then swallowed, her gaze on me. "That might be a good idea. Just get out of here for a while? Our cousin George is covering the business for me this week, and he could do it again. He's retired out of Burbank but is still licensed and has been really helpful."

"It gives him something to do besides fish," Kelsey agreed.

I pushed the remains of my late lunch away, starting to like these two women. Kelsey seemed a little young, but Krissy and Detective Pierce might make a good couple. If I wiped out as an attorney, I could always start a matchmaking service for locals. I loved setting people up, and there was no doubt Pucci was bad for Krissy. For now, I'd get ready for trial. "Okay. In your own words, tell me what happened the night that Rich is on trial for, Krissy."

She wiped mascara off beneath her eyes. "We were partying pretty hard, and this guy grabbed my butt at Dunphey's. Rich got mad, there was some pushing and shoving, and then they took it outside. When we were outside, the guy hit Rich, and Rich hit him back, and the guy fell down and didn't get up. Total wimp. So we left." Her gaze didn't meet mine.

Kelsey nodded. "Yep. That's exactly what happened." Her face was still pink.

Good people were usually bad liars, unfortunately.

"All we need to do is create reasonable doubt in one person on the jury," I murmured. "Just from reading everything, I feel like we have that. I see why Rich's earlier attorneys didn't want to plea it out." I couldn't let either one of them lie on the stand, so if they didn't tell me that they'd seen a gun, then I didn't know that. I didn't push either one for more information. Yeah, that was why I'd wanted to be a prosecutor to put bad guys away.

Kelsey gathered up the garbage and dumped it into the bag she'd used to bring the food. "So are we good?"

"Yeah, but you two have to know that the prosecutor is good and will cross-examine you. So my advice is to tell the truth. That's what you need to do."

"Right," Kelsey said.

The door opened and Rich stepped inside. "Do we need to practice my testimony?" Somehow he made it sound sexual.

Saber stepped in right after him and crossed his arms across his chest. He was big and wide, and I was suddenly happy he was watching the cabin.

I cleared my throat. "You aren't testifying, Pucci. It'd be a disaster. Let's see how far we get with the witnesses first." I glanced at the witness list from the state. "At the very earliest, you'd take the stand at the end of the week, so we don't even need to argue about it yet." I kept my voice calm and controlled.

"Okay." His gaze warmed. "Any chance you want to play tonight, lady attorney?"

I didn't know exactly what 'play' meant to Pucci, but whatever it was, I definitely didn't want it. "No." Why expand on that?

Saber's chest puffed out. "Are you finished with Pucci, Anna?"

"For now," I said, more than happy to let Saber escort the business owner out.

Pucci turned toward Saber. "You make a claim on Kelsey or not?"

"Up to her," Saber said shortly.

Pucci looked back and Kelsey nodded, her eyes wide. "Looks like you have. Great. Want to switch tonight?"

I couldn't help but look at Krissy. Her boyfriend wanted to have sex with her sister, and she was supposed to go off with Saber? None of this made any sense to me, and by her pale face, she wasn't loving her boyfriend's attempts. We really needed a girl's weekend away. Maybe I should try it for a week. It wasn't like I had a job, but everyone else might have trouble taking that much time off.

Krissy cleared her throat. "Rich—"

"I don't want your input right now," Pucci said. "I told you how it was with me, babe, and this is it."

Saber's jaw clenched. "I'm not trading. Not now or ever, Pucci. Not my thing." The Lordes member rose several notches in my opinion.

The relief that slid over Kelsey's face made my temper spiral.

Pucci motioned for the Walker sisters to follow him out, and they did. Once they were all gone, I sucked in a deep breath. "That guy is such an asshole." I couldn't care less if he had the place bugged or not.

Saber flashed a grin. "Keep that in mind and stick close to Devlin while we're here." Gunfire erupted outside, and he held up a hand when I jumped to my feet. "It's all good. Just some target practice away from the camp, and it was planned. I should've told you about it. Sorry."

"That was an automatic weapon," I said.

"Yep." He shrugged. "A little much if you ask me but not illegal."

I wasn't so sure about that. "Okay. Thanks." I turned back to my paperwork and went through the jury questionnaires, flagging the ones I'd want to excuse for sure. Then I started drafting an opening argument, and my stomach hurt even more. I really wasn't ready for this.

The door opened right when I was starting to get hungry again.

"Hey, Angel." Aiden walked in and before I could say a word, I caught sight of Pucci behind him. "Let's grab some dinner." He had a smudge of dirt on his cheekbone and what looked like motor oil on one thigh as he pulled a backpack off.

I stood, aware I was still wearing my suit from court.

He grinned. "I brought you some different clothes. Had to borrow from Kelsey, but she had more than any one person could want." He set the pack on the bed and drew out jeans and a sweatshirt. "It gets colder up here at night, so you should be all right with the sweatshirt."

"Thanks." I'd feel better out of the skirt, that was for sure.

Aiden partially turned to see Pucci. "We'll meet you outside." He gently clasped my arm in a quick squeeze that felt reassuring and then moved toward the door, herding Pucci out. Even so, I could see Pucci's grin. Oh, he had no idea I knew about possible cameras.

In a move women have perfected for years, I tugged on the jeans before sliding the skirt down over them and then undid my blouse and quickly yanked the sweatshirt over my head. If Pucci got off on two seconds of seeing my plain white camisole that covered my plain white bra, then he could have at it. Moron.

I looked into the pack and grabbed a thick pair of socks and tennis shoes. The socks fit, and the tennis shoes were a size too big, but I could make them work. So I opened the door and stepped outside where the smell of barbecued chicken and camp-fire smoke commingled into a sense of my childhood. I'd loved camping with my family every weekend, even after the kidnapping that had ended well because of Aiden.

He took my hand and led me toward the main lodge. Men and women milled around, many wearing a whole lot of camo. Many folks in my family hunted, so I was accustomed to seeing people in camo, but there were a lot of them at this camp.

There were also several women in too short shorts and tank tops that left nothing to the imagination. A couple tried to sidle close to Aiden. It was so weird. I have no problem with people choosing how to live their lives, but some things I just didn't understand.

The food was spread out over a picnic table with a cheery looking red tablecloth, and we grabbed paper plates and dished up. Chicken, salads, rolls and other camping staples looked delicious.

"Hey Anna," Kelsey called out from behind another table closer to the trees where she had a blender that was going nonstop. "Want a Margarita? They're my specialty."

"She's good," Aiden answered for me, digging two beers out of a cooler at the end of our table.

I almost protested and then thought about it. Oh. As somebody who'd unknowingly eaten pot-filled brownies not too long ago, it'd be smart to stay away from anything that wasn't bottled. I winked at Kelsey and then accepted the bottle from Aiden to set back into the cooler. I rummaged around and drew out a hard cider.

"My bad," he said, grinning.

I nudged him with my shoulder, feeling lighter for the first time that day. Until we sat around a campfire close to Krissy and Rich. Aiden sat on one side of me and Saber on the other, so I felt nicely bracketed.

The guy I'd learned was named Drag was on the other side of Krissy, already eating chicken. He reached behind his back and drew out a gun from his waist. "I beat your record of modifying by a second." He tossed the black gun over to Aiden.

Aiden caught it and flipped it over. "Doesn't count unless I see you do it." He angled his head. "Looks good, though."

Modified? I was pretty sure that was illegal, but I'd never had a gun case. Not yet, anyway. I looked over at the shiny part attached to the back of the slide. The gun was black, and the piece didn't look natural. "Is that a Glock?" I already knew that it was.

"Yep." Aiden tossed it back to Drag and dug into his food, his tone not inviting questions.

Fine. But we were talking later when we were away from other people. A walk after dinner sounded like a good idea. I sat back to relax and eat my dinner.

Until a smattering of more automatic gunfire pierced the peaceful evening. Nobody around me took notice.

Well. That wasn't good. How were they so accustomed to automatic gunfire when there weren't trainees around?

CHAPTER 30

*W*e hadn't gotten a chance to go for that walk. Aiden had matched beer for beer with Pucci, and by the time things got really wild at the fire, he'd been ready to turn in. By wild, I mean people making out, shooting guns, and stripteases. We'd gotten into bed and Aiden had kissed me, turned over, and started snoring.

Of course, if there were cameras in the cabin, it was the right move.

Morning had come too early, and we'd immediately driven to my cottage so I could change clothing before we all headed to the courthouse. I did so, and now I ran out to the truck dressed in a light green suit with yellow Naughty Monkey kitten heels. Nobody spoke as Pucci drove to the courthouse. Today he wore beige pants and a button-down shirt with no tie, while Krissy wore a pink sundress. I'd told Kelsey I wouldn't need her until the next day.

Aiden wore jeans and a t-shirt and was grumpy with a possible hangover. Or for some other reason. But we hadn't had a chance to talk privately, so I didn't know anything.

Since Krissy was a witness for me later, she couldn't be in the courtroom, so she went shopping.

We entered the courtroom as hearings were going on, so we took seats toward the back, and I ran through my *voir dire* questions in my head. I'd never done jury selection, and normally I would've had a more experienced attorney there to help. At least, back when I'd had a job.

I tried to remember what I'd learned in law school and caught sight of Alice at the prosecution table already in the middle of a hearing. She was arguing about jail time or something.

Judge Grizzio looked at the defendant, and something in the judge's expression caught my eye. "Are you sure you want to plead guilty, young man?"

I leaned to the side to better see. The defendant was a tall kid with short hair and bright red ears. He nodded.

The judge frowned. "You're entitled to a lawyer, you know."

The kid looked toward the door. "I thought I had one, but maybe not. I don't know. I just want to get all of this over with, okay?" From the back, he kind of reminded me of Pauley. The way he looked, anyway. Pauley would probably be arguing the law by now.

The judge sighed and looked down at his paperwork. "You're charged with violation of Idaho Code §18-7001 for malicious injury to property that amounted to more than a thousand dollars."

I sat up. Wait a minute.

"Yes, your Honor." The kid sounded miserable.

Alice leaned over to read from her casefile. "The defendant destroyed private property with his dirt bike, your Honor. He said he'll plead to the felony."

A felony conviction would get the kid a mandatory year in prison and up to five years. This wasn't right.

The judge shook his head. "Young man, are you sure you want to plead guilty?"

The kid nodded, his head down.

Before I knew what I was doing, I stood. "Wait a minute, your Honor. Please." I strode down the middle aisle and opened the swinging gate to the well, moving toward the kid. "Hey."

He looked up, his blue eyes miserable. "Hey."

"How old are you?" I whispered.

"Eighteen," he whispered back.

"Objection, your Honor," Alice said loudly. "This is inappropriate."

The judge shushed her.

I leaned closer to the kid, looking up at his clean cut face. "Why are you pleading guilty?"

He shrugged narrow shoulders. "We were riding across old man McLerrison's farm, and I guess we damaged the land by his pond. It was an accident, but we were trespassing, so I did the crime."

Oh, what a sweetie. "Where are your parents?"

He blanched. "Dead. My uncle raised me and died a couple months ago. I just want to get this over with, you know? I don't know how to do any of this."

I patted his arm. "That's okay. I do."

He shook his head. "I can't afford you."

"Sure, you can. I take stuff besides money all the time." I tried to look encouraging. "I need a bunch of heavy stuff moved, and you look strong. Don't worry—we'll work it out."

He shuffled his feet, looking like that Opie kid from the Mayberry show on the old movie channel. "I don't know."

"I do. We'll work it out. Do you have a dollar?" I asked.

"No." He reached in his pocket and drew out a shiny copper penny. "I saw this on the way inside and thought it would bring good luck."

I took the penny. "It will." Then I faced the judge. "I've just been retained by Mr...." I glanced at the kid.

"Duck. Oliver Duck," the kid said.

I blinked. "Mr. Duck. He'll be changing his plea, Judge."

The judge looked relieved, and I swear a hint of respect shone in his eyes. Good. "Mr. Duck?"

Oliver looked at me before turning back to the judge. "I plead not-guilty?"

"Good." The judge slammed down his gavel. "See you later."

Oliver looked at me.

I smiled and tried to appear like I knew what I was doing. A notepad rested on the table, so I quickly wrote my name and number on the bottom edge and ripped it off. "Here you go. Give me a call later in the week, and we'll figure things out. I can settle this one; I'm pretty sure."

He took the ripped piece of paper and then grinned. "This is your business card?"

"For now," I said, sharing his smile.

"Then you are the lawyer I can afford. Thanks, Anna. I'll call you." Looking much happier, he leaned over and wrote his number to hand over. "Here's mine." He turned and raced to the exit.

I pivoted to face Alice. "Seriously? What is wrong with you?" Her forced leave of absence had obviously gone to her head.

She rolled her eyes. "He destroyed property, Anna. The laws matter to some of us."

Ouch. Fair enough.

I exited and went to retrieve my file folders and notes before the judge called our case.

Aiden reached up and kissed me. "You are such a softie."

I rolled my eyes and motioned for Pucci to follow me to the defense table. I sat between him and the prosecuting attorney's table.

The judge handed off case files to his clerk, who handed him a bigger one. "Let's get this going. We'll have the same jury pool from yesterday, and I'll have them take seats in direct opposite of last time."

Fourteen people filed into the seats in the jury box. In Idaho, a jury was usually on the hook for a week, so they might hear many cases. The clerk came over to my table and handed me the list of who was in which seat, and I rifled through my notes on the jury questionnaire while Alice did the same.

Voir dire went off without a hitch, and I started to enjoy myself. While I'd never been in trial, I'd actually won the mock trial at law school. The prize had been a mountain bike, which I'd given to Pauley because he'd been interested in mountain biking at that time.

Then we were to opening arguments, and Alice's was good. She planted a nice question in the minds of the jury as to why a felon would own a survival business that included learning to shoot guns.

I stood up, introduced myself, and acted like my guy was a saint. I didn't like it. Yet the spirit of competition gave me a boost, and frankly, I didn't like that either. Even so, I smiled at the jury of seven women and three men. "My client does a service to the community, to many communities, and that's what we want, right? He has others deal with the guns, and he works with the survival aspect in the wilderness." Pucci had explained that to me when I'd asked. I finished up and took my seat.

"You're not bad," Pucci said.

I didn't answer.

The state called the guy Pucci had gotten into a fight with to the stand first. His name was George Dorsey, he was around forty, and he had a beer gut. His story was exactly what the charges had been. Alice got the story from him without my having to object often. Then she tendered the witness.

I smiled and stood. "Mr. Dorsey, how long had you been in the bar?"

"A couple of hours," Dorsey said, his blond hair slicked back and his face clean shaven.

"What were you drinking?"

"We had a couple pitchers of beer between the four of us," he said.

I paused because I'd read the entire police report. "Just beer?"

He frowned. "We may have had a shot or two of Jaeger."

One woman in the jury box shifted her weight. I ran him through the night, the bars they'd been to before that, and the fact that he grabbed Krissy by the butt. He adamantly denied it. I made a mental note to run through Krissy's statement again.

We worked through the afternoon, and the judge called an end to the day at around four o'clock, right after the state finished its case.

"We're on tomorrow," I told Pucci as we exited the courthouse. "Make sure both Krissy and Kelsey are here to take the stand."

"No problem." His hand rested at my waist as we walked outside, and I looked around for Aiden. "If you're looking for your man, he had business to deal with," Pucci said. "However, I'm fairly free right now. Why don't we go get a drink and celebrate the day? I think it went well."

"No, thanks." It had gone well. I'd been able to successfully cross-examine all of the state's witnesses and show that they'd pretty much been drinking all day.

"Your loss." Pucci released me as Krissy hurried our way.

She handed my car keys to me. "We had your car brought in, and here are the keys."

"Where's Aiden?" I asked.

"Haven't seen him." Then she leaned in and kissed Pucci. "We need to celebrate what looks like a good day, based on that smile you have going."

He had a smile going because the jerk had just made a move on me.

Pucci nodded. "All right. See you tomorrow, Anna." He slid his hand into the back of her linen pants, and they walked away.

I sighed and dug out my phone to call Aiden. It went instantly to voice-mail. The man was driving me crazy. He'd finally agreed to let me in, and now he'd disappeared. What business? Even if I had asked Pucci, he wouldn't have answered.

So I turned and strode along the sidewalk to my former office building, heading inside.

"Hey Anna," the receptionist said. We'd been buddies since I saved her picture of Stan Lee from a DEA raid the month before. "What's up?"

"Hi, Juliet. Is Alice around?" I asked. Maybe we could plea out Oliver Duck's case.

Juliet shook her head. "No. She planned to work from home tonight."

I glanced down the hallway. "What about Nick?"

"He's here. Go on back." She smiled.

At least I still had one friend left in the prosecuting attorney's office. "Thanks." I hurried off before she could think twice and soon knocked on Nick's door.

"Come in," he called out.

"Hey." I stepped inside and shut the door, quickly heading to what had often been my seat on the other side of his desk.

He looked up from behind his desk, still in a gray power suit with light green tie. "Hi. Alice called in and said you did a good job your first day in trial."

"Thanks." I wished I still worked with Nick. "Did she tell you I took on the Oliver Duck case?"

Nick's eyebrow rose. "What's an Oliver Duck?"

I gave him the whole story, and when I'd finished, he just shook his head.

"What?" I asked. "Come on. You grew up dirt biking, four wheeling, and snowmobiling anywhere you wanted. Probably on that farm at some point. You can't want that kid to get a felony."

"Of course I don't," Nick said, his eyes a light brown. "But I'm down one lawyer and I can't piss off Alice. I don't interfere with the cases of my attorneys, and the last thing you want is to go over her head, considering you're in trial together and probably will be again. Find a way to deal with her on this."

Frustration heated down my back. "She doesn't want to deal."

"Then go to trial," he said reasonably. "I'm not interfering." He reached for a file folder beneath a stack. "Now that you're out on your own, are you working on your sister's case?"

I wasn't exactly out on my own. In fact, I should start looking for a job. "Yes," I said.

"Good. File a Notice of Appearance, would you? For now, here's evidence I need to turn over." He handed me the file folder, and stress lines showed at the sides of his mouth.

Dread cut through my solar plexus. "What is it?"

"Lab results. We found Danny Pucci's prints on Tessa's toilet, and based on the timelines given by Tessa and Aiden of the day he was killed, somebody is lying." Nick sat back. "You might want to find out who."

CHAPTER 31

J grabbed pizza on the way home and met Clark at my front step, where I handed over the documents. "We're missing something."

Clark followed me inside and flipped through the documents. "So either Aiden is lying with the timeline of Danny going in and getting shot, or Tessa is lying about Danny not being at her place for so long." He walked and read, somehow missing the furniture. His phone rang.

I set the pizza down and tried not to freak out. My sister did not lie to me, so Aiden's timeline had to be off. But why would Aiden lie?

"Clark Bunne," Clark said, answering his phone. He straightened. "No. Sorry, Detective Pierce. My client has made the only statement she plans to make. Yes, I understand. Goodbye." He clicked off.

"You sound tough," I mused.

"I am tough." Clark slid his phone back into his pocket. "Pierce wanted to interview Tessa about the new evidence. I say there's no reason for her to talk to him, but I'll call her so she's updated."

It was so different being on this side of things. I dished out the pizza and we both sat to eat. While eating, I told Clark about my first trial. "I just don't think I can show that Pucci is innocent."

Clark shrugged. "Then don't. Show that it doesn't matter."

I drank some of the Chardonnay I'd poured for us. "What do you mean?"

He snagged another slice of pepperoni. "You're looking at the case like a prosecutor. Right and wrong, guilty or innocent. You're defending a guy, which lets the middle road in. Even if he had a gun, so what? If the jury wants to find a reason to let him go, they will find one. If you can show that the other guy really did grab Krissy's butt, which is a sexual battery, then they won't want Pucci to go to prison for defending her honor."

I sat back. Good point. "Pucci is such an ass."

Clark grinned. "You can't let that change how you defend him and you know it. Just do your job."

Another good point. "I don't suppose you want to second chair the trial?"

He shook his head. "No. Getting another attorney involved at this point would look bad to the jury. Like you couldn't handle it, which you can. Besides, I have a job interview tomorrow."

"Already?" I reached for another slice. "That's great."

"Hardly. I've been turned down so far, and this is my first interview and it's with a really small firm and probably not great pay. That newspaper article really screwed us. Have you tried for a new job yet?"

I shook my head. Then I leaned back and studied him. "You know—"

"No. We don't have any money and I need to eat," Clark said. "And I need health insurance and to be able to pay rent."

"Me too." I chewed the thought some more. "We could get a loan to start a business."

Clark tipped back the rest of his wine. "With what collateral?

My good looks and your penchant for ending up in the newspaper?"

I laughed. "There has to be somebody who'll lend us money."

"Nobody we want to owe money to," Clark countered. "A legitimate bank wouldn't look twice at us, unless you own a bunch of property somewhere that you haven't told me about."

"No property anywhere," I admitted. "Even so, think about it. We could rent a place downtown—"

"Which takes money," Clark said.

I sighed. "You need to be a dreamer." It'd be fun to own our own business and only take the cases we wanted. "Just think about it."

"I need to be a realist," he said, pouring us more wine. "No offense, but your life is never calm."

Who wanted a calm life? "Just think about it—okay? Albertini & Bunne."

He tilted his head. "Bunne & Albertini."

"I like it alphabetical," I protested.

He sat back. "If we do it my way, our initials would be B.A. Just think of the badass logo."

Oh, he had a point. Better yet, I had him thinking about it. "I'm sure our law degrees mean something, and a bank would give us a loan." I tilted my head. "Other than that, I don't have any assets." My Fiat was awesome but probably not great collateral.

Clark tossed his paper napkin on his paper plate. "We don't have the resources to start our own business. Maybe if we both got jobs and saved up for a few years we could create our own firm, but I don't see it happening before that." He paused. "I'm also not sure I'd want to start my own firm."

I'd never considered it before, either. My goal had been to seek justice, and maybe I'd have to do that case by case instead of by putting bad guys away.

Clark cleared his throat. "I need to take a run at Aiden. Without you there."

"Fine by me," I said. Both Aiden and Clark could handle themselves, and it'd be good to get me and my emotions out of the way. I trusted Aiden, but that didn't mean he'd told me everything so far, and I knew it. In fact, I expressly knew that he hadn't told me everything.

My phone buzzed and I glanced down to see the caller. "Hi, Kelsey," I'd answered. Both she and her sister had given me their contact info since we seemed to be on the same side now.

"Anna? We have a problem." Kelsey sounded like she was crying. "Can you come to my house?"

I looked at Clark. "What kind of problem?"

"You'll see. It's just Krissy and me here." She hung up.

"I have to go," I said.

Clark shook his head. "When somebody calls you after dinner and asks you to come over, it's a bad idea. See why I don't want to be your partner?"

"Yes," I said honestly. However, I was really warming to the idea of starting my own firm, and Clark and I complimented each other. I gave him Aiden's contact information. "Good luck. I hope you get him to open up."

* * *

My Lady Smith & Wesson was tucked in my overlarge handbag as I knocked on Kelsey's door. I might be big-hearted, but I wasn't a moron.

Kelsey opened the door, and her eyes were as red as her nose. "Come in." She sniffled and ushered me inside the cute living area.

Krissy sat on the sofa with a bag of frozen peas against her right cheek and eye. Her lip was swollen, and her hair crazily messed up. "I'm sorry Kelsey called you, Anna."

"She's our attorney," Kelsey said, going to sit on the sofa and take her sister's hand. Her sister's bruised hand—most likely a defensive wound. There were more bruises along her neck and down the arm that I could see, and maybe some of the hair from her temple had been pulled out?

My ears heated, and my lungs flared even hotter. "Did Pucci do this?" I set my purse down and moved toward her for a better look.

She nodded wearily and then winced before rubbing her neck. "We got into a fight. It was just as much my fault as his."

Somehow I doubted that. "Listen. We have to call the police on this."

Kelsey looked toward her sister.

Krissy shook her head. "No. I hit him, as well. They'd have to arrest us both, and we have too much going on. I wouldn't press charges, anyway."

Kelsey cuddled closer to her sister. "Maybe I shouldn't have called. Are you required to notify the police, Anna?"

Man, I wished I were required by law to notify the authorities. "No. I have to notify the police if I know of a crime being committed right now or one that's going to be committed in the future." Although, if Pucci had hit her once, he'd hit her again, so theoretically I believed there was a crime coming. But that didn't quite fit the requirements. "Although my professional advice to you is to call the cops on that bastard."

"What's your personal advice?" Krissy cracked a smile, and blood slid from her lip.

"To shoot him," I said, smiling back and dropping into a chair. "Seriously. Let's get him locked up and move on. I can help you." I had Detective Pierce on speed-dial and would be more than happy to have him cuff Pucci for good. After so many felonies, he would serve plenty of time, and there was no way I'd represent him again. Ever.

"No," Krissy said, holding her sister's hand. "I fought him, and he's hurting right now, too. We had too much to drink and started fighting about everything, and we both got out of hand. It's the truth." She lowered the frozen peas.

I winced. "That's going to be a glorious shiner." Wow. Under her eye and atop her sharp cheekbone, the skin was already turning a light purple. It'd been a deep amethyst by the morning.

"I'll keep ice on it," Krissy said, gingerly touching the bruise.

Kelsey's eyes widened. "Oh, no. We're supposed to testify tomorrow."

I reared back. "You two can't be considering testifying for him tomorrow after this. He hit you in the face, Krissy."

She straightened her shoulders and met my gaze head on. "I'm well aware of what he did. But I'm on the witness list, and I was present the night he was arrested, so either way I'm going to testify."

The woman had a point. If I decided not to call either Krissy or Kelsey to the stand, then the prosecution would wonder why and track them down. Not that they'd work with Alice. "Listen. If I choose not to call you two, then I still have two of Rich's guys who can take the stand and testify for him." Although I'd said in my opening statement that Krissy had been assaulted, and if she didn't testify about it, I couldn't get it into evidence. "Did Rich see that guy grab you?"

Krissy shook her head. "No. I told him."

It'd be hearsay, then. I sat back, my mind spinning. "Let me think this through."

Krissy set the peas to her face again. "No. It's a done deal. I'm going to plaster makeup on tomorrow, and then I'm going to testify like I promised. That moron in the bar really did clamp onto my butt, and he deserved to be punched by Rich. That's the truth." Her good eye glowed with determination.

I believed her. But I also thought Pucci had worn a gun in his ankle holster that night, although everyone was denying that still. "You might get him off this charge, Krissy. Are you sure you want to do that?" Putting him away seemed to be best for her.

She sighed and shut her eyes. "I love him. It doesn't make sense, but I think we can work things out."

As if on cue, her phone rang. She looked down. "It's Rich." Then she held the phone to her head. "Hello?" She shifted on the sofa. "Yeah. I know. Me too." She blinked and a tear slid down her face. "I know. Why don't you come here?" Then she giggled. "Okay. That sounds good." She set the phone down. "We've made up. Or we're going to make up, anyway."

I didn't want to be there when Pucci arrived, because I might just lose it. Helping a guy like Pucci was something I'd never wanted to do. I wondered what it would take for Nick to hire me back so I could put jerks like Rich Pucci into prison. That guy deserved prison. "Are you sure it's a good idea to see him tonight?" I asked.

Krissy rubbed one of the bruises. "I need him here. It'll be better if we're on the same page tomorrow, right?"

"I guess." I didn't know what else to say. "All right. I'll see you tomorrow. If you decide that you don't want to testify, just let me know. I'll figure something out." Then I retrieved my heavy bag from the floor and walked out into the warm night.

This totally sucked.

Swallowing, I drove back toward the main drag in town to my sister Tessa's apartment and remembered at the last second that she wasn't back home yet. So I flipped around toward an older part of town until I reached Donna's adorable Craftsman house and parked in her driveway.

Her door was already open by the time I exited my car, and Tessa stood there in cute pajamas.

I smiled as I walked toward my sister, stopping at the porch. "When was Danny last in your apartment?"

She paused in smiling. "Besides the night he ended up dead?"

"Yeah," I said softly.

"A couple of years ago when we were dating," she said, her brow furrowing. "Why?"

I studied her, looking for any sign of deception. Instead, only curiosity met my gaze. I knew my sister, and I knew when she was lying. Right now, she was telling the truth.

That meant that Aiden had lied.

CHAPTER 32

*W*hen I strode into the courtroom the next morning, I nearly tripped over my borrowed black and gold Louboutin pumps when I saw Aiden in the last row. Furious, I stomped toward him.

He looked me up and down and let out a slow and very quiet whistle. "Wow."

Yeah. The black suit was my serious one, considering it had gold hardware and a flirty slit to the side of the skirt. "You lied to me," I whispered.

His gaze flared hot and bright. "I doubt that. Man, you're beautiful when you're angry."

Oh, he was going to get punched. I paused in my thinking after remembering Krissy's black eye. Physical violence didn't solve anything. "I have to do this trial for your friend, and then you're going to tell me what really happened the night Danny Pucci died. Got it?"

"I told you." Aiden's brows furrowed. "Why are you thinking I lied?"

I leaned in to keep our conversation private. "Because Danny left a print on the toilet somewhere. That means he either was in the apartment before that night, which he was not, or that he was there long enough to use the bathroom, which contradicts your story. I believe my sister. I do not believe you."

Aiden cocked his head to the side. "Where was the print?"

"On the toilet," I hissed.

His blink was somehow threatening. "Where on the toilet?"

"Why does that matter?" My voice rose, and I fought to quiet down again.

He leaned toward me until I could see the different flecks of blue in his eyes. "It matters because if the print was on the handle, obviously he's been there lately. If the print was in the back, like he'd worked on the toilet at some point, it could be years old. So I suggest you ask your buddy Detective Pierce exactly where the print was found."

"How do you know I got the information from Pierce?" I asked, wondering where the print had been found.

"Please." Aiden sat back, his gaze still interested but now also pissed off.

I was just as ticked off. The last thing in the world I wanted to do right now was use my experience and brain to help Rich Pucci get out of breaking the law. "We are not done with this conversation." Without waiting for an answer, I pivoted on the excellent heels and stormed up to my table.

Pucci was already seated in his spot. He had that bad boy thing going on today and would probably charm a couple of the jurors. "What's your problem?"

"You are the exact wrong person to piss me off right now." I unloaded my case files and trial notebook from my tote. "Believe me." I turned to look at him.

He had long scratch marks down one side of his neck, and his bottom lip was a little bit swollen.

Good. He'd deserved it.

He leaned forward, and there were more scratches beneath his ear. "She attacked me, Anna. We were drinking, and then she just lost it. Completely."

What a freakin liar. "I saw her face, Rich. Her bruised and battered face."

"Well, you haven't seen my dick. She kicked me square on," he said, anger vibrating through his voice.

Oh, he'd no doubt deserved it. Now I was going to help him get off on another charge that he'd probably committed. The temptation to let him hang was strong enough I had to take several deep breaths and remind myself of the oath I'd taken when I'd been licensed as an attorney.

The bailiff entered and we all stood for the judge. Since there weren't any preliminary matters, the judge called the jury in, and we continued the trial. And I was correct. A couple of the younger female jurors smiled at Pucci, and when he smiled back, the youngest one twittered.

For goodness sakes.

I stood. "The defense calls Kelsey Walker to the stand."

The back door opened, and the officer let Kelsey walk down the aisle to the witness stand, where she was sworn in. She wore a pretty yellow dress with her hair curling nicely around her shoulders.

I ran her through the introduction questions about her name and where she was the night of the incident. "How many alcoholic drinks had you had that night?"

She kept her hands in her lap. "About three all night, I think. One with dinner and then two later at Dunphey's Bar. All margaritas." She turned to the jury and smiled. "I like margaritas. They're my favorite, and Dunphey's makes one that has extra spice."

Several jury members smiled at her.

"Would you say you were clearheaded later in the night at Dunphey's Bar?" I asked.

"Objection. Leading the witness," Alice said.

The judge looked at me. "Sustained."

Shoot. I smiled to keep Kelsey calm. "All right. Let's rephrase. Kelsey, how were you feeling toward the end of the night in Dunphey's Bar?"

"Clear headed," she said instantly, keeping her attention on the jury. Her face was earnest. "As well as tired. It was a long day, and I just wanted to go home."

"What happened before you left the bar?" I asked.

She took a deep breath. "I saw that blond guy grab my sister's butt, and she told her boyfriend, and he went to confront the butt grabbing guy."

A couple of older women in the jury smiled to encourage her. Man, she was a great witness.

"Did you later find out the blond guy's name?" I asked.

"Yes. His name is Mr. Dorsey, which is a name he does not deserve. Right?" She shook her head. "Anybody with such a cool name from literature should be a decent human being and not some guy who grabs a girl in a bar."

Oh, the jury was eating this up.

I nodded. "What happened after Mr. Dorsey committed a battery against your sister?"

She held up her hands. "The guy who'd assaulted my sister started swearing and pushing, and they took it outside. He hit Rich and Rich hit him back. That was all. Then we went home. The next day Rich was arrested for something, but that doesn't seem fair to me."

I waited for Alice to object again, but she must not have thought the last opinion really hurt her. "All right, Kelsey. Rich has been charged with taking a gun out of an ankle holster that night, as you know. Did you see a gun?"

She shook her head.

"I need you to answer audibly," I said as gently as I could.

She kept her gaze on me. "I didn't see a gun."

"I tender the witness," I said, striding around to sit by Pucci, that asshat.

Alice stood. "Ms. Walker, how do you know the defendant?"

Kelsey looked toward Rich. "Rich is dating my older sister. We do a lot of activities together, and I work for her at Walker's Funeral Home."

"I see. Is there any other way you are associated with the defendant?" Alice asked.

"Well, I was dating his cousin," Kelsey said, clutching her hands together.

Alice looked over at the jury. "You're no longer dating his cousin?"

"Objection, your Honor." This was going down the wrong path. "Relevance," I said.

"Approach," Judge Grizzio said, his bushy eyebrows rising.

Alice and I approached the bench, and I leaned up to talk before Alice could. "Danny Pucci's death has nothing to do with this case," I said.

Alice leaned up. "The defendant's overall violent lifestyle shows that it's more likely that he'd carry a gun."

I looked sideways at her. "Man, that's weak. You can't use past bad acts unless they're relevant, and you know it."

"Agreed," the judge said. "Follow a different line of questioning, counselor." He lifted back up and faced the jury. "The objection is sustained."

Alice and I returned to our seats. But now the jury looked curious at what I'd tried to keep from them, so the damage was done as Alice had intended. She had a lot more trial experience than I did, obviously.

Alice stared at Kelsey for a moment. "Where did Mr. Dorsey, also known as the blond guy, allegedly grab your sister?"

"On the butt," Kelsey said.

I coughed out a laugh before I could help it, as did several of the jury members. I could hear Aiden's low chuckle from the back row, and a new type of heat washed over my skin.

Kelsey turned beet red. "Oh. I mean, she was standing over by the dart boards in the bar."

Alice didn't lose stride. "Where were you standing?"

Kelsey faltered. "Over by the dartboards?"

"Are you asking me or telling me?" Alice asked.

"Telling you," Kelsey said, nervously pushing her hair away from her face. She faltered.

Alice stepped toward her. "Would you lie for your sister or her boyfriend?"

"Objection, your Honor," I said, defending Krissy and seeing a couple of the jurors nod. "Badgering the witness."

The judge looked up. "Objection denied."

Well, I'd gotten it across to the jury that Alice was mean, and Kelsey needed protection. Good enough.

Alice softened her voice in a very plausible manner. She sounded almost regretful to have to ask any more questions. "Please answer the question. Would you lie to protect your sister or her boyfriend?"

Kelsey chewed on her lip. "Probably but not in court under oath."

Excellent answer. I kept my expression stoic when I wanted to run up and high-five her. Sometimes the nicest people made the best witnesses, which actually gave me hope with the entire system.

Alice smiled. "All right. I assume you talked to the defendant's attorney before your testimony. What did she tell you to say?"

Kelsey pursed her lips before answering. "She just told me to tell the truth. That's all."

The bailiff stifled a grin. Yeah, I was new, but everybody learned that trick in mock trial and debate.

"I see." Alice didn't lose a step. "Let's go back to the night of the incident. You and your sister were in the bar. How close were you to your sister when Mr. Dorsey allegedly touched her?"

"He grabbed her. I was maybe a foot away from her?" Kelsey asked.

"And you were looking at her butt?" Alice asked smoothly.

"No. I mean, not really. Maybe I was more than a foot away, you know? We'd been drinking." Her eyes opened. "Not a lot, though. Yeah. I was a foot away."

I mentally sighed and listened carefully for possible objections to break up the line of questioning, and on redirect, I tried to rehabilitate Kelsey's testimony best I could. But Alice had dented her credibility, even while seeming to sympathize with her. Finally, Kelsey was excused.

She pretty much ran out of the courtroom.

Pucci turned toward me, keeping his voice low. "Is it just me, or did that not go well?"

"It went all right," I said. Kelsey had been shaky from the beginning, and it might've been a mistake to put her on the stand. But the jury had liked her, and they'd probably sympathized with her wanting to stick up for her sister and her sister's boyfriend, who'd been defending her honor. It was a strategy and possibly a good one. "She actually was more effective than you think," I said, my mind spinning. "We'll get your two buddies to set up the remainder of the night with their testimony, and then Krissy will bring it home."

"Good," Pucci said, leaning back. "She's solid."

She'd better be.

CHAPTER 33

$\mathcal{A}$fter a late lunch where my mind kept returning to Clark's statement the night before, I slightly altered my approach to the trial. I'd had one witness after Kelsey and before the break, and he'd done a good job of describing how upset Krissy had been when she'd been grabbed. I'd spent a lot of time with him and so had Alice, and he'd stayed strong. Making the trial about Krissy and not Pucci was the best strategy, and it seemed to be working.

As we settled at our table and waited for the judge to arrive, I glanced toward the back of the courtroom to see that Aiden had gone. He hadn't joined us for lunch, so I figured he'd be off doing whatever it was he did. I turned toward Pucci. "What's Aiden's deal, anyway?"

Pucci straightened his shirt and tried to look responsible. "He's who he says he is. The president of the Lordes."

I swallowed. "Yeah, but tell me the truth. I'm your lawyer now, and we have privilege."

Pucci looked my way, and his deep eyes were serious. "Listen. You're a nice person when you're not being all judgy. Aiden is a guy who gets things done. We have a deal going that will make us both a lot of money, and you should like that."

My head was starting to ache in both temples. "Is it a legal deal?"

Pucci studied me like he hadn't really looked before. "No."

For the first time, I felt like he was giving me the full truth. The reality smashed me in the chest, more specifically the heart. The pain was palpable. "He said he wants to go legit."

"We all want to go legit," Pucci said quietly. "But then opportunities knock hard and you have to take them. Guys like us can't help it. We don't want to help it." The rare display of wisdom seemed to open the floodgates. "You either need to get on board with that or get out now. Aiden ain't going to change."

I'd learned a long time ago that people didn't change, but how could Aiden go from being my hero at ten to breaking my heart at twenty-four? I wanted Pucci to be lying, but he seemed truthful. "What's the tattoo all about? The one both you and Danny have?"

He looked down at his arm. "It's the symbol of my company. Of the men involved in my entire business."

"And BGC?" I held my breath.

"Brotherhood, God, Country," Pucci said. "In that order." He shifted his weight on the wooden chair. "We're as tight as the Lordes are with each other, but we stay under the radar of the law much better than a motorcycle club does. It's a smarter way to go with the same benefits. No big and flashy leather jackets that act like neon signs."

"What's this deal you have with Aiden?" I asked, my stomach cramping.

Pucci shook his head. "We don't share info with our women. It keeps us safe and it keeps you safe."

"Aiden lied to me," I said, mostly to myself, still not quite believing it. The claw marks down Pucci's neck stood out, and I felt how dumb I'd been.

Pucci nodded. "I'm sure he did. You can't exactly tell a lawyer or frankly, a woman, that you're brokering illegal gun deals." He jerked. "Shit. We're covered by privilege. Don't tell Aiden I said that." He sat back and his lips pressed together.

Gun deals? They'd been talking about modifying handguns at the campfire, hadn't they? I knew that was illegal but needed to brush up on the actual statute. The sense of betrayal almost had me falling off the chair. Here I'd been lecturing Krissy about getting out, and I was facing almost incontrovertible truth that Aiden wasn't who I thought he was. Who I wanted him to be.

The bailiff entered along with the judge, and we all stood as the jury was brought back in. I called Pucci's other friend to the stand first and ran him through the night in question. He claimed there wasn't a gun, and he was pretty unflappable on cross-examination. It still took an hour or so longer than I'd expected. We were going to need another day for trial, but at least it'd be finished this week. Tomorrow was Friday. When Pucci's friend was finished, I turned to Pucci. "He did a good job."

Pucci looked calmer. "Yeah. Gram is solid."

I breathed deeply. "It's all up to Krissy. You picked the exact wrong night to beat her up."

Pucci rubbed the scratches down his neck. "She picked the night."

What an ass. I bit my tongue and called Krissy to the stand. The officer at the rear of the courtroom let her in, and she strode up the aisle wearing a pretty white sundress and strappy sandals. Her dark hair was around her shoulders, and her eyes were clear. The makeup job was phenomenal.

I could see bruises because I knew they were there. Otherwise, I don't think I would've noticed and would've thought the angles on her face were from shadows and light and not makeup. "You owe her better after this," I muttered.

Pucci just stared at her.

"Look loving," I hissed under my breath.

His gaze softened.

At the moment, I disliked myself more than I hated him. I stood and ran Krissy through the initial questions of her name, occupation, and relationship to the defendant.

"So, tell us what happened on the night in question," I said.

Krissy plucked at her skirt. "We were drinking at Dunphey's, and this guy grabbed my butt really hard. It, um, it freaked me out, and I, um, I told Rich." She looked toward him and then seemed to relax.

I kept my smile in place. "I know it's nerve-wracking to give testimony in any case. You're doing great." I needed the jury to know she was nervous and not lying.

She clasped her hands together. "Okay." Her small laugh was nervous but authentic.

"What happened after you told Rich that you'd been assaulted?" I asked.

She exhaled. "Rich went to confront the guy, and they started pushing each other around, and we all ended up outside. The guy hit Rich and Rich hit him back. Then we left." She settled back and looked like she relaxed.

"Good." I ran her through more questions to make sure her testimony was solid and then I tendered the witness. The jury was looking at her with sympathy, and so long as she stayed solid through cross-examination, we had a good chance of winning this thing.

Alice stood and scrutinized Krissy's face before questioning her. "I'd like to clarify a few things. Where were you when Mr. Dorsey, also known as 'the blond guy,', allegedly touch your butt?"

"In the bar," Krissy said. She cleared her throat and met Alice's gaze head on.

"Where in the bar?" Alice asked.

Krissy bit the inside of her cheek as if thinking. "Over by the pool tables and the bathrooms."

Alice paused. "Your sister said you were by the dart boards."

Krissy faltered. "The pool tables and the dart boards are in the same area."

Well, kind of. I'd spent my share of time in that bar, and I wouldn't say same area. But it was close enough.

Alice frowned as if she didn't agree. "All right. Let's move on from that for now. Where was your sister?"

"Um, over by the dartboards." Krissy blushed.

Alice's smile was a warning. "Guess I told you that one, huh? How often does your boyfriend keep a gun on his person?"

Krissy paled. "Never. He can't have a gun."

Nice reminder that Pucci was a felon who couldn't have a gun.

Krissy realized it quickly. "He's a good guy who's made mistakes. He's not perfect, but he's trying." She rubbed her face. "We all are. It's hard."

Alice walked closer to her. "Ms. Walker? Are those bruises on your face?"

Fuck, fuck, and double fuck.

Krissy jumped. "No. I mean, yes. Just one bruise." She unconsciously rubbed her neck.

Alice ducked her head. "And on your neck?"

Krissy's gaze darted to Pucci. "Um, yes. But, um, I fell."

"Oh God," Pucci muttered beneath his breath.

Alice slowly turned to look at Pucci and then returned her focus to Krissy. Nice theatrics. The jury leaned forward as one. "When I saw you outside yesterday, you didn't have bruises. Now you do. Did the defendant harm you last night, Ms. Walker?"

Pucci leaned toward me. "She's leading the witness. Object."

"You can lead on cross-examination," I said. "Shut up and let me work." Alice needed to say something to which I could object.

Krissy floundered and tears sprang into her eyes.

Alice softened her voice. "You need to answer the question, Ms. Walker."

"Wh-what was the question?" Krissy asked.

Crap.

"Did the defendant put those bruises on your face?" Alice asked.

"No," Krissy said. A couple of tears tracked down her cheeks, and she rubbed them off—along with the makeup. I'd been wrong. The bruise was more blueish than amethyst.

A couple of women in the jury box gasped.

Krissy reared up. "Honestly. I fell down the stairs last night. I'm so tired. I was up all night worrying about testifying and then fell, and I'm just not myself." She looked fragile and desperate. "Rich didn't hurt me. This is all a mistake." She looked imploringly at the jury, panic clearly across her bruised face.

In jury seat number four, an older man, who still worked as a farmer outside of town, turned and glared at Pucci. Even I could feel the heat from that stare.

Alice shook her head as if she couldn't believe it. "The defendant hit you, didn't he?"

"Objection," I said, standing up. I had to do something. "Relevance."

Alice pivoted to face me. "Relevance? The defendant physically harmed the witness before testimony today. It's witness intimidation at the very least."

"No," Krissy said, also standing. "He didn't hit me. It was my fault. Look at his neck. I scratched him. This is my fault."

"Oh, shit," Pucci muttered. "I'm going to kill her."

The judge looked at Krissy. "Has your testimony been influenced? Have you been threatened?"

Tears now streamed down her face. "No. None of that happened." She wiped off her eyes, revealing more of the bruise, and then looked at Pucci. "I love him. We're going to work all of this out."

It was just getting worse.

Alice ran her through more questions, but Krissy was pretty much a basket case after the initial questioning. Finally, Alice tendered the witness.

I looked at a visibly struggling Krissy. "No further questions, but the defense reserves the right to recall the witness."

"All right." The judge slammed down the gavel. "It's after four in the afternoon, and it looks like we'll need another day for trial. Let's start at ten in the morning." He stood, we all stood, and the jury filed out. Most of them averted their gazes from Pucci, but a couple of the older ones gave him a good glare on the way out.

"I'm screwed," Pucci said.

"Yeah. You are." I gathered my belongings and stuffed them in my briefcase. "I can call Alice and try for a deal, but I'm not sure if I'd grant one in this case." My mind spun on what to do next. "We could put you on the stand, but there's a good chance she'll shred you in cross-examination."

"Let's go and find Krissy," Pucci said, standing.

I walked down the aisle and out of the courtroom. "You two need to keep it civil," I said over my shoulder.

He didn't answer. All right. As a lawyer, I was duty bound to do my best. I'd done so for him, and I'd work hard the next day. Yet he was a jackass who probably deserved to go to prison. It was all right to feel two things at once. We walked out of the building and toward the parking lot in the still warm afternoon.

A note was stuck under the windshield wiper of his truck. He snatched it and read it. "Damn it. Krissy said she's sorry and needs time." He took out his phone. "Yeah. Hi. We need to get the deal done tonight. I have to split." Then he clicked off.

I took a step back. "You can't flee. I can't let you flee. We have to finish the trial tomorrow."

Pucci crossed his arms. "What could I get?"

It was surprising he hadn't asked any of his attorneys that question before. The guy must really be overconfident. "Another felony conviction, up to five years in prison, and up to a five thousand dollar fine."

He rubbed a scratch on his neck. "After all of that, the judge will nail me if I get convicted."

"True. Even if you're given five years, you could get out early with good behavior," I said. "I can call Alice to make a deal."

He grimaced. "Five years doesn't work for me. I'll have to go with plan B."

"You can't," I said. "You have to face this. Just get through it."

"No." He looked around the quiet parking lot. It wouldn't fill up until around five. "Sorry about this." Before the words sank in, he grabbed the back of my head and smashed me toward the grill of his truck. Pain exploded in my brain and I struck out, screaming.

He jerked me back, I caught my breath, and he smacked me against the truck again.

Everything went dark, and I fell into nothingness.

CHAPTER 34

I awoke with a blazing headache and a loud groan. "What the heck?"

"Ah, good. I was afraid you were dead." Pucci's voice came from far away.

I opened my eyes, and sharp blades of pain slashed through my irises right to my brain. "Oh, God." My stomach rolled over and I held it, shutting my eyes again. I was sitting on the passenger side of his truck, and it felt like we were parked. "Are we still at the courthouse?" I needed to reopen my eyelids but couldn't quite force myself to do it.

He chuckled and the sound was grating. "No. Man, you were really out. Sorry about that. What is today?"

"Thursday." I gingerly felt the two lumps on my forehead. "You just committed a battery and a kidnapping. Have you lost your mind?"

"No. It's self-preservation. Can you get out of the truck or do you need me to carry you?"

I forced my eyelids open to see the campground outside. People were hustling around and packing up chairs, tents, and belongings. "Touch me and I'll kill you." Since I'd been in court, I didn't have my gun. However, there were tons of guns in this place, and I could find one. "What's your plan?" I asked.

He sat back as he watched his people scurry around. "We're packing up and leaving first thing in the morning. I figure nobody will know you're missing until court starts, and even if there are cameras outside that building, nobody will look at the footage until then."

Dread swam through my nerves like a shark playing with prey. "Okay. Then what?"

"Well, that's up to you." He looked at my forehead and winced. "Geez. You really bruise purple and ugly. Are you seeing double?"

"No." My head hurt, but my vision had cleared. "All I see is one asshole in front of me." I didn't have the balance yet to jump out of the truck and run, so I took several deep breaths to regain some strength. "Why not scurry away now?"

He pointed at a couple of guys carrying large boxes toward a truck. "Money. I need to get paid for the business venture we've been creating and move on to rebuild all of this. We had a long-term deal in place, but I'm going to need to start my part over, and I need immediate funds to do so. This is just a temporary glitch."

"You'll be a wanted felon," I said, my head still swimming.

"Yeah, but I'll get a new identity and move on from there. It's not as difficult as you'd think." He sat comfortably as his people worked around him. "I can still do business with the Lordes but will have to do it from my secondary location. It's too bad. I like this campground and the other location needs a lot of work. Hence, the payment I'll get from Devlin today."

I turned toward him, which put my butt closer to my door. "Do you think Aiden will be okay with this? That he'll still do business with you after you've given me a concussion?"

Pucci's lip twisted with what actually looked like sympathy. "Oh, he'll be pissed, I know. But Devlin isn't going to lose millions because I've given you a little bump on your head." He leaned in. "Two bumps. Get over yourself."

That was fair. I ground the heels of my palms into both of my eyes, not caring if I smeared my mascara. "Considering you've brought me here, what's the business about? You've already kidnapped me, so it's not like I won't have worse things to say about you, and you'll have a new identity, so talk." This was assuming he wasn't planning to shoot me and dump my body in one of the abandoned cabins.

He chuckled. "You really are a curious one, aren't you? You know about cats."

"So I've heard," I said wearily, my whole body starting to ache. It was amazing what a blow to the head could do to the entire central nervous system.

He looked around. "We smuggle converter sets into the states and alter Glocks into automatic weapons. We also manufacture and distribute illegal weapons, and we're not picky who we sell them to. It's kinda illegal." He laughed at his own joke. "But very lucrative."

I shook my head and instantly regretted it as streaks of pain slashed behind my eyeballs. "The Lordes had a distribution system in place for drugs and were busted. Is the system still in place?"

"Somewhat but it's been modified," he said, then laughing at yet another joke. "We modify things. For now, the Lordes are involved as the investors because they had a whole boatload of cash the cops didn't find when they were busted for drugs. They also provide a good share of protection to us and the entire organization." He looked at me. "Aiden isn't who you think he is. If we need somebody to disappear, he's the one I call."

Right now, I needed to disappear. I'd deal with Aiden and my feelings for him later.

Pucci's phone buzzed and he lifted it to his ear. "Pucci." Then he glanced at me. "Are you sure about that? I may have somebody here at the camp who'd disagree. She put up a struggle, but it didn't last long." He handed over the phone.

"Hello?" I asked, already knowing who was probably there.

Quiet reined for a heartbeat. "Angel. Are you all right?" Aiden's voice was soothing and low.

"Not really," I admitted.

"How bad are you hurt?" The thread of calm command remained in place.

I couldn't stand him being nice right now. "Possible concussion and definite broken heart. I'm going to take you down, Devlin."

"It's a date. Give the phone back to Pucci."

I did so and then turned to eye the best route of escape. Probably along the river with the heavy underbrush. If I could get across it, they'd have a harder time tracking me.

"I want half the money for half of the shipment," Pucci was saying. "When I get set up again, we can continue." He looked at me. "Jesus, Devlin. She's fine. I won't hurt her so long as you bring what I want. We're good business partners and I don't want to ruin that. I just had to keep her from notifying the cops that I was going to run, and I also knew she'd be decent incentive for you in case you decided to cut bait here. This is a good business, and we can get through this."

I opened the glovebox in one smooth move, and papers fell out. No gun. I sighed.

Pucci looked at the papers. "In fact, I kind of like her. She has a lot more guts to her than that bitch I was dating. I'm gonna have to find somebody to replace her pretty fast."

I leaned back against the door again, ready to kick for his face if necessary.

Pucci rolled his eyes. "Yeah. I know. Yours." He shook his head. "Just be here in an hour with the cash." He paused. "Fine. I'll give you the extra hours, but we're leaving at first dawn. And Devlin?

If you don't show up, I'm taking the lady lawyer with me." He clicked off.

* * *

I SAT at the campfire next to Pucci and ate my steak, wanting to keep my strength up. A full moon illuminated the entire camp, although the floodlights set all around didn't need any help. It might as well be daylight. I'd been there for three hours and had tried to escape twice, until Pucci just up and tied me to a porch. Now that had gotten boring. He'd finally fetched me for a very late dinner.

"I like your spunk," he said, eating his steak with a plastic fork.

"Gee. Thanks," I muttered, taking a sip of my soda. My balance wasn't quite back, but my headache was now only a dull throb. "I have to ask. Aren't you even a bit sad to be leaving Krissy? She really loves you."

He snorted. "She's not half the person I thought she was, and I'll replace her easy enough. Well, not easy. But I'm better off without her. Never hitch yourself to a weak link."

Great. More philosophical advice from Rich Pucci. I took another sip. "Did Danny figure out you were running guns? Is that why you killed him?"

Rich paused with a beer almost to his mouth. "Kill Danny? He was my cousin. I didn't kill him." He scratched at a mosquito bite on his hand. "Danny was all in on the business and ready to make his fortune. I think his plan was to woo your sister with his millions." He shook his head. "Oh, I will find out who killed him, and when I do, they're dead."

I cocked my head to the side. "Aiden is a suspect, you know."

Pucci scoffed. "I'm aware of that, but believe me, if Devlin had killed Danny, he wouldn't be a suspect. Chances are we wouldn't even have a body."

Ug. All right. The boulder-sized pit that landed in my gut hurt as badly as my head. I wasn't so sure, but since Aiden seemed to be my last chance for getting out of this at the moment, causing tension between him and Pucci was a bad idea.

The moronic twins from before sat across the fire, both staring at me. In the moonlight, the red dye in their hair looked like blood. Rhino smiled at me. "What do you say, lady? Want a night you'll never forget with me and Spark?"

I couldn't help the shiver. "No." Rhino and Spark. Their mama must be so proud.

The sound of several motorcycles rumbled up the long road, and soon Aiden, Saber, and Drag came into view.

The relief that slashed through me held heat. They all wore jeans, motorcycle boots, and black leather jackets with the Lordes cut on them.

Pucci whistled. "It's a hot night for leather jackets. The boys are making a statement." He took another drink of beer.

Aiden dismounted and his gaze swung instantly to me. Top to bottom and so intense my toes curled.

The other two flanked him as he strode toward the fire, the angry embers in his eyes hotter than any natural fire. "We're here."

"The money?" Pucci asked.

Drag and Saber both held saddlebags.

"I have three million now," Aiden said, his gaze not leaving mine. "That's for half, and we take a truck with the goods out of here. Along with my woman."

I wanted to punch him—after we got out of there. So I didn't say a word.

Pucci's jaw jutted out. "That's fair. Hand over the money."

"Not until we see the guns and the converting kits," Aiden said.

Pucci pointed to a large gray truck with a canopy. "We already have it all loaded. You either trust me, or you don't."

"I don't," Aiden said shortly. "I'm not giving you a dime until you show me all of it."

Several guns emerged from the men at the fire.

Pucci stood. "You're outgunned."

"Not my first time in that position," Aiden said easily. "We wore the cuts on purpose, as I'm sure you know. I have fifty members ready to ride if I don't call in ten minutes, and we have a thousand affiliates preparing to jump on their bikes in several surrounding states and get here as fast as possible if the alert goes out. Are you sure you want to fuck with me?"

Pucci gulped in air. "Fine. Come with me." He started toward the truck, which was positioned beneath a light.

Aiden held out a hand. "Come on, Anna."

"She stays here at the fire," Pucci said.

Aiden leaned over and grasped my hand, pulling me up. My paper plate dropped to the ground. "She comes with me. Period."

Pucci chuckled and kept walking. "You have to watch that kind of attachment, Devlin. It's bad for you and for business."

"I'm aware," Aiden said.

I stumbled next to him but still managed to give him a look. A mean one.

"That's why we switch sometimes," Pucci said, reaching the truck. "Well, that and it's a lot of fun. How boring would it be to have only one chick for the rest of your life?"

"You really are a moron," I said.

Aiden squeezed my hand. "Knock it off." Then he pushed me behind him and to the side of the canopy. "Show me what you have."

Saber edged closer to me without seeming to move.

Pucci flashed a light into the truck.

Aiden cocked his head. "You're light."

Pucci sighed. "Fine. I didn't manage to get the full shipment of the converter kits, but I have half of them there. I'll get the rest to you on credit. I promise."

Aiden's jaw ticked. "What do you mean you didn't get the full shipment? Where the hell is the rest?"

"I don't know. There was a disruption in the distribution line, and I'm working on it. Somebody's head will roll, and I'll get you the rest of them. There's enough here to get you started."

"Fine." Aiden motioned for the other two to hand over the cash.

Pucci accepted the bags. "Well now, wasn't that easy?"

A bang echoed over by the fire, people yelled, and then the entire world lit up.

CHAPTER 35

a flash and bang blew up the ground around us.

"Duck," Aiden bellowed, bending over.

My ears rang and I cried out. Was that a flash grenade? People swarmed in from two directions, all yelling, all armed with large guns. I couldn't see or hear, and my head hurt worse than it had before. Somebody jumped off the top of one of the buildings to the right, followed by several other people.

I pivoted and almost fell.

Pucci grabbed my arm at the last second and yanked me toward him, pressing a gun to my side. It had all happened so quickly that I hadn't had time to think. He pulled me around the other side of the vehicle.

"Freeze!" Several voices yelled all around us.

A helicopter pounded through the night, directly above us.

I swayed, not sure where I was. My vision remained fuzzy, and the ringing in my ears made it impossible to hear anything that wasn't yelled. The cops had arrived? Part of me wanted to warn Aiden, and the other part wanted to kick him. Either way, I had to get away from Pucci.

"Let her go." It was Aiden's voice.

Gunfire erupted all around us, and several impacts hit the ground next to him, throwing up dirt.

I screamed and tried to fight Pucci, but my limbs were still numb.

Saber stood next to Aiden while Drag was on the ground, blood pouring from his leg as he inched around the other side of the truck and out of the line of fire.

Pucci's left hand pressed a knife beneath my chin, and I winced at the pain. He pointed the gun at Aiden.

"No," I whispered.

Aiden held up his hands. "Listen, Pucci. Let her go and I'll help you here. I know a way out but we only have seconds. Let's go."

"You set me up. Or you were followed. Either way, I'm out of here." Pucci leaned his mouth next to my ear. "We're going to bend down, and you're going to pick up both of those bags. If you move the wrong way or try to escape, I'm going to shove this knife up through your neck. Got it?"

"Yes." I didn't move my head and kept my gaze on Aiden's furious eyes.

Gunfights erupted all around us followed by more flash bangs and sounds of pain.

We bent and I fumbled for the bags, managing to nab both of them. Then we slowly stood, and the blade started to hurt my jaw. Blood slid down my neck, heating my skin. My vision was still off, and Aiden wavered in front of me. "Aiden," I whispered.

"You're okay, *Aingeal*. Just stay still and trust me," he said, his focus on Pucci. "Let her go. We can drive out of here."

"I don't think so. Our partnership is terminated." Pucci fired three times, hitting Aiden center mass. Aiden flew up and back, landing hard in the dirt. His legs kicked out, and his powerful shoulders threw up more dirt.

I screamed and fought, but the blade dug into my neck. Pain centered me. "Aiden," I yelled.

Saber grabbed him by the legs and pulled him around the truck. He left indents in the dirt.

"Let me go." I shoved back and tried not to impale myself on the blade. "I have to see if he's okay. Let me go." I freaked out, trying to see around the truck. More pain lashed through my neck.

Pucci pulled me around the truck and shoved me inside, grabbing the money bags and tossing them in the back. He jumped in and started the engine. I scrambled for the other door, but he manacled my hair and yanked my head to the steering wheel as he punched the gas and the truck lurched forward. My forehead hit the steering wheel, and agony exploded throughout my skull.

The truck bumped over rocks, and my body fell to the floor while he kept ahold of my hair with his hand on the steering wheel, so I was half on the seat and half off. My temple was attached to the damn steering wheel, and there was nothing I could do to get him to release me. My ribs protested, and my breathing was so off I could barely concentrate. The gunfire kept going outside.

Was Aiden dead? I hadn't seen any blood, but he'd fallen so fast I hadn't seen anything. Who was fighting out there? Was it the police or a rival gang or something? "Let me go, Pucci."

"Shut up." He punched the gas. Hard.

I gasped in air as tears flowed down my face. *Think. Breathe and think.* Angling my shoulder into the radio and pressing my knees against the floor, I twisted and punched him right in the groin. My hand glanced off.

He smacked me on top of the head with his free hand.

Agony shot from my head right down my spine, and I screamed. Then I struggled, panicking, hitting him with the hand that could reach him. He hit me again, and everything went dark. I fought to stay conscious.

"Stay still," he said. "Or I will shoot you." His words came from very far away.

The truck bumped and jerked, and water splashed inside his open window. He turned and drove down the shallow river, each river rock making him tighten his hand on the steering wheel as well as my hair. My whole head screamed in pain at this point. Bile burbled in my stomach and tickled up my throat, burning me. I blinked away tears and tried to clear my vision. In that position, I could see the bottom of his jeans and his boots.

I reached up and tried to pry his fingers out of my hair. He tightened his hold.

We went over a small embankment and both bounced. I flew up and then back down, more agony ripping through my skull.

The side of my face landed on the steering wheel this time. I whimpered and went limp, trying to stay alive.

"That's better. Just hold on." He turned the steering wheel, wrenching my neck, and we bounded over something hard, sending us flying again. Then we were clumping along a very rough area, but no more water splashed inside. Were we on the other side of the river? He swore and viciously twisted the wheel, nearly pulling my hair out. I bit my lip against the incredible pain. "Let me go, you asshole."

"I swear to God I am going to shoot you. Hold still," he barked.

Branches scraped the side of the truck, and we drove up and then down, then up and the truck bottomed out with a loud protest. Something scraped against the bottom of the vehicle, and we bottomed out again. If he didn't stop, maybe the truck would just break or flood.

My right arm fell to the floor on his foot. I looked at the brake. If I pushed on it, he'd just shatter my hand with his boot. I scrambled to get balance, my hand sliding beneath the seat. Something smushy was down there, but nothing that would help me balance.

He turned again, and water splashed through the passenger side window and spread across the seat. Were we back on the river? He twisted and my head twisted with him, once again putting me in a position to be looking at his boots.

A thought hit me out of the blue.

I bunched my shoulders.

When he turned again, I fell slightly, reaching for his ankle. My fingers touched metal. Going purely on instinct, I pulled the small handgun out of his ankle holster. I was unable to turn to face him, so I aimed at his driving foot and fired. Blood blew out of the hole in the leather.

The explosion in the small space was deafening, and I already couldn't hear. My ears rang and my skin stung.

He yelled and turned the steering wheel, crashing into something. We rocked back and forth, and I fell more fully onto the floor. "You bitch." He released me and shoved me away, kicking the gun out of my hand with his injured foot. The weapon fell to the floor and clattered beneath the brake pedal.

I fumbled to grab for it when he opened his door and ripped me out of the truck by my hair to throw me. I landed on the riverbank on my stomach and quickly turned over, crab walking backward up rough rocks.

Blood flowed from the top of Pucci's boot. Fury covered his face along with lines of pain. He limped toward me and drew another gun out of his pocket to point right at me. "I can't believe you fucking shot me." He kept coming as if in a trance, his body jerky and his once handsome face ravaged by darkness.

I tried to scramble farther away, but the rocks stopped me. "Don't shoot." There wasn't anything else to say.

"Oh, too late." He lifted the gun higher and pointed the barrel right between my eyes.

I hunched over myself and tried to protect my head.

A loud gunshot echoed through the night.

CHAPTER 36

I stilled. The shot had been loud. But I was still thinking and apparently not dead. Why wasn't I dead? Slowly, I opened my eyes to see Pucci face-down in the river with blood flowing from his head. I turned to see Aiden and Saber running toward me through the river, and Aiden's gun was still in his hand. Confusion bore through my brain like a hundred buzzing bees.

Aiden landed on his knees in front of me. "Anna? Anna, talk to me." His hands were everywhere. On my arms, my legs, my face. "Say something."

I blinked. "You were shot. Three times."

Aiden looked over his shoulder. "She's going into shock."

Saber flipped Pucci over, and his eyes were wide in death. "Jesus. Nice shot. You got him right in the temple."

Aiden shrugged out of his leather jacket. "Put this on, sweetheart. It's warm and it'll keep you from shock. Just hold on." He gently pushed my arms into his sleeves, and I settled into the safe smell of leather, motor oil, and man. Aiden's scent. "There you go." He zipped up the enormous jacket, and warmth began to seep into my bones.

The moonlight shone over his rugged face, bringing out the light and dangerous hues of his eyes. "The cops are coming," I whispered.

He gently brushed a couple of curls off my face. "They're already here, Angel."

I tried to concentrate, but between the concussion and apparently the shock, it was difficult. "You were shot." Hadn't I already said that? My gaze dropped to his chest, which should be covered in bullet holes. Instead, a black bulletproof vest spread across his wide chest with the letters ATF across it with POLICE in big letters beneath it. A silver badge was stamped next to the letters. "ATF?"

He nodded, lowering his head to better see my eyes. "You're definitely concussed."

Hope leaped into my confused brain. "They let you borrow a vest?" Maybe he was an informant, and they'd let him off. "I don't want to stop dating." Tears filled my eyes. If they took Aiden away, what would I do? "We can fix this." Wait a minute. I'd said that before, too.

Saber stood over Aiden's shoulder and peered into my eyes. "Yeah. She's definitely concussed. We have paramedics en route."

Aiden ran his palms down my legs again. "Are you hurt anywhere else?"

"I have no idea," I sighed, scrapes on my hands starting to ache. "I don't understand what's happening, and my head hurts."

A couple of men wearing full assault gear and ATF uniforms jogged up in the middle of the river. Water splashed all around them. "We have the camp under control. Three of theirs dead, none of ours. Drag was hit, but it isn't fatal," the first guy said. "Looks like Pucci isn't going to face racketeering charges after all."

"No," Aiden said, his hand remaining reassuringly on my thigh. My entire thigh. "But he has second and third in commands who are just as dirty, and I want everything thrown at them. Start with charges of violating the Organized Crime Control Act, and we'll go from there." He looked over his shoulder. "Looks like the locals are arriving?"

The first guy scouted the area with a world-weary gaze. "Yeah. We coordinated quick, and you're going to need to handle it."

"I've got it," Saber said, pulling off his Lordes jacket to reveal a bulletproof vest just like Aiden's. His silver badge had a scratch through it, obviously having had been used before. "You're gonna need to bring her to the ambulance. They can't get down here. I'll be right back."

Aiden wiped dirt off my shirt. "No. I need you on the body. Pictures, diagrams, and interviews. Also, take my service weapon out of my holster and clock it in for evidence. There'll be a hearing for the shooting. Clancy? Go deal with the locals until I can, all right?"

"Yep." The first guy turned to head back up the river with his buddy by his side.

I tilted my head and reached out to touch his badge. Surprise and relief and a whole lot of other emotions I couldn't quite track spread through me. "You said you weren't ATF."

He grasped my chin and turned my head to the side, examining my forehead. "You never asked about ATF. You asked about the FBI, DHS, and the CIA, I believe. And I told you I wasn't an informant."

So he hadn't lied to me. Wait a minute. Yes, he had.

Saber leaned over Aiden and took a gun out of the back of his waist. "We like to stay under the radar, you know?"

They were good at it. "You're a Fed," I murmured.

Aiden ran his knuckles across a bruise I could feel on my cheekbone. "You're bruised but nothing is broken, I don't think. To answer your question, I've been undercover for almost three years for this campaign, and I had to go through the Lordes to do it. I'll explain everything later. Right now, we need to get you checked out."

Yeah, everything was still pretty numb, including my brain.

But my heart was beating fast and out of control, and for the first time that day, it wasn't because of terror. It was because of Aiden. "I knew you were a good guy."

Saber snorted. "Ha. Boy, do you have her fooled." He took a picture of Pucci's dead body with his phone.

"Nah," Aiden said, cupping my jaw. "She's had me figured out since the beginning." He frowned and brushed a finger along my neck. "You're bleeding. It's not bad, but we need to go." Then he stood and lifted me, grunting when I settled against his chest.

"You're hurt." I tried to remain still and stiff. While I didn't know a lot about bulletproof vests, I had seen on television where somebody could have a couple of broken ribs after being shot while wearing one.

"The vest took most of the impact," he said, turning and starting up the river. When the brush receded along the shoreline, he strode that way and became more surefooted on land.

I gave in and snuggled my face into his neck. "Pucci said he didn't kill his cousin."

"I don't know who killed Danny," Aiden murmured, tucking me closer. "I told the truth about when I showed up that day and saw the shooter jump out the window, and I was just using Danny to get to Rich. From what I could tell, I don't think Rich had any reason to kill Danny."

I lifted back up to look at Aiden's face in the moonlight. His nose was straight, his jawline strong, and his eyes bright. Everything about him was masculine and sexy, even more so now that I knew my instincts had been on track with him. He was a good guy. "You have to know."

"I don't, and it's not my case." He pressed a kiss to my nose. "I know that Tessa didn't shoot Danny because she came in right after me, and I know that I didn't do it. Danny was an asshole who hit women and probably had a ton of enemies. I didn't know him very well, but he seemed like a screwup to me."

I coughed and my ribs ached. "Why were your knuckles all bloody?"

He smiled, and the sight was slightly less than pleasant. "Oh, Rich Pucci arranged a fight between Danny and me the night before, just to get some bets going. I didn't mind because I wanted to beat on Danny a little bit." Aiden grimaced. "Of course, I didn't know he was going to get shot the next day."

Obviously. This undercover situation was even more dangerous than I'd feared.

"Who killed Danny?" I whispered.

Aiden lost the deadly smile. "I really don't know. The local cops will figure it out. Detective Pierce is a pain, but he's good at his job."

I ran my hand through the hair curling below Aiden's ears. "Pierce is going to be so pissed you're a Fed."

Aiden chuckled. "I know." He found a trail and started following it back to the smell of fire. "I hope I'm there when he finds out, although it does prove his instincts were right, too. He knew something was off with me, and he just didn't know what. He'll still be angry, though." Aiden sounded like he was looking forward to the conversation.

I closed my eyes and rested my cheek against his ATF vest. "What's ATF again?"

"Bureau of Alcohol, Tobacco, and Firearms," he said, carrying my weight easily.

"Do you go undercover a lot?"

"Yeah." He didn't expand on the statement.

At the moment, I didn't want to know anything more than the fact that he was one of the good guys and wasn't going to prison right now. The huge lightness of relief almost made me giddy—or maybe that was the bruise on my brain. Either way, this was almost too good to be true. But it was true. "You guys fight drug trafficking, gangs, and gun violations." It all fits with the Lordes club as well as mixing it up with Rich Pucci. "Wait a sec. So you're not a Lorde?"

"Most women with a concussion or three are usually quiet," he mused. "Figures you'd want to chat."

I would've slapped him lightly, but my hand was busy playing with his thick hair. "I'm trying to ignore the pain."

"All right. I was never in a club. We created the cover with the Diablos right before they were patched over by the Lordes, and I took it from there."

I sighed and let my body relax completely. "All right." My voice was sleepy.

He jostled me. "No, you don't. No sleeping until we get your head checked out."

But I was tired. "I'm not sleeping." I sank lower into a meditative state.

He pinched my butt. "Stay awake. Keep talking."

I frowned but didn't open my eyes. "Fine. You were working with the Lordes and trying to take down their drug operation, which you did."

"Yeah, and during that investigation, we discovered Rich Pucci and his side business. So after we disbanded most of the Lordes, I recruited a few new members, most of whom work for the ATF. We then set up this undercover op to infiltrate and work with Rich Pucci." He turned suddenly, and I opened my eyes to see a trail between trees. "That leads us to today and what happened to get you here."

I snuggled into him more, although it wasn't easy with the tactical vest in my way. "I was in court, and then Pucci smashed my head against the truck and here we are." I relented. "You probably need a better statement than that."

"No. I won't be the one to interview you." He ducked beneath some sweeping branches. "Considering our relationship, somebody else will take your statement *in the hospital*." The last was said firmly.

My head hurt badly enough that I didn't argue. What was our relationship exactly? Where did Aiden live when he wasn't pretending to be a gun-toting criminal who sold drugs, ran guns, and hung out with murderers? Where did he want to live? Was there an ATF unit close by? I didn't think so.

"Are you still awake?" His hand was precariously close to my butt, which I had no doubt he'd pinch again.

"Yes. I was just thinking." The thoughts ran through my head, and even though it hurt, I dropped into legal thinking. "Are you a good agent?"

"I do all right." He ducked beneath branches again and stepped out into the clearing. Several of Pucci's soldiers were being loaded into a dark sheriff's van with their hands zip-tied behind their backs. Agents moved around, going through different trucks and storage bins.

I tugged on his hair. "I'm not looking for you to be arrogant. I want to know if you have a good reputation."

"I do. Solid. Why?"

"Because you're a solid ATF agent, one who just took down a major illegal gun manufacturing operation as well as a drug distribution gang, so you probably have some juice." The world was looking up right now. Big time. I smiled.

"So?"

I leaned back so I could see his pretty blue eyes. "So? You're the perfect person to clear Tessa. If you say she arrived at her apartment after Danny Pucci had been shot, then you're an excellent reference. See?"

"Yeah. I see." He pressed a kiss to my nose. "I'll make sure to add my official title to my statement with the police."

Perfect. It was just perfect. With that thought, I finally let the darkness take me. The last thing I heard before unconsciousness totally won was Aiden calling my name.

He had such a nice voice.

$\mathcal{I}$ woke up in the hospital, not for the first time this summer. Something beeped and my arm hurt. I looked to the side to see Aiden sprawled in a chair, his head back and his eyes shut. He wore an ATF T-shirt, black cargo pants, and a gun strapped to his thigh. It was a good look on him.

Slowly, he lowered his head and opened his eyes as if knowing I was looking at him. He had great instincts. "How's the head?"

I gingerly pressed on my forehead. "Okay. How long was I out?"

"Long enough." He rubbed through the scruff on his angled jaw. Dawn peeked in through the blinds behind him, sliding into the room with more than a hint of the summer heat to come.

A doctor poked his head in, and I didn't recognize him. "You're awake. I'm the on call doc. Dr. Springfield." He strode inside and checked me out, his hands and tone gentle. He had to be in his mid-sixties with a neatly trimmed white beard that matched his short hair. "Your pupils look good and have excellent response."

So long as they continued to keep an eye on Aiden, I didn't care. "Did he have his chest checked out?"

The doctor looked over his shoulder at Aiden. "No. Are you injured?"

"No." Aiden lifted his shirt to reveal his stone hard chest and abs, which were marred by three deep purple bruises with interesting striations of color spreading out from the middle.

The doctor craned his neck to see better. "Bullet-proof vest?"

"Yep." Aiden dropped the shirt.

"All right. Anna, I'd like for you to stay a couple more hours, and then you can be discharged with orders." He tapped notes into a tablet and turned on what looked like hiking boots for the door.

I sat more fully up and pushed my hair out of my eyes. "Where's my family?" It was shocking that nobody had arrived yet.

Aiden remained in his relaxed position with his legs extended. "I didn't call anybody. Three of Pucci's guys weren't at the compound, and while I don't think you're in danger, we're keeping you locked down until they're found." He rolled his neck.

Heavy footsteps preceded Saber arriving at the door and then smiling. "Hey. You're awake. How's the head?"

"Pretty good," I said, liking him more than ever now that I knew he wasn't a criminal. In fact, he was pretty cute. Maybe I should introduce him to Donna if Bud didn't get off his butt and make a move.

"Good." He focused on Aiden. "Hey, boss. We found the three missing BGC members buying drugs in east Spokane, and they're all locked down right now. We rounded them all up." He shrugged. "Or we shot them. Either way, she's safe."

"Nice job." Aiden stretched to his feet like a lazy lion.

More footsteps sounded and Detective Grant Pierce stormed into the room, elbowing Saber to the side. "Anna? You okay?" Tension rolled off him in palpable waves.

"Yep," I said.

He looked me over and then turned toward Aiden. "Are you fucking kidding me?"

Aiden sighed.

Pierce set his hand on the butt of the gun at his waist. "You're a Special Agent in Charge of an ATF SRT?"

Wow. That sounded pretty impressive. "What's SRT?" I asked.

"Special Response Teams," Aiden and Saber said at the same time.

Then Aiden stepped toward Pierce. "Yeah. I am. Sorry you can't arrest me."

Pierce took a step toward Aiden. "Me, too. Have you ever heard of professional courtesy? That if the ATF is conducting an op in a local jurisdiction that they let the locals in on the action? You know? So we don't accidentally shoot them?"

"It was a three-year op," Aiden said.

Pierce lowered his chin and looked every bit as pissed off as he sounded. "I want the guys you rounded up at the camp. Unlike you, I still have a crime to solve."

Aiden's expression didn't change. In fact, it didn't reveal anything. "Not a problem. They'll be made available to you as soon as we're done processing them. I am more than happy to work with local authorities, Pierce."

Pierce pivoted to look at me. "I need to interview you."

"Not yet," Aiden said. "She needs rest."

"She can speak for herself," I said quietly. "I'm fine being interviewed, Grant. It might be better while it's all fresh in my mind." Especially the part about clearing my sister of the murder.

Pierce took a notepad out of his shirt pocket and moved to claim Aiden's vacated seat.

More footsteps announced the arrival of another person, and Nick barreled into the room. "What the hell, Anna? Are you okay?"

"I'm fine. I don't work for you any longer," I reminded him. Even so, it was nice he'd shown up.

His brown eyes narrowed. "I know, but even so, as the prosecuting attorney of Elk County, I'd like to interview you about this."

I swept my arm toward the other vacant chair since Saber had decided to lean against the wall. "Join the club." Maybe I could call Tessa to come and see me.

Aiden looked my face over and his jaw tightened. "Are you sure you're up to this?"

"Yes," I said.

"Then Saber is going to stay and interview you for the ATF," Aiden said. "At least about the kidnapping and your dealings with Pucci."

Saber nodded. "I already was interviewed about the shooting. I think they're waiting for you, anyway. We're using the police station's conference room."

The sound Pierce made reminded me of a ticked off grizzly bear. They had a distinct snapping sound of frustration when they tried to intimidate other animals away from food sources. He looked at me and his gaze softened. "Are you sure you're up to this? We could wait until later."

"I'm fine. Let's do this." I kept the blanket covering me in the hospital gown.

Aiden reached the doorway. "Call me when you're released and I'll take you home, Angel." Then he was gone.

Saber grinned, making his almost black eyes dance. "He's a charmer, right?"

"Right." I settled my hands on the blanket. "What's your real name, anyway?"

"Saber," he said. "Well, that's my last name. My real name is James Saber. It's easy to have an undercover name when it's really your name."

Now that made sense. "Okay. Let me have it. When we're finished, Grant, please go interview Aiden in his capacity as an ATF agent about Danny's death. His word should carry some weight that my sister arrived at her apartment after Danny was shot."

"Fine," Grant said. "For now, start at the beginning."

* * *

THE GRAPEVINE GOT to my family before I could call anybody, and by the time I was released from the hospital, more and more people kept arriving. I let Tessa drive me to Donna's house where we met my parents, grandparents, and too many aunts and uncles to count. We ate a bunch of pizzas delivered from McQuirk's, and everyone babied me for more than my share of time. It was awesome.

Donna sat next to me on her sofa, finishing her pizza. "I can't believe Aiden is with the ATF. I hope he knows what he's in for with the family now that he's on the right side of the law."

I glanced to the side to see Tessa arm wrestling Uncle Sean. "I say we fix Tessa up with Nick. They're a good pair."

Donna reached for her wine off the coffee table. "If you're talking to me about it, you already approached Nonna Albertini. Let her take the reins. Tessa won't kill her, unlike you."

That was fair advice. I ate quietly and then approached Uncle Sean after he'd let Tessa beat him, which was an impossible feat considering his muscle. Uncle Sean was tough. He was also a very successful businessperson, and I had a bunch of questions for him. We had a great chat.

My phone buzzed and I looked down to see that Aiden was calling. Trying to be as casual as possible, I slipped outside to Donna's vacant front porch and sat on the steps. "Hi."

"Hi. Sorry I couldn't pick you up at the hospital." It sounded like there was a lot of wind in the background, which didn't make any sense.

"No problem. Want to meet at my place?" I asked, wanting to ask him so many questions I couldn't catalog them all.

The wind grew louder. "I can't, Angel. I have to head to the Seattle Field Office for a debriefing, and it'll probably take all weekend. I promise I'll return Monday night and we can have that talk then."

That talk? What talk? I was glad I was sitting. "Are you based out of Seattle?"

"No. Los Angeles," he said, and there was shouting in the background. Not angry shouting but shouting over an engine?

"Where are you?"

"Fairchild Air Force Base," he said, sounding farther away than that. "I'm catching a ride to Seattle."

I really didn't want him to go. It was like if he left, then it was all done. I didn't want it to be all done. "You're not going to head undercover again and not say a word, are you?" It was like something out of a movie. One with a crappy ending.

"No." He chuckled. "I'm just going to Seattle. I'll call you when I land Monday night. Bye."

"Bye," I said softly, turning as Pauley came out to the porch and sat next to me.

He tapped on his pants in his usual rhythm and watched something I couldn't see. "That was Aiden?"

"Yes. He has to go to Seattle to the field office, whatever that is," I said, my chest aching just enough to give me pause. "I hope he comes back."

"Did he say he would come back?" Pauley leaned down to make sure his tennis shoes were double knotted.

I nodded. "Yeah. I should look to see if there are any field offices here."

"There's one in Spokane," Pauley said. "I don't think it's full time, though." He sat perfectly straight and watched a ladybug crawl across the freshly cut grass. "I looked it up when Tessa told me Aiden worked for the ATF SRT."

"Oh." It figured Pauley would get to it before I could. "What did you find out?"

He set his hands on his knees. "There are five locations for the SRTs. Los Angeles, Dallas, Miami, DC, and Detroit. At least, that's what I found on the Internet. My guess is that Aiden is out of Los Angeles?"

"Yeah." I rubbed my stomach. "There's no base close to here?"

"No." Pauley blinked into the sunny day. "I texted Aiden and asked him how he started working for the ATF. I might want to do that someday, but it would be in intelligence and not tactical."

I leaned back. "You and Aiden text each other?"

"Yes. Sometimes. He started texting me after you and I got kidnapped in June, and I text him back sometimes. We just check in." Pauley started tapping again. "He was in the marines, was discharged, and went to work for the ATF. I find that impressive. You should not give up on him even if you have to live in different cities."

"What makes you think I won't move?" I asked.

Pauley thought about it. "Your family is here."

Yeah. My family was right here. Aiden was not. I sighed. "Let's go back inside and see if your dad wants to arm wrestle me this time."

My phone buzzed and my heart leapt. Was it Aiden? "Hello?"

"Hi Anna, it's Saber. Boy, do I have some news for you. There was an award for putting Rich Pucci away. Congrats."

CHAPTER 38

*a*fter a weekend of being babied by my entire family, I was grateful that Monday morning came finally. I dressed down in white capri's and a frilly blouse to deliver the papers regarding Pucci's death and subsequent dismissal of the case against him. While I hadn't lost my first trial, having my client kidnap me before being shot to death by my boyfriend probably didn't belong in the win column.

If Aiden was my boyfriend. It wasn't like he'd called during the weekend.

I drove down Main Street and parked in front of the three-story building where Cousin Wanda had her office.

Clark was waiting on the sidewalk for me. "Why are we meeting here?"

"I'll show you." I walked inside the cool interior and up the old fashioned stairs to the third floor. Then I moved down the hallway to the second door on the right, reached in my purse for the keys, and pushed it open.

"What have you done?" Clark followed me inside the dusty space and instantly sneezed.

I looked around, seeing the dust mites sparkle like diamonds from the sunlight streaming between the blinds. "It's our new office. The Bunne & Albertini Law Firm." I twirled around. "This is obviously the reception area." Dusty boxes littered the filthy floor, and the wallpaper peeled in several sections. I moved to the doorway beyond the reception area. "Come on. There are supposed to be two offices."

Clark sneezed again and then followed me. "This is crazy."

We came to one office that had a nice view of the street outside with a tree by the window to the left. To the right was an empty conference room with wide double doors. Beyond that were a kitchenette and bathroom. The final office was past that on the left, and it too had wide windows that looked out onto Main Street with mature trees. "The other office," I breathed.

Clark looked around. "Okay. It's pretty nice. How much does it cost?"

"That's the beauty," I said, giving him the good news. "The ATF called, and we actually got a reward for helping to take down Pucci. Well, I earned a reward, but since I got you fired, I figured we did. It's ten thousand dollars, and that's enough to get us started. My uncle owns this building and won't charge us rent for three months because this is vacant. We have to do this, Clark. What do you say?"

He looked tempted. Dust settled on his still bald head, and he wiped it off. "I'm thinking."

That was good. I tended to jump right in, and he was more cautious. We'd make a great team. My phone buzzed and I read the screen. "This is about our first client." I set the phone to my ear. "This is Anna Albertini."

"Hi. It's Alice at the prosecuting attorney's office. You called?"

"Yes." I kept my tone professional. "I'd like to talk to you about a plea for Oliver Duck on the trespass case. He was just a kid goofing off, Alice. Would you give him a break?"

She sighed. "Kids like that should be taught a lesson. So, here's the plea. A thousand dollars and six months in prison."

I blinked. "Are you kidding me?"

"Nope. Take it or leave it," she said. "I won the trial against Pucci. Are you sure you want to try again?"

Oh, she hadn't won. Irritation clawed up my still aching neck. "Definitely. I'll talk to my client, but I'm going to advise him to reject your offer." I clicked off. "What a jerk."

Clark put his hands in his pockets. "All right. I'm in."

I leaped for him in a hug, and then we both sneezed. "All right. I'm off to earn our first penny." It probably wasn't a good idea to tell Clark that I meant that literally. But I couldn't keep the finances from him since we were about to be partners. "Also, our first client is working off his fee, so he can help us clean up this place. And I thought we'd hire my cousin Pauley to answer the phones and conduct some research. He's brilliant. Literally."

Clark looked a little befuddled.

I tossed him his set of keys. "We're having a party for Uncle Sean's birthday Tuesday night at mom and dad's over in the valley. You're his favorite golfing partner and now his tenant, so you should come."

Clark made a gurgling sound.

I kept talking like I hadn't noticed. "We should get letterhead and business cards. And hats. We definitely need hats with a cool BA logo on them." Before Clark could back out, I hustled to the door and all but ran down the hallway and out of the building. This was going to work out. I just knew it. Now, if I could get my personal life on track, life would be good.

Exiting the building, I almost ran into Tessa. "Hey. What are you doing here?" I caught her by the arms.

Her eyes burned, and her cheeks were a bright crimson. "I called Cousin Wanda for a session. You wouldn't believe what a complete ass Nick Basanelli is."

I gulped. "He is?"

"Yes." She looked like she wanted to stomp her foot. "I figured that Aiden's signed affidavit would get me off the suspect list in

Danny's death, but Nick refuses to drop the charges right now. Something about a fingerprint on the toilet. For Pete's sake. Danny fixed the toilet eons ago when we were dating, the fingerprint is near the twisty thing on the wall, and I read that prints can last for years. I am so mad at that jackass."

Her temper really was glorious. "Did you tell him that?"

She emphatically nodded and her eyes were fire-filled emerald. "I did. I stopped by just to make sure I was off the list, and actually, I was going to ask him to grab a coffee after he said yes. Can you believe that?"

Man, she really was pretty. I tried not to smile. "Then you yelled at him?" Looking like this?" Looking absolutely glorious, in fact.

"I did."

"What did he do?" I asked.

She blinked. "Nothing. He just sat there looking kind of stunned. I don't think people yell at him very often."

Yeah, that was it. Not. I smiled and patted her arm. "Everything will be okay, Tess." Yes! I made a mental note to call Nonna Albertini to ramp up our plan.

* * *

I DROVE AWAY from town and my phone buzzed. "Albertini," I answered. Yeah. I liked that. Now that I owned my own law office, I'd answer with my last name.

"It's Grant. How's your head?"

I smiled. "Detective Pierce. It's kind of you to call. I'm a little achy, but all right overall. Thanks for checking in."

"That's not the only reason I called," he said.

Yeah, I already figured that. Pierce was a good guy but not exactly empathetic. "What's up?"

"Just wanted to give you a heads up that the fingerprint on the bullet that killed Danny Pucci matched one of the guys caught up in the ATF raid. I'm having him brought in later today for questioning. All I know is that his name is Spark. What a dumb name."

Relief felt nice and cool through my heated skin. "What time?"

"The feds are delivering him around three. You're welcome to watch the interview because I know you will, anyway. Just be careful until then, all right?" Paper shuffled in the background. "I'm not sure we've caught all of the BGC men yet, and more than one will want a little revenge for the death of Pucci. They had that whole brotherhood thing going on, and most of it seems illegal."

The hair rose at the back of my neck. "So long as you have Spark's twin brother, we're fine."

Silence came from him.

My heart sank. "You don't have Rhino?" God, what a terrible name.

Pierce audibly flipped over papers. "No. I have the mugshots and names, and there's no Rhino or guy who looks like Spark. I'll let the ATF know he's still out there. For now, keep out of sight."

My great day was turning crappy. "You think I'm in danger?"

"I don't know. Between the ATF and us, we'll have everybody even remotely linked to BGC caught up in a net very soon, so just stay under the radar if you can. I know it'll be difficult." Sarcasm came naturally to Pierce. "I'll let you watch the interrogation if you then go under until I say it's safe to come up for air. Deal?"

I twisted my lip and thought it over. "Deal. After the interrogation, I'll head over to my parent's house for the rest of the week. But that's it. Today is Monday, and I'll give you the week." I could order furniture and office supplies while relaxing at my mom's. "All right?"

"Yeah. We'll have them before that." He disengaged the call.

I looked down at my phone. That man never said goodbye. Rolling my eyes, I reached for the address and asked Siri to give me a hand finding it. My Siri had a male Australian accent, and he quite kindly directed me to my destination. The entry to the farm was out in the vicinity of Walker's Funeral Home, and I navigated it easily until reaching a private drive with a square log entryway.

Flower beds overflowing with weeds lined the drive up to the white clapboard house, while fields extended in two directions, dotted with cows. It was peaceful and pretty, except for the neglected flowers.

I took a deep breath and parked my car near the steps to the wraparound porch. Cheerful yellow cushions covered the porch swing.

A man stepped out onto the porch, his hair grizzly, his overalls stained, and his expression grumpy. "Who are you?" He wiped down what looked like some sort of engine part with a dirty rag.

"Mr. McLerrison? I'm Anna Albertini, and I represent Oliver Duck. He's the kid who rode his dirt bike on your land?"

McLerrison kept wiping off oil. His eyes were a faded blue, and laugh lines extended out, but it was hard to imagine him as happy. "I know who he is. I had him arrested."

"I know." I smiled and tried to use charm, but it didn't seem to be working. "I'd like to ask you to drop the charges."

"Why would I do that?" McLerrison asked. "The kid damaged the dirt right by my pond. He deserves a slap on the wrist."

I jumped at the language. "True, but the prosecutor has lost her mind and wants to get him prison time. Like real prison time." I moved toward him. "This is a good kid who lost his uncle, who was his only relative, a year ago and is alone. He feels awful about your land and was going to plead guilty until I pushed up next to him to keep him from going away for five years." Although, now that I'd had time to really think about it, the judge wouldn't have let that happen. He probably had been about to order someone to represent the kid, and I just got there first.

McLerrison frowned. "How'd he afford you?"

"He gave me a penny." For the first time, the man's lips twitched. "And he insisted on working off the fee. I figured maybe he could work for you for a while? The flower beds could use some tending, and he could use a friend. A good example."

McLerrison's eyes softened. "I lost my Twillie two years ago and haven't had time to work on the flower beds." He studied me. "All right. I'll call and drop the charges, but that kid needs to be here tomorrow morning at five. No later. Got it?"

Oh, thank goodness. "Yes. You're the best, and thank you." I made a mental note to bring him some cheesecake the following week when I was back in town. "I think you'll be good for him." Maybe Oliver would be good for the old farmer, too.

"All right. Drive carefully out of here. The turkeys are running wild."

"Okay." I smiled and returned to my car, driving very carefully out of there. Once I reached the main road, I put my car in neutral and called Oliver.

The kid was overjoyed at the turn of events and couldn't wait to be at the farm in the morning. Yeah, I was patting myself on the back. Then I sat there and planned what to pack to stay with my folks.

The idea of Rhino out there made me shiver. Sometimes morons were more dangerous than smart criminals. The language he'd used about women being BGC Property still made me nauseous. I quickly dialed Kelsey and held my breath until she finally answered.

"It's Anna," I said quickly. "Rhino is still out and is definitely dangerous. Are you okay?"

"I'm fine," she said, sounding tired. "The doors are locked, and I have a gun under my bed. I'm taking the day off." She sounded drugged but calm.

"What did you take?" I asked.

"Valium. Night, Anna." She hung up.

I shook my head. That woman needed help. I looked toward the private drive to the Walker Funeral Home. Did Krissy have the tattoo as well? If so, she could be in danger. Setting the car in drive, I made a right turn to go give her a heads up.

Then I'd go home, see my mom, and figure out what to do with Aiden.

If he returned to Idaho.

CHAPTER 39

The funeral home was quiet except for a loading truck over to the side. I walked into the front reception area to see Krissy at the desk, rifling through the calming cream file folders. She looked up. "Remind me to give my sister a raise. The paperwork on this side of it is a pain." Today she wore the scrubs again and looked all professional with her hair up, although the bruises had gotten even deeper across her pretty face.

I faltered. "Hey, I talked to the police, and Rhino is out on the loose, so I wanted to give you a heads up to watch out for him. Maybe he's fled the jurisdiction, but he definitely had a hard on for any woman involved with the BGC group."

She blew out air. "Wonderful. Rhino is on the loose. That guy is nuts."

I totally agreed. The woman was too pale. "How are you feeling, Krissy?"

She set the files down and pushed a wayward strand of hair out of her eyes. "My face hurts and I'm not sure how I feel about Rich. I think it's my fault he's dead."

"No." I rushed forward. "It's not your fault. He made his choices."

She sighed. "Yeah, but if I wouldn't have lost it on the stand in court, then he wouldn't have wanted to run, and everything wouldn't have exploded. I loved him. But he beat the crap out of me. This is all so confusing because I'm not that woman, you know?"

I nodded. "What you need is a vacation. Let's plan that trip to the coast." I'd made a new friend, and she needed some help.

The door to the display area opened, and a man dressed in overalls poked his head in. "We have almost all of the coffins loaded up and will be done in a few. Does the plain pine one with the embossed flowers go?"

"Yes," Krissy said, stiffening. "Thanks."

The guy disappeared. He was kind of cute with a goatee and firm build. Maybe there was hope for Krissy after all. He seemed decent, and she was blushing a little bit.

"Want to grab lunch?" I asked.

"I would, but I have to get this finished." She gestured to the paperwork.

I tried to think of a way to suggest she ask the hot guy to lunch. "Why are you getting rid of coffins?"

"They were faulty. Can you believe it? The seal wasn't working." Now she sounded disgusted. "Can't anybody do what they're supposed to these days?"

I gave her a sympathetic smile. "Give me a call when things calm down, and we'll plan that trip." I turned to head to lunch.

The door opened again, and another man walked through.

Then everything happened in slow motion. My brain clocked him, reality hit, and I yanked my gun out of my purse and pointed it right at Rhino. "Krissy? Get behind me."

Rhino stepped back and then his chin jutted forward. "Well. If it isn't the bitch who's too good for everyone."

Krissy looked up and between us. "What's going on?" She pushed to her feet and the bruises along her arm scrunched. "Rhino? What are you doing here?"

"Behind me, Krissy," I ordered, keeping the gun level. "Then call the police. Right now."

Rhino apparently found his balls because he took a step toward me. "I don't think you'll shoot me."

"The last guy who said that ended up with lead in him," I gritted out, widening my stance for better balance. "I've been training with a gun since I was strong enough to hold one. Don't think for a second I couldn't put one between your eyes." Even so, I aimed for center mass as I'd been taught. "You're a jackass, Rhino, and my day would vastly improve if you give me reason to shoot you." He'd obviously shown up to take Krissy, since she probably had that stupid tattoo.

Okay. The police should be there in fifteen minutes or so. "Call 9-1-1, Krissy."

"Yeah. That's not going to happen." The barrel of a gun pressed against my lower spine.

I blinked. Confusion rioted through me. "Krissy? Rhino is the bad guy. What are you doing?"

She sighed. "Rhino? Lock the front door." Then she pushed me with the gun. "Drop your gun, Anna. I haven't been training for long, but I'm pretty sure I could cause some damage with a bullet to the spine. Certain of it, actually."

I lowered my weapon as realization slapped me. "What are you doing?"

"Walk into the display room," she ordered, prodding me with the barrel. "Rhino? I said to lock the door." The snap in her voice made me jump.

Rhino grabbed my gun and then moved past us to lock the door. I stumbled into the coffin display room and tried to wrap my head around the fact that Krissy Walker had a gun in my back. The display coffins were in place, and only two of the newer ones that I'd seen last time still remained. The shrink wrap had been removed.

"Sit down." Krissy shoved me.

I tripped and sat down next to a display coffin. "I can't believe this."

She smiled, and with her bruises, the sight was ghastly. "Oh, I'm sure."

The cute guy came into the room and looked at the situation. Any hope I had that he'd help me out disappeared when he turned back to Krissy like I wasn't even there. "We're all loaded up. The buyer is ready to take delivery at eight tonight, so we need to get on the road."

I blinked. "Delivery? Oh, Krissy." Facts from the other day at the compound ran through my brain. "You have the other half of the converter shipment."

"Yeah." She laughed. "The converters are made up of three tiny metal pieces that you attach to a Glock that turns the weapon into an automatic. It's so simple."

"You deliver illegal goods in coffins," I murmured. It was brilliant, actually. Coffins as a delivery system.

Rhino came back into the room.

Krissy continued. "It's also an efficient way to transport rifles and explosives because of the shrink wrap. Inspectors rarely want the mess of unwrapping everything to get a peek."

Rhino looked me up and down. "Please tell me I get to have some fun before you put her in the oven."

Oh, God. My stomach lurched. The cremation oven?

Krissy motioned toward the door with the gun. "Not this time, Rhino. You guys have to get on the road. Now."

He grimaced but ambled toward the doorway. "Fine. We'll call you from Seattle." Then he was gone.

"You're completely in charge," I murmured, shocked that Rhino had just left that easily.

"I know," Krissy said, her plain tennis shoes shiny clean. "This is a great front, and believe it or not, selling illegal weapons is much more lucrative than funerals." Now that the truth was out, she seemed to want to talk.

I looked for anything that could be used as a weapon in the room. "I had no clue you were involved," I admitted, trying to keep her talking. "The whole battered woman farce worked well." Then I paused and stared at her. "Wait a minute. In court, did you try to send Rich up the river on purpose? With your testimony?"

Her laugh was low, and then tears filled her eyes. "I love him, you know? Yeah, he beat the crap out of me, bu-bu-but we're going to work it out." She laughed harder.

"Wow." So much surprise filled me that it might've been shock.

She preened. "I know."

I thought back to my discussion with Pucci. "He said you started the fight the night before."

She rolled her eyes. "I had to scratch him twice before he'd even push me. Oh, don't get me wrong. That dick had no problem hitting a woman and had done so before. But yeah, I set him up. Him going to prison would've made things a lot easier for me. Of course, your boyfriend shooting him in the head worked just as well."

Aiden could've died. I could've died. "You are such a bitch," I said, my body tensing to attack.

"That's just not nice." She flicked her wrist to read her watch. "We're going to have to make this quick. I told Kelsey I'd bring her lunch."

I tried to focus and not drop into a panic attack. "Is Kelsey in on any of this?"

"Of course not," Krissy scoffed. "Kelsey has never been able to deal with reality. She actually loved that moron Danny, if that tells you anything."

Danny. I'd forgotten all about him. "You really disliked him." I ran through the entire case. "Did you get in a fight with him in a bar?"

She laughed, and the sound was tinkly. "You mean when his neck got scratched? Yeah, that was me. The idiot told Kelsey that your sister had scratched him, and since I didn't want her mad at me, I didn't tell her the truth."

Wow. What a wench. Wait a minute. Just how bad of a person was Krissy? I tilted my head and just stared at her.

Her smile was catlike. "Yes."

My mouth dropped open. No way. "*You* killed Danny?"

She chuckled. "First, he hit my sister. Second, he figured out I was the one who'd taken the other half of the shipment. He threatened to tell Rich if I didn't split the extra money with him. So much for family loyalty. That guy deserved to be put down."

I levered up onto my knees and threw my arms out like I was angry. "Why did you kill him in Tessa's apartment? Why get her involved?"

She kept the gun pointed at my head. "I slipped Kelsey's phone from her at the concert and texted him that she wanted to keep him and figured out how. That she'd talked to Tessa, and they wanted to have a threesome. Can you believe it?"

"No," I said. "He wasn't that dumb." Yet he probably was.

"I knew he kept trying to get back together with Tessa because Kelsey cried about it every freaking night."

Even more anger started to uncoil inside me. "So you killed him there to cause Tessa problems? It wasn't her fault."

"Yeah, but the fact that she exists hurt my sister, and it was an easy way to get Danny where I wanted him. Your sister had left her window open, and the fire escape was close enough to climb in, so I just opened the door when he got there. Then I shot him." Krissy sounded matter of fact now. "I had to get out of there fast, and I went back to the concert."

The woman would have no problem shooting me, apparently. "Danny didn't have time to use the toilet, so his fingerprint must've been there from a year before." Another mystery solved.

"Hell if I know," Krissy said, taking aim. "I'm sorry about this. You really tried to help me."

"My car and phone are here," I reminded her. "I'm traceable.

Don't do this. Let's voluntarily contact the police, and I'll defend you."

She looked at me like I was nuts. "Um, no. How about I shoot you, burn the evidence, and drive your car and phone out to the Lordes apartment complex? Your disappearance will be a mystery."

The woman was a freakin criminal mastermind. "My family won't stop with the search, and you know it."

She gestured me up with the gun. "Yeah, but nobody is going to look at me. Come on. I can't shoot you here. Let's go downstairs."

"Seriously?" I didn't move. "You want me to meekly walk down to the crematorium and just let you shoot me? Should I climb in the oven first?"

"That'd be great," she said. "Thanks."

My legs went rigid. "No."

"If you don't, I'm going to have fun shooting you. First the ears, then the knees, and then your boobs." She licked her lips.

I blinked. What kind of woman shot another woman in the boobs? Fear made me lightheaded and I fought to stay calm. "Fine." I started to rise and then lunged for her, ducking my head.

She fired and pain blew across my shoulder. I hit her mid center, and we crashed into the coffin on the floor, sending it careening toward the wall. Panic full on took hold of me, and I punched and clawed, grunting with the effort to get the gun out of her hands.

Her scream pierced the day and almost froze me in place. She swung the gun around, and I punched her square in the wrist. The weapon flew out of her hand to dent the coffin on the stand. Then she clipped me in the forehead with her knuckles, and my still damaged forehead exploded in pain.

I fell back.

She jumped for me, and I kicked up, nailing her beneath the

chin. Going on instinct again, I rolled and tackled her against the coffin. She landed with a pained oof.

Then in a move I'd learned from her dead boyfriend, I grabbed her head by the hair, lifted it, and smashed it back down on the coffin. Twice. She yelped and her eyelids fluttered shut. Grunting more, I yanked her to the side, opened the coffin and shoved her inside.

I ran into the other room and grabbed my purse, quickly returning to sit on the coffin and dial Detective Pierce to explain the situation. He immediately called in reinforcements and promised to be there in record time. I clicked off the call to press both hands on the coffin on either side of my hips.

Krissy started screaming and kicking the lid, and I pushed my feet down on the tiled floor to keep my balance and not fall off.

My phone buzzed, and I fumbled for it with one hand. "Hello," I grunted, trying to listen for sirens outside.

"Hi, Angel. It looks like I'm going to be out of town for a few extra days. Have to fly to DC for a more extensive debriefing," Aiden said. "Also, I heard that Rhino is on the loose, so please stay low until we catch up with him."

I struggled to keep the lid on the coffin and glanced at the top of my bleeding shoulder. "Rhino's getting picked up as we speak, and I was wondering if you knew how much oxygen was in a coffin."

Aiden was silent for a second. "No. Why?"

Sirens finally trilled in the distance. "Just curious." Krissy kept kicking, so I figured she could breathe. I sighed at my bloody shoulder. "It looks like I got burned by another bullet." Darn it. I really liked that shirt.

CHAPTER 40

$\mathcal{I}$ sat in the shade at my usual table by the river at the family Sunday barbecue next to Pauley, who finished reading the front page expose about Pucci, Krissy, and the illegal gun operation.

"This is a good picture of you," Pauley said, setting the paper aside.

I glanced down at it. Last week after I'd called Pierce, the media had arrived with the cops, and the photographer had caught a snap of me still sitting on the coffin before Pierce had ushered him out. "Yeah, but Jolene made me sound like a creepy coffin lady." Although she'd had to give me props for taking down Krissy, the article was mostly positive. Even better, it mentioned that I was with the Bunne & Albertini Law Firm. Once we got phones, we'd hopefully have calls. If Krissy called searching for a defense lawyer, I'd hang up on her, however. That woman deserved jail time, and there was no way I'd defend her. Ever.

I sighed and moved the food around on my plate.

Pauley looked my way. "Has Aiden not called?"

"No." Would he call? I'd had more than one bad thought about him being undercover again and not making contact for another ten years. The thought made everything inside me hurt like I'd been gutted like a trout. I must really look miserable for Pauley to guess what was wrong with me.

"That is too bad." Today Pauley wore his customary white shirt and beige pants. Our table was toward the river in my folks' backyard, set off slightly from the hustle and bustle, and beneath a sweeping tree that provided shade. There were three chairs, and different people joined us different days.

Tessa moved our way, fury in her eyes.

"Uh oh," Pauley said, looking down at his chicken salad on a paper plate.

She stormed up. "I can *not* believe you did this to me."

I opened my eyes really wide. "What? I didn't invite him." I looked over to where Nick Basanelli and his grandma ate at a long picnic table along with our Nonna Albertini. "Nonna and his Grams are old friends who play Bridge every week," I said. "This is her doing." Since Tessa would never mess with Nonna, I didn't feel bad about throwing her under the bus.

Tessa faltered. "Oh. Sorry."

"Contessa Fiona," Nonna called out. "Come eat. I saved you a spot." Right next to her and across from Nick.

I barely kept from smiling. It was difficult, but I did it.

Tessa rolled her eyes, plastered on a smile, and turned to walk toward the table.

"I do not know how, but I have no doubt you engineered that situation," Pauley observed, eating his salad once again. "Tessa has a temper and likes getting revenge. You should remember that."

"If she ends up happy, then she won't want revenge," I said reasonably. My gaze caught on Uncle Sean and Clark near a tree with a pad of paper stuck to it by an arrow. They diagrammed, sat back, discussed wildly, and then drew more on the paper. "I'd go save Clark, but he looks as engrossed as Uncle Sean."

Pauley looked up. "They are planning next week's tournament up in Sandpoint."

I frowned. "How do you plan a golf tournament? You hit the ball and try to get it in the hole."

Pauley turned back to his food, obviously finished with the conversation.

A slight twittering came from the kitchen, and then Aiden walked out onto the deck with Donna smiling at his side. My mom, the ultimate hostess, immediately stood to greet him. He held out a bouquet of flowers for her.

I gaped and my heart went all mushy. "Aiden brought my mom flowers."

Pauley looked up. "Aiden brought your Irish mom Irish roses."

Oh, I melted right then and there.

Mom and Donna escorted Aiden to the buffet table and started piling food on a plate. He looked over his shoulder at me, his eyes pleading for help, but I just smiled. Yeah, he should've called.

"You should rescue him," Pauley advised.

"Ha. He's a big and tough ATF Special Agent in Charge. He can handle it," I said, liking how his ears turned red.

When they brought him over to my table, there was a promise of retribution in his eyes. Instead of giving me warning, it intrigued me and might've turned me on a little. "Welcome back," I said.

"Thanks." He took the third chair and accepted the napkin from my mom. "Thank you, Mrs. O'Shea."

She patted his shoulder. "It's Moira, Aiden. You know that." She barely kept the hop out of her step as she walked across the grassy yard to her table.

"The flowers were a nice touch," I said.

"Hi, Aiden," Pauley said.

Aiden smiled. "Hi, Pauley. Heard you got a job at Anna's firm. You sure you want that kind of danger?" He looked pointedly at the bandage poking out of my shirt from my shoulder wound.

Pauley smiled and put his napkin on his plate. "Probably not. Now I am going to play X-Box with Donna. Bye." He stood and maneuvered his way back into the house.

My dad made it five minutes before coming over to shake Aiden's hand. My dad was a miner, and a miner could break a hand with a shake. Aiden made it through without wincing, and by the end of the extra-long shake, there was respect shining in my dad's eyes. He handed Aiden a beer, welcomed him to dinner, and returned to where my mom was glaring at him to leave us alone.

Aiden twisted the top off the beer. "I've been in combat situations that were safer than this."

I laughed, feeling free and happy. Very happy. Oh, life would get complicated with the new business, but today was Sunday and I'd worry about that on Monday. I already had Oliver Duck on the schedule to help us clean out the office. Right now, I had a hottie ATF agent next to me who was hopefully coming home with me that night. "I'm glad you're here."

Aiden looked at me, and those blue eyes warmed even more. "I'm glad I'm here too. I landed two hours ago and headed right here, figuring you'd be at the family barbecue."

I had to give that to him. He'd shown up in front of both sides of my family. For me. "How long are you staying?"

He took a bite of the twice-baked potatoes and then had a drink of his beer. "I'm on the current assignment for at least a month to gather evidence on the remainder of the Lordes members as well as Pucci's gang. It'll take a week for Drag to stop complaining about being on crutches for a short time."

I sipped my wine. "Then it's back to Los Angeles and going undercover?"

He ate some of the steak and watched my family. "It doesn't have to be. What do you want?"

I wanted him to stay and see what we had or could have, but I wouldn't like it if he asked me to quit my job. "You. If you're in LA and I'm here, then I want the long distance thing for now." My hand shook, so I put down the wine glass. "What do you want?" My nerves jumped all over inside my body.

As if he knew, he reached out and kneaded my nape with his very capable hand. "I'm with you. Let's see if either one of us can manage...us. It's a lot."

That was the understatement of the day. I grinned. "Yeah. Definitely."

His gaze dropped to my bandage again. "Nice job bringing down a murderer on your own, by the way. I didn't suspect Krissy Walker for a second."

"She was good at it all." Hopefully she'd find a nice path in prison. Witch. "Did you get the rest of Pucci's guys?"

"Yeah. They're all off the street, so you're safe. From them, anyway. Who knows what'll come our way next." He ate more of his dinner while leaving his hand nicely on my nape.

I liked that. A lot.

He also seemed to manage warning looks from my dad and hopeful glances from my mom with ease. "Also, I'm working on being stationed out of the Spokane office."

Hope burst through me along with a ridiculous thread of caution. "I thought the closest SRT is out of Los Angeles."

"It is," he said. "There are about 160 full time members, and I have a team within the team. It'd be something new and different, but I think I have enough pull after the last two busts to relocate my team to here. It's by an airport and we can get anywhere across the country from here as easily as from Los Angeles." He tipped back his beer. "I'm trying anyway."

I patted his thigh. "That would be awesome, but I don't want you to change your life for me." Not yet, anyway.

He chuckled. "I'm not asking for anything, Angel. I'm tired of the city and I want to be here, whether or not we work out. My team needs to get out of the city and enjoy some time in the country, and their health is on my shoulders. Everything else, we'll figure out later."

I snuggled into him. It was a start, and like he said, we'd figure it out as we went.

Aiden Devlin was finally home.

ADVERSE POSSESSION

THE ANNA ALBERTINI FILES BOOK 3

Adverse Possession

The plural form of Nemesis is Nemeses

Anna Albertini never thought she'd have to look up the plural form of nemesis. In fact, she never thought she'd have one, much less three. But as she and her new partner try to make a go of their fledgling law firm, enemies come from every direction.

First, there's a newspaper reporter trying to earn a name for herself by dogging Anna's every move. Second, there's a lawyer on the opposite side of every case who just doesn't like Anna. And third, there's Aiden Devlin's ex-girlfriend, who decides to descend upon the sleeping Idaho town like a bird of prey. It's too bad she's discovered dead...after finding herself on the wrong end of a potato gun, putting Anna top of the suspect list.

Anna deals with every day as it arrives while juggling her developing relationship with Aiden, trying to pay her rent by finding at least one client who pays, and finally by partnering with her Nonna Albertini in the world's most chaotic plan to match-make her sister with the Elk County's prosecuting attorney, Nick Basanelli. It's a good thing Anna has learned to thrive in chaos.

PURCHASE where all books are sold: Adverse Possession

HAVE YOU STARTED THE DEEP OPS SERIES YET?

HIDDEN - BOOK 1

Hidden

Chapter 1

The day he moved in next door, dark clouds covered the sky with the promise of a powerful storm. Pippa watched from her window, the one over the kitchen sink, partially hidden by the cheerful polka-dotted curtains. Yellow dots over crisp white background—what she figured happy people would use.

He moved box after box after box through the two-stall garage, all by himself, cut muscles bunching in his arms.

Angles and shadows made up his face, more shadows than angles. He didn't smile, and although he didn't frown, his expression had settled into harsh lines.

A guy like him, dangerously handsome, should probably have friends helping.

Yet he didn't. His black truck, dusty yet seemingly well kept, sat alone in the driveway as he removed the crates.

She swallowed several times, instinctively knowing he wasn't a man to cross, even if she had been a person who crossed others. She was not.

For a while, she tried to amuse herself with counting the boxes, and then guessing the weight, and then just studying the man. He appeared to be in his early thirties, maybe just a few years older than her.

Thick black hair fell to his collar in unruly waves, giving him an unkempt appearance that hinted nobody took care of him. His shoulders were tense yet his body language fluid. She couldn't see his eyes.

The question, the damn wondering, would keep her up at night.

But no way, there was absolutely *no way*, she would venture outside to appease the beast of curiosity.

The new neighbor stood well over six feet tall, his shoulders broad, his long legs encased in worn and frayed jeans. If a man could be hard all over, head to toe, even in movement, then he was.

A scar curved in a half-moon shape over his left eye, and some sort of tattoo, a crest or something, decorated his muscled left bicep. She tilted her head, reaching for the curtains to push them aside a little more.

He paused and turned, much like an animal going on alert, an overlarge box held easily in his arms. Green. Those eyes, narrow and suspicious, alert and dangerous, focused directly on her.

She gasped. Her heart thundered. She fell to the floor below the counter. Not to the side, not even in a crouch, she fell flat on her butt on the well-scrubbed tiles. Her heart ticking, she wrapped her arms around her shins and rested her chin on her knees.

She bit her lip and held her breath, shutting her eyes.

Nothing.

No sound, no hint of an approaching person, no rap on the door. Her throat closed, making it nearly impossible to breathe.

After about ten minutes of holding perfectly still, she lifted her head. Another five and she released her legs. Then she rolled up onto her knees and reached for the counter, her fingers curling over.

Taking a deep breath, she pulled herself to stand, angling to the side of the counter.

He stood at the window, facing her, his chest taking up most of the panes.

Her heart exploded. She screamed, turned, and ran. She cleared the kitchen in three steps and plowed through the living room, smashing into an antique table that had sat in the same place since the day she'd moved in.

Pain ratcheted up her leg, and she dropped, making panicked grunting noises as she crawled past the sofa toward her bedroom. Her hands slapped the polished wooden floor, and she sobbed out, reaching the room and slamming the door.

She yanked her legs up to her chest again, her back to the door, and reached up to engage the lock. She rocked back and forth, careful not to make a sound.

The doorbell rang.

Her chest tightened, and her vision fuzzed. Tremors started from her shoulders down to her waist and back up. *Not now. Not now. God, not now.* She took several deep breaths and acknowledged the oncoming panic attack much as Dr. Valentine had taught her. Sometimes letting the panic in actually abated it.

Not this time.

The attack took her full force, pricking sweat along her body. Her arms shook and her legs went numb. Her breathing panted out, her vision fuzzed, and her heart blasted into motion.

Maybe it really was a heart attack this time.

No. It was only a panic attack.

But it could be a heart attack. Maybe the doctors had missed something in her tests. Or maybe it was a stroke.

She couldn't make it to the phone to dial for help.

Her heart hurt. Her chest really ached. Glancing up at the lock, a flimsy golden thing, she inched away from the door to the bed table on her hands and knees. Jerking open the drawer, she fumbled for a Xanax.

She popped the pill beneath her tongue, letting it quickly absorb. The bitter chalkiness made her gag, but she didn't move until it had dissolved.

A hard, rapping sound echoed from the living room.

No, no, no. He was knocking on the door. Was it locked? Of course it was locked. She always kept it locked. But would a lock, even a really good one, keep a guy like that out?

Definitely no.

She'd been watching him, and he knew it. Maybe he wasn't a guy who wanted to be watched, which was why he was moving his stuff all alone. Worse yet, had he been sent to find her? He had looked so furious. Was he angry?

If so, what could she do?

The online martial arts lessons she'd taken lately ran through her head, but once again, she wondered if one could really learn self-defense by watching videos. Something told her that all the self-defense lessons in the world wouldn't help against that guy.

Oh, why had Mrs. Maloni moved to Florida? Sure, the elderly lady wanted to be closer to her grandchildren, but Cottage Grove was a much better place to live.

Her house had sold in less than a week.

Pippa had hoped to watch young children play and frolic in the large treed backyard, but this guy didn't seem to have a family.

Perhaps he'd bring one in, yet there was something chillingly solitary about him.

Of course, she hadn't set foot outside her house for nearly five years, so maybe family men had changed.

Probably not, though.

He knocked again, the sound somehow stronger and more insistent this time.

She opened the bedroom door and peered around the corner. The front door was visible above the sofa.

He knocked again. "Lady?" Deep and rich, his voice easily carried into her home.

She might have squawked.

"Listen, lady. I, ah, saw you fall and just wanna make sure you're all right. You don't have to answer the door." His tone didn't rise and remained perfectly calm.

She sucked in a deep breath and tried to answer him, but only air came out. Man, she was pathetic. She tapped her head against the doorframe in a sad attempt to self-soothe.

"Um, are you okay?" he asked, hidden by the big front door. "I can call for help."

No. Oh, no. She swallowed several times. "I'm all right." Finally, her voice worked. "Honest. It's okay. Don't call for anybody." If she didn't let them in, the authorities would probably break down the door, right? She couldn't have that.

Silence came from the front porch, but no steps echoed. He remained in place.

Her heart continued to thunder against her ribs. She wiped her sweaty palms down her yoga pants. Why wasn't he leaving? "Okay?" she whispered.

"You sure you don't need help?" he called, his voice rich and deep. Definitely sexy, with a whole male edge that went with that spectacular body. "I promise I can be all sorts of helpful to damsels in distress."

Was that a line? Was he trying to flirt with her or put her at ease? What could she say back? Something equally flirty so he'd be at ease and not curious about her? Nothing came to her fuzzing mind. "I'm sure." *Go away.* Please, he had to go away.

"Okay." Heavy bootsteps clomped across her front porch, and then silence.

He was gone.

***

Hours later, Malcolm West kept moving boxes into his house, wondering about the pretty lady next door. She hadn't reappeared in the window for hours.

He knew the sound of terror, and he knew it well. The woman, whoever she was, had been beyond frightened at seeing him in the window. Damn it. What the hell had he been thinking to approach her house like that?

A fence enclosed their backyards together, and he'd wondered why. Had a family once shared the two homes?

He grabbed the last box of stuff from the truck and hefted it toward the house. Maybe this had been a mistake. He'd purchased the little one-story home sight unseen because of the white clapboard siding, the blue shutters, and the damn name of the town—Cottage Grove. It sounded peaceful.

He'd never truly see peace again, and he knew it.

All the homes the real estate agent had emailed him about had been sad and run-down...until this one. It had been on the market only a few days, and the agent had insisted it wouldn't be for long. After a month of searching desperately for a place to call home, he'd jumped on the sale.

It had been so convenient, it seemed like a stroke of fate.

If he believed in fate, which he did not.

He walked through the simple one-story home and dropped another box in the kitchen, looking out at the pine trees beyond the wooden fence. The area had been subdivided into twenty-acre lots, with tons and tons of trees, so he'd figured he wouldn't see any other houses, which had suited him just fine.

Yet his house was next to another, and one fence enclosed their backyards together.

No other homes were even visible.

He sighed and started to turn for the living room when a sound caught his attention. His body automatically went on full alert, and he reached for the SIG hidden at the back of his waist. Had they found him? Somebody had just come in the front door.

"Detective West? Don't shoot. I'm a friendly," came a deep male voice.

Malcolm pulled the gun free, the weight of it in his hand more familiar than his own voice. "Friendlies don't show up uninvited," he said calmly, eyeing the two main exits from the room in case he needed to run.

A guy strode into the kitchen, hands loose at his sides. Probably in his thirties, he had bloodshot eyes, short, mussed-up brown hair, and graceful movements. His gaze showed he'd seen some shit, and there was a slight tremble in his right arm. Trying to kick a habit, was he?

Malcolm pointed the weapon at the guy's head. "Two seconds."

The man looked at the few boxes set around the room, not seeming to notice the gun. Even with the tremor, he moved like he could fight. "There's nowhere to sit."

"You're not staying." Malcolm could get to the vehicle hidden a mile away within minutes and then take off again. The pretty cottage was a useless dream, and he'd known it the second he'd signed the papers. "I'd hate to ruin the minty-green wallpaper." It had flowers on it, and he'd planned to change it anyway.

"Then don't." The guy leaned against the wall and shook out his arm.

"What are you kicking?" Malcolm asked, his voice going low.

The guy winced. "I'm losing some friends."

"Jack, Jose, and Bud?" Mal guessed easily.

"Mainly Jack Daniel's." Now he eyed the weapon. "Mind putting that down?"

Mal didn't flinch. "Who are you?"

Broad shoulders heaved in an exaggerated sigh. "My name is Angus Force, and I'm here to offer you an opportunity."

"Is that a fact? I don't need a new toaster." Mal slid the gun back into place. "Go away."

"Detective—"

"I'm not a detective any longer. Get out of my house." Mal could use a good fight, and he was about to give himself what he needed.

"Whoa." Force held up a hand. "Just hear me out. I'm with a new unit attached to the Homeland Defense Department, and we need a guy with your skills."

Heat rushed up Mal's chest. His main skill these days was keeping himself from going ballistic on assholes, and he was about to fail in that. "I'm not interested, Force. Now get the hell out of my house."

Force shook his head. "I understand you're struggling with the aftereffects of a difficult assignment, but you won. You got the bad guys."

Yeah, but how many people had died? In front of him? Mal's vision started to narrow with darkness from the corners of his eyes. "You don't want to be here any longer, Force."

"You think you're the only one with PTSD, dickhead?" Force spat, losing his casual façade.

"No, but I ain't lookin' to bond over it." Sweat rolled down Mal's back. "How'd you find me anyway?"

Force visibly settled himself. "It's not exactly a coincidence that you bought this house. The only one that came close to what you were looking for." He looked around the old-lady cheerful kitchen. "Though it is sweet."

Mal's fingers closed into a fist. "You set me up."

"Yeah, we did. We need you here." Force gestured around.

Mal's lungs compressed. "Why?"

"Because you're the best undercover cop we've ever seen, and we need that right now. Bad." Force ran a shaking hand through his hair.

"Why?" Mal asked, already fearing the answer.

"The shut-in next door. She's the key to one of the biggest

312

homegrown threats to our entire country. And here you are."
Force's eyes gleamed with the hit.

Well, fuck.

Buy Hidden where all books are sold.

HAVE YOU LOOKED AT THE SCORPIUS SYNDROME YET?

MERCURY STRIKING

CHAPTER ONE

Life on Earth is at the ever-increasing risk of being wiped out by a disaster, such as sudden global warming, nuclear war, a genetically engineered virus, or other dangers we have not yet thought of.
—Stephen Hawking

Despair hungered in the darkness, not lingering, not languishing . . . but waiting to bite. No longer the little brother of rage, despair had taken over the night, ever present, an actor instead of an afterthought.

Lynne picked her way along the deserted twelve-lane interstate, allowing the weak light from the moon to guide her. An unnatural silence hung heavy over the barren land. Rusting carcasses of vehicles lined the sides; otherwise, the once-vibrant 405 was dead.

Her months of hiding had taught her stealth. Prey needed stealth, as did the hunter.

She was both.

The tennis shoes she'd stolen from an abandoned thrift store protected her feet from the cracked asphalt, while a breeze scented with death and decomposing vegetation lifted her hair. The smell had saturated the wind as she'd trekked across the country.

The world was littered with dead bodies and devoid of souls.

A click echoed in the darkness. About time. Predators, both human and animal, crouched in every shadow, but she'd made it closer to what used to be Los Angeles than she'd hoped.

A strobe light hit her full on, rendering sight impossible. The miracle of functioning batteries brought pain. She closed her eyes. They'd either kill her or not. Either way, no need to go blind. "I want to see Mercury." Since she'd aimed for the center of Mercury's known territory, hopefully she'd find him and not some rogue gang.

Silence. Then several more clicks. Guns of some type. They'd closed in silently, just as well trained as she'd heard. As she'd hoped.

She forced strength into her voice. "You don't want to kill me without taking me to Mercury first." Jax Mercury, to be exact. If he still lived. If not, she was screwed anyway.

"Why would we do that?" A voice from the darkness, angry and near.

She squinted, blinking until her pupils narrowed. The bright light exposed her and concealed them, weakening her knees, but she gently set her small backpack on the ground. She had to clear her throat to force out sound. "I'm Lynne Harmony."

Gasps, low and male, filled the abyss around her. "Bullshit," a voice hissed from her left.

She tilted her head toward the voice, and then slowly, so slowly they wouldn't be spooked, she unbuttoned her shirt. No catcalls, no suggestive responses followed. Shrugging her shoulders, she dropped the cotton to the ground, facing the light.

She hadn't worn a bra, but she doubted the echoing exhales of shock were from her size Bs. More likely the shimmering blue outline of her heart caught their attention. Yeah, she was a freak. Typhoid Mary in the body of a woman who'd failed. Big time. But she might be able to save the men surrounding her. "So. Jax Mercury. Now."

One man stepped closer. Gang tattoos lined his face, inked tears showing his kills. He might have been thirty, he might have been sixty. Regardless, he was dangerous, and he smelled like dust combined with body odor. A common smell in the plague-riddled world. Eyeing her chest, he quickly crossed himself. "Holy Mary, Mother of God."

"Not even close." A silent overpass loomed a few yards to the north, and her voice echoed off the concrete. The piercing light assaulted her, spinning the background thick and dark. Her temples pounded, and her hollow stomach ached. Wearily, she reached down and grabbed her shirt, shrugging it back on. She figured the "take me to your leader" line would get her shot. "Do you want to live or not?"

He met her gaze, his scarred upper lip twisting. "Yes."

It was the most sincere sound she'd heard in months. "We're running out of time." Time had deserted them long ago, but she needed to get a move on. "Please." The sound shocked her, the civility of it, a word she'd forgotten how to use. The slightest of hopes warmed that blue organ in her chest, reminding her of who she used to be. Who she'd lost.

Another figure stepped forward, this one big and silent. Deadly power vibrated in the shift of muscle as light illuminated him from behind, shrouding his features. "I didn't tell you to put your shirt back on." No emotion, no hint of humanity echoed in the deep rumble.

His lack of emotion twittered anxiety through her empty abdomen. Without missing a beat, she secured each button, keeping the movements slow and sure. "I take it you're Mercury." Regardless of name, there was no doubt the guy was in charge.

"If I am?" Soft, his voice promised death.

A promise she'd make him keep. Someday. The breeze picked up, tumbling weeds across the lonely 405 to halt against a Buick stripped to its rims. She quelled a shiver. Any weakness shown might get her killed. "You know who I am," she whispered.

"I know who you say you are." His overwhelming form blocked out the light, reminding her of her smaller size. "Take off your shirt."

Something about his command gave her pause. Before, she hadn't cared. But with him so close she could smell *male*, an awareness of her femininity brought fresh fear. Nevertheless, she again unbuttoned her shirt.

This time, her hands trembled.

Straightening her spine, she squared her shoulders and left the shirt on, the worn material gaping in front.

He waited.

She lifted her chin, trying to meet his eyes although she couldn't see them. The men around them remained silent, yet alertness carried on the oxygen. How many guns were trained on her? She wanted to tell them it would only take one. Though she'd been through hell, she'd never really learned to fight.

The wind whipped into action, lifting her long hair away from her face. Her arms tightened against her rib cage. Goose bumps rose over her skin. She was accustomed to being vulnerable, and she was used to feeling alone. But she'd learned to skirt danger.

There was no doubt the man in front of her was *all* danger.

She shivered again.

Swearing quietly, he stepped in, long, tapered fingers drawing her shirt apart. He shifted to the side, allowing light to blast her front. Neon blue glowed along her flesh.

"Jesus." He pressed his palm against her breastbone—directly above her heart.

Shock tightened her muscles, and that heart ripped into a gallop. Her nipples pebbled from the breeze. Warmth cascaded from his hand when he spread his fingers over the odd blue of her skin, easily spanning her upper chest. When was the last time someone had touched her gently?

And gentle, he was.

The contact had her looking down at his damaged hand. Faded white scars slashed across his knuckles, above the veins, past his wrist. The bizarre glow from her heart filtered through his fingers. Her entire chest was aqua from within, those veins closest to her heart, which glowed neon blue, shining strong enough to be seen through her ribs and sternum.

He exhaled softly, removing his touch.

An odd sense of loss filtered down her spine. Then surprise came as he quickly buttoned her shirt to the top.

He clasped her by the elbow. "Cut the light." His voice didn't rise, but instantly, the light was extinguished. "I'm Mercury. What do you want?"

What a question. What she wanted, nobody could provide. Yet she struggled to find the right words. Night after night, fleeing under darkness to reach him, she'd planned for this moment. But the words wouldn't come. She wanted to breathe. To rest. To hide. "Help. I need your help." The truth tumbled out too fast to stop.

He stiffened and tightened his hold. "That, darlin', you're gonna have to earn."

_____

Available Now: Mercury Striking

YOU'LL LOVE ALPHA MALE VAMPIRES WHO ENJOY THE SUN, EAT STEAK, AND DON'T NEED TO TAKE YOUR BLOOD TO SURVIVE!

The Dark Protector Series

The Dark Protectors are Back in a new ARC!

Vampire Ronan Kayrs wasn't supposed to survive the savage sacrifice he willingly endured to rid the world of the ultimate evil. He wasn't supposed to emerge in this time and place, and he sure as hell wasn't supposed to finally touch the woman who's haunted his dreams for centuries. Yet here he is, in an era where vampires are hidden, the enemy has grown stronger, and his mate has no idea of the power she holds.

Dr. Faith Cooper is flummoxed by irrefutable proof that not only do vampires exist . . . they're hot blooded, able to walk in sunlight, and shockingly sexy. Faith has always depended on science, but the restlessness she feels around this predatory male defies reason. Especially when it grows into a hunger only he can satisfy—that is if they can survive the evil hunting them both.

READ NOW: Vampire's Faith

"Hot and fast from beginning to end."

—Kate Douglas on *Fated*

"Sizzling sex scenes and a memorable cast."
—*Publishers Weekly* on *Claimed*

"A fast-paced, excitement-filled explosion of action... Zanetti keeps getting better."
—*RT Book Reviews* on *Marked*, 4.5 Stars Top Pick

ALSO BY & READING ORDER OF THE SERIES'

I know a lot of you like the exact reading order for a series, so here's the exact reading order as of the release of this book, although if you read most novels out of order, it's okay.

THE ANNA ALBERTINI FILES

1. Disorderly Conduct (Book 1)
2. Bailed Out (Book 2)
3. Adverse Possession (Book 3)
4. Holiday Rescue novella (Novella 3.5)
5. Santa's Subpoena (Book 4)
6. Holiday Rogue (Novella 4.5)
7. Tessa's Trust (Book 5) - TBA
8. New Anna & Aiden Book - TBA

* * *

LAUREL SNOW SERIES

1. You Can Run (Book 1)

2. You Can Hide (Book 2) - 2022
3. You Can Die (Book 3 - 2023)

DEEP OPS SERIES

1. Hidden (Book 1)
2. Taken Novella (Book 1.5)
3. Fallen (Book 2)
4. Shaken (in Pivot Anthology) (2.5)
5. Broken (Book 3)
6. Driven (Book 4)
7. Unforgiven (Book 5)
8. Unforgotten (Book 6 - TBA)

REDEMPTION, WY SERIES

1. Rescue Cowboy Style (Novella in the Lone Wolf Anthology)
2. Christmas story 2022 (subscribe to newsletter)
3. Novellas 2&3 in summer 2023
4. Book # 1 launch in 2024

Dark Protectors / Realm Enforcers / 1001 Dark Nights novellas

1. Fated (Dark Protectors Book 1)
2. Claimed (Dark Protectors Book 2)
3. Tempted Novella (Dark Protectors 2.5)
4. Hunted (Dark Protectors Book 3)
5. Consumed (Dark Protectors Book 4)
6. Provoked (Dark Protectors Book 5)
7. Twisted Novella (Dark Protectors 5.5)
8. Shadowed (Dark Protectors Book 6)
9. Tamed Novella (Dark Protectors 6.5)

10. Marked (Dark Protectors Book 7)
11. Wicked Ride (Realm Enforcers 1)
12. Wicked Edge (Realm Enforcers 2)
13. Wicked Burn (Realm Enforcers 3)
14. Talen Novella (Dark Protectors 7.5)
15. Wicked Kiss (Realm Enforcers 4)
16. Wicked Bite (Realm Enforcers 5)
17. Teased (Reese -1001 DN Novella)
18. Tricked (Reese-1001 DN Novella)
19. Tangled (Reese-1001 DN Novella)
20. Vampire's Faith (Dark Protectors 8) *****A great entry point for series, if you want to start here*****
21. Demon's Mercy (Dark Protectors 9)
22. Vengeance (Rebels 1001 DN Novella)
23. Alpha's Promise (Dark Protectors 10)
24. Hero's Haven (Dark Protectors 11)
25. Vixen (Rebels 1001 DN Novella)
26. Guardian's Grace (Dark Protectors 12)
27. Vampire (Rebels 1001 DN Novella)
28. Rebel's Karma (Dark Protectors 13)
29. Immortal's Honor (Dark Protector 14)
30. Garrett's Destiny
31. Warrior's Hope - 2023

* * *

STOPE PACKS (wolf shifters)

- 1. Wolf
- 2. Alpha (TBA)
- 3. Shifter (TBA)

* * *

SIN BROTHERS/BLOOD BROTHERS spinoff

1. Forgotten Sins (Sin Brothers 1)
2. Sweet Revenge (Sin Brothers 2)
3. Blind Faith (Sin Brothers 3)
4. Total Surrender (Sin Brothers 4)
5. Deadly Silence (Blood Brothers 1)
6. Lethal Lies (Blood Brothers 2)
7. Twisted Truths (Blood Brothers 3)

SCORPIUS SYNDROME SERIES

**This is technically the right timeline, but I'd always meant for the series to start with Mercury Striking.

Scorpius Syndrome/The Brigade Novellas

- 1. Scorpius Rising
- 2. Blaze Erupting
- 3. Power Surging - TBA
- 4. Hunter Advancing - TBA

Scorpius Syndrome NOVELS

1. Mercury Striking (Scorpius Syndrome 1)
2. Shadow Falling (Scorpius Syndrome 2)
3. Justice Ascending (Scorpius Syndrome 3)
4. Storm Gathering (Scorpius Syndrome 4)
5. Winter Igniting (Scorpius Syndrome 5)
6. Knight Awakening (Scorpius Synd. 6)

MAVERICK MONTANA SERIES

ALSO BY & READING ORDER OF THE SERIES'

ABOUT THE AUTHOR

New York Times and *USA Today bestselling* author Rebecca Zanetti has published more than sixty romantic-suspense and dark paranormal novels, which have been translated into several languages, with millions of copies sold world-wide. Her books have received Publisher's Weekly starred reviews, won RT Reviewer Choice awards, have been featured in Entertainment Weekly, Woman's World and Women's Day Magazines, have been included in Amazon best books of the year, and have been favorably reviewed in both the Washington Post and the New York Times Book Reviews. Rebecca has ridden in a locked Chevy trunk, has asked the unfortunate delivery guy to release her from a set of handcuffs, and has discovered the best silver mine shafts in which to bury a body...all in the name of research. Honest. Find Rebecca at: www.RebeccaZanetti.com

Made in the USA
Las Vegas, NV
21 July 2022